Kindersoldat

Robert Faulk

Book four in the four-book series

The Songs of War

KINDERSOLDAT

To Create a Warrior, you must first
Banish the Child

ROBERT FAULK

Kindersoldat
Copyright © 2024 by Lady's Slipper Books Inc.

Galleon Publishing, Moncton, Canada
www.galleonbooks.ca

ISBN
    Print book: 978-1-7780781-1-8
    ebook: 978-1-7780781-2-5

CONTENTS

Foreword

The background framework used in this book and The Songs of War series is as accurate as I can establish, and I have used those historical events as the backdrop for my fictional characters who lived and died in that terrible war. None of the characters' stories is factual, and although the names of some of the historical characters are accurate, the actions and words attributed to them are not.

I based the books on the experiences and perceptions described by friends I met in Germany while studying and working there. I was an opera student at the Northwest German Music Academy in Detmold from 1973 to 1980 and worked in Germany until 1983. Some people I met had lived through the 1939-45 war, and many were willing to tell their stories. I fictionalized them, sometimes merging characters to be unrecognizable from the original. None of the series' characters directly represent any specific person, living or dead, but all are based on people I knew...Germans, Russians, British, Americans and Canadians.

For more specific information, join me on my website:
thesongsofwar.com

Prologue

Dad taught me to operate a bulldozer as soon as I could reach the steering pedals and pull the clutch. At fifteen, I couldn't wait to get home from school to dig a basement or fill in the sewer line the backhoe crew had dug. I became addicted to the brute force of twenty tons of steel and a powerful diesel engine.

The first thing my father taught me about operating such a formidable machine was that it would kill me if I gave it the slightest opportunity. He said, "Never forget, not even for an instant...that machine has no heart or soul, and the strongest man has no chance against it; flesh and bone mean nothing to steel. And no matter how much you love a machine, it will not love you—make a mistake, and it will kill you without remorse!"

I have never gotten over my addiction to machines or dad's warning. I love to drive a well-handling car, dig holes with an excavator, and fly airplanes. A therapist would probably say it's about power and control. If I were a soldier, I would want to fight in a machine.

◇◇◇◇◇◇◇◇◇◇◇◇◇◇◇◇◇◇◇◇◇◇◇◇◇◇◇◇◇◇

Stalingrad was the beginning of the end for Hitler and his world—his generals and the German people knew it. But Hitler's megalomanic personality would not allow him to admit defeat. A sane man would have negotiated peace, but with bodies piling up in the death camps and the trail of atrocities his armies had left behind them in Russia, no negotiated terms could allow Hitler or his henchmen to live.

On 24 January 1943, when the fall of Stalingrad was a certainty, Churchill, Roosevelt, and Stalin, in absentia, released a statement following a strategic planning conference in Casablanca. In it, they demanded the "...complete and unconditional surrender..." of the Axis powers, or the Allies would "annihilate" them. Churchill and General 'Bomber' Harris's later speeches indicate there was no expectation of a German surrender, and that the Casablanca statement's singular intention was to justify the fire-bombing of German civilians.

A few days later, on 14 February, Goebbels responded to the Casablanca declaration by coining the phrase *Totaller Krieg,* 'Total War,' in front of a crazed crowd at the Sportpalast in Berlin, effectively assuring the German people that they must fight to the death of their country to save Hitler.

There followed a period of intense patriotism. The horrifying news from Russia was 'modified' by Goebbels Propaganda Ministerium, and the SS and Gestapo crushed spoken doubts of an ultimate German victory without exception or mercy.

In an attempt to bring the Germans to their knees and avoid the slaughter that would be the inevitable consequence of occupying Germany, British and American bombers attacked city after city, killing hundreds of thousands of German civilians, but accomplished nothing except to harden the resolve of those who survived.

Germany's armies retreated in battle after battle, but the stoic German people defiantly joined hands with Hitler, as the English had done for Churchill. Of course, the Germans had the added incentive that to do otherwise was a death sentence, or worse.

The casualty rate for the German armed forces was unsustainable; the need for trained replacements exceeded the supply. Consequently, Goebbels' propaganda machine responded by increasing the emphasis on fanatical patriotism. A righteous Germany fought against the world. Goebbels convinced the German people they must sacrifice everything to defend Deutschland and the Führer—to do otherwise was treason.

It was the birth of the "Kindersoldat." It was unpatriotic for the children's mothers to oppose it, and to be 'unpatriotic' was to invite a visit from the Gestapo, the SS, or one of the increasing number of militant Nazi gangs roaming the streets, taking care of business the Gestapo and SS were too squeamish to tackle.

Chapter One

23 May 1943

Erlaube mir, feins Mädchen....

(Allow me, beautiful maiden....)

Johannes Brahms

Lucas Schwartz was a skinny fifteen-year-old boy when, on the 23rd of May 1943, life threw him into the deep end of the pool and forced him to learn to swim or drown. Just short of an awkward one hundred and eighty centimetres tall, with brown eyes and brown hair, Lucas was so average in appearance that he wouldn't have needed a mask to rob a bank. He stood out only because he wore his hair long, against the unwritten but strict rules of the day, and he dressed in an open-necked shirt and vest. If Lucas hadn't been a unique music student, he would have been in the Hitler Jugend, had his hair cut short, and been wearing a uniform.

Lucas made short work of his Abendessen of black bread and gouda cheese, washed down with diluted apple juice. It was better fare than most Germans enjoyed in this time of rationing, and he thanked his mother for the meal and went to fetch his violin from the living room. When he passed the kitchen on his way out of the house, his mother and aunt were discussing the health merits of Brennnestle soup. Lucas beckoned to his sister, who wanted no part of a debate on soup, and she left the table to see him off.

"I'm going to Hartwig's house to practice with the quartet; we're going to start working on the Brahms tonight, and I might be late. Tell mother not to worry."

"And will Katrina be there?" Lucas's sister, Anna, started to smile, but his red face turned it into a laugh.

Lucas loved his older sister; he confided in her whenever he had a problem. Lucas's problem-solving hierarchy began with his sister, then reluctantly his mother, and then, as a last resort, he went to his father. He trusted his sister to relay his trouble up the line if the problem merited it, and his parents knew enough to pass their advice down through the proper channels.

Anna was nineteen and in the middle of her Abitur year, theoretically an adult and wise beyond her years. She knew that two quartet members were girls and that one of the girls had an irresistible influence on her brother—more specifically, Katrina. The other girl, Corinne, was a force of nature that baffled Anna. She wasn't like any other person Anna had ever met.

Lucas said, "Yes, we're starting to work on the Brahms quartet, and Corinne is playing the viola." Lucas avoided mentioning Katrina, knowing that Anna knew how he felt, but tactfully wouldn't mention it unless he did.

She smiled and messed his hair, then stroked it back into place when he tried to push her hand away.

She said, "Schöne Grüsse an alle." Although it was only good manners to send greetings, Lucas knew that Anna meant it; she cared for other people and took care that they knew it.

He looked through the kitchen door, but his mother was in the process of making a point and didn't see him wave goodbye. His grandmother cleared the table, ignoring the discussion but taking time to wave the cloth she was using to clean the table. She mouthed the words, "Viel Spass," and gave him her "I love you unconditionally" smile. He returned it, and she turned her attention to her daughter's enthusiasm for Brennestle soup, something unimportant to a crumbling world.

Lucas let Anna peck his cheek, opened the heavy door and left, looking forward to an evening with his friends. The sun was still high, and darkness wasn't coming for another two hours.

When the light faded, British bombers would drop their deadly loads somewhere in the industrial heart of Germany, but the citizens of Dortmund believed they had earned an exempt status. The British had given them their beating three weeks earlier, and as time passed with no attacks, they became complacent. They told themselves that the raid had given them immunity.

Two or three nights a week, Dortmund's citizens listened to the distant rumble of bombs and watched the gruesome spectacle of cities south of them burning. The fires grew out of the horizon in a continuous line of yellow and orange fire, occasionally bulging and bursting upward, like lava erupting over the edge of the world. Like storms on the sun's surface, bright flares reached into the black sky, sketching the outline of hills against a black velvet background. The fires reduced the factories, homes, hospitals, and schools which fueled them to piles of ashes and broken walls.

The dull crump of distant bombs had been constant since the beginning of the year. The radar warning system at Deelen tried to guess which city would die and alerted every possible target, setting off wailing sirens in cities that would not see a bomber. The sirens sent people running for the shelters, just in case the British had turned over their city's card.

An interconnected network of basements served as shelters in Dortmund's 'Old City' center. The citizens crouched there, fearful when the bombing had begun more than a few months ago, but when the scene replayed night after night, familiarity became contempt, and worry if this were the 'big one' became more abstract than real. They told worn-out jokes about the inaccuracy of the British bombing—they said there were spies in England who knew the British target, and the Luftabwehr, air defence authority, used that information to advise German citizens to go to that area, the only place no British bombs would fall!

Born of exhaustion, Schadenfreude dominated the conversation. It had been weeks since anyone in Dortmund's Old City had slept through the night, and the atmosphere in the confines of the cellars sometimes boiled over. Underlying tension and fatigue caused friendly discussions to mutate into animated disagreements, and sometimes even to physical altercations.

Night after night, no bombs fell on Dortmund, but the persistent sirens howled and sent people running for shelter. And every night, fewer people left the comfort of their beds.

The certainty that their number would soon come up pushed half the city into depression, deeper because so many ignored it. If the Luft-waffe couldn't stop the bombers at Düsseldorf, Cologne, Wuppertal and Essen, they wouldn't stop them when the British General Harris chose the total destruction of Dortmund as his next objective.

Lucas and Hartwig's families built comfortable safe rooms in their cellars and stayed there when the sirens sounded rather than make the fifteen-minute walk to an overcrowded public shelter. Lucas became so used to the sirens and the faraway bomb explosions that he slept through them on a bench in the shelter. He lived his life as though war were something far away—it would never happen to him. He shut his ears and brain to his parents' pessimism, believing they exaggerated the danger.

◇◇

Lucas arrived at his friend's house at seven, precisely on time. Hartwig greeted him at the door and followed him into the foyer. He took Lucas's coat, hung it up, and then led him into the living room, where he had set up music stands around an old upright piano. Lucas was the last to arrive; the other quartet members had already begun unpacking their instruments and scores.

Hartwig, blonde and the same age as Lucas, was ten centimetres taller but twenty pounds lighter. Lucas and Hartwig had taken an American literature class in which they had studied Washington Irving's mid-nineteenth century short story, "The Legend of Sleepy Hollow," and spontaneously, everyone, including the teacher, had nick-named Hartwig "Ichabod."

From the moment his mother sat him on the bench and showed him where to hit it, Hartwig and the piano had become a single homogenous instrument. His life became a constant search for complex piano music, and his teacher at the Musikgymnasium, a music school for gifted students, worked hard to stay ahead of his thirst for progress.

Katrina Müller, Lucas and Hartwig's stunningly beautiful class-mate, played the cello, a deadly combination for her testosterone-hyped classmates. Compared to the others in the quartet, she was not an outstanding musician, but her beauty rendered that irrelevant.

Her father had rescued her instrument from a pile of discarded junk outside a Jew's confiscated house and a carpenter friend had done his best to repair it, but the tone suffered despite, or more likely, because of the man's best efforts.

Lucas, not yet capable of understanding girls, didn't react when Katrina looked at him and smiled as he put his violin case on the sofa and released the snaps. He instantly regretted so obviously ignoring her, but his embarrassment wouldn't let him correct the error. Corinne, the fourth quartet member, said, "'tag, Lucas," and waved, giving Lucas no option but to return the greeting.

Corinne confused Lucas and made him nervous. She played the viola well, and a benefactor had given her a beautiful instrument, but her aggressive nature was her nemesis when it came to music and Lucas. It constructed a wall around the musician in her, allowing only tiny bits of musicality to escape at unpredictable times.

But for some reason that Lucas could not fathom, he had found her soft spot, as she had found his, and he could work with her in a way that baffled their friends. For reasons known only to Corinne, Lucas softened the lioness in her, and she brought out the peacekeeper in him.

◇◇◇◇◇◇◇◇◇◇◇◇◇◇◇◇◇◇◇◇◇◇◇◇◇◇◇◇◇◇◇◇◇

Corinne played all the notes precisely on pitch and on time, but her insistence on that precision restricted her musical expression to exactly the notation on the page. Her stoic aggression and determination limited Corinne's dynamic expression to loud or louder, but criticism of her playing was a challenge only the unenlightened or truly brave would face.

Hartwig awakened the Brunhilde warrior in Corinne. At the previous weekly rehearsal, he had narrowly escaped decapitation by viola when he dared to explain sarcastically that the distinction between "pianissimo" and "fortissimo" was equivalent to the difference between "Katrinissimo" and "Corrinnissimo" and that he vastly preferred the former in this particular phrase.

The viola flew out of Corinne's hands, dead on target—Hartwig ducked sideways, and the instrument missed him by a cat's whisker. Its flight stopped when it struck the blackout drapes behind him, landing on its back on the thick Persian carpet. Lucas retrieved the undamaged viola and carefully handed it to Corinne. Shifting from Hartwig to Lucas, she immediately softened her black stare, thanking Lucas with a plea for forgiveness in her eyes. No one dared say a word about the incident, and Hartwig diligently avoided criticizing her for the rest of the rehearsal, leaving that bit of delicate diplomacy to Lucas.

Corinne, almost the same height as Lucas, was built like Wagner's epic warrior heroine, Brunhilde, and projected the same sense of raw power. She had a strong face and a mane of blond hair that loudly reminded one of the Germanic legend's mythological origin. People and animals instinctively knew better than to mess with Corinne, and the warrior in her revelled in her dominion over them. Corinne's mother had respected her daughter's authority since she was twelve.

For some reason, evident to no one, Corinne loved music and, in particular, the viola. The only thing in her life that she loved more was Lucas. And he was the only mountain she was afraid to climb.

Today, she was in a playful mood and, having seldom seen this side of Corinne, her friends were understandably nervous. She joked with Hartwig about his agility when ducking her viola missile and even squeezed the comparatively delicate Katrina in an affectionate hug. Katrina winced and forced a smile. When Lucas crossed the room to take his position beside the piano, he neatly avoided getting his hug but pecked Corinne on the cheek as a precautionary measure. She blushed, a sight that made everyone laugh but Corinne.

Katrina removed the mediocre cello her father had rescued from its battered case and slid the lucky instrument between her legs. Lucas and Hartwig became as nervous and attentive as collie dogs when she stroked it with her bow, testing the tuning. Lucas crossed his legs and looked at the floor; Hartwig made a slight sound as he swallowed.

◇◇◇◇◇◇◇◇◇◇◇◇◇◇◇◇◇◇◇◇◇◇◇◇◇◇◇◇◇◇◇◇◇

Hartwig coughed and gave the quartet an "A" from the piano, beginning the tuning process. Corinne and Lucas quickly picked up their exact tuning and waited while Hartwig repeated the note for Katrina. He sounded it patiently at the start but hit the key progressively harder as she overshot, then undershot the pitch. Although she tried, she couldn't find the proper tuning, even when Hartwig embarrassed her by banging the note while holding down the sustaining pedal. Hartwig and Lucas exchanged glances, and Corinne looked at the floor as Katrina tried higher, then lower, missing the tuning on every string.

Finally, as Katrina showed signs of a meltdown, Lucas leaned against her and gently twisted each peg until the pitch was perfect while Hartwig plunked the corresponding key. When Lucas finished, Katrina smiled at the boys and said, "Thank you," so sweetly Hartwig forgot his resentment of Lucas, and they both melted. Katrina was exquisitely aware of her effect on Hartwig and Lucas and made no effort to hide it.

Corinne looked at the ceiling with her teeth bared.

◇◇◇◇◇◇◇◇◇◇◇◇◇◇◇◇◇◇◇◇◇◇◇◇◇◇◇◇◇◇◇◇◇◇◇◇

Tonight was the first ensemble rehearsal for the demanding piece, but the quartet members' respective teachers were the most brutal taskmasters in Dortmund, and they had been working on the parts for weeks. Hartwig and Lucas, fast learners of familiar patterns, had memorized most of the piece. Hartwig had sight-read it nearly perfectly the first time he'd seen it and, for the past week, had played it without the score. Brahms had written his Second Piano Quartet for virtuosic piano, and Hartwig's playing fit that description. He learned and played Brahms as though he had written the music himself.

Lucas, an excellent ensemble player, was a perfectionist in his playing. He studied the nuances and expression of his part not only from the violinist's perspective but also as it related to the other instruments. He was the ideal chamber musician for Brahm's romantic style.

Corrine would undoubtedly play all the notes correctly but have no idea how the parts fit. The saddest part for Lucas was that she seemed to have no interest in finding out what the other instruments were doing—as far as Corinne was concerned, they should do their thing, and she would do hers. Today, Lucas had decided he would find a way to change that. There was something in Corinne that awakened his desire to do something meaningful, like making a beautiful musician out of her.

After three months of working with her teacher, Katrina seemed lost; she still had problems with notes and cadenzas. Her tuning was approximate, and Lucas thought this piece would be a stretch for her. To put it kindly, she was not a fast learner, and sometimes Lucas wondered how she had won the right to study at the most exclusive music school in Germany's heartland. Occasionally showing a sense of logic that stopped conversations in mid-sentence, her beauty never failed to save her. Hartwig, her most enthusiastic victim, made it clear to Lucas that to mention Katrina's faults in his presence was verboten. Tonight, Katrina's playing would test that rule.

There is no fixed leader in the art of ensemble playing. The ideal is for the individual artists to become so sensitive to the ensemble's musicianship and interpretation that they think and feel as one. There are no formal signals to begin and none indicating when to move within the phrases. These things crystallize with rehearsal, attention, and a shared sense of timing and musical logic. This group had been playing together for three years and knew each other well—they tolerated one another's weaknesses and emphasized strong points, an approach that yielded a cohesive, satisfying result. This specific piece, a reach for everyone but Hartwig, would require months of preparation, and tonight, all they could hope for would be to establish the structure for the hard work ahead.

Her instrument tuned, Katrina poised herself to stroke her strings with the bow Lucas's parents had bought her, and all eyes turned to Hartwig. He raised his hands, struck the first octave chord in one smooth motion, and Katrina stroked her bow. Hartwig immediately lifted his hands, but Katrina continued playing the theme for another bar. She stopped mid-note, turned her head, looked at Hartwig, and lifted her bow from the strings, pressing her breasts against the edge of the blessed cello snuggled between her legs. Katrina pouted; Hartwig looked at her, opened his mouth, hesitated, and let a witty sarcasm die before it reached his lips. Her breasts wiggled on the varnished wood as she straightened to take her punishment, wearing the pitiful expression of a child expecting a beating; Hartwig grunted something unintelligible, and Katrina relaxed. She smoothly transformed her expressive face with a curious and sexy smile, spread her hands and looked from Hartwig to Lucas.

"What," she said in a childish voice, "did I do wrong?"

Hartwig looked from Lucas to Corinne, begging for help, and Lucas saved him.

"The piano plays the first statement before we come in." Lucas pointed to the vacant beginning bar marked with a '4' on her score. He patiently illustrated the entry by stroking it on his violin.

Corinne turned her head away from Katrina, lowered her eyes, and, obviously using a significant amount of effort, said nothing.

"Oh," Katrina said in a small voice, "I thought it was like the first Brahms quartet. I'll wait next time." She returned to her music, readied her bow and cuddled against the cello. Lucas looked at Hartwig, whose breathing through his open mouth had become audibly ragged. He waved his bow to get Hartwig's attention and nodded when he turned his head. Hartwig looked down at the keys as though discovering them for the first time, and it took him two tries to play the opening octaves correctly, something he could have done perfectly when he was six, if his hands had been large enough to stretch that far.

Each player entered the first phrase at the correct time. Katrina played with her eyes on Lucas's bow, matching his movement but a split second behind him. The second phrase was a reiteration of the octave theme that the piano had just played, and Hartwig stopped again at the end of it. He looked at Lucas, his eyes pleading for mercy. Lucas tried not to stare at Katrina—her breasts were close to spilling out of her dress as she pressed them against the cello. He turned to Corinne; she scowled, breaking his concentration, and he returned to Katrina. Focusing above her neck—he tried for her eyes, but his attention wandered to the edge of his peripheral vision, where temptation led him, and he had to force himself to look at her music score.

He asked, "Katrina, are you sure you're playing what's written?" He tried to see the notes on her score as he leaned toward her. She turned the music toward him and leaned in his direction in a way that brushed her long blonde hair against his face. He had to push the locks aside to see what was on the sheet. He couldn't help but note Hartwig's jealous loathing out of the corner of his eye.

"That's what I played!" Katrina said emphatically, pointing at the notes.

From her other side, Corinne leaned over the music. "It can't be! Brahms didn't write that phrase!"

"I played those exact notes!" Katrina's voice quivered defensively. She turned to Hartwig—her whole demeanour shouting 'help' like a drowning kitten.

Hartwig stammered and eventually found his voice. "Perhaps you could play the passage for us again, Katrina; we'll try to solve the problem for you." He looked at Lucas and quickly said, "If there is a problem." Then Hartwig further added, "Of course, I don't think you would intentionally play something wrong...your teacher should have picked up the error...if indeed there is an error..." Lucas vigorously nodded, hoping Hartwig would stop talking, but he didn't. He continued, "But, just in case, I would like to hear it again." Hartwig dug deeper... "but of course, only if you want to..."

Lucas interrupted him, embarrassed that his friend had become a jabbering fool. "Don't worry, Katrina, it's nothing we can't fix." He straightened, putting the violin under his chin. "Let's go through the section slowly."

Hartwig thanked him with a helpless expression but added something that told Lucas to be careful.

Katrina said, "Thank you both for being so kind. I'll try again."

"Ach! Du lieber Himmel!" Corinne muttered, not entirely under her breath.

Hartwig played the introduction again, but slower. Katrina began on time—Hartwig played the piano part softly—making the cello part dominant and clear. Everyone in the room already knew the problem, except Katrina, but Hartwig wisely didn't interrupt—he let her play the short passage to the end. Hartwig turned on the bench and looked hopefully at Lucas, then Corinne. Lucas realized what Katrina was doing and decided not to bail Hartwig out. Corinne smiled wickedly.

✧✧✧✧✧✧✧✧✧✧✧✧✧✧✧✧✧✧✧✧✧✧✧✧

Katrina, pencil in hand, prepared to note the corrections she knew would come. Lucas smiled, confident now that he was right, as he watched Hartwig squirm when she leaned over him with the music in her hands.

It was noticeable Katrina had sneaked out of the house without a bra. She gauged the degree of lean to stretch her thin cotton blouse tightly over her full breasts, knowing she had neglected to fasten the top three buttons. Lucas noted that Hartwig sneaked a look down her cleavage as she twisted in her chair to show him a little more than the score. The side of her skirt slid up her thigh, and her bare skin rubbed on the beautiful varnished cello. Hartwig's eyes dropped, marking the spot.

She handed the pencil to Hartwig. "Would you please mark the notes I played wrong?" She asked so sweetly that Lucas half-expected Hartwig's heart would stop. He noted that his friend's arousal showed and worried that his problem was also noticeable, but he didn't dare to look.

Hartwig didn't respond, so Katrina turned to Lucas and offered the pencil. Lucas noted with horror that her eyes flicked downward, and when she raised them to look at him, he detected a hint of triumph on her face. Lucas suddenly knew Katrina was playing him and Hartwig like she played her cello.

"Please help me, Lucas." She flashed a victorious smile, and Lucas felt his face redden. He made the situation worse when he tried to cross his legs inconspicuously. At that moment, he couldn't decide whether he loved or hated her.

Corinne busied herself by noisily adjusting her music stand and chair to see Hartwig and Lucas simultaneously without lifting her head. Her demeanour gave Lucas the clear impression that if she looked up, she would probably do something they would all regret.

With an impressive burst of willpower, Lucas tore his eyes away from Katrina's breasts, painfully aware that Corinne was dangerously close to murder—the only question was who she would kill first. Lucas suspected Corinne was as formidable as she looked and probably physically stronger. Somehow, that hypothesis simultaneously fascinated and frightened him.

Lucas's hand shook as he took the pencil from Katrina and pointed the tip at the notes. His voice reverted to falsetto when he began. "I believe the problem is quite simple, Katrina." He paused and found his man's voice, but not before he heard Corinne groan.

"You are missing the accidentals. The pitch is wrong on those notes." He made a heroic effort, tapping each accidental note with the pencil. He mistakenly looked into her eyes, and his voice shifted back into falsetto, eliciting another moan from Corinne. "Try the passage once more, one note at a time, and I'll show you." Katrina had won; he had sold his soul to the devil and would play her game to its end.

Corinne almost twisted the neck off her viola; a low, menacing growl rose from somewhere below her throat.

"All right, I'll do that," Katrina said, "but I'm sure the notes are right." She turned back to the music stand and picked up her bow. Her skirt, however, remained high on her smooth white thigh, and Hartwig's eyes instantly found the spot he had marked.

"Shall we begin again?" Hartwig's voice broke as he swung his hands in an arc over the keys, accurately nailing the opening phrase with a flourish. Katrina began, but Lucas touched her bowing hand, instantly stopping her.

"That note is sharp," Lucas said as gently as he could, careful not to expose the farce. "You're playing the A major chord when it should be F-sharp minor, a minor third lower. We are in A major, but the phrase is minor." He caught her looking at Hartwig in a way that told him Hartwig was her mark, not him. He said, "I'll play it both ways so you can hear the difference," then played the phrase first in the A major key, then in F-sharp minor. Katrina appeared to listen intently, but Lucas noted that she looked at Hartwig's problem while stroking the cello gently and slowly, correcting each note until she played it perfectly.

"I've been playing that wrong for weeks!" Katrina looked at Lucas, convincingly surprised, her eyes wide. Her face was so expressive that her bewitching feminine emotions radiated through the room as she switched to a pitiful plea for understanding. "I've been missing a lot of my lessons with those awful bombs falling all the time. My mother makes me stay home at night, and my teacher has no time in the afternoons."

Lucas smiled as he watched Hartwig become a puddle at Katrina's feet.

Katrina's mother struggled for the money they needed to survive, and Katrina's lessons outside of school hours came out of a limited pot. Lucas began to doubt his assumptions about her motives and even felt a tiny twinge of shame for suspecting her. Her childlike apology seemed so genuine that Lucas thought he saw a fleeting hint of sympathy cross Corinne's face, but it all passed so quickly that he wasn't sure.

"Na... alles ist gut Katrina..." Hartwig, eyes glistening, turned back to the keyboard, adjusted his bench a couple of millimetres, then reset it back where it had been. Katrina and Hartwig exchanged looks that embarrassed Lucas.

Hartwig reluctantly focused on Lucas and said, "Let's try that again from the beginning." The victorious expression on Katrina's face was undeniable, and she played perfectly, with every nuance smoothly executed.

◇◇◇◇◇◇◇◇◇◇◇◇◇◇◇◇◇◇◇◇◇◇◇◇◇◇◇◇◇

Hartwig's father, Karl, and his mother, Lenora, listened to their son and his friends practicing the difficult piece, proud of the musical skills he had inherited from his mother. They worked in the kitchen, where Lenora baked a plum torte for the young musicians while Karl shuffled papers at a corner table. The plums were thanks to a giant plum tree that dominated the small backyard, and Hartwig had helped his father pick the fruit the previous autumn so his mother could fill a long shelf in the cellar with bottles of plums.

Karl, the son of a master carpenter from a long line of professional tradesmen, was fanatical about detail. His job as the chief chemical engineer at the Hoesch-Benzin GmBH synthetic oil plant in Dortmund required perfection and precision. All aspects of Synthetic Oil production were complicated, and Karl had the temperament needed for the revolutionary technology. He was responsible for the yearly production and quality of over fifty thousand tonnes of gasoline, diesel and lubricating oil extracted from coal products that varied in quality and content. He used that same meticulous attention to detail in every aspect of his life, including cutting up plums. The little wedges were so perfect they looked unreal.

Karl received rewards for accomplishing production goals, including all the gasoline he wanted for his car and all the ration cards his family wanted. Consequently, the family lived as though there were no war, and, on this occasion, he was thankful for the sugar and cream. To Karl, the Pflaumentorte symbolized his family's just reward for the talent and hard work he gave to Adolph Hitler's war effort.

Lenora beat the cream into a pile and added precious beet-sugar crystals until it was sweet. She spread a thick layer over the Kuchen, deliberately swirling it into lavish and wasteful ridges. Leonora laughed when she caught Karl wincing as he looked at the unevenness and intentionally made it worse.

"It's time for the musicians to take a break." Lenora turned to her husband, who watched her from his small table in the corner. "Bring them to the kitchen while I set the table."

Karl was happy to interrupt his work on a plan to train and use a hundred additional Zwangsarbeiter—slave workers he would receive in the next few days. They would be predominantly Polish Jews in good health but with almost no skills he could use. The letter in his hand instructed him to work them fourteen hours a day with no day of rest, a mistake in Karl's experience. He had no love for slave labour; it was cruel and inefficient. But the Wehrmacht had conscripted all the men capable of working, and there weren't enough women to take their place. The war meant there were no German workers available. He had tried to convince the SS officer in charge of the Zwangsarbeiter that if he allowed his men to treat the workers better, they would work more efficiently, and the SS officer reminded him that their upkeep was none of his business.

Karl watched, frustrated, as many of them became weak and sick, then disappeared for good. He knew these miserable wretches received no real food while working in his plant, and he was equally confident they got less than enough to eat when they weren't there. A steady flow of replacement workers came from lands that the German army had overrun, keeping the plant in a constant state of instability. The situation forced Karl to constantly train replacement workers who couldn't speak German and had no interest or skill necessary to do a good job.

◇◇◇◇◇◇◇◇◇◇◇◇◇◇◇◇◇◇◇◇◇◇◇◇◇◇◇◇◇◇◇◇◇

"Okay, I'll get them." Karl gladly put down the letter and stood up quickly, stepping around the corner into the living room just as the quartet completed a second attempt at the dramatic ending of the first movement. The effort would have made Brahms proud.

When the last chord died, the quartet looked at one another and laughed, titillated by the unexpectedly perfect outcome. Karl waited while they congratulated one another, and as they swung their attention to him, he said, "Das Kuchen ist..." but they were already on their way, pushing past him with Hartwig in the lead. Karl closed his mouth and trailed behind them until they reached the kitchen, where he waited until they seated themselves at their usual places. A large beer mug filled with milk sat in front of each plate, all of them covered with a generous rectangle of the Pflaumentorte.

Katrina said, "Thank you for the Kuchen, Frau Zimmermann," her fork poised to strike. The others already had their mouths full when they realized Katrina had successfully made them look like Neanderthals. They stopped chewing and, mouths conspicuously full, mumbled their apologies and thanks as best they could. Lenora smiled—Karl stood beside her, his arm wrapped around her waist, family pride written all over their faces.

"Thank you for everything," Karl kissed her cheek. Above all, through war and uncertainty, he was deeply in love with his wife.

◇◇◇◇◇◇◇◇◇◇◇◇◇◇◇◇◇◇◇◇◇◇◇◇◇◇◇◇◇◇◇◇◇◇

Anxious to start the second movement, the musicians ate their Kuchen and drank their milk in record time while simultaneously talking about the Brahms quartet like excited children. When Katrina, the slowest eater, had swallowed the last bite, they stood and, buzzing enthusiastically, headed for their instruments.

Karl and Lenora kept their distance, proudly watching their son lead the quartet back to the living room. Karl gave his wife a squeeze of affection as the musicians rounded the corner and disappeared, then pointed at the empty Kuchen pan.

"Those gluttons ate all the Kuchen; they didn't save us a crumb!" Karl feigned a catch in his voice. "Now, what can you do to make that up to me?"

Lenora spun out of his arms, opened the oven door, neatly slid a pan of Kuchen onto the counter and picked up a roller cutter. "This," she said, "is for us."

She gave him a sly sideways look as she neatly cut the hot torte. "If that's not enough for you, you must earn what you want."

Chapter Two

23 May 1943

All mein Gedanken...sind bei dir

(All my thoughts are of you)

Johannes Brahms

Like his father, Hartwig tended to cut a job into segments, perfecting each part before joining them. He ran his long, bony fingers up and down the piano, playing an A Major run through two octaves to warm them up. He turned his head to Lucas and spoke while playing the scale at blazing speed. He said, "Let's play a few phrases before deciding what to do next."

Lucas could play the piano passably well, and he had been making music with Hartwig since he was in britches, but Hartwig, without intending to, still found ways to make Lucas drop his jaw. Hartwig hadn't the slightest idea that what he was doing was something the average pianist could only fantasize about, and Lucas held back an impulsive laugh as he said, "Sounds like a good idea to me."

Lucas, like Hartwig, had also inherited the engineering gene. His father, Andreas Schwartz, a mechanical engineer at the Hoesch Eisen und Stahlwerke, was close friends with Hartwig's father. Because they thought in the same structured way, Lucas was happy to agree with Hartwig on almost everything except Katrina. Her beauty fascinated him, but his friend Hartwig was head over heels in love. Katrina had both boys wrapped up in her seductive power, but Lucas knew he couldn't win.

When Lucas picked up his violin and began to tune it to the 'A' Hartwig played. Corinne gave him a warm smile that had nothing to do with learning music, and he momentarily forgot about Katrina. He corrected the tuning with a strange feeling filling his chest. Hartwig banged the 'A' until Katrina found the pitch, then verified it with a crooked grin.

<hr>

The quartet began the second movement exactly together, which was extraordinary considering it was the first time they had tried it. Katrina watched Lucas's bow and Hartwig's hands out of the corner of her eye. Her concentration pout returned, the tip of her tongue pushed slightly through her parted lips, and Lucas forced himself to concentrate on his violin. Hartwig glanced at her a dozen times before they finished the first page, missing notes every time he did.

Corinne ignored everything but her viola, marching ahead like an "oompah-pah-pah" orchestra at a Bierfest, a harsh counterpoint to the sensitive playing of the other instruments. Hartwig stopped after the first page, almost a full beat behind Corinne. He looked at Lucas as though his friend was the only hope for humanity's survival.

Lucas placed his violin on his left thigh and turned to Corinne with no idea what he would say until he started talking. Choking the violin's neck and turning the knuckles on his left hand white, he looked down, prayed for inspiration, and then raised his head with a troubled expression painted on his face. "Corinne, I may have a problem; could you hear whether I was in tune? I might have played that passage a little flat."

Amazed and pleased that Lucas would ask her such a question, Corinne responded judiciously. "Um…I don't think I heard any bad notes." She looked at him curiously, her tone and hesitation reserving her right to change the verdict.

Lucas put his violin under his chin and poised his bow. "Could we play the passage again? I would be grateful if you would listen carefully. I've been having a problem with the tuning in the adagio." He said it with such sincerity that Hartwig had to look over the piano and con-centrate on a flower hand-painted on the feminine wallpaper.

They began again—Katrina fiercely concentrating on her tuning and Lucas playing just enough off that he knew Corinne would notice. As he played, she listened intently, softening her tone so she could hear the sweet tones of Lucas's violin. There were indeed a few slightly sour notes, and when the passage concluded, she pointed them out to him. He carefully played them correctly for her as she smiled and nodded.

"Thank you, Corinne; your sense of pitch is phenomenal!" The gratitude and compliment were honest, cementing Lucas's credibility. He touched her hand, and she beamed like a lighthouse on a stormy night.

The sweet passage created the romantic mood that Brahms had intended, and Hartwig winked at Lucas. When they tried to include Katrina in the conspiracy, she stared at her music, nodding to the beats as she studied the notes, the tip of her tongue barely visible between her slightly parted lips. Except for the grinding of Corinne's teeth, there was a moment of silence as the boys' attention diverted to Katrina.

The other quartet members realized that Katrina was painfully aware of her position as the weak link in the ensemble and that she dreaded the inevitable day they would find another cellist. Hartwig, in particular, took every opportunity to soothe her fear, but still, Lucas knew that Katrina lived in terror that she would disappoint her friends. Lucas sneaked a peek at Hartwig as Katrina concentrated on the lines where her cello would dominate and found it pitiful to see how badly Hartwig wanted her to play up to the quartet's standards. The pain on his face was Katrina's pain.

◇◇◇◇◇◇◇◇◇◇◇◇◇◇◇◇◇◇◇◇◇◇◇◇◇◇◇◇◇◇◇◇◇◇◇◇◇◇

Corinne and Katrina lived on the long, parallel street behind Hartwig and Lucas's. Corinne lived toward the town center, while Katrina lived closer to the Hoesch factories, where rent was cheaper. Katrina's father, killed in Russia more than six months before the Brahms rehearsal, had not been living with the family since 1940, and her mother worked for Lucas's father in the office at the steel fabrication plant. Despite help from her friends and their families, life was difficult for Katrina. Her mother chose to drink Schnapps every night in a misguided struggle to dull her loneliness and usually fell asleep in a chair.

Katrina's mother slept through the siren on the night of the May fourth raid. Katrina couldn't get her to the shelter and spent the night cowering in the cellar under the stairs. She cried for most of the two hours of explosions and could not stand when it was over. Eventually, exhausted, Katrina slept on the damp floor and awakened just in time

19

to rush to school. When she left the house with a bun and a piece of cheese, her mother was still asleep in her chair, an empty Schnapps bottle on the floor between her feet. The bombs destroyed several houses close to theirs, killing five people, but their home was untouched.

Since that night, Katrina jumped at loud noises, and the slightest conflict in her life caused a panic attack so severe she required help. She worked hard at everything she did, and although she never asked for help, protectors and admirers surrounded her like ants around sugar.

Corinne's father was a steel fabricator, built like a truck, with a similar IQ. He drank beer by the litre mit den Jungen, 'with the boys' from the shop. He hated Jews, faggots, Communists, and the French pigs, in no particular order, but the pecking order in his home was simple. He came first by a long shot, then the dog, the car even though he had no gas, his wife, and last was Corinne. He had never shown a flicker of affection for his wife or daughter, but in fairness, he showed no respect for anyone who couldn't beat him in a fight. And no one had ever heard him thank anyone or apologize for anything.

Corinne hated her father with such passion that, given the opportunity, she could and would certainly kill him without remorse. He carried out a weekly beating of his wife in every room of the apartment. Corinne's mother took it without a sound, avoiding the embarrassment of answering prying neighbours' questions. Corinne had more than once tried to come to her rescue, but her father had then beaten her.

Corinne's beatings stopped when she turned thirteen. On that occasion, she had tried again to help her mother, and her father had chased her, cornering her in the kitchen. He upset the table and the evening meal in his eagerness to get at her, but Corinne's mother stepped behind him with a long butcher's knife, reached around his neck, and pressed the sharp blade against his jugular hard enough that she drew blood. He stood very still while she hissed, "You will never strike my daughter again, or I will slit your throat as you sleep! This I promise to you and the Virgin Mary!" She threw the knife to the floor, where it stuck upright in the pine planks.

That night, and every night after that, Corinne worked on a plan to kill her father. She lay awake, imagining scenarios, but could think of none that she could get away with. Two years later, when the British bombers came, Corinne envisioned a picture that became a plan she was convinced would work.

She would wait for the opportunity, then kill her father with the pickax in the cellar during the bombing, and she and her mother would drag him outside so it would look as though a British bomb had killed him.

◇◇◇◇◇◇◇◇◇◇◇◇◇◇◇◇◇◇◇◇◇◇◇◇◇◇◇◇◇◇◇◇◇◇◇◇◇◇

Hartwig suggested a fresh beginning before they played the following passage, and happily, Corinne played while watching and listening to Lucas. The result was magical, and Corinne was in a groove when they transitioned to the cello-dominated section. She reduced her sound to a soft pianissimo, allowing Katrina's cello to dominate. But this time, Hartwig's enthusiasm broke the spell—he played the virtuosic passage as though he were the only musician in the room. At the end of the section, Lucas lowered his head and rested his violin on his left thigh with his hand wrapped around its neck, squeezing it as though he wanted to kill the instrument. Hartwig knew he was in trouble and waited for it; Lucas didn't disappoint him.

"Confidence, born as natural ability, raised by hard work and expressed as arrogance with consideration for those less talented, can be forgiven. Selfish arrogance, born and raised out of the greatest talent but expressed without consideration for others, is the most abhorrent of human personalities. That kind of arrogance makes the most wonderful talent into something despicable."

He and Hartwig knew he had just quoted Karl Zimmermann, Hartwig's father.

"Say what you're trying to say!" Hartwig tried to seem exasperated, but every member of the quartet knew he was aware of what Lucas meant. They waited for him to swallow his pride as he always did, and finally, Hartwig waved his hand in submission. "All right, I know, I know." He looked at the keys, took a deep breath, raised his head and looked at Katrina while Lucas and Corinne waited.

"I'm sorry, Katrina." He sounded contrite, and that was enough. "I was carried away with the music. If you forgive me, I promise not to do it again."

Katrina looked at Lucas with, at the very least, intense disgust, then turned to Hartwig and gave him the warmest smile she could manage. "Thank you, Hartwig. I understand, and of course, I forgive you."

There was no forgiveness in the look she gave Lucas, and he suddenly realized that his own stupid arrogance had not only cost him the battle, it had lost the war.

Chapter Three

23 May 1943

In Stiller Nacht

(In the quiet night)

Johannes Brahms

PATHFINDER MOSQUITOS CROSSED THE DUTCH COAST undetected; they were thirty-five minutes from their target and cruising at four-hundred-and-fifty kilometres per hour. The bomber stream was two hundred kilometres ahead of them, flying on a course that suggested to the German radar controllers in Dielen that Hannover would be their target. Hannover is one hundred and fifty kilometres north of Dortmund on a course that would take the bombers west of the Ruhr. But General 'Bomber' Harris had designed an intricate plan to fool the Luftschutzwarndienst, the air raid warning system.

Every raid taught RAF Bomber Command how to kill civilians more efficiently. The bombers carried 2,000 tons of high explosives and incendiaries, in the most destructive ratio of explosives to fire. The explosives would create the fuel that incendiaries would set on fire. The bombers would change course too late to warn the citizens of Dortmund, the intended target. The timing was the key—Bomber Command planned to kill as many civilians as possible when they were most vulnerable—before they could reach the shelters. The intricate attack plan was for the bomber stream to take a hard right simultaneously with the Mosquito pathfinders' arrival over Dortmund, and the armada's lead squadron would arrive over Dortmund four minutes after the Mosquitos' twelve tons of target-marking firebombs and coloured flares had struck the ground.

The mosquitos, difficult to identify on a radar screen because of their wooden construction, avoided the German radar defences, and the air raid siren sounded five minutes before Dortmund residents heard the 'crump' of bombs landing in the old city centre.

A minute-and-a-half later, the bomber stream—eight hundred-and-twenty-six bombers carrying the ideal combination of high explosive and incendiary bombs—completed its turn to line up on a course that would take them over the flares and burning buildings in the heart of Dortmund.

The raid proceeded precisely as planned; the people in the condemned city had less than five minutes to find shelter before death rained from the sky. General 'Bomber' Harris's plan worked perfectly—only a few people would reach the shelters.

It was with a sense of foreboding that Karl Zimmermann heard the air raid siren, nick-named Meier's Trompete, and then, minutes later, aircraft engines. And then, in the kitchen window, explosions and fire in the city's centre, the Stadtmitte.

Since May, Karl counted down the cities; every raid brought the British bombers one city closer to Dortmund. But days, then weeks and months passed without the dreaded bombers. Hope grew, only to die in the explosions and flames of the Mosquitos' bombs.

During the May fourth raid, Karl had seen enough to know that the destruction from a determined direct attack would be beyond where his imagination could go. When Meier's Trompete wailed on the twenty-third of May, his heart rate accelerated, and he said to Lenora, who didn't look up from tidying the kitchen. "I think we should get everyone into the cellar as fast as we can." A minute later, when the sound of explosions came from the Stadtmitte, he knew this was 'the big one!' This was not a false alarm; the bombers were close.

<hr>

The Zimmermann home was on Wambelerstrasse, two houses northeast of Andreas and Stephanie Schwartz. The street ran directly northeast, straight to the Hoesch complex, and Karl and Andreas walked together to work every day. They lived on a direct line between the harbour, northwest of the city centre, and the Hoesch industrial complex. When he thought of how the British would bomb the city, targeting the port and the Hoesch plant, Karl Zimmermann's engineering mind recognized something sinister in the symmetry.

The siren's howl drove Karl and Lenora from the kitchen to the living room, where the quartet played Brahms. Before they reached the Wohnzimmer, the unmistakable distant explosion of bombs landing in the centre of the city removed any doubt that Dortmund was tonight's target, and Karl fought a sense of panic. He shouted into the living room, his forceful voice magnifying his rising anxiety. "We've got to get to the cellar! Now!"

Another crump punctuated the sentence, this time closer but from a different direction. Karl didn't know precisely, but using the human species' incredible ability to estimate the direction and distance to a sound's source, he estimated that the explosions were close to the Hoesch Complex.

The musicians began packing their instruments in their cases as though they were getting ready to go home, frustrating Karl. Hartwig helped Katrina with her cello; she rewarded him with a smile, deliberately leaning over in front of him so that he could see far down between her breasts. British bombs were the last thing on both their minds.

Infuriated with the relaxed mood, and to be sure they heard him over the rumble of approaching aircraft, Karl shouted, "This one is REAL! MOVE!"

Hartwig gave his father a sour look as he snapped the catches on Katrina's cello case and then calmly pushed the piano bench into its place under the piano's keyboard.

A tremendous explosion shook the house, and Karl knew from the direction and magnitude that it could only be a Benzin tank exploding at the plant. Katrina left her cello and bolted, her hands over her ears, passing Karl as she ran into the hallway, and, when she spotted her, Lenora's arms.

◇◇◇◇◇◇◇◇◇◇◇◇◇◇◇◇◇◇◇◇◇◇◇◇◇◇◇◇◇◇◇◇◇

Pilot Officer Byron Johnson knew all he cared to about the maelstrom he was flying toward. Bright orange bursts of flame surrounded by black smoke ravaged the night sky ahead of him. Pieces of metal blasted outward in all directions, shrapnel designed to shred aluminum, fabric, and the Perspex in front of his face. Many brave men faltered when they saw the cauldron nick-named the Wrath of God for the first time—and many could not face it again. When confronted with climbing into the bomber, they cried like babies, refusing to get into the aircraft. In previous wars, these broken men were jailed, sometimes shot, but this war was different. Bomber Command was populated with men who had flown their thirty missions and landed behind a desk, and they understood the injury that terror could do. They sent those damaged souls to desk jobs, training facilities or hospitals.

The sky ahead was a wall of explosions, red and orange fire shooting through clouds of black smoke. To the uninitiated, it was an impenetrable barrier. But Byron Johnson had many times successfully defeated the logic that told him not to fly into that vortex, the closest thing to hell that existed. He had flown through that kind of flak many times, but the wall of fire terrified him as it had the first time. Byron fought the urge to turn off the autopilot and turn the airplane around... reason screamed at him... "Turn around, before it's too late!" but experience had proven the logic wrong. Fear screamed at him to get the hell out of there, but experience kept him on course.

The airmen of Bomber Command referred to the Ruhr as the valley of death, a lethal combination of flak and prowling night fighters. The average bomber mortality rate in the valley was almost ten percent, technically the losses of a decimated army and a defeat of tragic proportions. And yet, the carnage continued night after night. Byron put out of his mind the theory of accumulator odds—that each time he cheated death, the odds accumulated against him—that before he flew his thirtieth mission, his death would become inevitable. He took the optimistic position that every night he flew over a German city, God gave him a fresh ninety percent chance of survival.

◇◇◇◇◇◇◇◇◇◇◇◇◇◇◇◇◇◇◇◇◇◇◇◇◇◇◇◇◇◇◇◇◇

Five long minutes from their target, the men in Johnson's Wellington had already seen two bombers fall in flames, victims of Luftwaffe night fighters. The sight motivated them to strain their dry eyes, trying to pick out shadowy forms creeping up on them in the darkness. If the prowling night fighters picked out their Wellington, the gunners in the turrets were all that stood between the crew returning to England and death. Knowing and seeing the consequences of overlooking a fighter before it fired was enough encouragement for the gunners to meticulously search the dark night for black apparitions. George Cunningham, the rear gunner, and Paul Burns, the mid-gunner, never strayed from memorized scanning patterns developed to pick out the slightest abnormality in the night sky surrounding them.

If the rear or mid-gunner picked a night-fighter out of the blackness before it could kill them, the gunner shouted into the intercom, "Corkscrew! Corkscrew!" and the pilot threw the plane into a twisting dive and didn't pull out until the airspeed reached the structural limit. If the Wellington hadn't lost the night fighter or torn off a wing, the pilot kicked the bomber into an opposite heart-stopping spiral aimed straight at the ground.

The early Wellingtons had no top turret, making them helpless against an attack from overhead or either side ahead of the tail, but Johnson's plane was the Mark IC; it had a mid-gunner turret on its back, with a clear field of fire over the top of the fuselage. In the past three raids, the Wellington's mid-gunner had notched two kills...the attacking German pilots, unaware of the new "Wimpy" design, had flown straight into a torrent of .303 bullets spitting from the twin barrels of Paul Burns' Browning machine guns. The turret sitting on the back of the 'Wimpy' had paid for itself.

The bomb run officially began when Eddie Goodrich, bombardier, forward gunner and flight engineer, took directional control of the aircraft. Until the bombs dropped out of the Wimpy's belly and the camera aperture clicked, avoidance of flak and night fighters was impossible. Straight and level over the target terrified every man on the plane.

◇◇◇◇◇◇◇◇◇◇◇◇◇◇◇◇◇◇◇◇◇◇◇◇◇◇◇◇◇◇◇◇◇

Eddie looked through the perspex nose one last time before lying down on the floor and taking the lens cap off the bomb site. A searchlight's white beam lit the Wellington's interior, destroying Eddie's night vision, then passed on to find a bomber ahead of them and glue itself to it. A second light found the hapless bomber; light spilled around the bomber, silhouetting it between the shattered white shafts that stretched upward. Seconds passed; flak burst around the plane, and then a shell struck the aircraft in the centre of the fuselage. The fuel tanks in a

Wellington had no self-sealant and exploded with little encouragement. The direct hit sent fire and red-hot shrapnel through the aircraft, igniting the fuel tanks, and the exploding high-octane gasoline sent pieces of wings, fuselage, and men outward and downward.

The light found a second Wellington, and it immediately released its bombs, raised its left wing and dove through the formation, twisting and turning like an eel. Before Eddie put his eye on the bombsight, he saw the Wimpy fly out of the light and disappear.

The low and slow Wimpy, designed before the war, was by 1943 outdated technology. Their fifteen-thousand-foot service ceiling put them a mile below an aluminum ceiling of Lancaster bombers. A mile closer to the searchlights, the white beams found them first, and night fighters picked them off like sharks taking the outside fish in a school.

As Eddie Goodrich guided Pilot Officer Johnson along the approach course to the Hoesch-Benzin GmbH synthetic oil complex, a fifty-thousand-litre tank at the fuel plant exploded, and his sight suddenly filled with light. The haze that perpetually blanketed the Ruhr Valley scattered the light from the explosion in a miles-wide circle. Black smoke from flak bursts around the Wellington further blurred the target, and Eddie decided to make a judgment call. He made his best estimate of time and distance, counted down from five, flipped the switches, and notified Pilot Officer Johnson, "Bombs gone!"

The aircraft lifted as a four-thousand-pound 'blockbuster' and five hundred pounds of incendiaries fell out of the bay. The entire load would reach terminal velocity in ten seconds and, leaving the sound waves generated by their stabilizing fins behind, struck the ground in under a minute.

◇◇◇◇◇◇◇◇◇◇◇◇◇◇◇◇◇◇◇◇◇◇◇◇◇◇◇◇◇◇

Eddie had guessed wrong—he had released his bombs three seconds early. The blockbuster continued forward two hundred yards, carving a smooth arc until it fell almost vertically through the roof of Andreas and Stephanie Schwartz's home, stopping when it had buried itself four metres below the cellar floor.

Andreas led his family to the reinforced room he and his friend Karl Zimmermann had built in the cellar. Anticipating this day, they had decided that the nearest public air-raid shelter, a twenty-minute walk, was too far away, and, if properly built, a refuge in the basement would be a safe and convenient alternative. Andreas somehow found old and rusty but serviceable steel beams at the Hoesch steelworks where he was the chief engineer, and he and Karl had constructed steel and concrete rooms in a corner of their cellars, stocked with enough water and preserved food to last a week.

His mind on the safety of the room and frustrated with their dallying, Andreas waited for Stephanie, who waited for their daughter, Anna, who, despite the sound of aircraft overhead, muttered that she didn't have time for this nonsense. It would just be another false alarm, and she had to study for her Abitur. She stepped leisurely down the cellar stairs; her aunt and grandmother followed her, chattering about a needlework pattern while the ominous sound of bombers grew louder and the distant thud of bombs reached into the cellar. Andreas's foot stepped on the cellar floor at the same instant an explosion rocked the house, and he knew the source had to be the complex where he worked. He reached for Anna's arm and opened his mouth to shout at her when the Wellington's massive 'blockbuster' bomb crashed through the house and embedded itself in the ground below the concrete floor. The two seconds that the delay timer ticked off before it exploded didn't give him and his family enough time to grasp that their death was imminent.

◇◇◇◇◇◇◇◇◇◇◇◇◇◇◇◇◇◇◇◇◇◇◇◇◇◇◇◇◇◇◇◇◇◇◇◇◇◇

The explosion converted four attached houses into an enormous hole and a rising cloud of dust and debris. And the instantaneous release of energy reduced the Schwartz family to the molecular level.

The blast peeled stucco and dust from the end of the Karl Zimmermann house, the first in a block of six. The end wall faced the hole that had been four connected houses that the Schwartz's home had been part of. The Zimmermann's end wall, separated from the hole and a short stub of surviving wall by a narrow driveway, shook, but the combination of Gitterstein and reinforced concrete held. Superheated supersonic air, dust and debris deflected upward and sideways, flowing around the Zimmermann house, peeling the first two rows of overhanging roof tiles off the roof and flinging them away into the dark night.

The only window in the wall disintegrated, but two layers of heavy blackout drapes deflected some of the bomb blast and absorbed most of the countless glass fragments. The curtains saved Hartwig's life, but the wall of air that blew under the drapes, throwing them aside, tossed him across the floor and left him piled awkwardly against the far wall. Corinne, bent over her viola case and facing the window, snapped the final catch at the exact instant the explosion lifted her, then pushed her back to leave her sitting awkwardly on the sofa. A few small glass fragments embedded themselves in her cheek, but she didn't notice—all of her attention was on sucking enough air to refill her empty lungs.

The upright piano stood between Lucas and the window, and the blast knocked it over, narrowly missing his feet. He fought to stay upright without relaxing his grip on the precious violin he had in his hand, and although the piano had absorbed some of the force, Lucas felt himself falling backward. Fighting to keep his feet under him, Lucas back-pedalled to the sofa and sat down hard on Corinne's lap, his eyes as big as apples.

When the first explosion shook the house, Katrina left her cello on the floor and ran to Lenora's arms; she was there when the 'blockbuster' detonated. Karl, urging the musicians to hurry, was standing in the doorway with his mouth open when the bomb exploded. Lenora and Katrina screamed, but their screams went unheard.

The explosion smashed Karl against the doorjamb, then bounced his body against the wall, bruising him in a half-dozen places. Katrina and Lenora, protected by the hallway, fell against the opposite wall with their arms around one another. Karl couldn't hear Lenora and Katrina's screams, but the looks of terror and the open mouths told him everything he needed to know. Karl left them, wild-eyed and screaming, and stepped into the living room, forgetting the pain his injuries caused. The first person he saw was Corinne, pushing Lucas to his feet and gasping for air. She grabbed Hartwig's arm in her formidable grip, and Lucas laid his violin on the sofa and grabbed Hartwig's other arm. Together, they dragged him into the hallway.

Karl moved his mouth and motioned them to follow him, the sound of his voice lost from shocked, injured eardrums and the now continuous thunder of exploding bombs. The desperation in Karl's movements conveyed an infectious sense of anxiety. He grabbed Katrina's arm, supporting her as Lenora opened a solid oak door at the top of the dark cellar stairs. Lenora held the door open as Karl passed her, instinctively turning on the light, but the flipped switch changed nothing. He picked up the flashlight he kept beside the switch and shone it on the steel and oak door to the shelter. He went down the stairs, took three steps and grasped the cast iron handle, yanking it open. Katrina waited in the doorway while Karl turned to the right where the kerosene lantern would be. He lit it with matches kept in a bottle beside it, and in its yellow light and everyone crowded in behind him. He checked each terrified face. Everyone was inside.

Lucas shepherded Katrina and Corinne to a bench against the wall opposite the door. Lenora lit two candles and held them over her head as she toured the small room, checking that everything was as it should be.

Karl and his son pulled the massive steel and wood shelter door tight to its stop, then dropped two heavy steel channel beams into their sockets to hold it.

Karl took a deep breath and took the time to look around the room.

"Is everyone okay?" He shouted, his hearing still compromised. Everyone except Corinne nodded; She smiled.

Chapter Four

23-24 May 1943

Wie komm' ich denn zur Tür herein?

(How do I get through your door?)

Johannes Brahms

A BLINDING WHITE LIGHT SUDDENLY FILLED THE COCKPIT, retreated, then returned to stay. The bombs were gone, the camera had taken pictures of the devastation, and Pilot Officer Byron Johnson pushed the column forward as he applied full right rudder and aileron. The now unladen aircraft reacted nimbly, corkscrewing clockwise as it accelerated.

The light shone directly into Byron Johnson's eyes, destroying his night vision. He had to accept the spinning directional gyro, the needle stuck in the corner of the turn and bank indicator, and the 'G' forces that pushed him into his seat as proof that the Wellington was in a tight right-hand spiral.

All his senses told him he was flying straight and level—he was not plunging earthward in a right-hand turn—but Byron Johnson knew that he and his crew would die if he obeyed his instincts. The engines increased their pitch from a dull roar to a scream, and the wind noise became deafening, even with earphones; the aircraft was in a twisting dive with the airspeed on the red 'never exceed' line. Johnson pulled the throttles back, applied left aileron and let the column find its natural place, dictated by the elevator trim setting. The danger of a collision was over; the Wellington was below the stream.

George Cunningham screamed, "What the hell is going on?" into the intercom as the aircraft twisted. Stuck on the plane's tail, as far away from the centre of rotation as a man could be, the turret whipped through a bizarre world of alternating light and dark. The effect disoriented him, leaving him with a confused sensation of the aircraft's position and attitude. Shafts of bright light and pools of fire twisted around him while he remained stationary, pinned to the floor of his cramped turret. His senses screamed at him, but he couldn't understand what they said. Confusion threatened to become panic.

"Searchlights!" Eddie Goodrich yelled back from the bomb-aimer's prone position on the floor—"Byron's getting rid of them."

<hr>

Eddie hailed from Canada, from Northern Ontario, where bush pilots were folk heroes. Before the war started, he had volunteered for a five-year stint in the Royal Canadian Air Force, intending to learn to fly, put enough money away to buy a plane, and, in five years, get into the business of hauling gold miners and their equipment around. He struck a bargain with the Canadian Air Force recruiting officer, who promised him a flying career.

Unfortunately, Canada declared war on Germany before Eddie finished basic training. RCAF priorities changed, and, deal or no deal, the Royal Canadian Air Force needed bomb aimers, flight engineers, and rear gunners more than they needed pilots. Faced with thirty missions in a cramped rear turret where life expectancy was measured in weeks, he reminded the Air Force of the recruiter's promise. They compromised by giving him the option of flight engineer and bomb-aimer, close to the pilot and the exit, or five years in the brig.

Eddie became very good at his job, but his dream of becoming a pilot remained burned into his brain. On every mission, before and after the danger of fighters, he sat in the flight engineer's jump seat beside the pilot, and the more he flew, the more his frustration grew. He knew he could fly the plane if he could get his hands on those controls.

His incessant questions to pilots about everything from takeoff to instrument flying earned him a reputation among the pilot fraternity as a 'fucking nuisance,' and they scattered when they saw him coming. But, despite the two hundred hours in his log book, this was the first time Eddie had been in an 'unusual attitude,' where he wasn't sure of anything. Bouncing off the aluminum and 4130-grade steel paraphernalia designed to break bones, he pulled himself into the forward gun-ner's seat, fastened the lap belt, and then stared at the twirling tapestry of fire and light rising to meet him.

◇◇◇◇◇◇◇◇◇◇◇◇◇◇◇◇◇◇◇◇◇◇◇◇◇◇◇◇◇◇◇

Pilot Officer Byron Johnson's talents combined the tenacity of a pit bull and the awareness of a cat, and he put all of his will into flying the wildly twisting bomber in the dark. And then, at a point where John-son thought he had things under control, the radio operator shouted "fighters" over the intercom and Burns, the mid-turret gunner, opened up with his twin Browning machine guns.

Cannon shells blasted holes in the aft fuselage as Johnson fought to undo what the plane was doing. He had to leave the fighter problem to the gunners. He checked that the throttles were back and, using the spinning fires in the city to orient himself, levelled the wings. Bracing his feet on the rudders, Johnson pulled back on the column, and the fires slid under his feet. The plane pulled out of the dive and climbed; Byron added full power, held the nose up until the airspeed dropped below maximum maneuvering speed, and headed for a stall. He kept the nose there as long as he dared, but the Wimpy bomber was still in the light. Johnson swore, glanced at the altimeter to see how much room was under the aircraft, threw the ailerons hard left and kicked the rudder while pushing forward on the column. He glanced at the placard that said, 'Unusual attitudes and aerobatic maneuvers are for-bidden' as the plane skidded sideways, dropped the wing and momen-tarily stood on the left wingtip before beginning a tight spiral in the anti-clockwise direction. It obeyed the law of gravity and headed for the ground. Johnson reduced power as the speed built, praying the wings would stay fastened to the fuselage.

"Jesus Christ, we're on fire! Boys, I'm trapped!" George Cunning-ham yelled into the intercom from the tail where the almost three hun-dred mph wind created by the plane's forward motion blew tongues of flame back toward him, cutting off his escape forward.

Johnson could see the fire's glow in his side window—he levelled the wings, backed the throttles and pulled out of the spiral. The speed quickly bled as the Wellington climbed, and Byron trimmed and set the throttles for level flight at a hundred and fifty mph—bailout speed.

He spoke into the intercom. "We've had it, boys…Abracadabra, jump! Jump! Everybody out!" Being a small man, Byron Johnson slid the sliding side window next to his seat back to the stop and pulled himself out, disappearing in the darkness.

◇◇◇◇◇◇◇◇◇◇◇◇◇◇◇◇◇◇◇◇◇◇◇◇◇◇◇◇◇◇◇◇◇◇◇◇◇◇◇

Following standard operating procedures, the wireless operator and bombardier/forward gunner/flight engineer followed the navigator to the escape hatch on the bottom of the fuselage. They had it open when George, the rear gunner, shouted, "Wait…don't jump!"

George Cunningham stood two metres behind them as he repeated, "Don't jump…the fire's almost out!" He had abandoned the rear turret, run forward of the dying fire, and now stood beside the navigator, bracing himself in the fuselage.

"The fire burned the cloth and stopped at the metal tail when it had nothing to burn. The way this thing's built, that fabric was just something to keep the rain out. She'll get us home… Hey, guys! Where's Byron?"

Fortunately, the Wimpy's geodesic fuselage frame didn't rely on the fabric cover for strength, so the naked, drafty Wellington was still structurally intact. The plane, trimmed for straight and level flight, had found a stable state on its own—the nose sat solidly pointed back over the city they had helped destroy; the fires and the searchlights they had flown out of were in front of them again and getting closer by the second.

Eddie said, "The contortions that Byron put us through must have turned the plane around. We're headed west, hopefully below the bomber stream. The planes attacking the target are a few thousand feet above us, going in the opposite direction. At least we should be okay for a few minutes, but we shouldn't jump until we're clear of those fires… Hey! Byron isn't in the cockpit! If he isn't here, where the hell is he?"

No one disputed his optimistic scenario until Cunningham said, "What about the bombs those guys are dropping? If no one does anything, they'll drop them on us! We've got to turn around! …And did you say Byron isn't in the cockpit?"

The fire at the center of the city sent tongues of flame a thousand feet above the buildings. Thousands of feet above the city, with an outside air temperature near freezing, the fuselage was becoming uncomfortably warm.

"Jesus!" Bill Parsons, the navigator, had gotten the hatch open before George announced that the fire was going out. He looked at the sea of flame devouring the city under the bomber and shut and locked the hatch. "I'll take my chances with the bombs. Where the fuck is Byron? He isn't in his seat. Who's flying the plane?"

Eddie climbed up to the empty pilot's seat to get out of the way in the crowded fuselage. "Christ Almighty!" He yelled as the starboard wing of a Focke Wulf 190, climbing up to the bomber stream, cleared the Perspex in front of him by less than ten feet. He clamped the pilot headset on his head and yelled into the intercom, "A fucking German fighter almost rammed us!" The crew was still standing in the fuselage beside him. Embarrassed, Eddie removed his headset, looked from one crew member to another and pointed at the open window. "Byron's gone. Can anyone fly this thing? We should turn around as soon as possible." He asked hopefully, knowing the answer.

There was no response—he repeated the question, but the answer was the same. He looked down at the expectant faces of the crew. "Come on, guys; I don't know what the fuck to do! Can't anyone here fly an airplane?" The crew shook their heads. "Has anyone here even read a book about flying?" They shook their heads again.

Bill Parsons spoke up, yelling over the engines and thrashing propellers. "You know damned well none of us can even fly a paper airplane!" There followed a long silence, and then Bill's voice yelled again, "I nominate Eddie as our new pilot because he's in the seat, everyone knows he wants to be a pilot, and he is the only one here who knows which way is up... Do I hear any ayes?"

Every crewmember but Eddie said, "Aye," and Eddie swallowed the bile rising from his stomach.

Bill added loudly, "Motion carried! Congratulations, Eddie, you're elected to be the man who has to get us home. But first, turn this thing around!"

"Jeeesuus Cheerist, boys, I can't fly a real airplane! I've never touched the controls of a bomber—I hadn't even soloed when they demoted me to bomb aimer—and you guys know I'm just a bullshitter!" Eddie pleaded, "Somebody come up here and fly it! Better yet, let's jump out and take our chances!"

George said, "Not me—if I jump, who will look for fighters?" He spun around on his heel and returned to his drafty, smoky turret.

Paul Burns spoke, now on the intercom in his mid-turret sling. "I have to protect the roof."

Navigator Sergeant Bill Parsons said, "I can't even drive a car, and my wife won't let me push the baby's carriage. They hired me to show you where home is if you can figure out how to get us there without hitting something."

Bill loved planning routes through the air where no markers existed, and he had never lost the excitement of having the destination show up on the windscreen exactly where and when he predicted. But, fly an airplane? He had never had any interest in machinery of any kind; in fact, the thought of pulling and pushing levers and switches terrified him.

"Eddie..." Angus McLeod looked up from his wireless operator's position beside Bill Parsons. "...Aw ye hae tae dae is gie us back tae Vera Lynn lain, an' we'll jump intae 'er lap." Every bomber had at least one Scotsman who couldn't speak English

All but two or three of the half-dozen gauges Eddie had in front of him might as well have been in a Chinese aircraft. He knew what the engine and fuel gauges meant—he was the flight engineer, the bomb aimer and the forward gunner—but most of the flying instruments were a mystery. The Tiger Moth Eddie had logged five hours in hadn't even had an airspeed indicator, and Eddie rested his hands on a flying bomber's control wheel for the first time in his life, and the first thing he did was hit it with the butt of his hand. "Fuck." Eddie's frustrated voice went over the intercom. "Fuck! Fuck! Fuck!" The plane oscillated like a porpoise every time he hit the column, and Eddie pulled his hand back.

The new pilot's frustration wasn't comforting, and the crew remained silent. He was their only chance to get home, and every man reasoned that if he couldn't get them there, they would have to jump into Hitler's lair. Vera Lynn's lap would be preferable and probably worth the risk that Eddie would screw up and kill them.

Chapter Five

24 May 1943

"Lasciate ogne speranza, voi ch'intrate"

(Abandon all hope, ye who enter here)

Dante Alighieri, from Inferno, the first part of 'Divine Comedy.'

KATRINA CROUCHED ON THE BENCH, hands clamped on her ears in a vain attempt to dampen the rumbling vibrations reverberating from the cellar's stone walls. She leaned ahead, elbows on her knees, her wild eyes focused on the floor at her feet. Corinne sat next to her, one hand resting on Katrina's arm and rubbing her back with the other.

Lucas envied Corinne's strength and admired her selflessness. He stood up, intending to go to her, but froze when a bomb landed so close it shook the house, followed by a sound that could only be dishes crashing to the floor in the kitchen above. Pale yellow lantern light projected Lucas's shadow on the girls, not entirely hiding the sad expression on Corinne's face when she looked up at him. She didn't move her eyes from his when another bomb landed close.

A string of overlapping explosions knocked bottles of preserved meat off a shelf beside Hartwig, part of the emergency rations. Lucas tore his eyes away from Corinne to look at the puddle of identical cubes surrounded by spiced brown gravy and pieces of broken glass. His overloaded senses dragged him to a place where crushing fear threatened to paralyze him. Turning to Hartwig's father, then his mother, Lucas felt a desperate need for an adult's assurance that everything would be alright. Hartwig stood beside him, wide-eyed and scared. Lucas felt sorry for his friend until he suddenly realized Hartwig probably saw the same in him.

Lucas turned to Hartwig's parents, hoping for a sign that they would survive. Karl sat on a chair beside the door, watching Corinne and Katrina, leaning forward with an elbow on each knee. He turned toward Lucas, lowered his head and folded his hands together, wringing them in a washing motion. Lucas looked at Lenora, sitting on a folded blanket beside her husband's chair. She covered his hands with both of hers, and it seemed to Lucas that she was comforting him and saying goodbye.

◇◇◇◇◇◇◇◇◇◇◇◇◇◇◇◇◇◇◇◇◇◇◇◇◇◇◇◇◇◇◇◇◇◇

The explosions went on without pause, a loud rolling thunder whose relentless intensity and volume came from everywhere at once and nowhere in particular. Lucas wanted to believe that bombs couldn't fall at this rate for long, but on other nights, listening from his bed, the sound of distant raids on nearby cities seemed endless.

He thought of his family, crouched in their basement shelter, two houses from where he fought to control his fear. The blast that blew the window into the living room had come from the direction of the Schwartz home, but Lucas took solace in the fact that the bomb had destroyed the house between them. He told himself that if the bomb had hit the house next door, his family had a fire-proof double masonry wall between the blast that destroyed the adjacent house and their home. He reasoned that they would be as safe in their shelter as he was in Karl's.

A nagging worry made him wish he had looked out the window after the blast, but there had been no time, and he tried to convince himself that darkness would have prevented him from seeing anything, even if he had looked.

Corinne and Katrina sat together on a wide padded wooden bench bolted to the outside cellar wall and intended as a sleeping platform. As Lucas watched, Corinne put her fingers under Katrina's chin and lifted her face so she could look into her eyes. The lamp's steady yellow light revealed a wild emptiness, an expression of pure unrestrained terror that turned Katrina's beautiful face into a pitiful mask. Corinne said something to Katrina, And Lucas knew even without reading her lips that she was comforting her friend with the promise that the bombs would stop soon and they would be alright.

Feeling like an intruder, Lucas looked away but couldn't help himself and let his eyes return to Corinne, who looked at him with sympathy or perhaps disappointment. His heart jumped when she lifted the corners of her mouth in a secret smile. Still smiling, she took Katrina's head in her hands and pulled it down to her lap. Stroking Katrina's hair, Corinne began singing. Lucas doubted Katrina could hear her—he certainly couldn't—but she was singing when she looked again at Lucas, and he smiled despite the horror around them. A tiny spark of hope glowed between them, threatening to become a flame.

Disturbing noises carried down through the kitchen floor, punctuating the continuous roar of exploding bombs—dishes, and occasionally something more substantial, crashed to the pine floor reinforced with a twelve-millimetre-thick steel plate fastened to the shelter's ceiling. The concrete cellar floor, the stone walls, and the steel-supported roof vibrated independently, out of sync with the overlapping blasts. But periodically, the tremors worked together to shake the building like an earthquake that didn't stop.

The vibration of steel 'I-beam' ribs bolted under the ceiling plate knocked dust from the beams' seats—mortared sockets built into the concrete and stone walls. Andreas Schwartz and Karl Zimmermann had estimated the force from a five-hundred-pound British bomb erupting in the cellar, and his father had assured Lucas and his mother that their shelter would take everything but a direct hit. The room was small, just a little over two metres square, which reduced the mathematical possibility of a direct impact to infinitesimally small.

Lucas and Hartwig had carried the Gitterstein and mixed the concrete and mortar for the walls separating the shelter from the main cellar, walls built with thirty centimetres of masonry blocks filled with concrete and reinforced with steel rods. Lucas's father had used a big hammer and stonemason's chisel to break the concrete floor and stone walls so he could key the Gitterstein blocks into them. Andreas and Karl had bolted oak beams outside the masonry block walls; Lucas vividly remembered the weight of the thick oak timbers, staggering under the load even with Hartwig carrying the other end.

Karl and Andreas, builders by nature and scroungers out of necessity, had found the old beams, the steel and the 'Gitterstein' in the

Hoesch industrial complex. Lucas recalled how he and Hartwig had complained to their paranoid fathers, but the short discussion always ended with, "Sicher ist Sicher," 'safe is safe.' He and Hartwig had tried to get a more technical answer from their engineer fathers, but now, with the room shaking and dust finding its way through every crack, Lucas appreciated his father's engineering logic.

Lucas reasoned that the same strength would apply to the identical shelter where his parents, sister, aunt and grandmother huddled, and he knew they would worry about him. Looking around at the construction, he tried to find a weak point but decided he was insulting Karl and his structural engineer father—those two would have gotten it right. The shelters they built were likely the safest in the city, if not in Germany. The specialist engineers who regulated them had inspected their bomb shelters and left the house laughing and shaking their heads. Neither Karl nor Andreas had to wait long for their stamped approval, and Karl's framed Erlaubnis hung on the wall behind Corinne's head.

◇◇◇◇◇◇◇◇◇◇◇◇◇◇◇◇◇◇◇◇◇◇◇◇◇◇◇◇◇◇◇◇◇◇◇◇

Lucas was surprised when the sound of explosions retreated only fifteen minutes after they had begun. Only the occasional isolated explosion broke periods of eerie silence. He looked at Karl, and they met in the middle of the room, looking around and listening but saying nothing. The sound of a swirling wind, a storm more frightening than the bombs, grew out of the silence.

Lenora stood up but found it difficult to walk. She lurched across the room to her son, swaying like a sailor searching for a handhold on a heaving deck. She put her arms around him, said something Lucas couldn't hear, then turned drunkenly to her husband. He placed his hand on Lucas's shoulder for a brief moment, then wrapped his arms around her, held her, and then led her back to the blanket beside his chair. He gently lowered her to her knees and whispered something in her ear.

Lucas thought of his parents, always partners in adversity, embarrassing him and his sister when they chased one another around the house, playing like children. The children tried to separate them and divert their attention to their offspring, but despite their efforts, they could not drive a wedge between their parents, and watching Karl and Lenora, Lucas could see the same mutual trust and devotion.

His mother had enviously told Lucas that when Hartwig was born, Karl had coerced the doctors into allowing him to experience the birth with his wife. She told him, with a bit of sarcasm, that Andreas didn't seem to regret her doctor's refusal to grant him the same privilege.

Stephanie insisted on the existence of soulmates' love, but Andreas never mentioned it. Lucas turned his head to look at Corinne, wondering if she could be his soulmate. She sensed him, looked up, their eyes locked, and they smiled.

Lenora used Karl's arm to pull herself up on her knees, leaned over, put her mouth close to his ear and asked, "What's that moaning sound?" She had to speak over what was now a howl, loud enough that Lucas heard what she said. Karl answered normally, without trying to prevent anyone else from hearing.

"It's the wind feeding a fire...probably in the Stadtmitte. The wind originates outside the centre of the heat; it's simply air rushing in to replace oxygen devoured by the flames. The buildings on this street are modern, built using stone, brick and concrete. In the old city, wood is the primary building material, and the fire follows the fuel." The words' simplicity brought back a disturbing conversation he had recently had with his father.

◇◇◇◇◇◇◇◇◇◇◇◇◇◇◇◇◇◇◇◇◇◇◇◇◇◇◇◇◇◇

Everyone who waited for the British bombers to fly over their city had heard rumours and read the newspapers' terrifying description of firestorms. Following the attack that destroyed Köln a year ago, Lucas asked his father, "Is there such a thing as a firestorm?"

Andreas gave him a newspaper with an account of what the paper called a firestorm in Essen on the twelfth of March, forty kilometres from Dortmund, and Lucas's father explained the article in simple terms.

"This account is nothing more than Goebbels' propaganda and selected witnesses' hyperbole. The bombers' target, the Krupp steel plant, was out of commission for only a week. The newspaper printed pictures of burned victims of the 'criminal British bombing of innocent German citizens.' The account of every raid has at least one picture of a burned child. More often than seems possible, there's a picture of a dead mother with a child in her arms."

"But those are real pictures, aren't they?"

Andreas said, "Look closely. Goebbels' Reichsministerium für Volksaufklärung und Propaganda chose the images to sow hatred for the 'Verdammnt Englander' and similar, and often the same pictures are there week after week. Whether they are fabricated or not, most intelligent Germans think the articles are exaggerations and turn the page."

But the photographs still disturbed Lucas. He wanted to believe the pictures were fake, and he began his quest for the truth by asking his father what caused a firestorm.

Andreas explained: "A burning building or two can't create a significant firestorm. A genuine firestorm covers blocks, theoretically, a whole city or thousands of hectares of dry forest. It resembles a thunderstorm on the ground, fed by hot air rushing from the edges to rise in its centre. A firestorm begins when a large fire creates a vortex of rising burning air, creating a vacuum near the ground.

Later, when you stop playing the violin and begin studying engineering, you will learn the phrase, 'Nature abhors a vacuum.' In this case, oxygen-rich cool air from around the fire surges into the vacuum left behind by the rising hot air, filling the void and nourishing the fire. If the fire has enough fuel and is big enough and hot enough, the air moving to the centre and rising over the fire creates a strong wind blowing toward the centre. The cycle grows in intensity, width and height until the fire runs out of fuel. If it had enough fuel, it would take all the water in the Rhine to stop it."

"Then it is possible," said Lucas, "that Goebbels is right... the British start the fires intentionally?"

"Yes, it is not only possible—that's what the British designed their bombers and bombs to do! The bomber releases hundreds of small incendiaries—phosphorous firebombs that burst outward when they hit, burning slowly and at a super-high temperature for five minutes or more. The high explosive bombs hit the target with two-or-three-second delay fuses, blowing buildings into small pieces, creating instant kindling for the incendiaries. The scattered burning phosphorous sets fire to the debris, and if they set fire to a big enough area of largely wooden buildings, it is theoretically possible, even likely, that the fire will generate a so-called 'firestorm.'"

Horrified at his father's cold-blooded explanation, Lucas shouted, "But that's inhuman! Hitler is right... The Englander are animals!"

Andreas looked up from the apple he was peeling. "I gave you a theoretical example of something that hasn't happened yet." He put the peeler down and looked into his son's eyes. "And what do you think war is? Do you think that it's a game with rules? Do you think one side uses weapons that the other side won't use because those weapons are inhumane?" He finished peeling, put the knife down and laid the apple he had peeled in the bowl. Stephanie took it away. Apfel Kuchen was on the menu.

"Son, you live in an unreal, romantic world of music, school and friends. Before you condemn the Englander, remember that the Luftwaffe bombed the first civilians for Franco in Spain and then Polish women and children in Warsaw. Our Luftwaffe destroyed half of Rotterdam—the half with the most people—to convince the Niederlander to surrender. We tried to defeat the English by attacking their airfields and industries, but they wouldn't surrender, and they replaced aircraft faster than we could destroy them.

The English pilots shot our bombers and fighters down, so Hitler bombed London at night, creating what we could call small firestorms, terrifying the English civilians. But the British still didn't quit, so he flattened Coventry and Plymouth. Coventry, a small city filled with refugees, mostly women, old men and children from London, was essentially destroyed because Hitler thought that this would break the English will, but he was wrong. Churchill used the bombing to stiffen the English resolve."

Lucas's shock prevented him from speaking, and his father waited. Suspecting he might be stepping into another minefield, Lucas said, "But we didn't use delay fuses and incendiaries!"

Andreas smiled sympathetically at his fifteen-year-old son. "Lucas, we invented the modern version of the incendiary in 1918, and we used it during the Great War. We also invented poison gas warfare during that war, thinking the British and French would surrender, but the British put on gas masks and used gas against us. We were the first to use long-delay fuses—in Warsaw, some of them set to explode hours later when people would be digging their friends, relatives and children out of the rubble. In England, we dropped thousands of fire bombs to light fires that became beacons for hundreds of bombers. We sent a thousand planes in a single raid, but still, the Englander wouldn't quit!"

Stunned, Lucas waited for his father to go on. Finally, Andreas said, "The raids killed thousands of people, but the English people still didn't quit, did they?" He waited, but Lucas couldn't find his voice. Finally, his father said, "And, unfortunately, neither will we!"

Lucas's mind went off the rails. He fought to find a way out but knew there was none when he asked, "But if no one will quit, how does it end?" His father smiled, put his hand on Lucas's shoulder, and said, "One side will get tired; its people will refuse to fight as happened in the Great War. When enough soldiers refuse to go on the battlefield, and their wives, children and parents refuse to work for the war, the war is over. The fuel for firestorms is wood; for war, it is hate. Every bomb the English bombers drop feeds that hate. And Germans are the only people more stubborn than the English!" He looked outside at a cold drizzle falling on the rotting seeds he had planted in the garden. "It probably has something to do with the climate."

◇◇◇◇◇◇◇◇◇◇◇◇◇◇◇◇◇◇◇◇◇◇◇◇◇◇◇◇◇◇◇◇◇◇◇

The conversation, indelibly burned into Lucas's consciousness, rushed back to him, and he concluded that the howl could only be the wind his father had told him about, a massive volume of air pouring into the bottom of an enormous fire. But all the houses where Karl and Andreas lived were brick and stone, with a minimum amount of flammable material, most of it in the roof structure. The wind was blowing away from them toward the fire in the city's centre, and he let his hopes rise.

Lenora spoke, connecting the dots and breaking Lucas's rumination. "My God, Karl, how will anyone survive? What about Andreas and Stephanie? The first explosion came from their house!"

Lenora looked at Lucas, realized what she had said, and, overwhelmed, began crying uncontrollably. Karl slid down from the chair, knelt beside his wife and wrapped his arms around her. Lucas leaned against the post that Karl had put in the centre of the room and listened to him as he directed his comments to Lucas and his wife.

"They are in a shelter like ours, and we can't do anything to help them until the bombing is over. I believe we are far enough outside the core that we will survive." Karl looked into Lenora's streaming eyes. Lucas wondered if Karl actually believed his theory but decided to accept that Hartwig's engineer father was right. The fear that nagged Lucas was the timing. The bomb had hit his house before the musicians had finished packing their instruments. Had his parents reached the shelter before then?

Leonora asked, "But what about our friends in the Stadtmitte?"

Karl hung his head, slowly shaking it back and forth as he said sadly, "I fear the worst."

Chapter Six

24 May 1943

Somebody do something!

A shape climbed past Eddie's windscreen, its twin exhausts lighting tiny patches on the trailing edge of the Messerschmitt's wing. He thanked God for whoever had invented the flame arrestors on their Wellington—the exhausts were invisible to an attacking fighter unless it flew straight and level directly behind the bomber—a practice that would dramatically shorten a fighter pilot's life expectancy. To night fighters above, the Wellington's outline contrasted against the firestorm below, but only if they took the time to look down. Fortunately, the fighters were busy chasing targets flying in the opposite direction and thousands of feet above Eddy's Wellington. The single dark shape of the bomber, flying in an unexpected place and on a course reverse to everything else in the vicinity, would probably flash through a night fighter pilot's consciousness so fast it wouldn't have time to register. That's what Eddie told himself.

Eddie dreaded the searchlights and the flak more than the fighters. The lights, probing the sky for targets, occasionally flashed past, sweeping in the opposite direction at close to the speed of the attacking bombers. A shaft of light flicked over the Wellington quicker than an eye could blink, in less time than a brain could identify it. With so little time to see the aircraft, decide whether it was a bomber or a friendly fighter, and then reverse the light's direction, Eddie decided that men on the ground would never recognize the retreating Wellington as a bomber. They wouldn't keep the light on it until the flak gunners or a fighter shot it down. Eddie convinced himself the lights were interested in attacking bombers, not retreating ones, then put them out of his mind and concentrated on the job he had wanted since signing the papers in Canada that had gotten him into this mess.

He took a deep breath, exhaled, and touched the controls, then pulled his hands back as though the wheel were hot. He breathed deeply, looked out the side window at the port engine's whirling propeller, and thought of home. He pictured his mother knitting mittens and socks in front of a fire in their stone fireplace, built by his father using rocks he had dug out of the fields and split with a hammer and wedges. He saw his father walking behind his prize-winning team of horses, pulling a set of bobsleds loaded with logs he had cut on the hundred acres of the farm that wasn't a field.

Something different in the plane's movement told Eddie to get back to business. The bomber had been flying a mile above the fires, bouncing along on updrafts, bucking like his father's chev farm truck on a dirt road. And then, Eddie realized the bumps had become less frequent and severe. A few minutes later, the plane left the fires behind and droned along as steady as a rock.

Calm now, Eddie returned to what was becoming a problem. The ground ahead of them disappeared, and darkness, a black void, slid beneath them. With the fires and lights behind the wimpy, Eddie had lost his reference points—the cockpit had become a black hole.

Eddie fought his senses, approaching panic—they told him the plane was falling—his brain told him he had to get out! He slid the window back, breathed the cold air, and was forming the words to tell the crew to bail out when Bill Parson's calm voice said on the intercom, "How you doin' Eddie?"

◇◇◇

Eddie hesitated, then looked at the instruments. He checked the altimeter, the airspeed, the turn and bank indicator. According to the compass, the Wellington was still flying west; England was west of Germany, so that was probably good. Nothing moved on the instrument panel; nothing had changed but his perception. He relaxed against the back of his seat and closed the window. The engines droned on with the same comforting moan; every instrument looked normal as Eddie examined them.

He said into the intercom, "I thought we were turning and falling;

I'm beginning to understand why they wouldn't let me stay in pilot training." His nervous laugh betrayed the helplessness he felt. "Bill, I don't have any idea what to do. We could jump now; it's dark under us, and we probably should get out before the fighters find us or we run into a hill."

Bill's soothing voice was the same one he used in the pub when they drank beer together. He could have been talking about his mother.

"Eddie, I was just thinking: who would have taught the Wright Brothers to fly? Forty years ago, who else knew how an airplane worked? They were the only ones who didn't think that something heavier than air would fall out of the sky. Hell, that's why I still hate getting into an airplane!"

Bill waited while Eddie considered that, and the more Eddie thought, the more he relaxed. He chuckled, the panic gone, but a healthy dose of fear remained.

"Okay, I admit you've got a point, but they only stayed in the air for twelve seconds. I read a book about their troubles getting that crate in the air, and they did almost everything wrong—they were just lucky. The only luck I have is bad." Eddie picked out the altimeter. The needles weren't moving; if the instrument wasn't broken, that had to be good.

The intercom was silent for a few seconds. Everyone, including Eddie, waited for Bill.

Bill finally said, "So, Eddie, isn't this easy? You've been sitting in a modern airplane watching Byron for months, and I was in the bar when Cliff talked you through a landing without using the control wheel. Like Cliff said, the plane is okay without your help! So, why don't you relax and enjoy the ride? Take your time—look at the instruments and figure them out. Take all the time you need—we've got lots of fuel, we're going in the right direction, and we can bail out anytime. In fact, according to Cliff, if you do nothing, we will probably make it to England."

Eddie took a deep breath, let Bill's logic sink in and put his hands on his lap. The instruments were all steady; the altimeter needle was frozen on what looked like six thousand feet plus a bit, the airspeed said one hundred fifty and wasn't moving, and the compass rocked gently on a westerly course, where his limited memories of school geography told him England should be.

Bill laughed as though they were all playing cards and drinking beer. "I would bet you my father's farm that you will figure it out—if he had a farm."

George Cunningham couldn't resist. "I didn't know you had a father... or maybe it's just that you don't know who he is."

Bill paused while everyone laughed, then became serious. "Eddie, We're okay for now—we're high enough that we won't hit anything, and we're flying toward England. If we wait, we can jump out where we will get a hero's welcome and all the beer we can drink. That beats a hard prison bunk and potato soup once a day!"

Eddie cautiously laid his hands on the wheel as Bill said, "Meanwhile, why don't you get the feel of the controls? Nothing fancy, just nudge them here and there to see what they do." A stretch of silence followed in which every man in the bomber asked God to help Eddie.

Eddie gently tested the resistance in the wheel. The plane moved, and Bill broke in. "But please, Eddie, no aerobatics." Nervous laughs came from everywhere; Eddie was acutely aware that he held all the cards and was playing with his friends' money. He hoped he wasn't overbetting an offsuit hand.

Angus MacLeod, the wireless operator, spoke up. "Eddie, don't ye fuss abit it. We coods hae bailed it ower a burnin' city, an' awreddy we can dae better than 'at! Aw ye need tae dae is gie us athwart th' channel, an' e'en Bill can fin' a chunk ay lain as big as Englain! We'll jump it, an' ye won't hae tae pay fur a swally fur all yer life."

Eddie wasn't sure he was right but assumed that Angus had wished him well. He grinned in his mask and said, "Thanks, Angus; I'll figure out how to get us home." He thought he heard a collective sigh of relief over the intercom. Each member of the crew keyed his mike and wished him good luck.

Eddie let the weight of his hands rest on the wheel. The altitude needle moved; he put them in his lap, and it was steady again.

Eddie pictured the Wright Brothers flipping a coin to see who would fly the contraption they had built. But total immersion on his first flight was not what Eddie had in mind when he enlisted in the RCAF. The control wheel felt strange—not at all sensitive, it resisted a small effort to try and move it—and it was nothing like his limited experience at the sensitive controls of the Tiger Moth they had let him fly until they discovered he had no talent.

Eddie put his feet lightly on the rudders but didn't push on them. He nudged the wheel to the left and right and was surprised when the aircraft barely tipped. When he slightly increased the deflection, the plane banked a few degrees each way. Eddie put his hands on his lap and decided to think before doing anything more.

The hours Eddie had spent badgering Byron Johnson to explain the instruments had resulted in him learning the basic information each instrument had on its face. He had learned enough that he knew he should restrict himself to standard turns on the turn-and-bank indicator—Byron had rated it the most useful flying instrument on the panel. He hadn't tipped the wings half of that, but he reasonably thought that the second half would not be any more exciting than the first.

"Okay, Bill," he reported to his navigator, "I'm pretty sure I can turn without killing us—now I'm going to try up and down."

Bill replied, with a hint of trepidation, "Roger, Eddie. Understood, but there's no need to turn for a while; England is straight ahead. Good work, buddy!" He added as an afterthought, "Careful with up and down... especially down... Even I know that too much of that could be bad."

Eddie grinned; he began to believe he could fly an airplane.

◇◇◇◇◇◇◇◇◇◇◇◇◇◇◇◇◇◇◇◇◇◇◇◇◇◇◇◇◇

He had grown up driving a kerosene-powered Case tractor on his father's farm near Thunder Bay in northwestern Ontario. His father had left the tractor-driving to him, preferring his team of Belgian horses, so the feel of machinery controls in his hands was nothing new to Eddie. His perfectionist father had made him learn to drive the ancient beast with precision, plowing a furrow as straight and even as his father could with his team of horses, something that Eddie discovered took more skill and planning than one would think.

His father taught him that plowing was an analogy for good work. He said, "Plowing is something you need to get right the first time; you can't replow a bad furrow; you must live with it. It will haunt you as you harrow it, fill holes, and turn over the skipped places with a fork. Planting is a lot harder on a badly plowed field."

Unfortunately, a farm tractor lives in a two-dimensional world, and adding a third dimension changes everything.

Eddie hadn't given up on learning how to fly when he joined No 431 Squadron as a bomb aimer. As his mentor, he picked Cliff Bulmer, a thirty-five-year-old Canadian bomber pilot, an old man by 1943 RAF standards. To Eddie's delight, Cliff befriended him, taking him under his metaphorical wing. Eddie listened, captivated by Cliff's tales of bush-flying adventures in the wilds of northern Canada, and Cliff rewarded him by answering an endless stream of flying questions. Sitting in the pilot's seat in the Wellington, Eddie directed his mind to the flying library Cliff had drilled into his brain.

When Eddie began experimenting with the aircraft controls, the altimeter had shown six thousand two hundred feet above sea level, but the sea wasn't what was under the Wellington. The ground was another matter—it was closer than that by at least a thousand feet—still enough if he kept his mistakes to a few hundred feet. Eddie checked the airspeed... the Wimpy was flying through the night sky at a hundred and fifty miles per hour. He tapped the altimeter like Byron did every time he looked at it—the needle bounced down the width of itself—and Eddie discovered they had descended two hundred feet. He told himself that the descent was a consequence of his incipient turns.

Eddie decided he didn't have a problem with six thousand feet, but the rate-of-climb indicator showed one hundred feet per minute down, and he had no desire to get any closer to the damned searchlights and flak that were everywhere in Germany. He had to fix that, but he decided to think first.

◇◇◇◇◇◇◇◇◇◇◇◇◇◇◇◇◇◇◇◇◇◇◇◇◇◇◇◇◇◇◇◇◇◇◇◇

Eddie's friend, Cliff, was the best pilot in the squadron and the only one who would answer Eddie's questions. He had verbally published his basic flight rules three months before Byron jumped out the Wellington bomber's window. Cliff's lecture in the pub, intended as entertainment, had more than a trace of education behind it. Cliff's "Fuckup Rule," the first one on the list, stated: "If in doubt because you have fucked everything up, take your hands off the controls and put your feet on the floor. Any aircraft is smarter than the average pilot." Eddie let go of the column, put his hands in his lap, and the rate of climb went to zero. He smiled. So far, Cliff's course got an 'A-plus.'

He decided that he would feel safer if he were to climb a little—that trying down first was probably, as Bill had made clear, not a good idea. He wasn't sure that all the bombers in the stream had passed them on their way to the target, and he didn't want to get among them, but some extra altitude would probably be a good thing. He heard Cliff saying, "The only thing more useless to a pilot than the air above him is the runway behind him!"

Cliff Bulmer had been a bush pilot since he was eighteen. He learned to fly in a surplus World War I biplane, the worst possible training platform but the only one available. After five hours with the smooth side up and the wheels hanging down, and having survived two landings, he decided he'd had enough lessons and bought the plane. Cliff immediately christened his bush pilot career by making his maiden voyage from Thunder Bay to Red Lake, following roads and rivers on a government-published Ontario road map. Eventually, he built a business flying freight and mail into the gold-mining hubs north of Lake Superior near the Manitoba border. By the time war broke out, he owned and operated a profitable flying business in the part of Canada that seldom thawed.

On a spring day in late May, with the ice in Trout Lake down to a few scattered rafts, the airplane gremlins killed the engine in Cliff's friend Ronnie's little Piper Cub, and he successfully landed on one of the smallest patches of ice floating in the lake. He radioed the gold mine in Red Lake, and they called every bush pilot in the area. A couple of them flew over and declared the ice floe too small to land on and the ice too thin. They recommended someone find a canoe and rescue Ronald before the ice melted, but Ronald refused to leave his little yellow plane. "Get Cliff," he said into his dying radio, "I won't leave my baby! I'll die first!"

Cliff, returning from Thunder Bay in his new Norseman C-64 freight aircraft, called Red Lake to tell them he was coming. The radio operator told him about Ronnie's problem, leaving out the details other pilots had described. Still equipped with skis, Cliff landed his Norseman on the last bit of snow next to the mine, off-loaded half a ton of dynamite, a couple of gallons of nitro-glycerine, and other less dangerous cargo, and then took off for Trout Lake.

With darkness approaching, Cliff decided to skip the usual fly-over to check the ice—if Ronnie could do it, he could— and landed on the little patch with his big Norseman. He took off with Ronnie and fetched the spare engine Ronnie had bought with the little Piper Cub. They worked all night, and the next day, Ronnie's little yellow darling took off from the rotten melting ice behind the Norseman, making Cliff an instant legend.

Six months later, for a reason known only to him, Cliff enlisted in the RCAF, leaving his bush-flying business and his new Norseman in the hands of his wife Carolyn and his friend Ronnie. Cliff trusted Ronnie with the flying, but the jury was out on whether he could trust him with his wife.

Cliff drafted a will, just in case, detailing how everything should play out should the Germans get lucky. In that case, he sincerely hoped there was an afterlife because, assuming he hadn't gotten too many demerits in this life, Cliff planned to torment Ronnie and Carolyn for as long as God would let him.

A year later, Cliff flew a Wellington bomber from England to Germany for the first time.

◇◇◇◇◇◇◇◇◇◇◇◇◇◇◇◇◇◇◇◇◇◇◇◇◇◇◇◇◇◇◇◇

Eddie rechecked everything. Nothing was out of place; the aircraft still pointed its nose toward England and had lots of air under it, although the Wellington descended slightly. While he stared at the turn-and-bank, trying to figure out what the '2 min' on each side of the centred needle meant, Eddie remembered Cliff's voice—they were at the pub, and he had asked him a question about climbing and descending...

"Eddie," Cliff explained, "a good pilot is a lazy pilot." Cliff put his beer down and turned to his student, as did every man in the room; they knew the routine. Eddie had asked a simple question, and Cliff, his voice a little too loud to be intended only for the young wannabe pilot, addressed the room with his concentration ostensibly on his student. It had been five days since their last victory over death, and the next mission couldn't be far in the future. The quiet bar radiated more of the uneasiness of a graveyard than the exuberance of rowdy young aviators. Cliff drank a swallow of his beer and then went on.

"Eddie, Most pilots move the controls way too much. An airplane is like a woman; you must move slowly and smoothly until emergency time. Understand how she moves, and she'll be nice to you.

"Horse shit!" said someone in the corner; "Crapolla!" said a man at the bar; "Coonshit!" said a Canadian who had just entered the pub. Further lively, less-repeatable comments echoed around the room.

The Canadians, a raucous, colourful bunch, acknowledged Cliff Bulmer as the best pilot in the squadron, although his approach was somewhat unconventional. The average bomber pilot didn't "give a shit" about honing his flying skills; an attitude pounded into them when they began bomber training. Most couldn't qualify for a driving license and weren't interested in anything that didn't involve a woman or required more than five minutes of concentration.

The program taught the would-be aviators that the pilot's solitary objective was to get the bomber to the target without running into any of his comrades and then drop the bombs when they were vertically over the target. Whether or not they made it home was preferable to the alternative but optional. The British were building new, more capable airplanes every day, and the old ones were soon outdated.

The naked truth, as every airman in the room knew, was that it didn't matter a whit how well the pilot could fly—flak and night fighters were indiscriminate enemies. The pilot rarely saw them coming, and in the infrequent instances where they did, running away was frowned upon, and in any case, it was futile. The RAF instructed them to get bombs to the target, but the redundant fine points of flying were left out. The Germans were defeating the Allies everywhere, and there was no time to waste teaching pilots to understand the delight of precision flying. Any landing the crew could walk away from was considered a good one.

Pub-bound bomber crews wanted nothing more than enough beer to dull their anxiety. Entertainment was a side dish, consumed after their minds were sufficiently numb that quality wasn't a factor. Depending on the listeners' point of view, Cliff either cloaked his flying instructions as theatre or disguised the theatre as instruction. The crowd pretended to enjoy themselves as long as the bar provided the mind-numbing beer.

"Yep, it's true..." Cliff knew his crowd... "if you learn to control things until the time is right, you will succeed—you oversexed, underserved studs should appreciate that!" A chorus of boos and jeers greeted Cliff, and then the men laughed. He had trained his audience well. Their attention diverted from fear of their next mission to Cliff's caricature of a professor lecturing his students.

"You want to climb..." He directed the question at Eddie but said it loud enough for everyone but the deaf or the dead to hear." So, tell me, what do you do?"

Eddie waded bravely into the shark pool. "I would pull the column back, of course." He spoke loudly and positively, but Cliff's grin erased his confidence.

A ragged, drunken chorus rang out. "Of course!" Cliff raised his hand but kept his eyes on Eddie. Instantly, the room became silent. But there was something wrong—Cliff was grinning, and then he wasn't—Cliff's tone changed; he feigned deep sadness.

"I've wasted all of my excellent teaching; you haven't learned a fucking thing, and I am very disappointed." He wagged his head as he walked around Eddie, then suddenly cheered up and turned to the crowd. "Not to worry...the second rule of flying according to Cliff's laws of flight, the rule of 'up and down,' is the one you must use here. No, you do not pull back on the column because it's a two-handed steering wheel..." He put both hands in the air..., "and you only have one hand available for the plane. Like a sailor in a storm...one hand for the ship and one for the sailor. Gentlemen, your other hand is busy." He raised one hand in the air and put the other on his crotch. The room roared.

Eddie remembered trying to appear curious, looking around the room as he asked, "Okay, learned one, oh eagle incarnate—what do I do?"

The silent room waited while Cliff faced his student, leaning over so that his face was a hairsbreadth from Eddie's (Eddie vividly remembered the stink of Cliff's breath) and growled, "You only need one hand to push the fucking throttles in!" He looked around the room, pushed his shoulders unnaturally back and paced forth, then back, holding his professor pose.

When he got back to a puzzled Eddie, he said, "The airplane has to do something with that extra power, and if the pilot doesn't fuck it up—rule one, remember?—it will fucking well climb! And that, my boy, is the first half of the 'up and down' rule."

No one had dared to challenge Cliff, not even the pilots in the bar—they knew better than to contradict a 'real' pilot, Cliff's description of himself. They had tried that, and Cliff had humiliated them. With two thousand hours flying through blizzards, landing on postage-stamp-sized clearings while carrying loads that mocked the aircraft's gross weight limit, the pilots in the room conceded to Cliff's right to arrogance.

Eddie still didn't understand why the plane climbed by adding power without pulling the column back. Cliff's next question completely flummoxed him—he didn't understand the logic. Cliff stuck his finger in Eddie's face and said, "Now, tell me, Eddie, what will be the airspeed in the climb?"

Eddie distinctly remembered considering, "How the hell should I know?" but knowing that humiliation would then be a sure thing, he wisely kept his mouth shut.

A voice in the corner said, "The same as it was...it won't change."

Eddie was sure the voice was wrong. He waited for Cliff to give the voice his 'comeuppance.'

Cliff looked toward the interrupter, moved his pointed finger to the speaker and said, "Correct, but if you interrupt Eddie again, I'll break your nose and drink your beer!"

Eddie still thought that the voice was wrong, but that would make Cliff wrong, which, according to Cliff, wasn't possible.

Cliff turned back to him and said pleasantly, "Now, that wasn't so hard, was it? I will give you fifty percent on that one, a bare pass because you used an outside source of information." A chorus of boos followed the announcement.

Then Cliff lifted his foot and placed it on the chair beside Eddie's. He leaned forward, bent his knee, repointed his finger at Eddie's face, and then turned right to look at every face in the crowd before anyone could ask a question.

"New topic, same rule—let's return to level flight." He straightened his back."How many of you would push the column ahead to descend?" Eddie looked around the room, but not a man dared to raise his hand, and he was pretty sure that none knew why.

"You can raise your hand without getting your nose broken."

Still, no hands.

"How about you?" he asked the voice in the corner. How would you descend?" He waited, but there was no answer, so he turned to Eddie. The corner piped up at the same instant Cliff's mouth moved.

"Pull the throttles back...using your free hand, of course."

Cliff pointed at the voice. "Okay, the smartass in the corner is right again, but what if Eddie's pilot is that you, Johnson?" Cliff pointed toward the corner and got a weak "Yep, that's me." Cliff shook his finger at Johnson.

"What if Byron gets wasted by a night fighter or, more likely, shits his pants in a flak storm and is so scared he can't fly?" He stared at Pilot Officer Byron Johnson, and Johnson laughed like he was supposed to.

◇◇◇◇◇◇◇◇◇◇◇◇◇◇◇◇◇◇◇◇◇◇◇◇◇◇◇◇◇◇◇◇◇◇◇

Eddie looked at the altimeter; it told him the plane was a hundred feet under six thousand. He tried to remember the altitude assigned to their Wellington and came up with nothing—he decided to check.

"Bill, how high are the lowest bombers in the stream?"

"Good question. Give me a minute—I'll look in my briefing notes." Eddie only had to wait a few seconds. "The lowest assigned altitude was ten thousand feet. If you're going to climb, don't trust anything above nine thousand until you are sure we're past the stream."

Basing his theory on the unknown proximity of the black ground, Eddie decided that three thousand feet up would put them in less danger than staying where they were. Byron had trimmed the Wellington to fly straight and level at a hundred and fifty miles per hour; it would be a while before they reached the coast, so Eddie took time for a review.

He went through the possibilities using Cliff's laws. The first rule was the 'fuckup rule,' for use when the pilot fucked up beyond his ability to fix it. It read: "If a properly-trimmed aircraft gets ahead of a stupid pilot, his troubles will go away if he takes the cause of the fuck-up out of the equation—the pilot. Because a stupid pilot can fuck up in very creative and unpredictable ways, said pilot must admit he has a problem and take his hands off the wheel, put his feet on the floor, and wait. If left alone, any stable airplane, including a Wellington, will return to its original trimmed position and stay there until it runs out of gas or hits something."

Eddie put his hands back on the column, and the plane began descending. He let go, and the altimeter froze on five-thousand-nine-hundred feet.

He decided to test Cliff's 'up and down rule.' It stated: "To fix a tendency to descend, first observe the 'fuckup' rule." Eddie had done that, and it worked. "Second, add throttle; if you add enough, the plane will climb, and third, if the second part doesn't work, recheck the fuckup rule!" Eddie decided he had the rule's theory covered—it was time to, as Cliff put it, "think or sink."

Noting two-thousand-two-hundred rpm on both engine tachometers, Eddie pushed the throttles ahead until the gauges read two-thousand-five-hundred, then put his hand on his knee. The airspeed initially dropped slightly, then returned to one-hundred-and-fifty as the plane climbed, passing through six-thousand-five-hundred feet in about a minute. He grinned and congratulated himself. He had proven Cliff's second rule, the 'up' part, the part he hadn't believed.

The night was clear, and the air was stable—perfect conditions for learning to fly. With Cliff's laws of flying as his reference, Eddie figured the only way the odds could be better would require an instructor. For now, he felt he had the plane under control.

He sat with his hands on his knees, looking at one instrument after another, watching the altimeter climb, thinking about Cliff's rules and the night at the pub. Then, the cockpit began to tilt. He leaned opposite the tilt to compensate and reached for the control column. This wasn't supposed to happen!

Chapter Seven

24 May 1943

Bush flying

EDDIE REMEMBERED CLIFF'S INSTRUCTIONS and caught himself before he touched anything. He put his hands in his lap, looked at his feet and let the feeling pass. When he looked up, the turn-and-bank indicator was centred, the compass gently rocked on the westerly heading, and the altimeter passed through eight thousand feet.

As he stared at the controls, his eyes went out of focus, and desperation overwhelmed him. The Wellington had passed the fires, the lights, and the bomber stream and now climbed straight ahead without his input. Everything was stable according to the instruments, but the black hole that imprisoned him seemed to be shrinking, pressing against him. His sense of up and down, turning, and balance were all gone. They told him the instruments were wrong, that the aircraft was turning, and he reached for the column to correct the wing he thought was tipping into a steep right turn. And then Cliff's voice came to him from the pub…

"Eddie, when you are not sure, always remember the first rule—the most important one—the 'fuckup rule.' Cliff spoke to him quietly over a beer. "There are three instruments that you need to watch, and only three. The others are nice to have, but you don't need them to keep the airplane in the air. You need the altimeter, the airspeed, and the turn and bank indicator. Having an artificial horizon and a rate-of-climb for precision flying is nice, but the first three are essential. Don't do anything unless more than one of those essential instruments says you are right. If the altimeter is winding down, look at the turn indicator—if you are turning and descending, you are in a spiral, and the airspeed will increase. An increasing airspeed is bad because it means that whatever you're doing is wrong, and the ground will eventually ruin your day. Go immediately to the 'fuckup' rule."

Eddie leaned back and closed his eyes. A few seconds passed before he peeked, and the first thing he looked at was the altimeter—it was still going up. He looked at the airspeed, frozen at a hundred-and-forty-five. The turn needle was centred, and the ball sat quietly at the bottom, centred between two black lines. Everything was fine, so he closed his eyes. He saw himself on the ground, climbing out of the hatch and standing beside the airplane. The men took turns slapping his back...

◇◇◇◇◇◇◇◇◇◇◇◇◇◇◇◇◇◇◇◇◇◇◇◇◇◇◇◇

Like every member of every aircrew bombing Germany, Eddie experienced an enormous sense of relief following every mission. If the mission had been a bad one, the airmen acted like giddy children as soon as their feet were back on terra firma. They kissed the ground, congratulated one another with whacks on backs and backsides, and jumped around like first-graders when the recess bell rang. Grown men acted out in ways that peacetime society considers foolish.

Sitting in the Wellington, listening to the labouring engines, Eddie longed for that feeling. He looked around at the dim red light on the panel, felt the vibration of the thrashing propellers, heard the drone of over two thousand unmuffled horsepower, and dark despair returned. He longed for the pub, a beer, friends and a cheerful woman's face, things he feared he would never again experience, and it took all his emotional strength to hold back his tears.

Eddie was young, under normal circumstances too young to fear death. But halfway through a thirty-mission tour, many crews, some of whom were Eddie's friends, hadn't survived. But, following a mission, rather than mourn missing friends, Eddie and his comrades-in-arms celebrated their victory over the War Gods. They drank beer, told silly stories, and raised their voices in song and unrestrained laughter. Every man knew that he was happy because it had been someone else's turn to die. They couldn't help celebrating and thinking, "Better him than me."

The morning after, when unbridled jubilation ended and euphoria crashed and burned, depression, the price for climbing too high and flying too fast, vanquished all comers. The countdown to the next deadly crapshoot began, and each night, each beer brought them closer to the day they would crawl into their bomber for another attempt to cheat the reaper. Eddie would have to repeat the cycle fifteen more times before Bomber Command commuted his death sentence and chained him to a desk.

◇◇◇◇◇◇◇◇◇◇◇◇◇◇◇◇◇◇◇◇◇◇◇◇◇◇◇◇◇◇

Eddie reached for the throttles as he said, "Bill, we're almost at nine thousand." Bill answered, "We're past the stream, and we are flying west, the even-numbered-altitude direction; take her to ten thousand."

The needle swept past nine thousand, the rate-of-climb sat on six hundred, and the airspeed was one-hundred-forty mph. For the first time, Eddie compared the magnetic compass to what Byron had told him was the gyrocompass.

"Bill, something's wrong." Eddie tapped the magnetic compass, bubbling the kerosene it floated in. "The compass says two hundred and eighty, and the gyro says two-seventy-five—one of them is broken."

Bill laughed. "No, Eddie, you have to set the gyro to the magnetic compass heading... friction causes it to lag, and you have to adjust it every ten or fifteen minutes. Pull the little button on the front and twist it until the gyro heading is the same as the compass. Don't forget to push it back in."

While Eddie followed Bill's instructions, Bill said, "When you're ready, your new course is..."

"Not yet. I want to level out at ten thousand before I turn."

"That's good, Eddie. No hurry, we won't get lost. Keeping things simple is more important right now."

Eddie scanned the instruments. The course was two-eighty degrees; the long needle on the altimeter swept past five hundred, and the short one seemed motionless at nine thousand feet. He tapped it as he had seen Byron do, and the long pointer shook as it moved smoothly past six hundred.

Eddie waited, hands on his knees, watching the altimeter needle circle toward zero—ten thousand feet. When the needle was a hundred feet short of vertical, he slowly pulled the throttles back to twenty-two hundred. The plane's nose dropped, and the altimeter needle slowed,

65

then began to descend. He left everything alone—Cliff's first rule—and the Wimpy climbed slightly, sank slightly, then settled close to ten thousand feet.

"By God, he's right!" Eddie could not believe he had just climbed and levelled off without touching the flight controls. He decided to run through all the maneuvers Cliff had so colourfully described. But first, he needed to know what the cruising speed was supposed to be.

"Bill, Eddie again; I'm at ten-thousand, but the airspeed is only one-forty."

"One-ninety would be good at this altitude."

Eddie thought for a few minutes. If he just added power, he would climb. The Wellington needed fifty miles an hour, not altitude. Then he remembered Cliff... "The elevators control speed, and the throttles control attitude. Trim down to go faster and add throttle to level the plane at the desired altitude."

Eddie increased the engines' revolutions a hundred rpm—the Wimpy obediently climbed. He trimmed back to level flight fifty feet above ten thousand. The airspeed indicator stuck on one hundred and seventy. Excited, he set the throttles at twenty-four-hundred, then trimmed—one hundred ninety and the altitude steady a hundred feet above ten thousand. Eddie guessed that was good enough for a beginner.

Satisfied with himself, Eddie checked everything. Turn-and-bank, centred; airspeed, one-ninety; altitude ten-thousand-one-hundred feet; course, one-eighty. He pulled the throttles back until fifty rpm dropped off each engine, beginning a slow descent. He added power, the same fifty rpm, and after a couple of porpoise moves, the plane levelled off at a hundred feet below ten thousand. He smiled; he could now control up and down. It was time to turn—rule three. He went back to the pub...

◇◇◇◇◇◇◇◇◇◇◇◇◇◇◇◇◇◇◇◇◇◇◇◇◇◇◇◇◇◇◇◇◇◇◇

Cliff was still talking. "Next item: you've got everything where you want it...the plane is straight and level, the airspeed is perfect, and you've got a big smile on your face." A murmur went around the room. "You are straight and level with your hands in your lap, and your feet are on the rudder pedals...but you're going in the wrong direction!"

He waved his finger around the room, "And you're going to run out of gas a long time before you get home because if you don't turn, you need to fly around the world!" He smiled. "And your ailerons are jammed by a piece of flak junk."

He looked from one pilot to another. "Does anyone want to comment about that?" Byron Johnson, in the corner, raised his hand.

Cliff looked at him, grinning.

"You would be fucked, wouldn't you?"

Cliff exaggerated a nodding of his head. "Correct. If you hadn't taken my free 'After three beers at the pub' flying course." He steadied his head and stared at Byron. Turning so that he could move his eyes from one pilot to another, Cliff said, "Now, I know that in what passes for flight school in RAF Bomber Command, they taught you that a pilot must use the ailerons to turn, and the ball must be in the center...inferring that if you side-slip a little, you will die!" He swept his pointing finger around the room. "But those bastards lied to you! Eddie is in trouble... He has no time to learn how to fly using all those complicated controls and pedals! He will die if he doesn't turn, and without those ailerons, he can't keep the stupid ball in the centre!" He looked at Byron again and waited. Byron asked the question.

"So, he's fucked?"

"No, he's not because he has learned Cliff's third law of flying, the left and right law. He's going to ignore the fucking ball. He will let it slide around—a small sacrifice so Eddie can go home. He's got a sweet thing waiting for him, and I promise you, he ain't never been laid. Winging his wang is the only way he gets satisfaction." He grinned, trying not to laugh. "You can't expect him to die a virgin...that's an awful way to go!" He pointed at Johnson. "That's a corollary of rule number three, Cliff's law of left and right...a bit of slip in an uncoordinated turn won't put the plane in any danger, and it will turn..." No one said anything... "Do you agree?"

Byron reluctantly nodded and smiled—a laugh would have been too much.

◇◇◇◇◇◇◇◇◇◇◇◇◇◇◇◇◇◇◇◇◇◇◇◇◇◇◇◇◇

Eddie took a deep breath, gently touched the left rudder, and the ball in the turn-and-bank slid to the right half the width of itself. The turn needle moved to the left. He released the air in his lungs in a hiss, held the rudder slightly depressed and watched the directional gyro.

It slowly counted down from two-hundred-and-eighty degrees. At two-hundred-and-sixty degrees, he lifted his foot; the plane levelled itself on a more or less steady course of two hundred and sixty degrees. He realized he had been holding his breath, breathed, and smiled as though he had cheated the Devil.

"Hey, Bill, what's the course for England?" The intercom had been silent since the up-and-down drill.

Bill answered so quickly Eddie knew he had been waiting for the call. "I've already worked it out. Fly due west, two hundred and seventy degrees, until we cross the coast, and I'll tell you when to turn north. Try it easy, and see how it goes." Bill didn't sound as cheerful as he had before Eddie mentioned the turn maneuver.

Eddie was about to squeeze the mic button when Bill answered his question.

"I've decided to take us over the land of canals, windmills and tulips, away from the stream of bombers returning from the raid." The intercom clicked off, then on. "There's no need to complicate your job with other aircraft in the vicinity. The sky is big, England is a big target, and a single bomber is unlikely to spark the interest of German radar when there are eight hundred bombers north of us."

Eddie gave Bill the minimum "Roger" and applied a little right rudder; the course slowly wound to two hundred and seventy degrees, and he centred it. The directional gyro was at two-seventy, but when he checked the compass, its course rested at slightly under two-seventy-two. He set the gyro and asked Bill, "How close do I have to be?"

Bill laughed. "We're trying to hit England, buddy. Try for five degrees so we come close enough to find a darkie station if we need it."

Eddie touched the left rudder and held it until the directional gyro was precisely on two hundred and seventy degrees, then leaned back in his seat. Cliff's rule three worked—he could steer with the rudders.

"Now," Eddie said aloud, but to himself, "if a fighter doesn't find us, we'll be as right as rain."

Unknown to Eddie, he had left the intercom switch on.

He decided not to think about night fighters and concentrate on keeping a perfect altitude and course.

Chapter Eight

24 May 1943

Interminable

THE NOISE ABATED, THE SOUND OF BOMB BURSTS RECEDED, and Lucas prayed it was over, though logic told him it wasn't. He could still hear bombers and hoped they would have a distant target, but his father had explained how the British pattern of waves of bombers often caught people who left the shelter too early. He said, "You must assume that bombs will fall until you hear the 'all clear' siren."

Lenora stood and looked around as though searching for something outside the shelter. She touched Karl's arm, the optimism on her face so pitiful Lucas had to turn away. She asked, "Does this mean it's over?"

Everyone in the room watched Karl; he considered lying but then decided to say what he feared. He shook his head and said, "I'm afraid they've only begun..." confirming Lucas's worst dread. But then Karl threw out a bone. "We may be lucky; they might bomb targets farther from us... maybe the harbour and the factories...." He looked down at the floor to hide his face. "All we can do is wait."

Katrina stopped shaking, and as minutes passed with only occasional distant explosions, she progressively relaxed. After a few minutes of relative quiet, she lifted her head and looked at Corinne. Lucas, astonished at Corinne's composure and tender concern for Katrina, smiled at her, and when she returned it, his fears disappeared, and he became calm.

◇◇◇◇◇◇◇◇◇◇◇◇◇◇◇◇◇◇◇◇◇◇◇◇◇◇◇◇◇◇◇◇◇◇

The moan became louder as the sound of bombs and aircraft receded. The ominous nature of it left no doubt that it was something to worry about.

"What's that?" Katrina asked, sounding more curious than afraid. Lucas turned away so he wouldn't have to answer.

"It's the wind," Corinne reassured her, turning to Karl, who looked at her curiously. She turned back to Katrina and went on. "The blast of the bombs makes wind, but it will go away." Karl lowered his eyes as Katrina accepted the illogical explanation, then straightened up and looked around the room. "I smell smoke! Is the house on fire?"

Corinne put her arms around her. "No, the house isn't on fire." She turned her eyes toward the steel plate on the ceiling, then back to Karl. Her eyes stayed on him as she said, "The ceiling isn't hot. Air is coming in through the vent Mr. Zimmermann put through the wall—the smoke comes from outside—somewhere, other houses are burning, but not this one. We must stay here for a while yet. You should sleep now; there may be more bombs later."

Karl smiled and nodded his head just a little at Corinne and Katrina, and Katrina relaxed. "Okay, thank you. I'm sorry that I'm so afraid." The pathetic tone of her voice moved everyone in the room; they said nothing about their own fears as Katrina lay down with her head on Corinne's lap. Her hand went up to her mouth, and she twisted into a fetal position on the wide bench. Her thumb found her mouth for a second before she realized what she had done and quickly withdrew it.

Lucas sat down beside Hartwig, trying to look like he was in control but knowing he was failing. Terrified, he suspected that Hartwig was frightened too—and his friend's expression confirmed that he had made the same assumptions about the noise that Lucas had.

<hr>

He looked around to see what would burn and decided that clothes were the biggest offenders. Other than steel or concrete, there were four chairs, two benches and a small table in the room, and Lucas was confident that the flashpoint for clothing was lower than for wood. He hoped they would die of something less painful before their clothes ignited; asphyxiation seemed a better choice. But the smoke could be poisonous... Still, that would be preferable to burning. Perhaps the hot air would cause them to pass out before their clothes caught fire, but Lucas wasn't sure.

He tried to chase the macabre thoughts away, but the temperature in the room was becoming perceptibly higher with every minute. Sweat soaked through Lucas's clothes, and beads of it stood out on Hartwig's brow. In their light clothing, the damp, unheated cellar should have been uncomfortably cold.

Hartwig moved close to Lucas and turned his head so he could speak close to his ear. "Are you afraid to die?"

"Yes," Lucas whispered, "I would rather put it off for a few years." He grunted, close to a sarcastic laugh. "Do we have a choice?"

Hartwig shrugged. "We might. I'm not going to die today if I can help it!" He looked at Lucas, then at the floor as he asked, "Have you ever thought about killing yourself?" He picked at a sliver on the corner of the bench. "If we die, do you think we will be able to see everyone crying over us, even though we're dead?"

Lucas looked at his feet and then at Hartwig. "Yes, sometimes I think about killing myself, but only when I get depressed; when I get over it, the feeling goes away. I don't understand why I consider it at all... I would never do it. How about you?"

Hartwig looked at the floor. "Yeah, I've thought about it, and if I were standing on the edge of a cliff at just the right moment, I might jump." He grinned and looked at Lucas. "That's why I stay away from cliffs." He looked at the floor again. "I don't know why I get depressed, but it usually doesn't last long. Do you remember Michael? Do you think he fell as he crossed the track, or did he jump in front of the train?"

"He was playing chicken, and he made a mistake." Lucas and Michael had been best friends in Grundschule until the train ran over him.

"What about right now? Are you depressed?" Lucas smiled. He knew the answer.

"No, I don't understand it, but I'm not depressed. I don't think I will ever be sad again if we get through this. Right now, I feel like fighting! I want to live if only to piss off the bastards who are dropping bombs on us."

Lucas laughed. "Yeah, me too; I'm mad as hell." He put his hand on Hartwig's arm. "Let's sing when the bombs start again." He had a sudden epiphany. "How about The Two Grenadiers? Schumann would be impressed if we sang it when bombs were falling." Hartwig laughed, and Lucas said, "I know the Lied because when I was twelve, I taught it to Mr. Schlesinger, and he's the slowest learner I've ever seen!"

Hartwig laughed, his elbows on his knees, looking across the room. "Yeah, he sings it every year at the Meistersänger competition, and I always play it for him." He turned to look up at Lucas. "Do you remember the concert last spring?" He turned back to look at the wall. "God, it was awful; I wanted to crawl under the piano."

Both boys laughed as they thought of the fat old butcher yelling the dramatic song at the amateur singer competition he had never won. They reminisced and laughed until, what seemed like minutes later, the war Gods, using British flying orders and bombers, made another attempt to kill them.

Lucas looked at Hartwig, and they began to sing, "Nach Frankreich zogen zwei Grenadier..." singing the tale of two French soldiers returning from Napoleon's defeat on the Russian front, their patriotism undiminished.

The irony was not lost on Karl as he watched his son and Lucas, proud of the boys' bravery, or at least their attempt to give that impression in the face of almost certain death. He expected the end to be horrible, and his heart broke as he looked at his wife sitting on the floor beside him. He slipped off his chair, put his arm over her shoulder and pulled her close. She rested her head on his shoulder.

◇◇◇◇◇◇◇◇◇◇◇◇◇◇◇◇◇◇◇◇◇◇◇◇◇◇◇◇◇◇◇◇

Bombs rained down in a steady rumble, rolling across the city and shaking the house. Karl feared the fires of Armageddon would burn Dortmund to the ground. He and Lenora leaned against one another, silent, resigned to whatever God and General 'Bomber' Harris had planned for them.

As the minutes passed, the temperature levelled out, and Karl applied the theory of diminishing fuel, diminishing fire, and began to hope. He bowed his head and prayed, something he hadn't done since childhood, and then only at his mother's insistence. As a child, he had asked God to protect his friends, cousins, aunts, uncles, parents, sister, and two brothers every night. But many of them got sick, and some died. When his grandfather suffered a heart attack, Karl prayed that he would be all right, but he died without seeing his grandchild again. When he was twelve, Karl's mother died of cancer after six months of agony witnessed by her family. And then the train killed Michael, Hartwig and Lucas's best friend. Karl decided that either prayer was overrated or God was mean, and he hadn't prayed since. But now he prayed and thought he sensed the moaning diminish... but why wasn't the cellar cooler?

Chapter Nine

24 May 1943

A thousand tons of death

Bomber Command had assigned a hundred bombers in the second wave to attack the Dortmund-Ems Canal complex and the Hoesch synthetic fuel plant, targets separated by four kilometres of residential streets. They intended to destroy both targets using twelve-thousand-pound tallboys on the canals and a variety of smaller high explosive bombs equipped with impact-delay fuses on the factory buildings. Unfortunately, bombing at night from four miles above the target, through thick industrial smog and smoke, was more a matter of coincidence than science.

When planners considered overlapping impacts and near-misses, the mission required a hundred bombers to damage targets that ten could have destroyed. These accuracy problems caused civilian collateral damage; in this case, most of it would be on the line between the objectives. Wambelerstrasse, where Lucas and Hartwig sang like drunks in a pub on a Saturday night, lay precisely on that line.

Although Lucas and Hartwig sang as loud as they could without injuring their vocal cords, most of the time, they couldn't hear themselves, let alone one another. In the moments when the noise level was low enough that Lenora and Karl could hear them, they smiled at the boys as though they were enjoying a concert. Corinne, watching Lucas thumb his nose at fate, joined the irrational act of defiance and began singing the alto part, and Lucas switched to the tenor line. Katrina lifted her head to see what was happening, pushing herself to a sitting position. She looked at Hartwig in a way that told Lucas his friend had won, but Hartwig seemed oblivious to what was evident to everyone else.

Lucas felt the sound of their singing and laughter lifting a corner of the curtain of terror that smothered everyone in the room. Corinne smiled at Lucas as she sang, keeping her eyes on his, spurring him on. He increased the gusto, grinning at her like the schoolboy he was, blending his tenor part with her alto, and the bombs and overlapping resonance drowned out Hartwig's bass.

When they finished the song, Lucas was sure he detected a change in the odours coming through the vent. They were not as strong. An increasing number of gaps in the wall of sound meant fewer bombs. The eerie moan subsided to a sigh, and Lucas imagined the room was cooling. The explosions receded farther away; only a rare blast shook the house even a little. Encouraged and high on their continued existence, Lucas and his friends celebrated by singing a polka, filled with unreasonable hope and even confidence that the end of the horror was near.

◇◇◇◇◇◇◇◇◇◇◇◇◇◇◇◇◇◇◇◇◇◇◇◇◇◇◇◇◇◇◇◇◇◇◇◇◇

The respite they welcomed was short, measured in minutes. They had barely finished the first verse and chorus of the polka when a third wave of bombers hit the city's centre, where they knew the targets were women, children and old men, the only people left in the Stadtmitte of most German cities. One after another, the trio stopped singing until each of them waited quietly with their head lowered. They were safe for the moment, but knowing that their gain was at the expense of others dulled the relief they should have felt.

The third wave, aimed at civilians, was the largest, and the sound of bombs exploding in the old part of the city became a constant rumble at Wambelerstrasse 31. Lucas and his friends remained quiet, thankful that the British were targeting someone else, their imaginations mesmerized by the horror they knew those people were experiencing.

Thirty minutes later, the bombs stopped exploding as suddenly as they had begun; the sound of bombers' engines receded and died, and silence returned to the world an hour and ten minutes after the first bombs had landed. A sinister quiet lay over the city like a soft blanket respectfully spread to cover the dead and dying. Lucas had expected to feel joy, but with their minds still on those who lived in the Stadtmitte, no one in the shelter celebrated. They spoke in a respectful, quiet voice.

It occurred to Lucas that, sequestered in their armoured cocoon, they could be the only people in the city still alive.

He was suddenly ashamed; he hadn't thought about his parents since the bombing began in earnest. Lucas told himself again that his family had the same steel and reinforced concrete protecting them; he was safe, and they would be just as secure in their identical shelter. But he couldn't shake a black feeling—maybe they weren't alright—perhaps they hadn't reached safety.

◇◇◇◇◇◇◇◇◇◇◇◇◇◇◇◇◇◇◇◇◇◇◇◇◇◇◇◇◇◇◇

Despite the silence, Karl made his charges wait another twenty minutes until the all-clear siren screamed. He opened the shelter's heavy door, and they followed him through the rubble to the cellar stairs. Lenora held the lantern over her shoulder, casting a yellow glow on the cellar's walls and the solid wooden stairs. She shone the light on rubble piled on the stairs and waited while Karl and the boys began to clear a path to the door. The ceiling had fallen, and they had to move piles of plaster and wooden lathes.

When Karl reached the cellar door and tried to push it open...it wouldn't move,

"There's something against it. Hartwig and Lucas, help me push."

Lucas and Hartwig stepped on the second step and pushed on the door while Karl put his shoulder against it. It moved a few centimetres, then stopped.

Karl swore. "Scheisse, we need more power."

"I can help." Corinne stepped out of the darkness. "Let me push."

Karl said, "Thank you, Corinne, but there's not enough room for four people on the stairs."

She said, "Why don't you help Hartwig while I push on Lucas's back?"

Corinne ignored Karl's open mouth and said, "Lucas, why don't you stand sideways with your shoulder against the door?"

Karl said, "Good plan. Let's try it."

Lucas stood on the top step where he thought he would have the best angle, crouched and put his shoulder against the door. Corinne put her right arm over his, with her hand against the door. She leaned against him, wrapped her left arm around him and braced her feet.

Lucas immediately realized she knew more about this than he did. He felt Corinne's breast pressing against his back and forgot that if the door didn't open, they had a real problem—it was the only way out of the cellar.

Karl said, "Okay, I want everyone to push on my mark." Lucas raised the tension in his body, and Corinne leaned against him, her breasts solidly against his back.

"Okay, Push!"

The door scraped and then started to move—dirt and pieces of masonry fell into the cellar as it swung. Corinne pushed so hard she squeezed the air out of Lucas's lungs.

When the door stopped at a forty-five-degree angle, Karl said, "Stop! We must drag the debris back into the cellar. Hartwig, get the shovel."

Corinne stepped back to let Lucas go down the stairs. She quietly asked, "Did I hurt you?" and Lucas shook his head.

It took half an hour to clear the junk behind the door so they could swing it far enough to squeeze through the opening.

"Good job, everyone," Karl said as he and Hartwig stepped around the door and disappeared into the hallway. Marita followed with the lantern, Katrina in her wake, leaving Lucas and Corinne in the dark.

Corinne was close enough that Lucas could hear her breathing. She took his hand and said, "We have to go now," but didn't move. Lucas choked out a "Thank you for helping" and missed the first step with his foot. She caught him before he fell and led him up the stairs, around the door, and into the lantern's light.

Karl and Hartwig worked to clear a path through piles of rubble while Lenora held the lantern at shoulder height. Katrina, bent over in a most unladylike way, tried to clear away pieces of plaster behind Lenora but only succeeded in scattering it around.

Lucas and Corinne could do nothing but watch—there wasn't room for them where they could do any good. Neither seemed in any hurry to let go of the other's hand.

The walls were still vertical, but dirt, glass, and pieces of wood and plaster covered the floor. They worked their way down the hall to the kitchen by the light of the lantern, and when they passed the living room, the eerie glow of fires everywhere they looked outside lit up the room and spilled into the hall.

The main house door that should have hung at the end of the hallway lay on the floor six metres from its hinges. Lucas, close behind Karl and his family so he could share the lantern's light, tripped over it on his way into the living room. The lantern went into the living room with Lenora, and Corinne helped guide a shell-shocked Katrina through the debris.

Nothing remained standing in the living room except the sofa. It was still on its legs but jammed into a corner with a heavy oak cabinet leaning over its back. The glass shelves and front were missing. The Schrank had been the showplace for Lenora's collection of Hummel figurines and expensive crystal inherited from Karl's parents. The porcelain ornaments and crystal lay scattered on the floor—none had survived unbroken. The piano lay on its front, the keyboard smashed. Pieces of glass and ceiling plaster covered the back of the instrument and the floor around it.

The cello and viola, still in their cases on the floor, covered with ceiling plaster, appeared to be undamaged. Lucas's precious violin was on the sofa—he picked it up and examined it as well as he could in the dim light but could find no damage—he tried to remember putting it there but couldn't. He looked around the room for the case, but it wasn't anywhere the feeble light could reach. He suddenly remembered that the blast had torn it from his hand before he could put the violin in it. He searched for the bow and found it under the piano, broken beyond repair.

Karl, Lenora and the lantern went to the kitchen, followed by Hartwig, Lucas, and the girls. Lenora brushed the dirt off a section of the tabletop, put the lantern on it, and then wandered around the kitchen, assessing the damage to her domain.

Cooking pots and broken dishes covered the floor. Lenora picked up a broken cup, looked for matching pieces, gave up, and frustrated, lobbed it against the wall.

An oak cupboard had crushed two chairs. Lenora looked at Karl; he took the hint, and Hartwig and Lucas helped him stand the Schrank on its feet. Lenora found the broom and swept the area it usually occupied clean before they pushed it to its place against the wall. The broken chairs went into the corner Lenora used to pile the debris and dirt she accumulated with her broom. The work counters were intact, and the sink was still in place, but no water came from the tap when Lenora opened it.

Wherever he walked, broken glass crunched under Lucas's feet; ceiling plaster and dirt covered everything, and he looked for a place to start.

Karl lit a second lantern Hartwig found in the storage room, and the boys left the kitchen to search the bedrooms. The story of destruction repeated itself everywhere; bomb blasts had broken everything breakable, smashed all the windows, and glass, dust, and plaster covered every horizontal surface. A section of the roof was missing; the dark, smoke-filled sky was open above the master bedroom.

◇◇◇◇◇◇◇◇◇◇◇◇◇◇◇◇◇◇◇◇◇◇◇◇◇◇◇◇◇◇◇◇

When they returned, Karl was sitting in one of four usable chairs with his head lowered. He rose when they entered the kitchen, pointing to the door beside him. Lucas walked over to Karl and stood beside him while he waited for Lucas to understand what he was seeing.

Lenora, Corinne, Hartwig, and Katrina gathered behind them, staring at where the garden had been and where the city beyond had been an uneven horizon.

There was no backyard, garden, or buildings as far as they could see. The southern horizon was a burning line of flames licking upward, searching for fuel. Small fires scattered between them and the Stadtmitte burned single or smaller groups of buildings.

Two apple trees and the plum tree that had been in the yard for twenty years were gone as if they had never existed, and unidentifiable pieces of buildings covered the yard. Lucas imagined he could feel the radiating heat and fought the urge to run back into the house. The scene mesmerized him.

Karl took Lucas's arm, and Lucas reluctantly stepped outside. His eyes followed Karl's arm as he pointed toward Lucas's home. Dread clutched his heart as he saw by the light of the fires that there were no houses where there had been four of them; there wasn't even a wall; all Lucas could see were bomb craters.

While Lucas stared at the trash that used to be the buildings, he felt something grasping at his soul, telling him his life was over. He stared at the holes, questioning what his brain was trying to say to him.

Karl disappeared into the house but returned in a few seconds with the lantern. Lucas's voice broke, and a tightness gripped his chest so hard he found it hard to breathe as he said, grasping at hope beyond reason, "They'll be in the shelter—won't they?"

Karl put his free hand on Lucas's shoulder, looked into his eyes and said quietly, "We'll need candles, tools from the cellar, and the other lantern. Lenora and Corinne are looking for candles; you and I will get the tools." Looking at the holes, he added, "Andreas Schwartz is the smartest man I know…don't give up hope yet!"

The rescuers left the house with hammers, crowbars, an axe, and a wooden ladder. The women carried candles and one of the lanterns; Karl took the other and led the group with a long-handled four-kilo-gram hammer on his shoulder.

The backyards, a moonscape of overlapping craters, each more than five metres across and at least two metres deep, had to be carefully ne-gotiated. Two deep craters lay across the straight-line path to Andreas' house. Loose bricks, Gitterstein and timbers—pieces of what had been buildings a few hours ago—littered the ground.

Karl led the way with Lucas behind him, working around what he couldn't step over. The broken remains of roofs, floors and walls littered the ground and sometimes left no choice but to make a path by throwing aside pieces they could lift and crawling over those they couldn't. Karl pointed at a section of wooden floor, breaking the other-worldly silence when he said loudly enough for everyone to hear, "Be careful not to step on nails sticking out of the wood!"

◇◇◇◇◇◇◇◇◇◇◇◇◇◇◇◇◇◇◇◇◇◇◇◇◇◇◇◇◇◇◇◇◇◇◇◇

The perfectly still air carried the sound of a distant siren and the faint roar of fires burning. But no dogs barked, no people screamed or shouted, and no birds chirped. Two hours ago, the rescue crew lived in a busy metropolis. There were cars on the streets, people walked on the sidewalks, and because the night was unusually warm, the sound of recorded music carried through open windows. Now the city was dead, the air so still that the candles only flickered when in motion, throwing strange moving shadows on a landscape covered with the broken pieces of destroyed homes and lives. It was impossible to walk anywhere in a straight line.

There was no longer a visible border to the Zimmermann yard. Where the fence and a shed had been, there was only trash. As far as anyone could see in the light of the fires, there were craters, broken walls, and isolated houses sticking up through piles of bricks, wood and stone. The Zimmermann home was one of only a few they could see still standing.

<hr>

Karl stopped where he knew the Schwartz's house should have been and stared into a massive black hole. Lucas prayed Karl was mistaken—that the house was farther down the street. He looked back at the house they had left and estimated the distance, and his heart knew the vast crater had replaced the home he had left for the last time a few short hours ago. It was deeper and broader than the linked cellars.

A sizeable pool of water had formed from broken water lines trickling into the gaping hole, removing all doubt that houses had been there. A small section of one cellar wall remained intact, but everything else was gone. The blast had blown the house, the shelter and the houses attached on each side out of the crater.

"Are we sure this is where the house was?" Lucas tried to control the quiver in his voice. Neither he nor Karl had spoken for over a minute, waiting for their minds to accept the horrible truth.

Karl spoke softly, looking into the massive hole with his head down.

"Yes, I'm certain. I can see a tool hanger that I bolted to that wall." He pointed to the only remaining piece of cellar wall, and Lucas recognized the hanger.

Lenora and the girls stood away from Karl and Lucas, crying. Lucas desperately tried to rationalize a situation in which his family had survived, but the sense of logic he had inherited from his father killed every glimmer of hope. He surrendered to grief. Karl put his arm over Lucas's shoulder, and they wept.

Eventually, Lucas became aware of the group standing around him, wiped his face with his sleeve and turned to Karl.

"I think we should return to your house and wait for daylight. We all need to sleep." Lucas turned away from the crater and felt something dying inside. There was no time to grieve and no one who could help him, so he stubbornly fought the hopelessness he felt creeping into his soul. He had never felt so alone, and he wanted his life to end.

Corinne emerged from the darkness, stroked his hair and took his arm. She led him back the way they had come, and he gripped her arm as though it were the only thing that could save him. She followed Hartwig, who carried one of the lanterns. Karl and Lenora shepherded Katrina through the debris behind them with the light of the second lantern.

Lucas felt the ground under his life shifting as the glow from the fires in the Old City and the nearby Hoesch complex and smaller fires all over the city left black shadows that hid timbers, broken bricks and shattered glass. He followed Corinne as she pointed out the obstacles, steering him when he strayed. Lucas was no longer worried about getting injured or even death—nothing mattered. He sensed that somehow Corinne would make everything right.

A sob surging from his throat surprised Lucas, and he stopped, momentarily overcome by emotion. Corinne put her arms around him; Hartwig put his lantern on the ground and did the same on the other side. The little group of refugees stood and stared at the wasteland that a few hours ago had been their city, waiting for something, not knowing what.

Chapter Ten

24 May 1943

High Flight

Oh! I have slipped the surly bonds of earth
And danced the skies on laughter-silvered wings;
Sunward I've climbed, and joined the tumbling mirth
Of sun-split clouds—and done a hundred things
You have not dreamed of—wheeled and soared and swung
High in the sun-lit silence. Hov'ring there
I've chased the shouting wind along, and flung
My eager craft through footless halls of air.
Up, up, the long delirious, burning blue,
I've topped the windswept heights with easy grace
Where never lark, or even eagle flew—
And, while with silent lifting mind I've trod
The high untresspassed sanctity of space,
Put out my hand, and touched the face of God.

Written by: Pilot Officer Gillespie Magee, No 412 Squadron, RCAF

Killed in action on 11 December 1941

EDDIE USED TRIM TO SET THE WELLINGTON at one-hundred-and-seventy-five miles per hour in a gradual climb. The nose was barely up, and the climb rate was below three hundred feet per minute when he began to play with the control wheel, banked to both sides, increasing and decreasing the angle, always returning to a course of two hundred and seventy degrees. Gradually, Eddie fed in a bit of rudder until he could keep the ball in the center. He felt guilty—the coordinated turn violated Cliff's law of left and right.

"What the hell are you doing?" These were the first words he had heard on the intercom since Dortmund, and George Cunningham's voice was clearly agitated.

"I'm practicing my turns so I can land this thing." His confidence growing, Eddie began to consider the possibility. He asked, "Hey! What do you guys think?"

No one spoke.

Eddie pleaded, "Come on, boys, tell me what you think. I can land this crate without any problem. If we jump out, who knows what will happen…none of us has ever done it! What if our parachute doesn't open? Wouldn't you rather sleep in your cozy bed tonight?"

An incredulous Bill Parsons answered, "Eddie, you are an optimistic bastard! You haven't logged a full hour of flying yet, and you're telling me you can land this plane?" He didn't wait for an answer. "You go ahead and try, but you will do it without me! I'll tell you what... I will get you to the field; you fly over it at two or three thousand feet, and I'll jump out." Bill laughed, "Thank you for the offer, Eddie, but no thanks." The others remained silent.

Eddie took that for unanimity and said, "I've got a crew of frightened old women." He waited, but no one interrupted, so he said, "You're all cowards!"

Eddie's tone had a hint of humour, but no one laughed. He realized too late that coward was a term he should not have used, even in jest.

He was silent for a few seconds, then asked, "If we all jump out, what about the plane? It could land on someone's house!"

Bill replied so quickly that Eddie decided he must have been thinking about the problem. "I have a fix for that. You will fly out to the mouth of the river, point the plane at Germany, cut the throttles back so it will eventually come down in the channel, and jump out over terra firma. I speak for all of us when I say we wouldn't want you to spoil anyone's day by crashing your airplane on their house!"

Eddie said, out of arguments and resigned to everyone jumping, "Okay, that's it then." Eddie didn't have rank on his side, nor did anyone else. The aircraft had become a democracy, and he had lost the vote.

◇◇◇◇◇◇◇◇◇◇◇◇◇◇◇◇◇◇◇◇◇◇◇◇◇◇◇◇◇◇◇◇◇◇◇◇◇

The bored Focke Wulf 190 pilot couldn't believe his luck! Assigned to patrol over the Dutch border with no targets on the Deelen radar, the only challenge that kept him awake was keeping his fighter right side up. The aircraft cruised at twenty thousand feet with the throttle set at sixty percent and the mixture lean to save fuel. When he spotted a shadow below and ahead of his night fighter, he wasn't confident that he was looking at an English bomber until a tiny glimmer of light reflected from it.

He looked closer and decided it was a Wellington, and FW 190s ate Wellington's for lunch! The plane was either lost or crippled, and to the FW 190 fighter pilot, it didn't matter which! It would burn on the ground in a few minutes, and he would notch another kill.

The pilot muttered something about the idiots in Deelen sleeping, pulled the throttle back and trimmed the nose down so his angle of descent would put him on the bomber's tail when his fighter was five hundred metres behind it. His airspeed was over a hundred kilometres per hour faster than the enemy aircraft's, and he would catch him in minutes. He grinned from ear to ear and concentrated on getting the closing angle perfect.

◇◇◇◇◇◇◇◇◇◇◇◇◇◇◇◇◇◇◇◇◇◇◇◇◇◇◇◇◇◇◇◇

Eddie told himself he had to practice his turns. The need for turning would eventually come, and he would need to concentrate on other things simultaneously. Attitude and speed were vital to life when the plane was close to the ground, so maneuvering using the controls must be second nature. The Wellington would cross the Dutch coast in ten minutes, and he told himself he needed to know his limits.

Cliff had drilled in him that most flying errors that killed pilots started or ended with a 'fucked-up' turn. Eddie pushed the 'keep it simple' principle that Cliff had taught him to the back of his mind...the more he could learn now, the greater his chances when the hammer came down. He felt confident he could do more than fly straight and level.

Eddie was in a dangerous place for any pilot—he was beginning to believe he could control the airplane.

He made a couple of gentle turns at a third of the maximum rate on the turn-and-bank indicator, focusing on keeping the ball peacefully between the little black lines. He decided he could need twice that bank to keep the plane lined up on the runway, especially if he had a crosswind. He thought for a moment, rubbed his hands together and said to himself, "Eddie, it's time to shit or get off the pot." He turned the wheel left, estimating it would take twice as much as he had used so far, while simultaneously applying two inches of left rudder pedal, double what he had done until now.

The plane responded instantly, moving like a racehorse out of the starting gate! An unseen force yanked it to the left, pointed the wing at the ground, and launched the plane into a tight downward spiral through the blackness that hid the ground. Confused, Eddie reacted by yanking the wheel to the right and pulling it toward him, forgetting to release the left rudder and cross-controlling the now bewildered airplane. The control wheel told the Wellington to turn left, but the rudder insisted it turn right!

The airspeed wound counterclockwise, leaving the green, entering the orange, and then the red zone, where lift magically vanished. The weird dynamic forces a cross-controlled stalled aircraft generated would turn the bomber into a pile of burning wreckage if Eddie didn't fix the problem. The Wellington, its wings now useless baggage, sank like a stone, dropped its right wing and spun toward the ground like a shot-gunned duck. Eddie pulled harder on the column and forced the rudder to its stop, forgetting everything he had learned and entering the world of suicidal self-denial. When the right wing became vertical, pointing at the ground, Eddie turned the wheel hard to the left while holding the column back.

◇◇◇◇◇◇◇◇◇◇◇◇◇◇◇◇◇◇◇◇◇◇◇◇◇◇◇◇◇◇◇◇◇

Eddie's efforts to fly outside Cliff's or nature's laws got him nowhere; he didn't understand that he had taken the air off the right aileron and wing, losing all lift on that side. The spiral became a flat spin, tighter than the aircraft's design criteria could have anticipated. The airspeed wound down, and the Wellington fell like a fluttering leaf; the altimeter wound backward like a Whirling Dervish, and Eddie's faulty logic told him to pull harder on the column.

"Help!" Eddie yelled into the intercom, but no answer came back. The aircraft corkscrewed to the right—the engines moaned, straining to overcome the insane aerodynamic forces Eddie had set up in his efforts to stop the spin. Two hundred and seventy miles per hour became less than eighty in seconds, the Bristol radial engines thrashed helplessly, their two thousand horsepower useless in their fight against propellers set for cruise. Air came into the propellers from one side and exited the other; the engines vibrated, shaking the aircraft like a baby trying to break its rattle.

The Focke Wulf pilot pressed the button on his wing cannons, simultaneously firing bullets between his propeller blades with the synchronized machine gun. Expecting the bomber in his sights to disintegrate in front of him, he prepared to pull back hard on the stick so that the debris wouldn't kill him. Hot tracers left the nose and wings, but when they reached the spot in space where the Wellington was supposed to be, there was nothing but air. The shells, the power of gravity pulling them downward, arched harmlessly through the empty air to the ground. He released the firing button as his prize disappeared in the darkness, below and behind him.

"What the fuck was that?" Tracers sliced past and above George Cunningham as he braced himself against the aircraft's wild gyrations. The last ten feet of the fuselage had no fabric on it, and when Eddie forced the plane into its wild slip, it had presented its side to the airstream, and the resulting hurricane inside the tail would have blown George out of the turret had he not had his belt fastened. He grabbed the Perspex frame with his right hand and the handle of his machine gun with his left. He didn't have to think very long to conclude that a fighter had just made a pass and would return.

"Help!" Eddie's voice didn't sound like he needed more bad news, so George waited, knowing there was nothing he could do… the damned fighter was a bigger worry.

The plane thrashed for over two minutes while George prayed. He begged God to help Eddie, promising way too much if he would. When Eddie levelled off and began to climb, George looked up and said, "Thank you, God," instantly regretting the promises that concerned alcohol and women.

"Boys, we've got a problem!" George squeezed his mic so hard his hand cramped. "A fighter fired at us, and unless his mother called him for dinner, he's coming back!"

Paul Burns in the top turret shouted, "I saw the tracers, and his exhaust when he passed us. It's for sure he's not going home without trying again!"

⬦⬦⬦⬦⬦⬦⬦⬦⬦⬦⬦⬦⬦⬦⬦⬦⬦⬦⬦⬦⬦⬦⬦⬦⬦⬦⬦⬦⬦⬦

"God, please show me what to do!" Eddie suddenly realized that he only talked to God when he wanted something and hoped it wouldn't hurt his chances.

The Wimpy searched for equilibrium—Eddie couldn't decide whether to turn, push, or pull, so he did none of those things and instead pulled his hand back. He needed a review, but there wasn't time... the fighter would return... maybe they should get out—but could they get to the hatches in time?

Since Dortmund, Eddie had climbed steadily to reach twelve thousand feet, but two thousand feet disappeared in twenty seconds. Eddie was terrified. He heard Cliff's words through the fog of panic. "The airplane will fly itself if you let it. If you are scared—shitting your pants scared—stop fighting the airplane and let it save itself and you!" Eddie was very close to shitting his pants when he let go of the column, put his feet on the floor and gave the Wellington its head. Then he closed his eyes and prayed for something good to happen.

The Wimpy took over, rewarding Eddie by pointing its nose at the ground. He said, "Shit! No!" and reached for the column, then forced himself to pull his hands back—the spin stopped, the wheel centred. As the speed built, the nose rose until the indicator passed a hundred and seventy-five miles per hour, reached one hundred ninety, then fell and rose again as the plane porpoised to equilibrium at the airspeed Eddie had set the trim for. Eddie's hands shook as he reached for the column, then pulled them back. His eyes went from one instrument to another— everything was at peace, but the course was now one hundred and eighty degrees, due south, ninety degrees to the left of the two-seventy that would take them home. All he had to do was turn right.

⬦⬦⬦⬦⬦⬦⬦⬦⬦⬦⬦⬦⬦⬦⬦⬦⬦⬦⬦⬦⬦⬦⬦⬦⬦⬦⬦⬦⬦⬦

The FW 190 made a sweeping left turn, looking for the bomber. It took a few minutes to find it, below his Focke Wulf and heading south. He quickly planned to approach from above and on the bomber's rear quarter, lining up the fuel tanks. Every German night fighter pilot knew where to hit a British Wellington bomber. The tanks had no self-sealing membrane, and a single rifle bullet would send the plane to the ground in flames.

The young German pilot, with only two hundred hours in his logbook, twenty-two of them in a Focke Wulf, completed his turn in half a minute while keeping his eyes on the black shape. He could easily lose it against the dark ground if it pulled more shenanigans. The bomber would be his second kill, and already, his young imagination envisioned him telling the tale to his comrades.

Above and a thousand metres behind his intended victim, his heavy fighter closed fast on the bomber. As the bomber grew, he pulled the throttle off, approaching from above and slightly to the right of the tail. He identified it for certain as a Wellington and knew from the briefings that the wings were almost entirely fuel tanks; it would only take a short burst from the cannons to turn the plane into a fireball. He gained slowly, concentrating on the section outboard and behind the right engine. He put his thumb on the firing button.

As his instructors had taught him, the young pilot looked for the tail gunner, and something about the plane caught his eye. His eyes went forward to the fuselage... "Um Gottes willen! He could see inside and through the airplane! He stared at bare control cables leading to the tail, a narrow piece of floor, square beams... "Scheisse! There was no covering on the fuselage!" The geodesic frame's members were naked from the tail forward almost to the wing, and the young man made the fatal assumption that there would be no rear gunner. But it was his second assumption that assured his demise.

The fighter pilot's first kill had been a Wellington, and he had killed it from the top, where they were most vulnerable. He laughed, turned slightly to the left and pressed the cannons' firing button. The guns spit a stream of tracers that converged on the starboard engine of the Wellington. He released the button, pulled off a little more throttle, touched the right rudder to line up the tanks he had missed and was tensing his thumb when he died.

"Jesus Christ, there he is!" Paul screamed, swinging his twin Browning machine guns to line up on fire spitting from the fighter's nose. He pressed the firing button so the 190 would fly into two lines of steel three-aught-three machine gun bullets. Simultaneously, George Cunningham pressed the firing buttons on his rear turret guns, sending four streams of armour-piercing ammunition through the German's propeller. The impact crushed the top two engine cylinders, and oil flew out the top of the engine block as bullets ripped the cowling apart. Unhindered, the steady streams of bullets from six Browning machine gun barrels shattered the thick windshield. Paul's Brownings followed George's into the cockpit, tearing the pilot's body apart before he pressed hard enough to fire the fighter's guns. The weight of the dead pilot's arms pushed the stick forward, and the Focke Wulf's nose dropped. It fell under the Wellington and disappeared, absorbed into the darkness.

"The starboard engine's on fire!" Eddie yelled into the intercom as he pulled the mixture and shut off the fuel to the sick engine. He unbuckled his belt, leaned across to the engineer's panel and hit the fire extinguisher, the exact Standard Operating Procedure in the training manual. The fire went out; the RAF hadn't entirely wasted their time training Eddie to be a flight engineer.

Suddenly a handful, the Wellington, with a thousand horsepower on one wing and a dead weight on the other, turned sharp right as the left wing tried to pass the fuselage. Eddie corrected by pushing the starboard rudder, and things suddenly got a lot worse. Realizing his mistake, he tried the left rudder to its stop, but he had already done the damage. Twisting in a tight right-hand spin, the Wimpy headed for the ground, the altimeter spinning the wrong way at an alarming rate. Cliff's lessons hadn't covered this situation.

Eddie fought the airplane, pushing and pulling without rhyme or reason. Tears blurred his vision, panic gripped his brain, and his heart threatened to stop.

"God, I fucked up! Please help me!" Despite Eddie's straightened leg pushing on the left rudder, the Wellington continued to spin to the right through the darkness, falling so fast that the long needle on the altimeter was unreadable.

◇◇◇◇◇◇◇◇◇◇◇◇◇◇◇◇◇◇◇◇◇◇◇◇◇◇◇◇◇◇◇◇

Back in the bar, Cliff said, "No matter how bad you fuck up a Wellington, if you leave it alone, it will fly straight and level." Eddie let go of everything and waited, but this time, Cliff was wrong; the Wellington stayed on its winding path to the ground.

Cliff yelled, "Think, you arrogant southern pussy!" and a light shone.

"The engine," Eddie shouted back. "It's pulling us into the spin." He cut the throttle on the left engine and put his left foot on the rudder. The bomber snapped left, and when the wings levelled, Eddie lifted his foot. The airspeed climbed, and the nose raised on its own. The plane porpoised twice, and then they were gliding toward the ground, falling at 600 feet per minute. The altimeter showed 2,500 feet, giving the Wimpy four minutes before it ran out of valuable air.

Eddie added throttle and left rudder trim until the plane was flying level at one hundred and forty mph, with a little over two thousand feet of air under it. His hands shook, and he finally took a deep breath.

"The right engine is burning again," Paul's calm voice announced, "Is there anything left in the fire extinguisher?"

"Oh Jesus, no," Eddie felt the panic rise as he tried to keep thinking. "I can only fire it once!"

George said from the tail turret, "In that case, I think we should get out right now. I'll meet you at the hatch."

Paul Burns vented his frustration over the intercom. "We're over Holland, almost to the coast...we could be over England in ten minutes. I think we should risk it and try to reach English soil!"

Eddie shook his head, but no one could see it. "The fire will be in the fuel tank before then." He felt a surge in the left engine, and it lost two hundred revolutions. "And the left engine is sick; everyone out!"

The engine died with the last word. The Wimpy's altitude was under 1,800 feet and dropping fast. They now had seconds to get out!

"How high is the ground? If we jump, there may not be enough room for the parachutes to open!" George was already at the hatch with Paul, and without engine noise, his voice carried to everyone.

Bill pawed through his charts. "I'm not sure—probably enough, but I'm not sure." Time and air under the Wellington were running out.

"I'm riding her down." George climbed into the engineer's seat and buckled in.

Paul climbed into his turret and swung around to face forward, bracing his feet on the coaming. "Okay, I guess we take our medicine. Good luck, boys!"

"Good luck!" everyone repeated.

Eddie tried to remember Cliff's lesson on how to land. He knew the plane was going too fast, but maybe he shouldn't slow down yet. The Wellington needed to run out of air and speed at the right time, and Eddie had to review that part of Cliff's lesson. He desperately let his mind return to the pub...

Cliff said, "Now that you know how to slow the airplane, speed it up, and make it go up and down, you are officially a competent cruise pilot. And you will demonstrate the superior skill and knowledge you have acquired from your superior instructor by landing the aircraft without touching the column!" He smiled a cat-like smile, the one it smiles just before it bites the mouse's head off, and turned to face his audience.

No one in the room believed there was a pilot alive who could do it—a Wellington was a handful close to the ground. On the other hand, they knew that Cliff was about to tell them how.

Cliff said, quietly enough that the unruly bunch had to stay silent, "Okay, let's get this crate on the ground." Cliff dramatically raised his hands, illustrating the runway ahead of him. "You are lined up for the runway but still miles from the threshold—you have lots of time. You've got to slow the aircraft to flap deployment speed—about a hundred and thirty, give or take."

Eddy turned the trim wheel back until the airspeed was a hundred and thirty. He had no throttles to adjust, so he pulled the flap lever to the first notch. The nose rose, and the airspeed dropped to one hundred twenty.

Cliff's voice said, "...and this is important...you put the wheels down...we wouldn't want to land on our belly, now would we?" Everyone followed Cliff's lead by wagging their head.

Eddie found the gear lever but then decided to wait until he knew what he was landing on. He looked ahead, searching for a field, a road, anything he could put the Wimpy's wheels on.

"Next item," said Cliff." Set your approach speed by the book at one-point-three times the stall, which for the empty Wellington I drive is close enough at one-hundred-and-five miles per hour. You are straight and level with your feet on the rudder pedals—and you are going to use the rudder!" He waved his finger around the room. "You will use only the rudder to steer the aircraft to the ground!"

He looked from one pilot to another. "Does anyone want to comment about that?" Byron Johnson, still sitting in the corner, raised his hand.

Cliff looked at him, grinning.

"You would be side-slipping, wouldn't you?"

Cliff greatly exaggerated the nodding of his head. "Correct, but we already established that the ball in the centre is optional, and the slip won't be enough to mess up the landing."

◇◇◇◇◇◇◇◇◇◇◇◇◇◇◇◇◇◇◇◇◇◇◇◇◇◇◇◇◇◇◇◇◇◇◇◇◇◇◇

Eddie wound the trim up until the airspeed was one-hundred-and-five, straining to see through the darkness. He glanced at the altimeter—passing through a thousand feet—he had to find something to land on! Unless God intervened, the plane would meet the ground in ninety seconds.

When Eddie's eyes left the altimeter and looked through the windscreen, he spotted a bright patch of ground almost precisely in the centre of his windscreen; he trimmed for a hundred mph and watched it slowly begin to crawl down the windshield.

"I can reach that white patch...does anyone know what it might be?"

Bill could see through the windshield from his seat. "I think it's the moon shining on a wet beach; it has to be the Dutch coast."

Eddie took time to flash back to the pub in case he had forgotten something.

◇◇◇◇◇◇◇◇◇◇◇◇◇◇◇◇◇◇◇◇◇◇◇◇◇◇◇◇◇◇◇◇◇◇◇◇◇◇◇

Cliff turned Eddie and his chair away from the table, leaned over to face him with both hands on the chair's arms and turned his bum to the audience. "The end of the runway has arrived at the bottom of your windscreen—you have to do something, or you will leave it and the airport behind. What are you going to do about that?"

Eddie answered quickly. "Cut the throttles."

"Excellent answer...that's rule number two, up and down, in this case down...I had begun to give up hope." Cliff stood up and snapped the red-and-white striped braces that held up his pants. Eddie was pleased with himself until Cliff leaned over and put his face nose to nose. "How much?" The pleased look on Eddie's face disappeared.

"I don't know," Eddie said it too quickly, and Cliff smiled.

He shouted, "Think, you arrogant soft southern pussy!" and then waited for Eddie's brain to get into gear.

No one in the room made a sound. Eddie was from Thunder Bay—one of the coldest cities in civilized Canada, but it was three hundred miles south of Red Deer Lake, where Cliff and a few hundred friendly natives who thought the whole world got snow in July had their abode.

Cliff continued, "You won't live long in this business if you don't think, and neither will the four guys in the plane with you! Think, dickhead!" he shouted at Eddie, pressed his face dangerously close—they breathed the same air they exhaled. Eddie opened his mouth, then closed it again; he tried to hold his breath. He doubted that Cliff had brushed his teeth in the past week.

Eddie desperately tried to picture the situation; he hadn't had time to take a deep breath and needed air; his brain function was deteriorating. The room was silent...Eddie's face was beet red. He would fly over the airport if he didn't pull the throttle far enough—that wasn't good! Too much, and he would crash short of the runway... Eddie turned his head, gasped, yelled and slapped the table.

"I'll adjust the throttles to keep the end of the runway in the center of the windscreen! By God, that will work! If the runway goes up the windscreen, I will add power to make it go down—if it goes down, I'll pull the throttles back to make it go up! It's the second rule, up and down, but reversed because it's the runway that moves in the windscreen!"

Cliff leaned forward and slapped Eddie on the back. The room burst into applause, with a couple of 'bravos' sprinkled around. Cliff held up both hands; the noise stopped instantly.

He quickly turned back to Eddie and asked, "By the way, what's your speed?"

"One hundred and five miles per hour," the multitude prompted. Cliff turned back to the crowd and pointed at them.

"And that's going to be true unless you touch the trim or the control column, isn't it?" Cliff yelled at his audience.

"Yes, sir!" the inebriated men's choir answered—Cliff's law of up and down was confirmed.

Cliff turned back to Eddie, and the room went silent. He said, "Now, this is the tricky part, and you have to pay attention, or you'll die. You don't want to dive into the end of the runway... do you?" Eddie shook his head. Cliff repeated, "Do you?" louder as he stood up and turned around. He waved his hands upward. Everyone shouted, "No, sir!" as Cliff and various officers had taught them, then laughed because they were pretending to be happy drunks.

Cliff turned to Eddie and slowed everything down, carefully enunciating each word. "How do you know when to flare?" He leaned on the arms of the chair. "Too soon, and you will stall and fall on the runway, creating a lot of work for the cleanup boys, what with scraping up the blood and meat from five guys so they can send it back to their parents and wives. If you flare too late, the aircraft will strike the hard runway at a steep downward angle, with the same aforementioned result. Now, what the hell are you going to do?"

Eddie thought carefully. Finally, unsure of himself, he began.

"On short final, about a half-mile from the end of the runway, I'm going to gradually trim up until I'm close to stalling...about eighty-five? That will lift the nose and shallow the angle." Cliff nodded his head, and Eddie continued. "I will adjust the throttle to fly parallel to the ground until I pass the threshold. When I'm sure I will reach the runway, I'll pull the throttle a little at a time until the wheels touch; when they do, I'll pull them completely off." Eddie's uncertainty showed in his face, and Cliff let him sweat for a few seconds.

He stood up, grinning, and slapped Eddie on the back. "My God, you've made it! You've just saved those fine British factory workers a lot of work building a new airplane, and the crew gets to eat a steak dinner instead of becoming worm meat. Great job, Eddie!" A cheer rose, and the crowd clapped and laughed for a good minute.

Chapter Eleven

24 May 1943

You must not lose faith in humanity.
Humanity is an ocean; if a few drops
of the ocean are dirty, the ocean
does not become dirty.

Mahatma Gandhi

EDDIE ADDED A NOTCH OF FLAP and the patch became stationary in the center of his windshield. He said to himself, "I don't see any trees, and it looks flat. It will have to do."

The Dutch countryside on the edge of the English Channel was as black as midnight in a cave, but the tiny grains of wet, white sand on a wide beach reflected the starlight and the weak light of a rising moon working its way above the horizon. As the crippled plane approached, the brightness became an endless flat strip of sand, packed and groomed by the interminable pounding of waves. Eddie thanked God that the tide was out.

Eddie announced to no one in particular, "I'm going to use the wheels. The sand looks wet, so the tide must be out, and the sand will be hard." He pushed the gear lever down. Three seconds later, the left gear light announced that the gear was down and locked. The right gear light flickered, then went dark. The gear leg was part of the engine mount, and Eddie had no way of knowing if the gear was down or not. The FW 190's cannon shells could have damaged it, or perhaps they had only broken the switch that activated the light. He asked himself, "Even if the right gear is down, is it locked?"

Eddie tried to raise the wheels, but nothing happened to the starboard gear. He couldn't hear the worm gears and guessed no power was getting to the motor. Only the wormgear in the left wheel whined as it came up.

He said, "Shit," and lowered it again, hoping that the right one was down and locked.

Eddie suspected that the beach would be firmer next to the water, and as he approached, he could see darker sand next to the right edge. He decided to put the right wheel as close to the water as possible.

◇◇◇◇◇◇◇◇◇◇◇◇◇◇◇◇◇◇◇◇◇◇◇◇◇◇◇◇◇◇◇◇◇◇◇◇◇◇◇

Ludger Weiss was not a Nazi—he hated everything National Socialism stood for. He was a member of the regular German army, conscripted out of the University of Heidelberg's School of Medicine when his grades dropped below the threshold that would have kept him out of the Wehrmacht. He was less than a year from graduation when he received his official notification letter, and despite his professors' pleadings, he became a sergeant in the regular army.

Ludger's father died in a British gas attack in 1917, leaving his mother with two boys and three girls to raise. She worked as a seamstress at home, 60 hours a week, 52 weeks a year. She invested every pfennig she earned in a roof and food for her children and lived without the distractions of a man. None were interested in the burden of five children, and she had no interest in washing a man's clothes and buying his beer.

She pushed her children to work as hard as she did and taught them the value of money. Ludger, the youngest child, was the only one who failed to finish university, and he was determined to correct that when the war ended.

Every night, before they went to their barracks, Sergeant Weiss led a twenty-man patrol along the dunes at the edge of the beach near the town of Noordwijk, occasionally stopping to look out to sea with his binoculars. He often spotted a fishing boat, and occasionally, a British patrol vessel approached the shore, careful to remain out of the range of German guns. Ludger would write a description, the time, and relevant facts such as sea conditions in a notebook, then later transfer the information into a logbook. No one had looked at his records in the two years he'd been patrolling the beach.

Ludger stood on a dune, scanning the sea through his binoculars, thinking of his bedridden mother, when he heard a swishing sound on his right. He lowered the glasses just as the left wheel of a twin-engined British bomber touched lightly on the beach a hundred metres to his right.

The right wheel touched twenty metres after the left, held the wing up for a second, and then collapsed. The starboard wingtip dove into the water's edge, carving a long hole, ever deeper as its drag swung the aircraft toward the sea. As the furrow the wing plowed became deeper, a cascade of saltwater dowsed a fire in the right wing, and the left wheel collapsed from the sideways force on it. The tail lifted, pushing the front perspex into the sand, where it broke, allowing sand to jam into the fuselage as the plane's weight forced it deeper into the wet sand and mud. The plane stopped in front of Ludger with the forward fuselage half-buried in mud and water. Sand and seaweed covered the engines and wings.

Ludger closed his open mouth without a word and ran toward the wreck; his men were close on his heels. Except for Ludger, they were to a man over fifty years old, and most of them carried beer bellies, courtesy of the Niederlander bars, and they made no attempt to keep up with their young sergeant.

The strip of wet sand slid down the windshield as Eddie trimmed the nose up, holding the bomber above the smooth surface until its wing stalled, losing its ability to keep the plane in the air and dropping it gently on the sand. For a second, Eddie thought the plane would stay on its wheels, but the hope died when the starboard gear collapsed and the right wing dove into the English Channel, swinging the Wellington into the water.

The forward perspex burst inward; mud and sand pushed past the Browning machine gun, followed by saltwater. The force of the heavy, wet sand, driven back by the momentum of the bomber, pushed the instrument panel back and down, jamming Eddie's legs. George fared better in the flight engineer's position; the seat broke from its moorings, and the mud wall took him back into the fuselage. The goo stopped at Bill Parson's waist, and he waded to where a wide-eyed George was digging himself out. Paul Burns unfastened his harness and stepped out of the sling.

"What about Eddie?" Paul looked at George.

"I don't know." Bill began to dig at the wall of mud and sand in the direction of the pilot. George and Paul tried to help, but there was no room for a second man between the radios and a bulkhead opposite them.

Paul touched Bill's shoulder. "George and I will go outside and try from there." George went to work on the sand forced against the rear hatch, and it took only a few minutes to open it. When they crawled outside, they met Ludger, and his rifle pointed at their chests.

"Hände Hoch!" Ludger tried to sound confident, but his unsteady tone betrayed him.

"Our pilot's trapped." Paul paid no attention to the rifle and pointed at the cockpit window. Sand and mud covered the inside of the window with enough pressure to bulge it outward. George ran around Ludger just as his wheezing men got to him, leaving Ludger to decide whether to move his rifle from Paul to George. Ludger shouted, "Halt, oder ich schiesse dich!" Paul raised his hands but kept walking around Ludger. George beat at the window with his hand until a big puffing brute of a man grabbed him and spun him around. George broke free and went back to hammering his fists on the window. The big man put his hands on his knees and gasped like a steam engine.

"Ist jemand d'rin?" Ludger lowered his gun and touched Paul's shoulder. He pointed at the window.

"Yes, Eddie. He was flying... Pilot!" Paul yelled, and Ludger nodded. He pushed George aside, turned his rifle around and used the butt to smash the window. George and Paul broke pieces of perspex from the edge and began digging, throwing sand and mud behind them. Ludger and one of his men pulled the sand away to make room for more, and they reached Eddie in less than thirty seconds. Paul pulled sand away from his face, and Eddie breathed, swore, "Fucking mud!" sucked air into his lungs and spit gray goo.

Paul laughed, George laughed, and Ludger smiled. Twenty men

smiled and passed congratulations from one to another. Paul and George went back to digging around Eddie's face.

Ludger had spent two years watching the tide come in and go out, and an inner voice told him to hurry. He moved George and Paul aside and used the rifle butt to push sand back into the fuselage. Working like a madman, he soon tired, and when he stepped aside, he passed the rifle to George, now standing in a foot of water.

"Dass geht aber nicht!" One of the soldiers pointed at George, who now wielded the loaded German rifle, pushing sand away from Eddie. Paul reached past Eddie and pulled mud out with his hands.

"Ohne Hilfe schaffen wir's nicht!" Ludger yelled at his men. "Nimm die Hälfte der Männer und hol' Hilfe. Wir brauchen shaufeln, seil, Äxte...werkzeugen!" When the men turned to obey his order, he added, "Er ist Britisher Flieger! Sagt ihr dass oder ihr kriegt nichts!"

"I think he's sending them for help." Bill could understand a few words of German. He had given up digging inside. He was ten feet of mud and sand from Eddie and figured he could help more from outside. "The fucking water is rising fast!"

A soldier broke the perspex out of the front of the fuselage with his rifle and began digging with the butt; another widened the hole so he could work beside him, pulling sand back with his bayonet. The water was up to his knees.

Fifteen minutes later, the soldiers returned from the village, surrounded by Dutchmen carrying shovels, hoes, axes, crowbars, and coils of rope. The villagers swarmed the wrecked bombers, chattering in Dutch, occasionally addressing a soldier in German. The soldiers laid their rifles on the beach; some dug with their hands, and others used the villagers' tools. They dug like madmen until they slowed, then stepped aside, replaced by a fresh set of arms and lungs.

The water reached the opening ripped in the front; a Dutch villager climbed on the aircraft's roof and began hacking at the aluminum beams. Unfortunately, the geodesic structure started at the nose, and the axe he swung was not the tool to cut structural aluminum. Nonetheless, the man chopped a hole big enough to get through. Someone passed him a new axe, and he widened it. Two men shovelled what they could reach; others pulled and pushed it away from the plane, making room for more.

The villagers knew the tide and became more desperate as it rose. A few began to shout and point, running around the plane, gesturing at a wingtip, then the tail. Men waded out to the end of the wing and dug under it, working in water up to their hips. A Dutchman and a soldier lay down in the cold water, snared the tip with a manila rope the size of a child's wrist, and dragged the end behind the plane and onto the dry beach. Four men pulled on it to test the tip, and it held.

Others, clearly men who knew how to work with their hands, worked on the other tip. The water had reached it, but it was clear of the sand and easily snared. They tested the setup, made a few adjustments and called 'Fertig! to signal they were ready.

Men ran down the beach with more rope, wrapping it around the tail. They pulled it behind the plane, adding a second rope.

◇◇◇◇◇◇◇◇◇◇◇◇◇◇◇◇◇◇◇◇◇◇◇◇◇◇◇◇◇◇◇◇◇◇◇◇◇◇◇

Eddie watched the drama around him, first with fear and then with wonder. Who were these people? Why were they trying so hard to help him? The German soldiers had laid down their rifles—Dutch villagers ran to perform tasks assigned by men who took charge because it was natural for them to lead. Paul, George and a German soldier had removed the mud and sand down to his hips, but he still couldn't move his legs. He couldn't feel them, and when he tried to wiggle his toes in his boots, he wasn't sure he had succeeded. When the water reached his hips, he couldn't feel its wetness and coldness, and he worried.

George dug around with his hands where he expected to find Eddie's knees, but the instrument panel was between his hands and Eddy's legs. They would have to remove the panel before they could remove Eddie, but water already covered the panel and flowed around Eddie's stomach.

Someone shouted a command—villagers and soldiers picked up the ropes, tightened them and waited. Ludger stood on the beach where everyone could see him. He shouted, "Fertig!" with his hand in the air. He looked at the men leaning forward...waiting...and then, "Ziehen!"

Every man pulled, surging, stretching the hemp ropes, digging into the sand with their boots. The plane didn't move. The mud and sand sucked on it, refusing to give it to the men, adding tons of weight to the load.

"Halt!" Ludger shouted, and the men stood up, relaxed, and waited for the inevitable second try. Ludger gave them half a minute and repeated the process, but the plane still didn't move, not even a little bit.

Men grabbed shovels, anything that would move dirt, and began moving mud away from the fuselage and behind the wing. Some worked in water up to their chests, others to their waists. Fifty men dug and pushed mud and dirt with their feet and hands, becoming more desperate as time and tide progressed. Panic set in, and men cried as they worked.

The water reached Eddie's chin; he tipped his head back. George hacked desperately at the instrument panel supports buried in the water while Ludger pried at the other side with a bar, but it didn't move.

Ludger, up to his neck in water, said to George, "Ich fürchte, wir müssen ihm die beine abschneiden." George didn't lift his head. He felt with one hand and hacked with the axe in his other hand. Ludger gently touched his face. "Legs. Off." He made a throat-cutting motion with his hand.

"No!" Eddie yelled at the fuselage's roof. He tried to turn to face the German, but water ran into his mouth. George put an arm under his left armpit, and Ludger lifted the other, gaining an inch.

"Shoot me!" It had been an hour since Eddie had resolved to die rather than lose his legs. He had given up hope in the hour since the wheels had touched, and peace had replaced it. "Please shoot me." He looked into Ludger's eyes, knowing the German understood.

"I cannot." The German officer's voice broke.

"What is your name?" Eddie pitied the man, who looked to be about his age, tears rolling unashamedly down his cheek.

"Ich heisse Ludger Weiss."

"Ludger, you must shoot me." Eddie turned his eyes to the roof. The discussion was over. Either Ludger Weiss would shoot him, or he would drown.

Ludger crawled out of the fuselage and picked up a rifle lying on the beach. Bill and Paul met him as he reached the bomber, and he offered them the gun. They shook their heads.

⬦⬦⬦⬦⬦⬦⬦⬦⬦⬦⬦⬦⬦⬦⬦⬦⬦⬦⬦⬦⬦⬦⬦

"Hurry, Ludger!" George was tiring, and the water was beginning to choke Eddie.

Ludger put the muzzle two inches from Eddie's temple, and before he pulled the trigger, Eddie said, "Ludger, I flew an airplane. I die a happy man."

He choked—Ludger pulled the trigger, and half the men on the beach fell to their knees.

Chapter Twelve

May to October 1943

Gott lässt uns sinken, aber nicht ertrinken.

(God will let us sink, but will never let us drown)

Gray pre-dawn light, dust, and smoke filtered into the living room through glassless windows. The musicians had converted the living room into a place to sleep, using mattresses dragged from the bedrooms and cushions taken from the sofa and chairs.

Lucas woke and had to step around sleeping forms as he went to the window opening that faced the crater where his home had been. Dust hung in the still air, and the smell of smoke permeated everything. In the morning twilight, he could see nothing but rubble, piles of it, and craters, some with water in them. He forced himself to look at the massive empty hole that marked his family's grave and tried to imagine life without his parents and his sister—knowing they were dead but harbouring a feeling in his soul that they weren't yet gone.

He heard movement and turned around to find Karl Zimmermann waking from a fitful sleep. Lucas couldn't remember sleeping, but pieces of the night were missing. He had heard others going to the bathroom and had gone once himself. Without water to flush the toilet, the bathroom was a stinky place, and he resolved to use the backyard as soon as there was enough light.

As far as Lucas could see, Katrina hadn't stirred, and he wondered whether she had somehow turned off her consciousness or if her mind had shut itself down in an attempt at self-preservation. Karl stood up and walked over to Lucas. He stood beside him, looking at the hole that had been his best friend's house. He put his hand on Lucas's shoulder.

"Lucas, I'm afraid we're on an island surrounded by death and devastation. We have no time to feel sorry for ourselves—we are the lucky ones who can go on with our lives."

The finality in Karl's voice dismayed Lucas. He understood the words but had no idea what 'going on with his life' would mean. He couldn't see past going outside to the relieve himself. All he could think of was his parents—he needed their help now more than he had ever needed it in his life.

Lucas swept his hand around the room. "Where do we start? Nothing is left; this house is ruined; we have no food or water, and there is no one to clean up the mess!" He looked at the hole in the ground. "And have you been to the bathroom yet?"

"Yes, once, and I think you and I should use the backyard and leave the toilet for the women until I get a bucket of water somewhere—broken waterlines will have made puddles in the bottom of a few craters."

Karl let his gaze move from left to right, looking at the sleeping figures. "There are six of us here, and others out there will need help." He pointed toward the devastation. "We must search for survivors; there is no time for what might or should have been. We will eat the food and water in the shelter, and when it's gone, we'll find more somewhere." He looked into Lucas's eyes and said, "I realize you should have ten more years to grow up, but you don't."

Lucas stared at the crater. "I hate those English bastards!"

"...and the English hate the German bastards, but neither has anything to do with our present situation." Karl leaned ahead to look into Lucas's face. "Don't waste your time on blame and hate. You can destroy the precious life you've been given by trying to figure out who to blame—or you can help yourself, your friends, and my family." He put his hand gently on Lucas's shoulder and turned him so that the boy had no choice but to look into his eyes. "We can't help those who died—but we can do something for the living."

Karl turned to face the room, clapped his hands, and raised his voice. "Everyone up! Others need help!"

Despite the imminent dawn, no birds sang, no dogs barked, and no sounds of human activity broke the silence. As the people in the room woke one by one, they began wandering. When Corinne returned from the bathroom, she asked Karl and Lenora, "Is it okay if I do what I must do in your yard?"

Lenora said, "Yes, that's what I'm going to do." Corinne nodded and disappeared.

The oppressive stillness weighed on the survivors in Wambelerstrasse 31. They spoke in subdued tones as though the dead were asleep, and they feared they might awaken them. Looking out the windows, it was clear that their house was one of few still standing. But the stillness, the absence of cries for help or screams of pain, removed the sense of urgency that they knew they should feel. Piles of debris, half-walls, damaged buildings, and craters spoiled the once-orderly landscape. There was almost no separation between streets and yards, and smoke rose from hundreds of piles of rubble. Water running out of a broken cast-iron pipe slowly filled an enormous crater in front of the house, where a beautiful street had been.

◇◇◇◇◇◇◇◇◇◇◇◇◇◇◇◇◇◇◇◇◇◇◇◇◇◇◇◇◇◇◇◇◇◇◇◇

Karl found two buckets and made two trips to the crater. When he arrived in the kitchen for the bread and cheese Lenora had located, enough to feed everyone but not fully satisfy anyone, he declared the bathroom functional but unpleasant.

While Karl was cleaning up the bathroom, Lucas and Hartwig had gathered an armload of tools, wire, cloth, a piece of rope, and general paraphernalia—anything they thought might be useful. The boys patched the table, and Karl jury-rigged the broken chairs. Using a tap in the cellar, Corinne drained the house's water system into a copper pot and put it on the table. Katrina found enough broken-handled cups, plates, and silverware to set four places— two would have to stand when they ate, and Lucas and Corinne volunteered.

The group talked in low tones as they ate, speculating about what they might find, dreading the reality that must be out there. No one talked about anything else; no one laughed or joked, and Karl stopped the speculation halfway through the meal.

"We need to structure our search for survivors. We will take whatever tools we can carry; if we find someone, we might not have time to return to get them." Everyone nodded, and he said, "I suggest we split up, with Katrina, Lucas, and Lenora going to Katrina's house while Hartwig, Corinne and I search for Corinne's parents."

Everyone agreed to meet back at the house with no set schedule. They went out the garden door and worked their way to what had been the street.

It was impossible to walk in anything that resembled a straight line, and Lucas led the way through narrow gaps between piles of scattered bricks, stone and wood. He didn't hear a cry for help or see a soul—the only sounds were the faraway noises of rescue vehicles and fire trucks.

Katrina's house was scarcely two hundred metres from the Zimmermann house, but it took an hour to find a pile of rubble that Katrina could identify as her home. They lifted timbers, threw bricks aside, and crawled into holes, searching for signs of life or death. The most massive pieces of the house were in the cellar, too heavy to move, and there was no answer when Katrina called her mother's name. Finally, they gave up, and Katrina said she still hoped her mother had made it to the shelter.

When they returned to Wambelerstrasse 31, Karl's group was already there, and he reported that Corinne had quickly found the pile of debris that had been her house, and they had found the bodies of her father and mother crushed under tons of rubble. Unable to lift the timbers and sections of the wall that had killed them, they left them there. Tears streamed down Corinne's cheeks as she told Lucas of their attempts to lift a heavy beam lying on her mother. Karl had rigged pulleys and ropes, and they pried with crowbars but had finally had to give up.

Karl said, "She's gone, Corinne. It would have done no good if we had gotten your parents' bodies out. The emergency people will get them, and they will receive the respect you would want."

Corinne sat down on a repaired chair, tears in her eyes. She told Lucas, "There was a couple in the cellar with my parents. They lived upstairs, and they helped my mother when my father beat her. He threatened to shoot my father, but my mother wouldn't let him. He was old and told my mother that they wouldn't put someone as old as he was in prison." She looked at Karl and sobbed. "If I had been home, I would have killed him and blamed it on the bombs. I've been planning it for months... ever since the bombing started."

Corinne stood up and wiped her face. "I think we should go out again; there must be something we can do for someone."

Karl looked to the northeast, where he could still see flames fed by the oil, gasoline, and coke stored at the plant he managed. "The bombs ruptured the fuel storage tanks, and the slave labour barracks probably burned to the ground." The agony on Karl's face mirrored his broken heart as he thought of the people locked in the wooden building while it burned.

Karl turned to Lucas and Hartwig, standing near him, waiting for orders. "This house is of no more use; we can't stay here…it will take months to clear the streets and find the bodies and years to replace the buildings."

Lenora returned from the shelter with an entire Mettwurst and a loaf of black Pumpernickel from the emergency supply—she had even found a jar of goose fat for the bread and two bottles of apple juice. Everyone attacked the food like starving dogs.

Katrina had eaten almost nothing when she stood up, stared into the garden through the opening where the back door used to be, and talked to no one in particular.

"My mother is dead, and it's probably better this way." She swept her eyes from one to another of her friends. "I'm on my own now; I have no money and no place to sleep. I will need help."

Lucas's mouth was full of Pumpernickel, and before he could grind it into small enough pieces to swallow and offer his help, he realized with a start that he was in the same sinking boat.

Hartwig, happy to be generous with his family's situation, eagerly said, "You can live with us as long as you want to!" as he looked at Katrina with a broad grin. "I'll sleep on the floor, and you can have my bed."

Lucas noted that Hartwig only directed the offer at Katrina.

Lenora closed the discussion without consulting her husband. "We will stay together for as long as it takes. Karl and I will find a house big enough for all of us; he will rebuild the plant, and I will take care of the rest. We will get through this together!"

Lenora reached across the table, took her husband's hand and looked at him with the love Lucas had seen in his mother's eyes when she looked at his father. He had been too busy to dwell on his family, but the love in her gesture brought his father and mother back, and it took all the will he possessed to control his sense of hopelessness. Since he had stood on the edge of the crater that marked the only grave his family would have, his urge to surrender to grief came and went like waves crashing on a beach, threatening to pull him out to sea.

Karl glanced at Lenora, then looked around the room as he said, "Lenora is right—we can't stay in this house any longer—we've got to find something north of here, away from the bombing. I'm afraid we must leave our home and start over."

"Of course I'm right…" Lenora smiled for the first time since the bombing started. "And you are also right—we can't stay here, and we are wasting time. Why don't we get moving!" It wasn't a question. She looked from one to another, still smiling. "There's no point in waiting for problems to find us…it's better to face them where they are." She reached for Karl's plate, but he pulled it away. Lenora waited while he swallowed and put his last piece of Mettwurst on a piece of bread, then took the plate and turned to Lucas.

Lucas drank the last swallow of juice, stood up, and handed his cup and plate to Lenora. He asked, "What about our instruments?"

Karl said, "You can carry them. We won't take any tools."

Still smiling, Lenora slammed the dishes on the floor, throwing them so hard that they broke into small pieces. She said, "Alle Anfang ist schwer, but we will begin again!"

Everyone met in the only flat spot in the garden. The musicians had their instruments; Hartwig carried Katrina's cello, and Karl, Lenora and Katrina brought the remaining food.

◇◇◇◇◇◇◇◇◇◇◇◇◇◇◇◇◇◇◇◇◇◇◇◇◇◇◇◇◇◇◇◇◇◇◇◇

Karl and Lenora led the way northwest, picking their way through piles of broken buildings and around bomb craters until they found a relatively open street heading in that direction.

A kilometre northwest of Wambelerstrasse 31, almost every house was still standing, most of them without damage. People walked on the streets, talking to one another, searching for food, asking everyone they met if they had seen missing friends and relatives. Everyone wanted to help, but the rescue and emergency authorities had everything organized and chased civilians away.

Eventually, two Wehrmacht soldiers stopped them. They asked Karl who he was and where he worked, then abruptly told him to wait where he was until they returned. They sat down on two benches in front of a shoemaker's store, and twenty minutes later, two Kubelwagen, open army vehicles with noisy little air-cooled engines, picked them up and drove them to a shelter in a school classroom. They slept on folding cots, and the Kubelwagen took Karl to the Hoesch site the following morning.

A week later, Karl, Lenora and the string quartet were in a large, comfortable Wohnung five blocks north of the synthetic oil plant. It had five rooms, three of them bedrooms. Katrina and Corinne took one, and Lucas and Hartwig another. The Third Reich desperately needed Karl's talents; it was in the National Socialists' interest to keep his family comfortable.

◇◇◇◇◇◇◇◇◇◇◇◇◇◇◇◇◇◇◇◇◇◇◇◇◇◇◇◇◇◇◇◇◇◇◇◇◇◇

On the day of the bombing, Lucas's only relatives were a great-aunt in Detmold and grandparents in Wuppertal. A few days after Dortmund's demise, his grandparents died in a bombing raid. With nowhere to go, he stayed with Hartwig and his parents until October when, following an exchange of letters with his aunt, Lucas and Corinne left Dortmund on scavenged bicycles, bound for Tante Waltraut's house.

It took three cold, rainy days to pedal the hundred and thirty-five kilometres, sleeping in Pensions and eating in Gaststätte using money Karl had given them. The north wind blew in their face, and Lucas quickly learned that Corinne could pull away from him. She led the way, periodically glancing over her shoulder, trying not to embarrass him. On the first day, Lucas was thankful when Corinne picked out a Pension in the middle of the afternoon, insisting that she was tired. He was exhausted but noted that she wasn't breathing hard.

The next day, Corinne insisted that Lucas lead while she pedalled effortlessly behind him. The wind had shifted to the southeast, carrying her words forward so he could hear her talking to herself. She spent most of her time obsessing over her hatred for her father. Corinne regretted not killing the "bastard" and said she hoped he "burned in hell!" The wind carried her bitterness to Lucas, and when she finally shifted from hatred for her father, he heard her blame herself for the beatings her mother had suffered. She cried and asked her mother's forgiveness, and Lucas had to fight the urge to tell her she was not to blame. He wanted to stop and put his arms around her.

The Pension had given them buns and cheese to eat on the road, and Lucas was ready to stop when Corinne asked him to pull over. The ground was too wet to sit on, so she pulled her bicycle ahead and turned it around to face Lucas. Reaching behind her seat, Corinne took the bag of buns from a wooden box tied on her parcel carrier and passed a Brötchen and a bottle full of water to Lucas. He leaned against his bicycle, unscrewed the top, took a long drink and began talking while wiping his mouth.

"I heard you talking about your mother and father."

Corinne also wiped her mouth with her hand. "I was talking to myself, not to you."

"I couldn't help overhearing you—you said you wanted to kill your father."

Corinne bit a piece from her bun, chewed it twice, and pushed it to the side of her mouth. "Unfortunately, it's too late for that—now all I can do is kill him in my imagination."

"I heard you say something about hitting him with a hammer."

Corinne seemed to consider what to say as she chewed on a piece of Brötchen, so Lucas waited until she decided to go on.

"Yes, I was going to kill him with the hammer he kept in the cellar. I planned to do it during an air raid and make it look like something had hit him."

"But if the cellar weren't damaged, that wouldn't work."

"I was going to drag him outside."

"What if no bombs landed near him? The police would know he had been murdered."

Lucas wanted to prove that Corinne wouldn't have killed her father even if the opportunity were there.

She didn't hesitate. She went on with the details she had worked out.

"Everyone would be in the shelters or their cellars, so I would drag his body to where there were bomb craters. I'm strong, and I could have dragged him a long way. Anyway, if they thought it was murder, they would never suspect me. I would steal his wallet, take out the money and leave it somewhere close to the body."

"I'm glad you didn't have to do that." Lucas kicked a stone off the bicycle path. He imagined Corinne killing her father and dragging him to a crater and realized she would have done it if the British hadn't interfered.

<hr>

They leaned on their bicycles while they ate bread and cheese washed down with a bottle of water. Their rubber raincoats and hats kept them reasonably dry in the wet drizzle.

Corinne rinsed her mouth and spat in the ditch. "I wanted to kill him with my own hands; The Englander cheated me by killing him before I could."

"I couldn't kill anyone." Lucas couldn't imagine taking a life. "Especially with a hammer or a knife."

Corinne took a long drink out of her water bottle. "What if someone were trying to kill your mother?"

She screwed the top on the bottle, put it in her backpack, and turned back to Lucas. "What if he did it every week, and he made you watch him do it? What if he beat you and then beat your mother when she tried to protect you?"

Lucas began to regret starting the discussion.

Corinne wagged her finger in Lucas's face. "You're a man, not a helpless woman or a child, and you don't know anything about it!"

Lucas thought about Corinne's father beating her in front of him and decided he could kill that particular man in that case. He said, "I could kill your father if he were beating you, but I can't imagine my father beating anyone, so I must say no, I could never kill my father. And I can't believe you could kill yours!"

Lucas checked the ropes holding his suitcase and violin on the rear carrier, straightened out the rubber sheet covering them, climbed on his bicycle, put his feet on the ground and waited for Corinne. "I don't want to talk about killing people. I could never kill anyone; I hate to even think about it!"

Corinne checked out her viola, made sure the rubber sheet covered it completely, and then looked at Lucas before getting on her bicycle.

"Lucas, you're too sweet to win a fight or to kill someone—I'm afraid you would let the other guy kill you first. If you want to kill a bastard like my father, you can't kill him in a fair fight; you need to kill him when he can't see it coming. You must do it quickly—don't hesitate or allow him to save himself. Otherwise, he will kill you and whoever you are trying to protect."

As Lucas drove ahead of Corinne, he tried to think through her murder scenario and decided she had never cared if the police caught her. She had intended to kill her father to save her mother, and the consequences for her were irrelevant. Lucas hated her father for beating Corinne, and maybe he could kill him, but Lucas's mind wouldn't allow him to consider hurting his own father.

On the afternoon of the third day, they climbed over a ridge and drove down a crooked, steep path through the Teutoburger forest into Detmold, turning up on Tante Waltraut's doorstep in the evening twilight, soaking wet and in driving rain. She welcomed them with tears in her eyes.

When they were inside, Lucas saw that Waltraut had only a kitchen, a living room, and one bedroom, and he didn't know what to say. Waltraut showed him a straw mattress ready for him on the living room floor and said Corinne would sleep in the bedroom with her. Corinne looked at the bed and said, "Thank you, Waltraut." Lucas followed her lead, saying, "I can sleep anywhere, so don't worry about me. Thank you for helping us."

Waltraut smiled and stroked his hair. "You look just like your father, Lucas. He was the finest man I've ever known." She paused and took his hand in hers. "I will take care of you as long as I can."

Chapter Thirteen

May 1944

In spite of everything, I still believe people are good at heart.

Anne Frank's diary

UNDER NORMAL CIRCUMSTANCES, Aida, the grandest of grand operas, would have been an ambitious undertaking for the small Detmold Theatre, but in the frustrating times of 1944, it was a mammoth enterprise, becoming out of necessity a community project. After four years of war, most of the town's population mourned the loss of someone—fallen sons and fathers taken from their homes to fight for the Vaterland and relatives and friends killed in the bombing of cities, and the distraction was welcome.

The need for a diversion created a large pool of volunteers, primarily seniors too old to otherwise contribute to the war effort. A local artist designed impressive sets, and local tradesmen too old to fight built them from scrounged material. The entire Detmold music community became involved in the production, bolstering the depleted opera house's chorus and orchestra. The average age of the men in the chorus was over sixty; the women were slightly younger.

Felix Schmidt, Aida's stage director, lost his wife six months before the Aida première. Their older son had died in the invasion of France, and when the younger son died in Russia, the loss of her second boy was too much for Amelia. On Christmas night, she walked into the Teutoburger forest without telling anyone where she was going and sat on a bench beside the gravel path she and Felix walked every Sunday. Sometime during the cold night, merciful death came for her, and Felix found his beloved wife lying on the bench with her eyes closed. When he approached, he thought she was sleeping.

For months, Felix walked to the spot every Sunday, sat on the bench, looked down at his feet while he drank schnapps and felt sorry for himself.

◇◇◇◇◇◇◇◇◇◇◇◇◇◇◇◇◇◇◇◇◇◇◇◇◇◇◇◇◇

Felix hit the schnapps hard, and his work at the theatre suffered. His friend, Theo Finke, lived on Gartenstrasse, as did Felix, and Theo walked him to the theatre every morning, rain or shine, drunk or sober.

Felix hated umbrellas, although it rained in Detmold three days out of four. Amelia had bought umbrellas for him, but one by one, he left them behind until he eventually lost them. Finally, she gave up. When Amelia died, Theo bought an enormous umbrella, the biggest one he could find, big enough to protect both of them when they locked arms and walked in step, forcing Felix to match his friend's pace, a difficult challenge when Felix was drunk.

Time passed, Felix's bitterness subsided, and he stopped drinking. Felix and Theo played chess as they had when they were young, and Felix's chess improved as his heart healed. His anger disappeared, and he again found the patience to deal with arrogant tenors and moody sopranos. The new Felix avoided conflict and aggression; he turned and ran rather than face them, and it didn't take long for everyone in the theatre to learn that they had to meet Felix more than halfway or watch his back leave the stage.

Theo was the only person with whom Felix could speak of his losses and loneliness. When he was home, and the black depression made the Schnapps irresistible, he walked up the street to Gartenstrasse 18 and banged the knocker. Theo always took time to play chess with Felix until the black despair passed. They talked about Aida's music, the elaborate scenes and sets and how they could stage it considering their limited human resources. They never spoke of the worsening war or mentioned the daunting financial challenge Aida would present.

No matter when Felix came to their door, Theo's wife, Maria, arranged to be busy, and except for making tea and cookies for them, Maria left Theo to do his magic.

◇◇◇◇◇◇◇◇◇◇◇◇◇◇◇◇◇◇◇◇◇◇◇◇◇◇◇◇◇◇◇◇◇◇◇

Waltraut Grönert, seventy-two in 1944, sang as a guest member of the Detmold Theatre chorus. She was a large, muscular woman, built to pull a plow. Blessed with an enormous alto voice, she occasionally sang tenor, as in the opera that the theatre was currently rehearsing. Theo desperately needed her resonant voice to carry the tenor section, and he conscripted Waltraut to play a soldier in an Egyptian army that had existed a thousand years before Christ was born—and Waltraut deserted.

She decided she owed Felix an explanation and came to the first staging rehearsal prepared to refuse a soldier role. She would tell him that she was okay with being a female slave.

At the costume fitting, she made her dismay known by refusing to accept the soldier uniform. Felix ignored her refusal, telling her he had too many slaves and too few soldiers. Finally, with Felix on the verge of a breakdown, begging with tears in his eyes, she agreed to take the costume home. But once there, Waltraut changed her mind and decided to quit the production if Felix insisted she play a soldier. She would agree to sing tenor while she played a slave, but she would never go on stage as a soldier.

◇◇◇◇◇◇◇◇◇◇◇◇◇◇◇◇◇◇◇◇◇◇◇◇◇◇◇◇◇◇◇◇◇

Waltraut arrived at the theatre early the next day, searching for Felix to give him the bad news privately. He wasn't in the theatre, and he wasn't in the cafeteria. But when she spotted Theo Finke nursing a coffee at a corner table, looking thoughtfully out the window, she decided to talk to him about her problem. The timing was perfect; he could solve the soldier conundrum and maybe find a solution for her other problem. She stopped at the counter to pick up a cup of coffee, dropped fifty Pfennig on the bar, and then walked over to where Theo sat brooding over a coffee. He stood up when he saw her coming.

"I'm going to sit here with you if you don't mind." She held the coffee in both hands and waited for him to be gracious.

Theo smiled warmly, pulled out the chair opposite him and gallantly gestured for her to sit. She was one of his favourite people.

"Are you going to scold me about something?" He smiled hopefully.

She said, "Of course I am! But you should look at it as expert advice from one who understands your situation better than you do."

Waltraut and Theo had bantered for thirty years. She was a founding member of the Singverein he had formed when he left the Wehrmacht but had drifted away from the community choir when her husband died. It had been two years since Theo had heard her voice, and this production of Aida would be her first singing adventure since her husband's death.

Waltraut became serious. "Theo, I have a problem."

"It's only a problem until it's solved."

"It's my grandnephew Lucas and his friend Corinne," she began, then stopped, trying to decide how to ask for his help.

Theo broke the ice to give her time. "Is he your sister's grandson? She lives in Dortmund, doesn't she?" Theo knew via the rumour mill that Waltraut had boarders from Dortmund but assumed she was doing it for money; her husband had left her near penniless.

"Yes, both Lucas and Corinne lived in Dortmund. My sister lived with her younger daughter Stephanie's family—Stephanie's husband, Andreas, was an engineer at the Hoesch Iron and Steel Works. They had two children, and sadly, when the house was destroyed in the raid last May, everyone, including Lucas's parents and sister, was killed. Fortunately, Lucas and his friend Corinne were at a pianist friend's house practicing a Brahms quartet when the bombers came, and when the raid was over, it was the only house on the street still standing. Corinne's parents lived on the street and were also killed in the raid. She and Lucas have no one, and the house is uninhabitable."

"The tragedy goes on... I am so sorry to hear that. I remember your sister well." He looked into Waltraut's eyes. "How may I help?"

Waltraut went on, suddenly full of hope. "They are both fifteen and have been living with me since October, but I have only one bedroom, and Lucas has to sleep in my living room. More than that, Lucas needs his music, a place to practice and someone to care about him. He is a talented pianist and violinist, and you could do worse than teach him. Corinne plays the viola and could also use some help—the kind Maria could give." She added a tiny piece of bait. "Lucas may even become a conductor with the right push!"

Waltraut was openly desperate. She squeezed a napkin with her left hand, and her right hand shook so that she had to put her coffee down. "I'm afraid I have no money to pay you, Theo, and, of course, they have no money either." She hung her head, and Theo sensed her shame. "I don't know how I'm going to feed Corinne—I had a little saved for a rainy day, but that's all gone. "

Theo put his hand on hers and, without hesitating, said, "Okay, bring him any time before rehearsal tomorrow morning…If he wants to learn, I will teach him. Bring his belongings, and he can have Johann's room." It occurred to him that he had promised to share their apartment without consulting Maria. "Don't worry about money for Lucas; I will take care of that. I will also see that Corinne earns enough with the orchestra to help you with her board. Only God knows how badly I need a viola, and Corinne will be the answer to my prayer."

Waltraut began laughing, soft and nervously at first, and then the laugh became full, and she leaned over the table to kiss him. He kissed her cheek, and she let him go, embarrassed, childishly smoothing the top of her skirt where it had crept up and wrinkled.

She said, "All right, that was too easy. What's the price?" Her nervous expression implied she would negotiate, but what could she offer?

Theo said, "It's alright, Waltraut," and was about to say he didn't want anything, but suddenly realized that she had something to offer, something valuable that wouldn't cost her anything but would benefit everyone.

"I've heard you don't think Egyptian soldiers are your bailiwick, but I must disagree…you would make a fine soldier!" He smiled, and when she didn't, he changed his tone.

"Felix is very fragile right now, and I think you could help him. You're a born leader; people follow you naturally. I must tell you that this has nothing to do with Lucas or the deal—I will do that in any case. But playing a soldier will benefit everyone—perhaps especially you." Waltraut shifted in her chair, knowing what was coming. She also knew that, no matter what Theo said about there being no connection with his offer to take Lucas in, she would have no choice.

He said, "I want you to lead the choir through this Aida effort, officially, for a paltry sum of money we could pay if you play a soldier, not exclusively as a favour to me. You will make or break this performance, and I need you to make it work in every way you can. Support Felix and me—don't criticize us publicly, no matter what you think of the crazy things we ask you to do."

Waltraut smiled broadly, let it become a laugh. "You knew that I don't like being a soldier?"

"Yes, you made it more than apparent to the whole opera house when they gave you the uniform. Everyone in the theatre pays attention to you, and that's why I need you to lead." He touched her hand. "I will announce you as the choir leader at the rehearsal tomorrow...but you must get me a couple of soldiers...it's okay if they can't sing."

Waltraut was suddenly excited. She knew several men who would gladly play soldier, but they couldn't carry a tune in a pail. "It's a deal! I'll give you a happy Felix and a great Aida, and you will make Lucas a musician!" She stretched her hand across the small table, and Theo shook it enthusiastically.

Waltraut and Theo had a half-hour before she needed to go to her first musical rehearsal, and they had just started reminiscing when Felix approached the table with a cup of steaming coffee. He pulled a chair back and sat down. Staring at Waltraut, he searched for the right words and the courage to say them. Waltraut and Theo waited.

Felix began, so desperate it was pitiful. "Waltraut, I don't know what to do if you won't be a soldier! I don't have enough men, and now that you refused, the other women don't want to be soldiers either. I don't know what to do if...."

Her smile stopped him in mid-sentence. Waltraut took his hand; he held his breath and began to hope. She said, "Don't worry yourself about this; just tell me what you need from me, and I will give it to you. I'll get you a whole army if that's what you need! They won't all be singers, but they can carry a spear."

Felix hesitated and looked curiously at Theo, wondering what he didn't know. "What did this cost you, Theo? Is it something we can discuss in public?"

Theo laughed, kissed Waltraut's hand and rolled his eyes upward to look into Felix's. "We'll never tell!"

Chapter Fourteen

May-June 1944

The Triumphant March

"How lucky I am to have something that makes saying good-bye so hard."

A. A. Milne, Winnie the Pooh

SEVEN MONTHS AFTER HE STOOD IN THE RAIN on Waltraut's doorstep, Lucas stood in the rain again, this time on Theo Finke's doorstep. In his excitement, he had left Waltraut behind, and by the time she huffed her way up the stone steps and stood beside him, gasping, he had slammed the knocker against the plate for the second time.

The door opened, and Theo Finke stood facing him. He bypassed Lucas's outstretched hand and wrapped his arms around him. "Welcome, son, welcome." He stood back to let Lucas and a puffing Waltraut through the door. Lucas, carrying an old leather suitcase, turned right in the large entrance and went through the kitchen door to where Maria waited to greet him.

Like her husband, she wrapped her arms around him. She said, "Welcome to your new home, Lucas." She turned him toward the door to the living room, and Waltraut threw herself into a kitchen chair.

Maria gave Waltraut a concerned smile and said to Lucas, who had put the suitcase down, "Bring the suitcase—I'll show you where you will be sleeping."

She led Lucas through the living room to an open door on the other side.

"This was our son's room before he got married. He's in Russia now and will live in his family's house when he comes home, so it's yours for as long as you need it." She kept a warm smile on her face as she motioned for him to go in. Lucas walked past her and set his suitcase on the floor in the middle of the room. A bed, a huge Schrank—a portable closet—big enough for all the clothes Lucas had owned in his lifetime, and a large desk still left enough space to dance. He turned to Maria and asked skeptically, "Is this room all mine?" When she shook her head positively, Lucas impulsively hugged her and then, embarrassed, let her go.

He tested the bed, then pointed to a photograph of a man in a Wehrmacht uniform surrounded by Maria, Theo, a woman and two children.

"That's our son Johann, his wife Barbara, and his children, Lisa and Thomas. Johann has been in Russia for almost three years, and you will meet Barbara and Thomas on Saturday."

Lucas stared at the man, imagining him playing violin, but couldn't see him killing men. He asked, "And Lisa...isn't she coming?"

Lucas let his eyes wander from one picture to another, on the bedside table, the desk, and hanging on the walls. The photographs documented Johann's life, from a naked baby to a family man to the soldier in a Wehrmacht uniform.

"We lost Lisa a year ago when a bomb destroyed her friend's house where she and her classmates celebrated her friend's birthday. The explosion killed all the children and two of their mothers."

Lucas's mind jumped to the hole where his family had died, and he couldn't stop a flood of grief. Tears flowed, he sobbed and said, "Oh, Frau Finke, I am so sorry!"

She wrapped her arms around him, and his tears flowed down his face in a river.

"Theo told me you lost your sister and your parents. You might not believe it now, but the pain will stop someday, and you will be able to remember them without crying."

<hr>

Lucas, Theo and Thomas played a round-robin chess tournament on Saturday morning, and Lucas finished last. Barbara and Maria fussed around him like mother hens, and when Mittagessen was over, Theo took him to the theatre to listen to an orchestra rehearsal.

Theo gave Lucas a week to adjust to his new home, then began his music theory and piano lessons. Maria gave him violin lessons, and his playing steadily improved. The instrument Lucas owned was full-toned and resonant, so Theo decided it was time to exploit him.

He began his pitch at dinner a few days later.

"How would you like to play in the theatre orchestra, Lucas? Maria says that Corinne is ready, and we need both of you."

Lucas put his fork down. "I've never played in an orchestra, except in school."

Theo wiped his mouth with a napkin. "I've lost three violins and half the violas to the Bundeswehr, and two violins I have are amateurs and not as talented as you are." He put the napkin down and concentrated his gaze on Lucas. "Lucas, I need you and Corinne in the orchestra, and Maria and I will help you learn the music. If you agree, I want you to start this evening after you lead the choir rehearsal."

Lucas blurted, "Choir rehearsal? I can't sing, and I've never had anything to do with choirs!" He looked at Theo, and Theo grinned.

"Yes, I know that, but you don't need to sing...I need someone to play the piano and bang notes into the choir every afternoon for the next few weeks, and I've volunteered your services."

Lucas didn't hesitate. "I'll do whatever you need me to do. My grades are good, and the homework isn't too hard; I'll give you all the time I can."

Theo smiled like a sneaky cat that had eaten the canary. Maria shook her head almost imperceptibly, but Lucas noticed.

Mittagspause was over at three o'clock, and Lucas started his first choir rehearsal while Theo watched. He sight-read the music, pounding notes into the choir phrase-by-phrase. Theo watched for thirty minutes without comment, then disappeared.

Theo stayed twenty minutes at the next choir practice, the last time Lucas saw him in the choir room. He became more comfortable with every rehearsal and suspected from comments Theo made at the evening meal that he had a spy within the choir. Lucas suspected Waltraut was the mole.

◇◇◇◇◇◇◇◇◇◇◇◇◇◇◇◇◇◇◇◇◇◇◇◇◇◇◇◇◇◇◇◇◇

Lucas had slept fitfully since the Dortmund bombing raid and some nights lay on his back looking at the ceiling for hours. When he finally drifted off, he saw people, usually his parents and sister, blown to pieces. He often woke in a sweat, crying and yelling senseless words. A few days after arriving at Theo's house, Lucas woke from a nightmare and found Maria sitting beside his bed. He speculated that she had been there for a while and that this was not the first time.

After that, most nights, Maria sat and talked with him before he went to bed, taking time to listen to ramblings about his dead family and the terrible night they died. At first, he told her every detail, sometimes through tears, but gradually, as time passed and Theo increased his workload, the talks became shorter, and he didn't remember her leaving his room. The topic changed, and finally, Lucas just said, "Gute Nacht," and slept soundly, dreaming of playing the violin and teaching the choir. Princess Aida sometimes crept into the dream, bearing a remarkable resemblance to Corinne, and he often woke up in the morning singing the chorus parts he was teaching.

One night, he was surprised when he dreamt amorously about Corinne and had to get up to clean the bed. Although Lucas thought he had hidden the evidence, when he went to his room that evening, he discovered that Maria had changed the sheet and the Federbett cover. At orchestra rehearsal, Corinne's smile made him wonder what she knew. Did she dream about him?

Lucas's independent nature didn't seem to bother Theo. On the contrary, he commented on how remarkably Lucas reminded him of his confident son Johann at that age. When Theo credited Lucas with self-discipline at least equal to his son's, Lucas felt a sense of pride he hadn't felt since his parents' death. Every morning from six until breakfast at eight, Lucas practiced the violin or worked on the choir music, and then again from when he got home from school until Mittagessen. Lucas made sure he was never late for anything and didn't waste a minute of the day. His devotion to Theo and Maria grew with every day they spent together, and he treasured every word of their encouragement.

Corinne began to show up at the house almost daily, ostensibly to work on her viola with Maria, but she spent most of the time talking to Lucas. After orchestra rehearsals, Corinne arranged to walk home from the theatre with him, and he found happiness and contentment with her that he couldn't imagine living without. It surprised him when even the little intellectual musical games they played while eating Maria's cookies aroused him sexually.

Corinne picked a note out of the air, Lucas raised it a half-tone, Corinne sang a minor third under Lucas's tone, and they modulated through the keys using patterns the other singer had to recognize and anticipate. They made rules, sometimes restricting modulations to those available to Bach or Mozart, and occasionally, they made the game more complicated, using Ravel, Tchaikovsky, and Stravinsky's modern and more flexible chord progressions. When Theo joined the game, he raised the stakes further, using quarter-tones and fascinating modulations found only in Arab and East-Indian music.

On one exquisite day, a particularly complicated game ended surprisingly back in the original key, in perfect harmony, using different routes. Excited, Lucas said, "That was wonderful, Corinne! I love..." His voice softened, and he said..., "doing chord progressions with you."

Corinne said softly, "I feel the same about you," and looked at their chaperone, who was knitting on the sofa, pretending she hadn't noticed anything. Without dropping a stitch, Maria asked Corinne, "Did you say something, dear?"

Corinne wagged her head; Maria looked over her glasses, smiled from ear to ear, and returned to her knitting.

Every evening, Theo discussed the choir parts' fine points with Lucas, explaining how to raise everything to performance standards. Theo and Lucas discovered that Lucas had a beautiful baritone voice with the true sense of pitch often found in string players. As Lucas's teaching and people-managing skills improved, he sometimes caught Theo secretly watching the choir rehearsal through the open door. Lucas worked hard at the musicianship his mentor insisted on, but most of all, he worked on dealing with people, especially old people with failing, shaky voices.

◇◇◇◇◇◇◇◇◇◇◇◇◇◇◇◇◇◇◇◇◇◇◇◇◇◇◇◇◇◇◇◇◇◇

Theo and Maria had not heard from Johann in months, and the news from Russia worsened daily. Lucas watched their deep longing for their son, with the feeling that his own successes were somehow irrelevant to the crumbling world. Lucas spent a lot of time looking at Johann's photographs, trying to understand how a sensitive musician could learn to kill. He was certain that he could never kill a man!

When the day that Lucas's choir had its first rehearsal with Theo's orchestra arrived, Lucas sat in the middle of the second row of violins, listening to Theo blend the interlacing parts into a beautiful whole.

Lucas was as nervous as a cat in a room full of rocking chairs, and when the rehearsal ended, he had chewed his fingernails down to the flesh on his fingertips.

Theo and Lucas walked home from the theatre in silence until they turned off Hornschestrasse onto Gartenstrasse, and Theo began talking about the latest war news from Russia. He still hadn't mentioned the rehearsal when he opened the front door to Gartenstrasse 18 with the beautiful round key that had opened it since 1867. When they stepped into the kitchen, Maria saw the anxiety on Lucas's face. She touched the back of his hand and turned to Theo.

Lucas, unable to control himself any longer, said, "Theo, I need to know what you think of the choir's singing." He spoke like a child asking if he could go to the circus, knowing the answer was 'no.'

"I heard the spots you pointed out to them, and yes, I know they do need work, but I can put in some extra time. Please, tell me what I need to fix, and I'm sure I can make it right if you help me." It took a supreme effort to win the fight against running to his room.

Theo laughed. "Lucas, I can't tell you what was wrong because that was the best-prepared amateur choir I've ever heard. I thought they sang very well, and I assumed you knew. They didn't miss an entry— you even had most of the dynamics worked out precisely as I wanted them. Son, you didn't leave anything for me to do! Congratulations, and thank you!" He put both hands on Lucas's shoulders, and Lucas felt his chest would burst.

When Theo looked into Lucas's eyes, Lucas could see the wetness in them. "There is another thing I would like to say..." his voice broke slightly... "I am as proud of you as I am of my son." He lowered his gaze but kept his hands on Lucas's shoulder. "My God, I wish he could meet you!"

Theo wrapped his arms around Lucas, and Maria ordered them from her kitchen before it became embarrassing. Lucas went to his room and took his violin out of its case but was too excited to practice. He picked up a picture of Johann dressed in his uniform beside his beautiful wife, with a smiling boy and girl standing in front of them. Was it possible that the Wehrmacht could make this man kill other men? If a Russian were about to kill me, would I shoot him, or would I die?" He decided he would probably die because he would take too long to make up his mind.

◇◇◇◇◇◇◇◇◇◇◇◇◇◇◇◇◇◇◇◇◇◇◇◇◇◇◇◇◇◇◇◇◇◇◇

Felix arrived at the opera house excited about the solution he had worked out to compensate for his manpower shortage. He would hold the first blocking rehearsal at three and had been worried that he wouldn't have enough people to carry off any semblance of the victory parade Verdi had written in the score! But he had worked out a simple, foolproof plan, and he was nervous but confident his plan would work when everyone lined up in the order he wanted them to cross the stage.

Felix sang Verdi's theme in the worst voice anyone in the choir had ever heard, and the group marched to the other side at approximately the music tempo. As each person reached the stage wings, Felix hurried them across the stage behind the scenery to the starting point, where they caught up to the back of the group waiting to cross the stage. They followed one another in the same order and spacing as they had used on the first crossing so the audience would see an endless line of soldiers, prisoners, and slaves that could theoretically go on forever. Felix was so excited he clapped and jumped up and down like a four-year-old high on sugar waiting to blow out the candles at his birthday party.

Felix let the Egyptian army and the captured Ethiopian soldiers and slaves walk through three circuits, enough to establish that a brisk walking pace behind the scenery would avoid a break in the line and create the endless belt of soldiers and prisoners that he wanted. The marchers seemed comfortable with everything, and he allowed them to rest a few minutes before running through the scene's beginning and end.

The timing of the ending was critical. Soldiers, slaves, and prisoners had to stop in front of the Royal reviewing stand at the correct spot in the music, which meant that the pace had to be perfect. He appointed Waltraut leader of the choir; she would lead the soldiers and set the pace. After the first circuit, the lead would be irrelevant, but the speed had to be spot on. He minimized the risk by marking the laps in Waltraut's score as "enter" each time she should begin a crossing. If she were ahead or behind when she stepped on the stage, she would lengthen or shorten the pace to correct it. And just in case, he would stand in the wings and cue every lap.

Felix planned the rehearsal for two hours, but the choir's older members began to tire after an hour, and so, satisfied that he had accomplished his objectives, he cancelled the last hour.

Red-faced from the exertion of the brisk walk behind the scenery, Waltraut was embarrassed to be out of puff. Felix expressed his concern to her, but she laughed at his worry. "I'll be okay by the time we perform it. Don't worry—I'll go for a brisk walk every day until the Premiere."

Two weeks later, during the dress rehearsal, the choir wore their full costume for the first time. Although built as light as the theatre carpenter could make them, the stiff leather armour added substantially to the effort. The wooden swords in the scabbards at their waists looked heavier than they were, but the seven-foot spears confiscated from a production of Il Trovatore were heavier than they looked and, in addition, were awkward to carry. The wooden shields, built for stationary soldiers in a Händel production of Samson, were cumbersome. Felix gave the soldiers a choice of whether to lug a spear or a shield and was ecstatic when they chose both.

On Wednesday, the evening was abnormally warm, and since the heat was rare in Detmold, most people moved as little as possible. Theo abbreviated each scene except the ensemble singing, which he wanted to polish. There was no singing in the long, repetitive marching scene, so Theo stopped it at a single circuit. After a satisfactory music rehearsal, he let the cast go home early so that he would have a fresh crew for the première on Saturday, thinking that surely the weather would cool off in the next three days.

But the heatwave not only lingered, it got more humid. On Saturday, the day of the première, the theatre was hot, and the evening didn't cool off. The weather, increasingly warmer and stickier for three consecutive days, had heated the building to the point where most of the opera patrons filling every seat in the Detmold Theatre were using their programs to fan themselves. Dominated by women over fifty, the audience didn't need heat.

Most of the patrons sweating in their seats had a vested interest in the performance and would have stayed seated if the theatre had caught fire. All of Detmold had been waiting months for this night. They had donated money, labour and time to the production, and they wouldn't let a little heat stop them from enjoying the results.

◇◇◇◇◇◇◇◇◇◇◇◇◇◇◇◇◇◇◇◇◇◇◇◇◇◇◇◇◇◇◇◇

Hannah Müller's husband, the only one she had in her more than eighty years, was killed by a gas attack gone wrong in the Great War. Her marriage at 19 had ended her aspirations of becoming an opera singer, and when her husband died in a futile attempt to save Germany from itself, she used his considerable wealth to support the Detmold Theatre. Her substantial donations guaranteed her the first seat choice, and the theatre reserved the center seat in the first row, less than a metre from the conductor, for her exclusive use at every Premiere. Even at eighty-six, she followed every note in the piano score she kept open on her lap.

Hannah was Theo's greatest critic and dearest friend. Standing with the back of his head a metre in front of her face, Theo felt inspired to find perfection, as is every true artist. Despite the amateur nature of the performance, he felt optimistic it would be a welcome occasion for the whole city. After all, even the world premiere in Cairo on Christmas Eve, 1871, was not up to Verdi's professional standards, and the great composer more or less disowned it as a piece of amateur theatre and not worthy of the 'Premiere' title. He approved the second performance in Milano as the Premiere—perhaps because he had personally mentored the project and attended the performance.

Aida, challenging for any opera house, and, most aficionados would agree, impossible for an opera house the size of Detmold's to produce, would need a lot of cheap help. Theo and Fritz had counted on the people in the audience and their friends, most of whom had some connection to the opera through donations and volunteer work. They were friends with people who worked in the theatre and had friends who would help a friend. They would own the performance as surely as the theatre did.

131

Theo made his way through the orchestra pit, stepped up on the podium and turned to bow to the usual applause. He smiled at Hannah and nodded. She returned his smile, he turned to face his musicians, and Hannah opened her score.

◇◇◇◇◇◇◇◇◇◇◇◇◇◇◇◇◇◇◇◇◇◇◇◇◇◇◇◇◇◇

Theo's sixty-six years had seen Germany struggle through the Great War, the Depression, Kristallnacht, and four years of a war he and everyone else in his country knew Germany could not win. No one spoke of the war because to whisper that Germany would or even could lose was a death sentence.

Hitler had ordered all theatres to close by the beginning of September, and Theo feared that this production marked the dying gasp of Detmold's opera theatre. He felt a sense of foreboding and finality as he swept his baton downward to begin the masterpiece, and a millisecond later, a solo violin began the emotional introduction to one of the greatest musical works ever written.

Act one and three scenes of the second act flowed flawlessly under the bridge of time; the Egyptians had won their war against the Ethiopians, and everything was ready for the triumphant return of Egypt's victorious soldiers. The soloists had set the mood and developed the plot; the stagehands changed the scenery; the choir and soloists quickly and quietly took their position behind the closed curtain, warning one another not to make a sound. But a soft "toi, toi, toi" still made the rounds.

Verdi wrote the fourth scene of the second act for a rousing chorus of townspeople who had gathered to welcome their victorious heroes. The Egyptian army had defeated the Ethiopian enemy, which called for a parade. The sweaty, smelly, apprehensive and excited Detmold Opera Chorus prepared to sing. Two soldiers flanked the King's entourage, dressed in golden armour, holding shields and upright spears. The rest of the chorus, dressed as Egyptian citizens, waited on both sides of the throne.

On the stage, at the audience's right, a group of young maidens prepared to dance for the King and the returning heroes. They whispered and giggled until their teacher, standing in the wings, threatened them in a loud whisper that carried to the back row of the theatre. She said, "Es gibt Nachstraffen..." "...There will be punishment for those who don't immediately shut up!" The Tanzmädchen knew where the end of Frau Richter's rope was, and she was there. While the audience smothered a laugh, the little girls shut their mouths and quietly took their positions.

Theo lifted his baton, and the theatre became as silent as a tomb. He gave two beats to set the tempo, and the orchestra played the opening bars of the opera scene which was the nemesis of every director who had ever put it together. The curtain opened, and the audience burst into applause, a good start. The adrenalin-charged chorus began singing their rousing hero's welcome as the curtain came to a swaying halt at the sides of the stage.

The chorus sang with the passion every performer reserves for the première, with enthusiasm seldom seen in a dress rehearsal. The marchers, lined up and waiting behind the scenery, sang to the beat of a junior conductor standing before them. He wasn't junior because of his age; he was at least eighty. But he could see the conductor's podium and wave his baton in time with Theo's. When the welcome-home chorus ended, the old man conductor put his hands up in a victory sign. The curtain closed, and every choir member took off to where they had stashed their swords, shields and spears. They felt a surge of pride and anticipation as they waited to march past the Egyptian King.

Theo waited for the inevitable and traditional applause to die before cueing the trumpets to begin the dramatic soldiers' entrance. He paused until the last ripple died, then killed as much time as he dared, looking from one orchestra member to another while holding his baton by his side. The "townspeople" rushed behind the scenery to change costumes and makeup, almost instantly becoming slaves, prisoners and soldiers. Finally, when the pause was about to become too much, Theo waved his baton and said a short prayer that he would have soldiers and slaves when the curtain opened. The curtain swung open as the trumpets played the thrilling repeated notes that began the march and signalled the soldiers' entrance. The trumpets filled the small theatre with a clear, resonant sound that bounced off the domed ceiling to the eager ears below.

◇◇◇◇◇◇◇◇◇◇◇◇◇◇◇◇◇◇◇◇◇◇◇◇◇◇◇◇◇◇◇◇◇

Waltraut proudly led a double line of soldiers from the audience's stage left, marching confidently straight ahead, a proud Egyptian soldier setting the standard for those who followed her. When she reached the

133

wings, she stepped smoothly behind the ballet girls, turned the corner and picked up her speed. She arrived at stage left in time to escort the last prisoner. She breathed deeply, attempting to build up a reserve of oxygen. Despite the walking she had done to condition herself, Waltraut was terrified she would fall or drop out, spoiling the show for her friends. She stepped on the stage again, full of confidence, at the spot in the music she and Felix had marked as "Enter."

Three minutes later, the magnificent trumpet march ended, marking the third circuit's completion, and Waltraut had led her soldiers to precisely where they should be at that spot in the music. But the line didn't stop.

While the children began their dance, Waltraut led the stream of soldiers across the stage for the fourth time, then hurried behind the scenery. Waltraut and the soldiers picked up the pace to match the faster tempo.

The slap of sandals running across the stage behind the scenery became thumps, rising in volume until the sound intruded on the delicate music. The marchers' pace flagged, the noise became louder, and the orchestra's power was not enough to compete with the clump of feet hammering the wooden floor as their owners leaned ahead, doggedly crossing behind the scenery.

Waltraut tried desperately to maintain the pace and her dignity—but she and her soldiers were sadly behind the music and long past worrying about anything but making it to the other side. They marched with a sense of mission—heads down, spears and shields low at their sides. A bar late for her entrance, Waltraut lifted her shield and spear just as she stepped on the stage, but within a few metres, she looked as though she were pulling a plough.

Most of the marchers breathed hard, but Waltraut puffed like a train, her face beet red as she forced herself to keep up. She made her fourth crossing with some dignity left, but hurrying behind the scenery was painful. She leaned her weight ahead, forcing her legs to move under her shifting centre of gravity so she wouldn't fall on her face. She tried to lift her numb arms—pain shot through her left arm into her chest—she almost dropped her shield as she stumbled forward on her fifth entrance. She willed her feet to catch up and correct her balance before she fell, stepped quickly, ran ahead of the march tempo, and caught up. The group behind her lost ground, and the sudden gap made the marching mob's difficulties embarrassingly noticeable to the audience.

Following her score and familiar with the opera, Hannah saw exhaustion in the faces of the seniors in the choir, most of them close friends. There were still several pages of marching music, and the endless ballet had to run its course. Hannah flipped ahead to see how many pages there were until the end, although she was agonizingly aware of what lay before the gasping marchers. As Waltraut stumbled at the beginning of her fifth circuit, Hannah watched her closely, and her friend's obvious distress almost brought the old lady out of her seat. She contemplated opening her mouth to shout that they should stop and considered hitting Theo with her score, but, against her instincts, she kept her score and her mouth where they were.

The fifth lap was hard work for all the marchers, but for the older ones, it was agony. They plodded their way across the stage behind the scenery, moaning as they arrived late, and entered in a straggled mess. A few slaves passed soldiers who fell back. There was no attempt to carry shields or spears high; the objective for most was only to make it to the other side. The audience grew restless; giggles and chuckles resonated above the orchestra. The dancing girls flitted lightly back and forth across the stage, in stark contrast to the calamity behind them. They cheerfully twirled and pirouetted their carefully rehearsed promises of rewards for the returning heroes, full of youthful energy, oblivious to everything else.

On the following circuit, what was to be the last lap, the second row of soldiers passed Waltraut. She couldn't get enough oxygen through her lungs to power her large frame, her tight chest and pain in both arms preventing her from lifting the spear. She entered stage left with the heavy metal point dragging on the floor—her shield hung loosely at her side. A soldier behind her, Waltraut's eighty-year-old neighbour, dropped his spear with a loud bang, tried to pick it up, abandoned the effort and passed Waltraut without it. He had already given up the shield behind the scenery.

The dancing girls began one by one to become aware that something was wrong, and the snickering became louder. The girls started to sneak glances at the audience, assuming that the dancers were the object of what was becoming almost continuous laughter.

The younger prisoners pushed the soldiers, trying to help them across the stage—the slaves and prisoners had nothing to carry and wore only light rags. As they entered for the sixth and final time, soldiers and prisoners bunched together, the prisoners assisting their captors. Two prisoners crossed the stage with a soldier slung between them, his arms over the prisoners' shoulders, his feet all but dragging. The audience laughed louder, out of control now, abandoning any pretence of trying to control themselves.

When Waltraut staggered on the stage, the audience was in a full-throated roar, heads back, slapping their knees. Prisoners carried soldier's weapons; the youngest slave marchers passed the entire group, attempting to fill in gaps.

Waltraut lurched ahead, summoning all her courage to face the agony. She reeled among the passing prisoners, her vision blurred, unsure of where she was. Her breathing became shallow; her legs turned to rubber; she staggered valiantly, stumbled, forced her legs to take another step, and then fell, directly in front of Theo and Hannah. She was no longer aware of anything but pain and her struggle to breathe. Her neighbour and friend, who had consented to dress as a soldier and march beside her, attempted to help her, but Waltraut's weak attempt to stand wasn't enough; she fell on her side, and her friend fell beside her. The laughing abruptly stopped, replaced by a collective groan, then silence.

As the scene disintegrated, Theo desperately tried to remain in control, but when Waltraut fell, he forgot about Verdi and thought only of her. He dropped his baton on the music stand, left the podium and ran for the exit to the stage. The orchestra went raggedly on for a couple of bars, then stopped playing. Buried under the stage, the musicians had no idea of the catastrophe above them. The first violin attempted to keep the music going, but the look on Theo's face as he rushed by him set off alarm bells, and he gave it up after a few bars. Lucas and Maria laid their violins down, jumped to their feet and followed Theo up the stairs, not knowing why. Corinne climbed over the woodwinds and caught them at the stairs.

Hannah was close enough to Waltraut that she could clearly see her face, and her friend was in pain. Hannah knew she was mortally ill. A soldier rolled her over on her back and placed his shield under her head. With a sense of dread, Hannah stood up, watching the irregular rise and fall of Waltraut's chest. She crossed herself and began reciting..."Mother Mary, full of grace..." The man sitting next to her, whom everyone knew to be a Gestapo spy—they all looked and dressed the same—stood up and asked what was happening, but Hannah ignored him and kept up her fervent praying. She thought she saw the hard lines of his face soften but decided that could not be possible.

◇◇◇◇◇◇◇◇◇◇◇◇◇◇◇◇◇◇◇◇◇◇◇◇◇◇◇◇◇◇◇◇

When Theo reached Waltraut's side, he knelt beside her. The dancing children, their music gone, stood on the side of the stage whispering, fascinated by the drama unfolding before them.

"Waltraut, please speak to me!" Theo pleaded with the dying soldier, his voice carrying everywhere in the otherwise silent theatre. Tears flooding her eyes, Corinne dropped to her knees and stroked Waltraut's hair.

Waltraut's eyelids fluttered, and her face relaxed. She tried to lift her hand to touch Theo's face, but her arm fell short. She smiled at him and Corinne; her hand dropped, and her chest became still. Theo cried out...the sound echoed from the stage throughout the theatre.

"No, Waltraut, don't leave. Please, don't go! Not now!"

Lucas and Maria knelt beside him, and Theo leaned against Maria, tears streaming down his face. Oblivious to hundreds of people watching her, Corinne kissed Waltraut's cheek and stroked her hair. Lucas knelt beside Corinne, not knowing what to do, so he did nothing and waited.

Hannah's eyes instantly filled with tears— she knew her friend had died—the rouge on her face became the only colour there. The Gestapo man put his hand on her arm; she wanted to lean on his shoulder but couldn't bring herself to do it. Behind her, the sounds of sobs carried throughout the theatre. Waltraut's friends had come to see her dressed as a soldier, to laugh and tease her about it after the performance.

Maria helped Theo to his feet and stood beside him as he gazed through tears at his friends in the theatre. They stared silently back at him, patiently waiting for him to speak. No one moved before Theo raised his head, looked at the top balcony and spoke.

"I am sorry, but we must cancel the performance." His voice cracked, but he went on. "Thank you all for coming, but we can't continue."

The stage manager slowly closed the curtain as Theo knelt beside Corinne and held Waltraut's limp hand. The last thing the audience saw was Theo's sobbing frame.

Gradually, people stood and slowly worked their way out of the theatre while speaking in soft whispers, tears in the eyes of most. Hannah's entire row left before she finally turned to the Gestapo man. She knew that her enemy had waited to help her, and when she began to struggle to her feet, he stood up, took her arm, and guided her to the exit. Outside the theatre, he twined his arm around Hannah's and, without a word, escorted her home.

Chapter Fifteen

10 June 1944

Wenn elephanten Kämpfen, leidet das gras.

(When elephants fight, the grass suffers)

African saying.

Maria, Theo, and Lucas walked home in silence, and when they entered the kitchen, out of bystander's earshot, Maria said, "I didn't want to ask this where someone could hear us, and I feel terrible about Waltraut, but you must decide what to do about Aida. The day after tomorrow is the second performance, and you must decide whether you will do it."

Theo searched Maria's eyes for her opinion, but if she had one, she successfully hid it. He touched Maria's cheek.

"Waltraut didn't quit until she died, and neither will we."

Theo's tone told his wife and Lucas that he had not thought about it until that moment.

"So, you're not going to cancel even one performance?"

"No, but I am open to your suggestions. I think we should do all four performances. Too many people have invested too much in this for me to cancel."

Maria put her finger on her lip, and Theo knew she had something on her mind.

"Why don't we dedicate the next performance to Waltraut? The choir could sing her favourite choruses before the performance, and her friends could say a few words. Perhaps we could think of something special to do for her."

The knocker hitting the brass plate on the door interrupted them, and Theo went to answer it. A Wehrmacht soldier stood on the landing.

"Can I help you?" Theo greeted the soldier, and his hand began to shake.

"Perhaps," the soldier answered, and a letter in his hand indicated nothing good. "Is this your home?" The soldier was over fifty and therefore assigned to non-battle duty. Theo looked at the letter, then into the soldier's sympathetic eyes.

"Yes, my name is Theo Finke, and this is my home. This boy lives with us." He nodded toward Lucas, who stood beside him, curious why Theo seemed so upset. "What do you want with me? I am too old to fight in Hitler's war!"

The soldier's face softened as he looked at Lucas and asked, "I am sorry, young man, but what is your name, please?"

"Lucas Schwartz, sir." Lucas felt the sympathy oozing from the old soldier and knew something unpleasant was about to happen.

The soldier held out the letter. "I'm afraid this is yours. Please do what it says."

Lucas took the letter when the soldier pushed it in his direction. His heart sank as far down in his chest as it could go as the man, standing at attention, solemnly recited his orders. "The Führer orders you, Lucas Schwartz, to report for training and assignment, and you must arrive in the Wehrmacht training facility in Würzburg no later than a week from Monday." He looked into Lucas's eyes, and the look reminded Lucas of his father. "The details are in the letter." Lucas opened the envelope, reluctantly letting his eyes go to the letter, and recognized the Bundeswehr Adler logo.

Theo took the envelope from Lucas, examined the seal and crest and said, "There's been a terrible mistake...Lucas is not yet sixteen!"

The soldier shook his head. "There is no mistake. The Führer has ordered that, as of today, Lucas Schwartz is a member of the Wehrmacht, and if he refuses to report, the Gestapo or the SS will come for him. We both know how they will handle it, and you don't want that. I'm fifty-five, and a year ago, they took me away from my family. Now, my wife and daughter are running our farm without a man's help."

The soldier saluted, turned, and walked to the Kubelwagen that he had left parked at the curb opposite the house. Theo stepped outside, and Lucas stopped on the landing beside him. They watched the soldier open the Kubelwagen's tin door and climb into the seat. He looked back at them, started the noisy little engine and drove away.

Theo said, "He at least had the good grace not to use the 'Heil Hitler!' salute."

◇◇

Lucas opened the letter, read the words demanding his service, and wondered what he could do in the Wehrmacht.

"I'll have to go, won't I?"

Theo nodded, tears welling in his eyes and a lump in his throat cutting off his air.

"I can play in the orchestra until next Saturday's performance, and then I must go to Würzburg." He looked at the floor, barely catching a sob before it became more. "This hasn't been a good day, has it?"

Theo put his arms around him.

When Lucas and Theo turned around, Maria stood in the doorway. She hugged Lucas, trying unsuccessfully to control herself. She took Lucas's hand and led him to the kitchen, talking as she went. "This is all a mistake...the Führer doesn't use children to fight his battles. Theo will go to the Bürgeramt tomorrow morning and find out what's going on." She checked with him; Theo nodded and said, "Yes, this must be a mistake. Lucas would be useless to any army, let alone one as professional as the Wehrmacht! What could a boy like Lucas possibly do? He's not exactly the warrior type!"

Lucas closed the kitchen door a bit harder than necessary, his ego wounded.

He hadn't reached the living room when the doorknocker rapped. Maria left to see who was there and returned with Corinne.

"She shouldn't stay alone in Waltraut's apartment." She said it as though that were a given. "Lucas, you will sleep on the sofa until you go to Würzburg."

Corinne screamed, "Is that why the Wehrmacht was here? I saw a soldier drive away—Mein lieber Gott, what's going on?" She looked more frightened than Lucas had ever seen her, even during the bombing in Dortmund. He tried to speak like an adult but soon realized he sounded like an idiot.

"I'm the führer's property now; I must report to the Wehrmacht in Würzburg a week from Monday." Lucas didn't feel as upset as he thought he should be. Why would Theo and Maria believe he couldn't fight if he had to?" He imagined himself carrying a rifle, dressed in a girl-catching uniform. He would be a man, and he would do a man's job.

Corinne looked from Lucas to Theo and then back to Lucas. "But, you are still a child! They can't ask a child to fight against men!" She turned back to Theo. "Theo, you must know someone who can fix this horrible mistake!"

Theo slowly shook his head. "I will take Lucas to the Bürgeramt in the morning, but I'm afraid not Corinne. I had much more power when they took Johann, but I couldn't do anything. Hitler calls, and you must answer or accept the consequences."

Lucas blurted out, angry now. "I am not a child! I can learn how to fight as well as any other soldier!" When he realized that he had his fists clenched, he relaxed his hands.

The pity on Corinne's face puzzled Lucas. She took his hand and kissed it.

"Lucas, you are not a soldier, and you never will be, no matter what age you are or how tall you grow. You cannot kill a man, and it would be criminal to put you in a situation where you had to kill or die!"

Lucas felt his face redden. "Johann was a musician, and now he's a soldier! Why do you think I can't do it if he could?" Lucas looked at Theo for support.

Theo put his hand on Lucas's shoulder. "Johann was almost thirty when the Wehrmacht conscripted him, and he is mature and resourceful. You are more sensitive, and you are young for your age. You will always be the wrong person to train as a soldier, and I'm afraid I share Corinne's fear."

Lucas felt the air going out of his balloon—he suddenly wasn't sure about the Wehrmacht or killing people, or worse, people trying to kill him! He tried to maintain the bravado, but if Theo and Corinne thought he would get killed... He was suddenly frightened.

"I don't have a choice, but I know I can do whatever I must. There are lots of jobs in the army that don't mean I have to kill someone! Maybe I will drive a big Lastwagen, or even a Panzer!"

Corinne looked at him with tears streaming down her face. "I don't want them to make a soldier out of you—that would be like telling Rembrandt to paint a house or forcing a brain surgeon to butcher a pig."

"I can do it just like Rembrandt could have painted a house, and who better than a surgeon to cut meat?"

"Yes, my sweet Lucas, but it would be a terrible waste! And it wouldn't kill Rembrandt or the surgeon. Even if you are the best soldier in the Wehrmacht, a bullet could kill you, and that is not something I could bear." Tears filled Corinne's eyes.

Lucas felt his throat tighten, and he didn't know what to say. He looked at Maria, then Theo, and they were no help.

"I'll be careful, Corinne. Anyway, the war will probably end before I finish my training."

When bedtime came, Lucas was glad of the opportunity to do something for Corinne. He moved his necessities to the coffee table, and Maria made a neat bed for him on the sofa.

Maria explained the intricacies of using chivalry to win a fair lady's heart to Lucas, and he gave his only pair of pyjamas to Corinne. He neatly folded them before he laid them on the bed.

"You may need these." Lucas was pleased when Corinne blushed.

No one wanted to sit on that sofa, let alone sleep on it, and when everyone had gone to their rooms, he tore the bed apart and moved the cushions to the floor.

◇◇◇◇◇◇◇◇◇◇◇◇◇◇◇◇◇◇◇◇◇◇◇◇◇◇◇◇◇◇◇◇◇◇

Lucas spent every afternoon of his last week in Detmold with his new family, playing chess with Thomas and going for long walks with Corinne to feed the ducks and swans in the Am Wall canal. Every day, he learned more about Corinne, and what he learned made him want to know more. On their second walk, she took his hand and held it every day after that until he kissed her goodbye at the railway station.

He said confidently, trying for a manly voice, "I will come back, Corinne," and she smiled despite her tears.

"You'd better!" She buried her face in his shirt and squeezed him so hard he had to grit his teeth so he wouldn't cry out.

Maria and Theo let their adopted son and daughter have their privacy, pretending to read the train schedule while the children kissed and cried.

When they moved apart, Theo embraced Lucas. "If you meet up with Johann, tell him to write." He shook Lucas's hand as he would a man who was his equal. "I will give you the same advice my father gave me. Never volunteer, and never show off what you can do! I fought in the last war, and I swear that was how I survived!"

"I promise I won't volunteer for anything." Lucas turned to Maria, who hugged him and whispered, "Please bring Johann home with you, Lucas," in his ear.

"Theo advised me never to volunteer, but for you, I will try." Lucas tried to laugh, but a half-sob came out.

Chapter Sixteen

June-July 1944

The Panzer Corps

In all chaos, there is a cosmos
In all disorder, a secret order

Carl G. Jung

Lucas arrived in Würzburg on 26 June 1944, scared, alone, and excited. His first thought as he stepped onto the platform was of Corinne. Since Hitler had called Lucas to fight for him, her Viking personality had peeled away, and the girl he found under it bewitched him. Her strength somehow made it bearable when two soldiers escorted him out of the Bahnhof and steered him into the back of a Lastwagen with eight other recruits.

The rigours of training Lucas's body began as torture and went downhill from there. Each passing day became more demanding and painful, reaching a level he had not imagined possible. Until now, the most laborious physical work he had ever done was bang on a piano or cut the meat on his plate.

Most of the recruits in his unit were graduates from the Hitler Jugend, a year and sometimes two years older than he was, and already trained to a high physical standard. Lucas had been exempted from the Jugend as a member of a Musik Gymnasium and found it impossible to keep up with them. They could shoot, swim, run, and fight with most adult soldiers—for them, the training was a 'tune-up' of skills they already possessed. For Lucas, it was the army's version of hell.

The Feldwebel who trained his squad, Sergeant Janzen, was not kind to Lucas. He relentlessly pushed him, but didn't ask more than his young charge could do. Lucas learned to respect his authority and did everything he could to please him. The Sergeant knew Lucas's limits, and every day pushed him a little farther than Lucas thought he could go.

Last to finish everything, an easy victim in self-defence class, always last across the finish line, he accepted that the first enemy soldier he saw would kill him. He decided he had to find a job that didn't involve fighting with a rifle, bayonet or knife as soon as possible.

However, worse than that for him was mindless, pointless discipline hammered into his numbing brain through repetitive, senseless physical tasks. His intellect revolted, but to no avail—the military left no room for individualism or interpretation. The system forced Lucas to conform, follow the lowest common denominator, and surrender his artistic creativity.

When he began basic training, the Sergeant pushed him; he resisted, and the Sergeant pushed harder. He fell on his face and vomited; Sergeant Janzen picked him up and forced him to go on.

◇◇◇◇◇◇◇◇◇◇◇◇◇◇◇◇◇◇◇◇◇◇◇◇◇◇◇◇◇◇◇◇◇◇

Eventually, the pain stopped, replaced by a feeling of power Lucas hadn't expected. Janzen urged him on, and Lucas began to enjoy driving his strong, healthy body to do more. He pushed the now useless sensitivity away, began to swear like the other soldiers, and deliberately used words in a way he had despised. Although Lucas still found dirty jokes abhorrent, he learned to laugh in the right places. Finally, when he mimicked the other boy's terrible grammar and learned to swagger like a bully, the men in the squad took him into the fold.

On a hot night two weeks into training, Lucas sat alone on a bench in front of the mess hall, thinking about Hartwig and Katrina. He had decided to write them and was about to get up when Sergeant Janzen sat beside him, pulled out a pipe, stuffed it with tobacco and lit it.

"Lucas, I see in your file that you are a musician."

Lucas said, "Yes, sir. I play the violin and piano; I was playing in an opera orchestra when Hitler sent me a letter asking for help." He smiled and looked at his feet.

"Ah, yes, the letter." The sergeant sucked on his pipe, blew a cloud of smoke away from Lucas and paused. Lucas waited. He had no idea where Feldwebel Janzen was going, so he sat quietly while the sergeant seemed deep in thought.

"I trained one other violinist; I remember him well because he was an outstanding rifleman and a natural leader of men. He came from Bielefeld. Detmold is twenty kilometres away, but music circles are small; perhaps you know him." He stood up, took his pipe out of his mouth and faced Lucas. "His name is Johann Finke. He should be a leutnant by now."

Lucas got to his feet; he was so excited he wanted to dance! "I live with his parents! I sleep in his room!"

Janzen smiled. "Small world. I haven't heard from Johann. He was in the Sixth Army at Stalingrad, and I doubt he would surrender to the Russians if he had a choice. Do you know what happened to him?"

Lucas, thrilled that this man knew and cared about Johann, felt his world suddenly shift. He wanted to hug the sergeant but restrained himself.

"Sir, he escaped from Stalingrad and is now fighting with the Fourth Panzer Army."

Sergeant Janzen brightened and put his hand on Lucas's shoulder. "I got him into the Sixth and was afraid that I had sent him to a Russian Gulag, or worse. They don't tell me when my students die, and I don't want to know. It's better to think that my work gives some of them the tools to survive."

Sergeant Janzen's hand shook as he took a long pull on the pipe and puffed smoke out of the corner of his mouth. "We start shooting tomorrow. Johann was the best shot I've ever seen, and he knew the Mauser rifle better than I do. When you shoot, we'll soon see if the violin has anything to do with it." He took the pipe out of his mouth, lifted his foot and tapped the bowl on the sole of his boot. The sergeant grinned from ear to ear as he put his hand on Lucas's shoulder, leaving him determined to learn everything he could about shooting. A rifle would eliminate the difference between men and boys. Lucas went to bed, resolved to be the best rifleman in the platoon.

◇◇◇◇◇◇◇◇◇◇◇◇◇◇◇◇◇◇◇◇◇◇◇◇◇◇◇◇◇◇◇◇

The following day, Lucas discovered that he liked to shoot and, to his delight, was good at it. Sergeant Janzen, a sniper in the Great War, took

Lucas under his wing, teaching him the art of caressing the trigger and firing without instinctively blinking. He became one of the best shots in the regiment and the best student of tactics, guaranteeing himself a job where intelligence was more important than brawn.

Lucas became a man physically, surprising himself when he came third in a platoon self-defence competition. He was 'sneaky fast' and earned the nickname Wiesel, a vicious little animal that was afraid of nothing. Pride in his newfound abilities gave Lucas an unexpected degree of confidence.

He stopped his fight against authority and learned the value of the chain of command and discipline. He learned there was no time to discuss tactics on the battlefield, and obedience without question was the only way an army could function. But he also discovered that leadership was a quality most men didn't have, and finally, he admitted to himself that he wasn't born to lead. The men he ate and slept with treated him as their equal, not as their leader.

Sergeant Janzen recommended that Lucas apply for the Panzer Corps. Janzen told him that if he joined the infantry, he would fight Russians as soon as the army could get him to the front. Janzen suggested that the training required to join the armoured corps would buy him time to develop his survival skills, and the 50-year-old sergeant hinted at an added benefit—the war might end before Lucas's training did.

Lucas wisely didn't ask the sergeant which side he thought would win.

In their search for tank crews, the army considered a soldier's intelligence an essential criterion, and Lucas displayed an abundance of that. He thought of Sergeant Janzen when the Wehrmacht immediately accepted his application and fast-tracked his transfer into the elite Panzer Corps. He suspected that Janzen had influenced the decision.

Following a month in a Panzer crew training facility near Berlin, the Panzer Corps cancelled Lucas's promised two weeks leave and sent him to join the Fourth Panzer Army, now fighting its way across Poland. He arrived at their camp near Warsaw early in August, and his compressed Panther training began the following day.

Kindersoldat

The Fourth Panzer Army, comprised of infantry and armour, consisted mainly of Waffen SS tank elements. Waffen SS regiments were the cream of the German army; their unique black uniforms with Totenkopf death-skull insignia aroused fear and hate in their enemies and respect in their friends. Waffen SS soldiers' skill, tenacity and ruthlessness were the pride of the German army and the bane of their enemies.

Lucas immediately heard gossip about the murder and rape of civilians by the advancing Red Army. Bored veteran soldiers repeated and embellished stories of unspeakable horrors, of neighbours turning against neighbours, giving them to the advancing Russians for a pack of cigarettes or a turnip. They told in gory detail of Russians pulling Waffen SS crews out of crippled Panzers and tearing them to pieces. The stories became more gruesome with each telling, and Lucas drew a picture of the Russians as animals that would eat him alive, making the decision of whether to shoot them a lot easier.

The war-weary soldiers saw Lucas as a child and amused themselves by scaring him with ridiculous exaggerations. They took turns gleefully describing in graphic terms what Russians did to women, children and Waffen SS soldiers, embellishing the already horrible scenarios to see the terrified look on the face of the child that the stupid Wehrmacht had sent them to babysit.

⬦⬦⬦⬦⬦⬦⬦⬦⬦⬦⬦⬦⬦⬦⬦⬦⬦⬦⬦⬦⬦⬦⬦⬦⬦⬦⬦⬦⬦⬦

The first day of Lucas's panther training began with a film on the tank's merits, the crew's duties, and the invincibility of a Panther. Lucas watched without reacting, as did the other prospective crewmembers. None dared to say it aloud, but even to their naïve and untrained minds, the film was ridiculous propaganda. The panzers violated irrefutable laws of physics, and SS soldiers performed impossible feats of daring. The film insulted the intelligence of the most ignorant recruit in the room.

When the film finally ended, the recruits exchanged looks as a Waffen SS officer in an immaculate black uniform stood before the screen to face them. He waited a few seconds before he spoke, and during the silence, Lucas tried to imagine what the officer would say. He expected a sales pitch on the Panther tank—an expansion of the film's propaganda. The officer scowled, showing his annoyance to the soldiers who dismantled the screen and projector. He waited until they had shut the door before he spoke.

"Now that the bullshit is out of the way, I'm going to tell you what it's like to fight in a Waffen SS Panther tank crew."

He paused, and Lucas smiled, sensing that the other trainees were equally relieved.

"And when I finish, you will wish you had chosen the navy."

The officer began to pace in front of the recruits, his hands folded behind his back. "Contrary to the propaganda you have just seen, a panther tank is not invincible; it is a death trap! The Russians know how to kill it, along with its crew."

He stopped, unfolded his hands, and leaned against the lectern. "And contrary to popular belief among the self-proclaimed experts in Berlin, the Russian T-34 is its equal and, under some circumstances, is superior to the Panther. The Panther has a longer, more accurate gun with a superior sight, but the T-34 is more maneuverable, and its gun swings twice as fast as a Panther's. The T-34 has a better engine and stronger final drives, and this detail is more important than you think!

The Russian tank is lower and therefore harder to hit. It is faster than the Panther, so don't try to run. It fires the same shell and has the same armament, but it can fire faster." He looked from one astonished face to another, then dropped the bomb. "I have driven a captured T-34, and I would swap two Panthers for one of them!"

The instructor waited for a moment, then stepped behind the podium. The shocked room had become as silent as space. He spoke slower, emphasizing every syllable. "Do not despair, for we do have one major advantage, and it is our well-trained crews. On the other hand, most of you will fail to meet those standards, and those unfortunate souls will get a new rifle and a free train ticket to where they will meet the Russians." He leaned ahead and grinned facetiously. "Does anyone have any questions so far?"

There were none.

The officer extinguished the smile and stepped away from the podium with his black leather gloves in his right hand. He slapped his left hand with them.

"The first thing you must accept is that your life is worthless; It doesn't matter if you die." He raised his voice. "It does matter if your comrades die, and it matters a great deal if you lose a Wehrmacht Panzer!" The Hauptscharführer locked his hands behind his back and waited.

Lucas and every other man in the room vowed to themselves they would do whatever it took to get into a Panther tank.

The instructor continued, his tone changing to that of a father speaking to his son.

"All of your lives depend on the tank surviving, and that won't happen unless each of you does your job perfectly. Perfection, my children, is the standard you must meet here!" He paused for effect. "A good job will get you a nice new rifle and a free ticket to the Russian front; a bad job will get you killed before your training is over!" He slapped the gloves against his hand again.

Lucas listened intently. Every German knew that Waffen SS criteria were the highest in the Bundeswehr, but now these boys who must become men would face it in real life-and-death terms. Every young man in the room felt a surge of pride in joining these professionals, mixed with apprehension that he might not measure up.

Lucas had learned the value and elusiveness of perfection by learning and performing complex music. He knew the importance of repetition and focus, which are the foundations of real skill. He was excited to join a group of men who set perfection as their goal.

The officer locked his hands behind his back again and silently paced, building tension before he stopped to examine the young recruits individually. "I want to clarify something before we begin with the dirty part of your training. You are not, and you probably never will be Waffen SS! You will not wear the Totenkopf, and your uniform will be the field grey you are wearing now." He paused and lowered his head to look at the young men eagerly staring up at him. Lucas thought he saw a glimmer of sadness in his eyes.

The SS officer put his hands in front of him, grasping his gloves with both of them while lowering his head to look at the floor. When he raised it, he spoke quietly.

"Until you earn the honour to sing the Panzer anthem, you will stand in silent respect when your comrades sing it. If you die, know your comrades will sing it for you." Lucas watched the instructor closely, detecting a sense of defeat and resignation.

The Hauptscharführer said, "Go now and do your job as well as you can. if you do that, you might return to your parents." He saluted with a loud "Heil Hitler," abruptly turned, and left the room.

A Wehrmacht corporal walked onto the stage and pointed out that he had posted their assignments on a board at the back of the room. They stood, exchanged a "Heil Hitler" with the corporal, then hurried to the board.

For the next three days, the recruits would work with the panzer maintenance crews, divided into groups of ten, each assigned to a different station for the initial phase of their training. They watched mechanics replace track segments and final drive gears, change and 'sight-in' a gun barrel, and replace a transmission. On the fourth day, they returned to the classroom.

◇◇◇◇◇◇◇◇◇◇◇◇◇◇◇◇◇◇◇◇◇◇◇◇◇◇◇◇◇◇◇◇◇◇◇◇◇◇

The speaker was a regular army Feldwebel with one arm missing below the elbow and the look of a tired old man. But when Lucas looked closely, he guessed the man was not yet thirty. The sergeant began using a tone that told Lucas he had memorized the speech.

"The Panther has a weak point that the Wehrmacht has not acknowledged and fixed, despite the loss of dozens of tanks, hundreds of men, and my right arm! During a battle, the worst thing that can happen—if we ignore artillery, aircraft and Russian T-34s—is losing power to one of the tracks. If a panzer stops, it becomes a stationary target for those Russian tanks, guns and aircraft, and we can no longer ignore them. They will destroy your Panther and kill you if you try to escape—but you might be lucky like me and lose only your arm." He held up the stub and waved it around.

He waited for his message to sink in, then went on. "If you leave the tank, the Russian infantry will probably kill or capture you. If the Russians capture you, do not expect the Geneva Convention to protect you because, contrary to what you have heard, it has ceased to exist as far as our little war is concerned. The Russians immediately shoot the lucky Waffen SS prisoners, but if they have the time and inclination, they will make you pray for the end!" He looked around at the smooth young faces. "Are there any questions so far?"

The sergeant raised his voice and continued. "You're probably wondering, so I will tell you the easiest way to ruin a Panther's day. It's remarkably simple…just break a final drive, the last set of gears that turn the sprockets that drive the tracks.

The quickest way to do that is to open the throttle, put it in first gear, pull one of the steering-clutch levers and apply the brake to instigate a pivot turn, especially if the tracks are on soft ground or the gears are old. If you do that with the tracks sunk ten centimetres into soft ground, you will hear a loud snap from one of the corners, and if a Russian gun or tank can see you, you and your friends will likely die in the next few minutes. If you are on friendly terms with God, no Russians will see you, and a recovery tank will tow your panzer back to maintenance. But if you were the driver, you would never again see the inside of a panzer!" The room was silent.

The instructor went on. "The second easiest way to break the gear is to overstress it by driving the tank too fast, in too much mud, or both.

If no Russians are shooting at you, and your panzer is on hard ground, you can use any gear up to and including fourth, but do not use any gear above fourth unless a T-34 is chasing you! If you are in even a little mud, do not use more than half the throttle when turning!" He stepped away from the lectern and then returned.

"The third easiest way to destroy the final drives is to allow them to run without oil. The seals on the output shafts are shit and don't last very long, especially in mud, and you must replace them as soon as you see oil on the shaft. You must check the gear oil in the final drives daily, along with the engine and transmission oil. And you must inspect the gear shafts for oil leaks every time you walk past them!"

The sergeant stepped from behind the podium and faced the boys as he spoke slowly and emphatically.

"The final and surest way of breaking the final drive is neglecting to change them. They will last one hundred and fifty kilometres if you are very careful and stay off the fields, but if you must drive off the roads, they will not last more than a hundred kilometres. If you want to live longer than a few weeks, you will learn to change both sides in three hours, and you will do it every seventy-five kilometres. You will keep a new set of gears as spares, packed in their original wooden box covered in the original grease and wrapped in waxed paper. When you replace the gears, you must get new ones to replace the spares. In that case, keep the old gears until the Wehrmacht gives you the new ones."

The sergeant spoke louder. "If you change or modify what I am telling you, you will probably die. I am alive because of a generous amount of luck and an understanding of what I'm doing."

He pounded the lecturn. "But you don't know shit from butter! It is my expert opinion that you will all screw up and be dead in less than three weeks anyway, but if you take care of your tank, there is a small chance you will prove me wrong."

Chapter Seventeen

August 1944

Two-two-seven

A great war shall break forth from fishes of steel...

Nostradamus

The training curriculum in Berlin had devoted three weeks to teaching the duties of every position in the tank. Lucas had driven around the fields in outdated Panzer IIIs, fired the gun at burned-out trucks and tanks and fought mock battles. The shortage of time and fuel abbreviated the in-tank training they received, leaving the young men with disproportionate confidence in their abilities. Lucas, aware of professional standards in a way that his comrades weren't, was painfully mindful that it would be madness to put them in tanks as crews to fight against professionals. Aside from losing men, it would mean unacceptable losses of desperately needed war machinery. The thought of him and his friends fighting blood-thirsty Russians terrified him. The initiation to the Panther helped Lucas's confidence but left what he knew was a gaping hole between where he was and where he had to be.

When Lucas left Panther training, he joined Panther two-two-seven under Obersturmführer Klaus Riker with a sense of relief. A short, skinny, dark-skinned Italian from a small town in the Dolomites, Riker had black hair and was so thin he joked that he could hide from the Russians by turning sideways. At thirty-two, Riker was old for a tank commander, but he and his crew had survived the encirclement of Stalingrad and killed twenty-one Russian tanks. They had been in a Panzer IV assigned to the Sixth Army during Barbarossa, when the German army crossed the Russian border. The

6th Army was no more, and Panther 227 was now part of the XXIV Panzer Corps, attached to the 4th Panzer Army.

Obersturmführer Riker held out a small, friendly hand before Lucas could salute. "I assume you're Lucas Schwartz… welcome to 227." When he saw Lucas's bewilderment, he smiled. "There will be no saluting. You could get me killed by a Russian sniper; they are very good at picking off German officers." His smile remained fixed as he said, "There's a fifty-fifty chance they'll shoot you."

"I understand, Herr Obersturmführer." Lucas stood stiffly at attention.

"You might as well salute as stand like a scarecrow. I would be pleased if you would relax."

"Yes, sir, I understand, sir." Lucas tried to relax, but the effort made him awkward. Riker's fixed smile didn't help, and Lucas was so tense he began to shake. Riker took his arm and turned him toward his new comrades, who seemed to enjoy the terror Lucas tried to hide.

"This is Max. He shoots the cannon that you'll learn to load."

Max was a big man with a dark beard. He smiled as he enthusiastically shook Lucas's hand. "Welcome to two-two-seven, and don't take that Italian bastard too seriously. I'm your boss, not him." He roughed up Lucas's hair with his big hand.

Riker pulled Lucas to a dark-skinned man with a neatly trimmed black beard, who smiled and revealed an ugly set of nicotine-stained teeth. "This ingrate is our wireless operator, Simon—don't trust him with your money or your secrets—he's from Bayern."

The wireless operator shook Lucas's hand once, showed his hideous teeth, then took back his hand and let the deceptive smile fade.

A tall, blond, handsome man with a square chin shook Lucas's hand warmly as the commander said, "As you can see, Kristian is the only Aryan here that Hitler would approve of. We keep him around in case Hitler visits, and because he's the only one who knows how to drive the tank."

Kristian took the cigarette out of his mouth to say, "If you call me Siegfried, I will kill you." But the warm smile gave him away, and Lucas decided he liked him.

The commander's fixed grin suddenly disappeared. "My name is Klaus; I will not answer to Obersturmführer or Riker. We'll take the tank on a short exercise tomorrow, and you will be the loader. Today, Max will teach you how to load the gun."

Lucas opened his mouth to say that he had already learned to load in Panzer Schule but decided to close it. Klaus stared at Lucas, and when his new charge said nothing, the smile returned.

"It is not my job to keep you alive, but I will do that because if I don't, I will have to write a letter to your parents. I hate to write letters, so I expect you to do your part by following my instructions without hesitation."

"I promise you will not have to write a letter to my parents, sir!" Lucas spoke perfect formal Prussian German while standing as stiff as a post. Klaus laughed at him and walked away.

An hour later, Lucas loaded the gun and then lifted his hand to tap Max's leg. Lucas's training had taught him to touch the gunner when he had the breech locked and ready, eliminating the possibility of the gun firing before the breech was solidly closed and locked and the loader was clear when the gun bucked and ejected the empty cartridge.

He yelped when the gun immediately fired, then reached for a fresh shell, drove it firmly into the breech, locked it solidly in its place, and then lifted his hand to tap Max's leg. The gun fired as soon as the breech slammed, the spent shell ejected, and Lucas reached for another round.

The engine revved, the turret swung to the right, and then suddenly reversed. Lucas lost his balance and missed the butt of the shell he intended to use. It slid sideways, jammed his fingers, and he yelled an expletive he had learned in Würzburg.

Max removed his intercom mouthpiece and shouted over the engine, "We're dead. I have a second T-34 on our flank, and I can't shoot. You've killed us!"

The loader's job in a Panther is difficult. The heavy shells are stored vertically in racks, and the loader must pull them up using the cap's edges. During training, Lucas had gotten accustomed to leaning against the cumbersome pipe rail used to protect the loader when the gun fired, but 227 had no such protection—only bare flanges where the factory had bolted it in place. The guard made loading more difficult and therefore slower, but crouched in the cramped space, without the guard to lean against or hold onto, the loader had nothing to grab or lean against.

Lucas opened his mouth to defend himself but decided against it. He suspected Max had intentionally removed the guard so the loader could work faster, so he remained silent while the gunner explained.

"The turret on this Panther will turn a complete revolution in fifteen seconds; therefore, 90 degrees takes less than four seconds. I need a shell in the barrel ready to fire in less than those four seconds, better yet, less than three, or you will fight the Russians with a rifle. Before you can do what I am trying to teach you, you must learn what they don't teach you in the training films.

The breech guard bar you are used to is not in this tank because it slows the loader down when he has to reach over it to slide a shell into the barrel. Safety has a different meaning when we die because you can't load faster than the enemy tank that's trying to kill us. The safest technique is the one that kills the Russian tank before it kills us, which means we must load and fire faster than he does! Brace your feet when you slam the breech so you can pick up another shell without getting killed when the gun fires!"

The edge went out of Max's voice. "If you aren't sure you can slam the breech shut, locked exactly right every time, then we will practice until you and I know you can."

Max waited for Lucas to say something, and when he didn't, Max went on.

"I am asking you now...can you close the breech perfectly every time? Do I have to worry about that?"

Lucas felt tears coming, swallowed them and reluctantly said, "I'm not certain. I did make a mistake in training when I didn't have the breech completely locked. The shell had no powder or cap, but if it had been live..." He waited, but Max didn't say anything, so he said, "Yes, you should worry...it could happen again."

Max put the edge back in his voice. "No, it can't happen again! During training, when you make a mistake, you take the time to discuss it and correct the cause, but if you make a mistake here, we all die!" He stared at Lucas, leaving the rest unsaid.

"Klaus and I will take the crew and sit in the shade under trees you will find in that direction when you can load the gun." He pointed to the side of the turret, and Lucas peeked through the slit. "We're going to eat lunch and shoot the shit for a while." He put his hand on Lucas's shoulder. "I will show you where to put your feet and how to load a round without moving them—and you will come over and get us when you know how to load and close the breech perfectly every time. Now, go out the rear hatch and leave it open while you watch me."

Max crawled out of the gunner's seat and into the loader's position while Lucas watched through the rear hatch. He positioned his feet, looked at Lucas to see that he was paying attention, and then, in one smooth motion, slid a shell out of its rack and into the barrel. Max slammed the breech, grabbed another round, and had it ready behind the barrel in less than two seconds, and at no time was he in any danger from the breech. He did it twice more before he put the shell back in the storage bin.

"Okay, I've got it," said Lucas, with as much confidence as he could muster. "I will practice, and it may take awhile." He stepped aside to let Max exit through the rear hatch. Kristian led Simon out the front hull hatch, and they walked over to the only trees in sight and sat in the shade.

An hour later, Lucas had loaded, slammed the breech, and unloaded the gun at least a hundred times without a mistake. He broke the motion into segments, then assembled the parts into a single fluid motion that felt like the flow of movement Max had shown him. Lucas's arms were sore, but he was confident.

When he crawled out of the rear hatch and walked over to his comrades, no one stirred except Max, who stood and motioned for Lucas to follow. They climbed into their positions in the tank, and Max said, "Load the gun." In one smooth motion, Lucas slid a shell into the barrel, slammed the breech, and resisted the impulse to tap Max.

But Max didn't fire. Without turning his head to look at Lucas, he said quietly, "Put your head behind the breech, far enough away that it won't hit you when I fire." Lucas hesitated, and Max repeated the instructions. "Put your head behind the breech, and be careful of the ejector." The ejector was beside and partially behind the breech, and Lucas did as instructed, avoiding its path.

The gun fired, and he instantly and smoothly reloaded. Max looked back at him, waited until his head was again in position, then fired. He fired two more shells before he motioned for Lucas to stop loading.

"What do you think? Kristian and Simon can find something to do for the afternoon if you want more time to learn how to load."

Close to tears again, Lucas answered quickly, "Yes, sir, I would appreciate it if you could give me more time!"

Max said, "Okay, Lucas, let's take the afternoon together, and I will teach you a couple more tricks so you can do that a little faster. When you've mastered loading, I'll teach you how to fire the gun. You must be able to do both." Lucas suddenly realized Max had tested him to see if he was worth training. He had passed.

◇◇

Two-two-seven spent most of the next three weeks patrolling west and south of Warsaw. Lucas fired the gun smoothly and accurately and learned to load faster than Max, but his arrogance grew faster than his ability. He loved to shoot, and his favourite was the most difficult shot for a tank gunner—firing over the side while the tank moved, the equivalent of shooting skeet from a moving vehicle using a rifle. His arrogance disappeared when Max nailed four empty barrels in a row from the wide-open Panther going 25 kph over rough ground in fourth gear.

After three weeks of local patrols and practice, Obersturmführer Klaus Riker announced that the crew and the tank were ready for battle. When he pronounced that Lucas would load the gun, Max slapped Lucas on the back hard enough to make him wince and stagger. Lucas was as happy as he had been in his short life.

They trained until the end of September when Klaus announced, "The Polish rebels in Warsaw are no more, and the city is burning. The Russians will soon cross the Vistula River, and they will smell blood. If Hitler and Stalin don't start talking to one another, we are in deep Scheisse."

Chapter Eighteen

5 October 1944

Warsaw

War is the science of destruction

Sir John Abbott, Prime Minister of Canada, 1891–2

Wehrmacht soldiers loaded Panther two-two-seven on a rail car, and the train took it and three others to Warsaw's western edge. It was October 2nd when they arrived at the railway yard, and Klaus left his crew to unload their Panther while he attended a meeting with other tank commanders.

Lucas asked, "Are we going to fight the Russians in Warsaw?" He had a bar in his hand that Max had given him to loosen a turnbuckle holding a 12 mm binding chain fastened to the Panther's tow bar.

Max saw the perplexed look on Lucas's face, took the bar from him and said, "I'll show you how to do that." He slid the bar into a hole in the turnbuckle and pried it around, lengthening the threads and loosening the chain. "Loosen them a few turns, and Kristian and I will take it from there."

Lucas pushed the bar into the turnbuckle holding the opposite side and tried to turn it. It moved a quarter-turn and stopped. Max said, "Wrong way... you're tightening it," grabbed the bar, reversed the direction, and the chain sagged.

Max laughed. "What did you do all day when you were a kid? Didn't you learn anything?" He expertly twisted the turnbuckle anti-clockwise, loosening the chain in seconds.

"I practiced piano and violin for three hours every day, some days more. My mother was a pianist, and my dad was an engineer—he always worked, and I wasn't interested in mechanical things."

"Was? Are your parents dead?" Max neatly removed the turnbuckle, laid it on the bed of the railway car, then pulled the chain through the hold-down bits in one smooth motion.

"Yes, a bomb hit our house when the British attacked Dortmund. The explosion killed my parents, aunt, grandmother, and my sister."

Lucas didn't want to discuss the bombing, so he tried his original question again.

"Are we here to defend Warsaw against the Russians?"

Most of the buildings Lucas could see were damaged; bombs and artillery had reduced them to piles of bricks and stone. "Did the Russians already bomb and shell the city?"

Max passed the bar back to Lucas. "No, we did that. The Russians are waiting on the other side of the Vistula River for us to eliminate the Free Polish Army."

Lucas tried the bar on the next chain, and Max patiently waited while he pulled without success. Finally, Max said, "If it doesn't turn one way, just try the other." Lucas reversed his effort; the turnbuckle turned, squeaking at first, then moving smoothly. Max pointed to the next hole. "Put the bar in there and pull it toward you." Lucas did as Max had told him, and the chain went slack. Max separated the turnbuckle assembly from the chain and laid it on the plank floor.

Max talked while Lucas studied the threads on the next turnbuckle. "Klaus is friends with General Nehring, and Nehring told him that the Russians made a deal with us—they will stay out of Warsaw until we get all the Jews and the Free Polish Army out of the city. They want to kill any chance the Poles have of resisting them after they take their country from us."

Lucas put the bar in the turnbuckle. "We're going to fight the Polish Army? Didn't we do that five years ago?"

"Yes, we did, but the Polish army of 1939 doesn't exist anymore. The rebels the Russians want to eliminate call themselves the Free Polish Army, and they have been working underground with the British since the war started. I guess we can say the rebels had an army until they decided to come out into the open and fight."

"Why didn't they stay underground? How could they hope to win against us and the Russians?"

"They thought the Russians, English and the Americans would help them if they openly fought the Germans. In fact, the Allies probably told the Free Poles they would help them. When the Russians advanced to the edge of the city, the Free Polish Army got their guns out of their cellars, and the battle began. But the Russians wouldn't cross the river. They grounded their planes, and the ammunition and guns promised by the British and Americans didn't arrive. The British and Americans didn't even recognize the Free Polish army as a legitimate army, and that meant when we captured them, we could shoot them as spies." Lucas opened his mouth to ask the obvious question, but before he could, Max answered it. "If the Allies don't officially recognize them as an army, the Geneva Convention doesn't protect them."

Lucas turned the next turnbuckle the right way on the first try and had another chain loosened almost as fast as Max could remove it.

"We shot unarmed prisoners?" He decided there must be more to it.

Max laughed sarcastically. "Why do you think the Russians hate us enough to chase us through Poland and back to Germany? We shot, starved and tortured most of the Russian soldiers we captured. Since I crossed the border into Russia three years ago, I've been fighting this war without seeing a prison for captured Russian soldiers. So, the question is: where are they? I've seen Russians working on the roads, digging trenches, and burying the dead, but I haven't seen the prison camps where they live!"

Confused and shocked, Lucas slammed the bar on the bed of the rail car. "I think that's all crap. We don't shoot prisoners, and if the Free Polish Army is defeated, why are we in Warsaw if not to fight the Russians?"

"We are here to clean everyone and everything out of Warsaw and then flatten it." Max put a chain in a wooden barrel, feeding it through his rough hands until the end clattered over the edge. "Our soldiers are loading trains with booty and people as we speak. The loot goes to Germany; the people either become slaves in German factories or go to work camps."

Lucas climbed over the car to the chains on the other side and had them loosened before Max and Kristian caught up to him. Furiously attacking a turnbuckle, he said, "I don't believe you, and you shouldn't spread such lies!"

Max and Kristian exchanged looks and shook their heads.

Lucas sat beside Max on the Panther's rump as Kristian drove the panzer through the streets, following a half-track and a Lastwagen filled with soldiers. Four Panthers and two truckloads of soldiers had left the railway yard, all belonging to 227's squadron, but each tank and a few soldiers stopped at a different street until the last tank, 227, reached its destination.

A dozen soldiers jumped out of the Lastwagen and joined those already there. A ten-tonne Lastwagen loaded with furniture passed 227, and three others were backed up to houses. Klaus parked his Panther in the street and ordered Kristian to shut off the engine. "We have to wait until all the trucks are gone. He looked at his pocket watch. That's supposed to happen in an hour."

A woman suddenly ran from a house and a younger woman followed her a few steps behind. Soldiers fired; the young woman dropped to the ground, and the older one returned to help her. Soldiers ran to them, forced the uninjured woman to her feet, and dragged the other woman's lifeless form to the sidewalk. The soldiers stopped the older woman from returning to the form lying on the sidewalk, pushed her into a Kubelwagen, and it drove away.

Lucas felt a shock that he hadn't known since Waltraut died. He cried out, "What's going on? Why did they shoot that woman? What will happen to the one they took away?" He fought to control himself, but his throat closed, and tears formed in his eyes.

Klaus's upper body was out of his cupola—his seat was as high as it would go on its adjustment. Lucas sat on the turret next to him, and Max sat on the other side of Lucas. Max lit a cigarette before he offered one to Klaus.

Klaus spoke before he lit the cigarette.

"There were over a million people in Warsaw a couple of months ago, about a third of them Jews. They are all gone, except for a few like these women... I suppose they were hiding in that house." He waved his hand in the general direction, then lit his cigarette.

Lucas asked, "Where did they go? Why did they kill that woman?" Confused and angry, he tried to understand what Klaus was saying, "We defeated Poland five years ago, and now we're fighting the Russians to save Poland, aren't we? Why would we shoot Polish women?"

Klaus looked at Max, then spoke to Lucas as he pointed down the street. "Lucas, what do you think those Lastwagen are doing?"

Lucas looked carefully at one of the trucks. Four men loaded a piano over the back.

"It looks like the people here are moving out. Where are they going? Did they sell their houses?"

Klaus said, with more than a bit of anger in his tone, "The people are either in slave camps or they are dead. Those Lastwagen..." Klaus pointed at the nearest truck... "are stealing everything that's left. The people with the Lastwagen are Germans, taking the Polish people's possessions to the railway station where the trains take them to Germany. Hundreds of railway cars, maybe thousands, are going to Germany with booty. Some carry slaves, some loot; Genghis Kahn had nothing on us!" He turned to Lucas.

"Okay, here's how it works: the top Nazis in the party have their choice of loot based on how high they are in Hitler's world. The jewelry and art are already gone, turned to cash or hidden somewhere by the top people in the Nazi Party. The furniture goes to furnish Nazi houses stolen from the Jews in Germany, and the factory machinery goes to German factory owners, for a price, of course. The glorious Third Reich is emptying every building..." He looked down the street and swept his arm to encompass the houses on both sides... "and then we are going to destroy them!"

Lucas stared at the street. The last three Lastwagen passed the Panther, leaving the houses open behind them—most of the front doors had been loaded on the trucks.

"But the people; surely a million Poles can't all go to Germany to work in the factories?" He spoke quietly, resigned, trying to reconcile the answer. Surely, he had misunderstood something!

Max took over. "When we took Warsaw, we put the Jews in a section of the city with a fence around it. It was called a Ghetto, and there was no way in or out without permission. A year ago, the Jews tried to fight their way out—many died, and many were taken away. The survivors hid until August, when the Free Polish Army came out of hiding, counting on the Russians, British and Americans to help them. But the Russians and the British made a deal to double-cross the Poles, leaving Hitler free to slaughter them. He ordered Warsaw emptied and destroyed, and that's where we come in."

"What about the rest of the Jews? The children?" Lucas felt his world coming apart.

"The SS murdered the Jews or took them to camps, and the non-Jewish citizens who weren't killed in the fighting became refugees or slaves." He waved the hand holding his cigarette across the scene before him. "And now we are going to knock down every building."

Lucas looked at his feet, his mind trying not to believe what had to be true. Klaus and Max puffed on their cigarettes, waiting for Lucas to lift his head. Finally, he did, and, sick to his stomach, said, "My country does this? I have heard awful stories about how we treat the Jews—my parents told me not to ask questions, or I might disappear with the friends they lost when the SA took them to a labour camp. But they wouldn't talk about it, not even to my sister and me." He tried to force the tears to stop. "My father worked with Polish Zwangsarbiter, in truth, slaves, and I have heard stories that we murdered Jews in Russia, but I didn't believe them. I didn't think they could be true, but now—I think they might be."

Klaus grabbed Lucas's shoulder so hard it hurt. "Don't ever say things like that! The Gestapo is everywhere, and even in the Waffen SS, you are not safe!" He squeezed Lucas harder. "They will kill you for saying much less than that!"

Lucas squirmed, and Klaus released him.

"Why do we fight for the bastards who do this?"

Klaus looked down the empty street. The soldiers had loaded the last truck and were leaving.

"We fight to defend our homes—The Russians will make this our fate too if they get to Germany before the Americans and the British. We must delay the Russians until the Western Allies are in Berlin." He looked at Lucas with something like pity. "We cannot win this war; we can only try to survive. When the Russians move again, they won't stop until they drive through the Brandenburger Tor and down Unter den Linden to the Reichstag. The Americans and British have already crossed the Rhine and are in Germany—If we do things right and have a lot of luck, they might be in Berlin before the Russians."

He raised his voice to speak to Kristian. "Start it up and drive down the middle of the street; I will tell you when to stop."

He turned back to Lucas. "We must see that the Americans get to Hitler first, but you must never talk about this again. Somewhere in Berlin, brutality has overcome reason. The maniacs in charge think it's more important to destroy what we hate than to protect what we love."

Lucas looked at Max, and Max nodded. "Everyone knows this, but you must never talk about it...there are Gestapo ears everywhere." He pointed to where Simon sat with his earphones on, listening to Rundfunk Belgrad.

Lucas tried in vain to understand. Klaus didn't seem bothered by what Lucas understood as murder. The commander's hatch lay wide open; he sat on its edge, relaxed, with his legs dangling, most of his body in the open, unprotected. A woman had died, another kidnapped, and Klaus seemed indifferent. They were going to destroy people's homes, and he didn't care.

✦✦✦✦✦✦✦✦✦✦✦✦✦✦✦✦✦✦✦✦✦✦✦

Klaus ordered Kristian to stop and swept his hand from one side of the street to the other. "There are your targets, gentlemen; begin at the far end and leave nothing still standing on this street." He smiled, climbed down from the Panther and walked to the doorstep of a house opposite it. He sat down with his back against a pillar.

Lucas loaded the gun, and Max carefully lined up a house and fired. The shell entered through the front door, Max's aiming point, and the roof and two walls exploded in a blast of brick, wood and roof tiles. He swung the gun to the right—Lucas loaded as the turret rotated—and hit the house on the nearest corner, destroying it with one shot. Klaus waved to Kristian, and the Panther reversed.

It took half an hour to fire seventy-nine rounds, all the ammunition they had, and when Max had fired the last shot, he stood up in the cupola and waved to Klaus. Klaus motioned the crew to come down and join him on the steps of the three-story house. They sat down on the steps and ate their Wurst und Feldbrot lunch.

"What are we doing blowing up houses?" Kristian directed the question to Klaus. "Is there some secret plan I don't know about?"

Klaus answered, "We are doing precisely what General Nehring sent us here to do." The crew turned their heads to look at the ruined buildings—half a kilometre of rubble lay between the end of the street and 227. Smoke curled up from the hot barrel of the cannon. "The plan is not a secret; we will blow up every building in Warsaw!"

Simon asked, "How many houses do we have to destroy? I will need better earplugs if we're going to do this much longer." He pulled a piece of rag out of his pocket. "What's the point in staying in the tank? Why don't I sit here with you and smoke?"

Klaus bit into an apple. "Our orders are to destroy as many houses as we can, and I interpret that to mean until we ruin the barrel on the gun—probably sometime late this afternoon if they bring us enough ammunition. That barrel is the original, and a new one would be nice. The new ones have a better sight, and the rifling is worn out on the old barrel." Klaus didn't address the second question.

On cue, Lucas heard an engine and turned to see a Munition Lastwagen dodging around piles of rubble, driving down the street toward them. The driver and his helper unloaded ammunition from the rear, and the tank crew filled the bins. They piled boxes of extra ammunition on the sidewalk—enough to replace the 75 mm shells again. Klaus looked at a hundred rounds of cannon ammunition and said, "Yes, that should do it, don't you think, Max?" Max grunted and smiled, dreaming of a new gun.

The Lastwagen driver held the cab door open while Klaus signed for the ammunition. He asked Klaus, "Will that be enough for today?"

Klaus smiled. "Yes, I'm quite sure that will be enough." He handed the board back to the driver.

Lucas wasn't surprised when time proved Klaus and Max correct: Max and Lucas increased the firing rate, cutting half a second from the time to reload. As anticipated, they ruined the cannon's barrel by the end of the day. Max lowered the gun to its limit and stood on an empty box to examine the grooves that spun the shell, stabilizing it on its way to the target.

"Climb up and look into the barrel, Lucas. See what a worn-out barrel looks like."

Lucas looked but couldn't see what was wrong. "What should I look for?"

"The grooves' edges are rounded off; they should be square and deeper. The shells aren't spinning fast enough, and they're tumbling before they hit the target. We can't hit anything with that barrel outside a couple of hundred metres, and a Wurst can would deflect it!"

Klaus leaned against the Panther's side skirt while he lit a cigarette. He blew a smoke ring and pointed into the setting sun.

"It's time to quit. Simon, tell the command centre that our gun is kaput." They parked the panzer and went into an empty house. The mattresses were still on the bedrooms' floors, a better place to sleep than cramped in the Panther. Max headed for the cellar, and when he returned, he reported that the bin was full of coal and that he had made a fire.

Shortly after daylight the following day, an officer in a black SS uniform stopped his Kubelwagon beside the doorstep where Klaus and his men sat opposite Panther 227. He gave Klaus orders to return to the front and drove away following a brief conversation. Klaus read the orders, smiled, and briefed the crew.

"We're returning to the front, but we won't fight until the maintenance engineers put a new barrel on our gun. But that doesn't mean Hitler has given up on his plan to level Warsaw. Someone convinced him that it would be cheaper and more effective to use explosives and flamethrowers to destroy the city, so he's sending Verbrennung und Zerstörung Kommando units to finish the job. They specialize in setting fires and blowing things up; they're experts with flamethrowers and dynamite!" He looked at the cannon barrel, then at the demolished buildings. "I must agree with Hitler's advisors—that will be a much more efficient way to accomplish their insanely useless objective." He stepped on the front armour plate, and the men followed him up the slope of the Panther. He waited beside his cupola until everyone was inside, climbed into his seat, and yelled down to his feet. "Kristian, take us back to the railway yard. I will give you directions."

That night, they slept in the tank, and the following morning, Wehrmacht soldiers loaded Panther 227 on a railway car and took it back to the front, which was becoming active again—the Russian Bear was stirring.

Changing the gun's ruined barrel took two days, and Max and Lucas spent the third day sighting it. Max was pleased, muttering that this was a good barrel, much better than the "piece of shit" that had come with the Panther. The new sight's magnification could be set at 2.5x for close shooting, usually under 1000 metres, and 5x for longer shots.

The long barrel and high-velocity armour-piercing ammunition Klaus managed to acquire generated a muzzle velocity that could penetrate the front armour of a T-34 at anything under a thousand metres and kill a T-34 two kilometres away by hitting it anywhere else. The Panther's new longer barrel and superior sight gave it a tremendous advantage over the T-34 in the open. But with its slower turret and inability to maneuver quickly without breaking something, the Panther was at a disadvantage in a close-quarters dogfight.

"I've got a great gun," Max rubbed the barrel affectionately, "but I need a faster turret."

"We need stronger final drives worse than a faster turret."

Kristian leaned over the axle to check for leaking oil; it had become a habit whenever he smoked outside the tank. "What's the point in having seven hundred horsepower if I can only use five hundred?"

Chapter Nineteen

17 October 1944

Combat

Whoever said the pen is mightier than the sword obviously never encountered automatic weapons.

Douglas MacArthur

Lucas woke an hour before dawn on the 17th of October. There was no pre-dawn light, and it was raining. And getting out of bed was the thing he hated most about the army.

Every night, just before turning out the lights, Simon listened to the weather forecast for the next day. Today, the 17th of October, it was sporadic showers, heavy overcast, ceilings below one hundred metres and patches of fog—a miserable day if one had beach plans, but driving a tank in the open would be less stressful with Russian aircraft on the ground.

The dawn was still an hour into the future when an orderly covered the table with food, dishes, and cutlery, poured coffee for everyone and left. Klaus ripped a Brötchen in half and began spreading a thick layer of butter on one side.

As with every morning, Klaus had read the day's orders before he joined his men in the mess for breakfast. He started to talk as he added jam. "It looks like we're going back to fighting Russians today, and there's a good chance we will fire our new gun." He bit a generous piece out of the Brötchen and drank enough coffee to make a slurry in his mouth. Everyone waited while he mixed coffee, Brötchen, jam, and butter before he swallowed.

"About fifty kilometres northwest of here, the Russians have set up the Sandomierz Bridgehead, a place that a few hundred thousand

Russian soldiers call home. As of yesterday, our scouts reported a small Russian tank and infantry unit on our side of the river. Four T-34s and a company of infantry are scouting and probing our defences. The weather makes an attack on them from the air impossible, and tomorrow, they will likely go home. Our orders are to discourage this type of activity by finding and destroying them, which means there is an excellent chance we will get into a fight."

The men looked at one another with big grins on their faces. Lucas looked from one man to another, surprised at the joy he saw on their faces. He grinned so he wouldn't stick out.

Klaus took another bite of the bun, washed it down with coffee and went on.

"We will take three Panthers with us and hopefully find those T-34s before they find us. I will command the mission." He looked up from piling more jam on the Brötchen.

"There will be no air support or infantry; we will travel fast, and we can't wait for men on foot. A Jäger unit travelling in a Demag will find them for us and tell Simon." He took a bite of his Brötchen and drank a mouthful of black coffee.

Max cracked two eggs and peeled them with his spoon. He cut the eggs into small pieces and melted a large chunk of butter into the pile.

Lucas said, "Max," blurting it out without thinking, "How can you eat that after the night you had? I heard you throwing up your guts in the bathroom!"

Max gave Lucas a look that made him wish he could crawl under the table. "Junge, that's none of your damned business!" He put a forkful of the eggs in his mouth.

Lucas tore a Brötchen apart while looking at Max out of the corner of his eye, noting that he was as pale as the white of his egg, and his eyes were dull.

Klaus cleared his throat, diverting Max's contemptuous stare away from Lucas. "Our assignment is to find the Russian reconnaissance group and destroy it...that means shooting, and shooting means I need a healthy gunner."

Max nodded at Klaus and said, "Don't worry—you've got a healthy gunner—I'm fine," and then stuffed a piece of Brötchen in his mouth.

Lucas suspected that Klaus and Max thought he was the weak link in the panzer, but he was confident they were wrong—all he needed was a chance to prove himself. When he tried to return Max's stare he had to lower his eyes and shift his attention to his breakfast.

Although Lucas hated coffee, the SS drank a lot of coffee, so he forced himself to drink it black in front of his comrades. He slurped a small Schluck, then quickly took a bite of the Brötchen he had coated with a thick layer of jam so the sweetness would moderate the battery-acid taste. He wondered if he would ever wear the black Waffen SS uniform

Simon ate noisily with his head down, ignoring everything but his food, shoving a thick piece of Wurst into his mouth behind a whole egg. He licked his dirty fingers, smacking his lips disgustingly. Overweight, with fat cheeks, narrow-set eyes, a flat nose and no neck, Simon bore an uncanny resemblance to Churchill's bulldog.

Max had told Lucas they had tried to teach Simon to shoot and load but, after a frustrating and frightening day, concluded that they would have a better chance of ramming a Russian tank than of Simon hitting it. Simon's intrinsic clumsiness also ruled out handling live ammunition as a loader.

There was a reason the man was still there doing a job that wasn't critical to the actual battle. Simon's father was a Gauleiter, a Nazi party leader in Munich—otherwise, Simon's ignorance would have long ago earned him a shallow grave in the Russian mud.

Consequently, if Max or Lucas couldn't fight, the tank couldn't. As the tank's commander, Klaus had to decide whether he could count on Max, and when they had finished breakfast, he decided that a sick Max was better than the best gunner in the 'spares' pool.

◇◇◇

Klaus took his tank squadron southeast, hoping to flank the Russian force and approach from a direction they would not expect. At breakfast, he told the tank crew that he doubted the information they had was reliable, and he didn't think a sizeable force could have pushed more than twenty-five kilometres from their bridgehead without opposition.

The Panthers would be in the region in less than two hours, and

Lucas's pulse rate increased as the minutes ticked away. For the first twenty kilometres, the Panthers drove in a line behind one another with a hundred metres between them. There was no other traffic, and they rode along at a relaxed pace in fourth gear, a quiet and smooth ride on the paved road. Klaus planned to spread out his forces once they reached the 'hot' area, with three of the Panthers taking to the farm roads running between the fields. He reasoned that the Russians would stay close to the patches of woods sprinkled between the fields, avoiding main roads.

At ten o'clock, the scouts reported on the radio that the Russian T-34s were northwest of them. Klaus sent his panzers on separate parallel paths northwest, still connected by radio but sometimes not in visual contact. As they drove slowly in a direction Klaus hoped would take them to the Russians' flank, he could still see two of the squadron's panzers, but the third had disappeared behind a small copse of trees. Panther 227 barely marked the hard-packed field road, and Klaus assumed that, although the harvested fields were wet from the rain, they were solid enough to carry a Panther. Nonetheless, he decided to avoid them unless there was an emergency. Even in a solid field, the heavy tank would sink a few inches, causing considerable rolling resistance, possibly breaking one of the fragile final drives if the Panther found it necessary to turn hard.

Klaus was perusing his 'what if...' options when Max yelled, "Jesus Christ, I've got to shit!" Every man in the tank's enclosed space could smell Max's discomfort and verify the statement, and none were surprised at his sudden outburst. Max bent over, hands on his abdomen, and a long, wet-sounding blat warned everyone of impending asphyxiation. Lucas held his breath, but there was a limit to that remedy.

Klaus was not happy. They were close to the Russians, and to stop the tank in the open would make it a sitting duck. Smelling Max's distress, he told Simon to inform the other panzers that two-two-seven would stop for a few minutes. Thankful that his position as commander necessitated having his head above the hatch,

Klaus spoke into the intercom. "Kristian, there's a bunch of trees just ahead; we will stop there." He took a deep breath and lowered his head to speak directly to Max and Lucas. "Max, you can leave the gun now and get out when we get there; Lucas will take the gun." He put his head out of the hatch and breathed fresh air before he spoke into the intercom.

"Kristian, when we stop, you will keep the engine running at two thousand revolutions in case we need to swing the gun. Lucas, you'll slide into Max's seat as soon as he leaves, and I want you and Simon to make sure the machine guns are loaded and ready. Take the safeties off."

The intercom was silent until they reached the trees. The Panther slowed and stopped smoothly; Klaus spoke into the intercom. "Everyone, keep your eyes peeled. Max will leave by the rear hatch, and I will watch him from here."

Max was barely out of his seat when Lucas slid into it and looked through the sight. He flipped it from 5x to 2.5x to double the field of vision. Through the open hatch above his head, he observed Klaus scanning the horizon with his Zeiss binoculars, stopping to examine every building and tree. Even Max's groans didn't shake the commander out of his routine. Lucas, sick from the stench, dared not mention it. Loyalty had kept this crew alive to Stalingrad and back, and it infected the boy.

Klaus put his face down so Max could see him. "All right, Max, as quickly as you can!" Klaus picked his Papa machine gun from the slewing ring shelf before straightening up.

Lucas had opened the rear turret hatch before taking Max's place. When the Panther stopped parallel to the trees, the big man pulled his muscular frame through the hatch, swung his legs over the hull, and ran straight for the trees as soon as his feet touched the ground.

Lucas was watching Max through the gunner slit beside the sight when Klaus yelled a warning and fired his submachine gun over Max's head. An instant later, bullets exited Max's back, fired from the trees in front of him. He stopped, his knees buckled, and he fell on his back, motionless, his legs bent back under him.

<hr>

Klaus's hatch cover clanged shut a second before a grenade landed on it, rolled down the spare track segments hanging on the side and exploded on the ground. Klaus scrambled to the rear hatch and closed it as bullets rattled everywhere on the tank. Lucas found the gunmen, betrayed by smoke trails coming from the trees on the right side of the road and from a barn 100 metres down the left side.

Klaus jumped back to his seat, looked through the ports under his hatch, and screamed into the intercom, "Reverse, Kristian! Now! Lucas, clear the tank!"

Lucas obeyed the order he had practiced in training, swinging the turret three-hundred-and-sixty-degrees with the pedal fully depressed to clear any unwanted passengers. Klaus sprayed a full magazine out of a gun port as the turret turned a complete revolution in 15 seconds, shouting, "Use the machine gun, Lucas! Kill them, or they'll kill us!" The swing was almost complete when Lucas realized his mistake and pressed the machine gun's trigger.

The engine, already revved, spun the tracks when Kristian slammed it in gear and released the clutch an instant after Klaus finished the order to reverse. The Panther jerked back; Kristian opened the throttle, accelerating as fast as he could. Unfortunately, the Panther had only one reverse gear, and its designers had selected its ratio for power, not speed. It reached terminal speed, slower than a man could run, in two lengths of the tracks.

Russian soldiers ran toward the tank from the trees behind the ditches, sensing they had only a tiny window of opportunity to kill their enemy. A few soldiers knelt on the road and fired grenade launchers at the slowly retreating Panther, but they exploded harmlessly, ineffective against a heavy tank like the Panther.

Klaus had a 360-degree field of vision through the ports under his hatch and spotted an anti-tank gun team towing their gun to the road, preparing to fire.

"Lucas, Swing the turret to the rear until I say stop." Klaus was the only crew member with a 360-degree field of vision, and Lucas swung the turret until Klaus shouted, "Stop!" He had the field gun in front of him and it fired before Lucas had the crosshairs lined up.

Klaus yelled, "Achtung! Granate!" as the incoming shell exploded harmlessly against the front armour. Lucas ignored the explosion, found the Russian gun crew in his sight, pressed the machine gun trigger, and a stream of bullets hit the road in front of them. Without slowing the hail of bullets, Lucas smoothly corrected, the dexterity in his sensitive fingers and hands manipulating the control wheels, steering twenty rounds of steel bullets every second into the men caught on the road without protection. He felled them like scythed wheat, then killed another five Russians as they climbed out of the ditch, trying to get to the gun. The turret machine gun on a Panther uses the same sight as the cannon, moving in synch with the big gun, which is not a good arrangement for accuracy. But Max had taught Lucas to watch where the bullets hit, and then swing the stream to the target like a high-pressure water hose. Lucas had learned the lesson well, and Russian soldiers paid the price.

He screamed his anger at the figures dying on the road, took a second to wipe his eyes and blink the tears away, and fired at the men running to the trees until the machine gun stopped. He fed a new belt into the breech of the MG-34 and pulled the trigger, instinctively killing the men closest to safety before he targeted those who had farther to go. Simon used his hull machine gun to complement Lucas's, sweeping a continuous line of bullets into the men trying to escape on the other side of the road. Only a handful made it to the relative safety of a stone farmhouse.

Klaus, watching the carnage through the slits below the cupola hatch, yelled over the screaming engine and the machine gun chatter, "Keep it up, Lucas…kill the bastards!"

Klaus used the intercom to guide Kristian. In reverse, the driver had no vision out the rear of the tank, which was the direction the tank was travelling. Klaus and Kristian had practiced the maneuver tirelessly. When in reverse, Kristian was blind, and the steering was reversed—left was right and vice versa. The commander had 360 degrees of sightlines under the hatch or through gunports, no matter where the gun and turret pointed, and he instructed the driver when the Panther drove backwards.

Lucas fired the MG-34 almost continuously, pausing only when he ran out of targets or ammunition. He followed Klaus's shouted directions, childish whimpers becoming adrenalin-fueled yells, filling Lucas with a sense of power he hadn't expected. Excitement drowned out his fear as he mowed down the bastards who had killed Max and would kill his friends if he didn't get to them first!

Lucas moved the turret using the foot pedal, whipping the stream of bullets back and forth, clearing the soldiers from the road, forcing the survivors to find cover where he couldn't see them.

Klaus yelled, "Use the cannon; shoot the corner of the barn!" Lucas fired the loaded 75 mm cannon the instant the sight found the target. He jumped from the seat, lifted a shell from its pocket, rammed it into the barrel and locked the breech in one smooth motion. As he slid into the gunner position, he shouted, "Gun is loaded and ready, sir!"

Lucas saw through the sight that the shell had destroyed the vertical beams holding the barn up, and the side and roof of the building had fallen on Russian soldiers. Lucas machine-gunned their comrades who were trying to help them.

Klaus shouted, "Lucas, swing right forty-five degrees!" Lucas swung the turret clockwise with the foot pedal until the sight found trees and Russian soldiers. He pressed the machine gun trigger before releasing the foot pedal, mowing down Russian soldiers trying to escape into the trees two hundred metres away. Simon's gun stopped; he bellowed, "Out of ammo!"

Klaus shouted, "Lucas, back to the road!" Lucas stomped the left pedal, bringing the cannon to bear on two soldiers trying to load the anti-tank gun. Although the sight was bouncing around, he took an average and fired; the shell hit the road at the soldier's feet, blowing them and the gun upward and outward. Lucas sprang sideways, pulled a round out of its pocket and was lining it up for the push into the barrel when Klaus shouted into the intercom, "Kristian, turn hard right on my signal!" Through the corner of his eye, as he slid the shell home and slammed the breech, he saw Klaus swing his hatch cover fully open and look over the edge of the cupola through his "Donkey ears" range-finder. Lucas dove into the gunner's seat, and when he looked through the sight, a T-34 was climbing out of the ditch a thousand metres down the road.

Explosions to the left of their position indicated the other tanks were under attack. The squadron had run into a planned ambush, and Max had spoiled it by exposing them before the Russians were ready.

"Lucas—range eight hundred fifty!" The fast T-34 had the receding slow-moving Panther to fire at, and if he hit it at this range, 227's crew would almost certainly die. The Russian stopped and took less than a second to target the slowly receding Panther before he fired—but he fired three seconds after Klaus shouted in the intercom, "Turn right now!" Kristian pulled the left clutch and hit the left pedal hard. The reversing Panther turned right and pitched down as it crossed the ditch, and the T-34's shell missed the corner of the hull by a handful of millimetres and hit the empty road 200 metres past the Panther.

Lucas had already adjusted the range to 850 metres when Klaus yelled, "Lucas, leave the gun over the front. The range is eight-fifty." The Russian could fire in less than three seconds and Klaus's timing had to be perfect. He said, "Kristian, turn left ninety degrees! Now!" Two-twenty-seven swung an instant before the Russian gunner fired— and the shot hit the ground in front of where 227 would have been if it hadn't turned. The Panther disappeared in a cloud of dust and smoke.

Klaus shouted, "Kristian, Stop! Lucas, fire as soon as your sight is on him!"

The Panther stopped in three metres, facing the T-34. Lucas put the point of the gunsight on the center of the T-34, pulled the trigger, and a streak of smoke from the Panther's long barrel followed the high-velocity armour-piercing shell. Lucas saw it strike the Russian's sloped armour under the gun, deflect to the joint where the hull meets the turret and explode inside the seam. The barrel of the T-34's gun lifted, skewed to the right, pulling the turret's track out of its ring.

Lucas jumped across the turret, pulled another shell out of the rack, rammed it into the barrel, slammed the breech, and leapt into the gunner's seat. The Russian tank plunged to the right, and Lucas followed with his turret. He stopped the turret with the sight just ahead of the retreating tank, checked the range, waited, and fired as the Russian dropped off the left road shoulder into the ditch. The shell entered the tank just above the track on the left side, exploding inside, igniting the ammunition in the hull side bins. The tank split open like a can of meat and fell on its side—smoke, then flames rising from the wreckage.

"Kristian, reverse and turn right! Infantry!" Lucas loaded the big gun while Simon focused on the retreating infantry, killing at least half before they reached the stone farmhouse.

Klaus yelled, "Stop!" and Kristian stopped the tank. "Lucas, two hundred metres, the farmhouse, as soon as you are ready!" Lucas set the range, sighted, and blasted the farmhouse with the big gun. He reloaded, hit it again, and it became a pile of rubble. Simon fired his machine gun whenever Russian soldiers stood up and tried to run. Lucas loaded the cannon, then swept the field with his sight on high power. Nothing moved.

Klaus looked down into the turret, smiling. "Okay, Lucas, everyone except us is dead or pretending to be; you can stop now." Lucas, panting, kept his hands on the sighting wheels to keep them from shaking. He had peed his pants, and he was terrified Klaus would see it.

Klaus smiled at him, then spoke into the intercom. "Let's get Max into the tank and move ammunition to the ready position. The scout Demag says there are three more Russian T-34s around here," and machine-gun fire from their left punctuated his sentence. "Simon, get our panzers on the radio. Tell them we're alright and ask for a report."

When they returned to Max, Lucas crawled out of the rear hatch while Simon left his position from the front. Klaus climbed into the gunner's seat, and Kristian kept the engine turning over at two thousand rpm.

Lucas and Simon rolled Max's body into a canvas body bag and carried him to the tank. They dragged him into the turret and strapped him in the loader's seat. There was nowhere else they could put him except outside, and Klaus wasn't willing to do that. Before Klaus gave the gunner position back to Lucas, he said quietly, "Now you know why they hate us." Lucas looked at him, his eyes still enlarged from the adrenalin. Klaus put his hand on Lucas's shoulder and said, "You'll do, Lucas." Then, as an afterthought, "If a soldier tells you that he didn't pee his pants the first time he was in a real battle, he is lying about one or the other."

Lucas let the tension release. He felt a bond with these men that quieted the nagging feeling he didn't belong. A mixture of a sigh and a sob escaped his lips, and he knew that his life had changed forever.

They moved the ammunition to fill the racks and the ring where Lucas could easily reach 24 rounds. Typically, the wireless operator would become the loader, but Lucas was relieved when Klaus decided to leave things as they were.

The road was smooth enough that Kristian could drive in fourth gear, and Lucas's heart rate had time to return to normal before the wireless operator in the Panther on their left flank screamed for help. Two Russian T-34s and infantry had the Panther pinned down, and its destruction was imminent.

Klaus calmly said, "Kristian, drive across the field. If we don't get to those T-34s, they will get our Panther."

The two other Panthers on two-two-seven's left flank were ahead of its position and were not under attack, but a small stream with trees on steep banks split the fields between them and the Russian tanks attacking the trapped Panther. Klaus's Panther was the panzer's best and probably only chance.

The two remaining T-34s assumed that the trap had killed 227; consequently, their crews didn't see the tank coming. Klaus pointed them out and shouted, "Lucas, when we stop, shoot the Russian on the left...Range...a thousand and fifty metres. Kristian, stop the tank... now." Lucas had the range set when 227 stopped, and he fired a second later.

From a thousand metres, the armour-piercing round hit the nearest Russian tank full on the side under the turret. The shell drilled a neat hole in the T-34 and exploded inside...none of the crew got out before the tank started to burn. The second T-34 swung its gun to bear on the Panther and fired before Lucas had the gun loaded. Klaus ducked his head into the cupola as the Russian shell hit 75 mm of plating on the 55-degree sloped front, jarring the Panther with an ear-splitting explosion.

Lucas ignored the hit, lifted a fresh round to line up with the barrel and slammed the breech shut. He jumped into the gunner's seat and sighted using the fine-adjustment wheel and five-X on the Zeiss lens. He centred on the soft side of the T-34 and fired at the same instant it moved forward. The shell struck just behind the exact center of the

Russian in its fuel tanks. The combination of range, the long 72 calibre barrel, and high-velocity ammunition spelled doom for the Russians; the shell penetrated to the center of the fuel tank, where it exploded, and the T-34 spectacularly spewed flames sixty metres in the air.

Lucas loaded the gun while Klaus guided Kristian toward the trapped Panther, now freed from the T-34 problems and firing at its infantry tormentors. Klaus ordered Lucas to train his guns on the only escape route the now-exposed infantry would have, and the Russian soldiers retreated right down Lucas's gun barrel. He and Simon fired until nothing moved.

The two wayward Panthers found a way over the brook and travelled as fast as they dared toward 227. The few scattered Russians who left the battlefield alive fled into a small patch of forest.

◇◇◇◇◇◇◇◇◇◇◇◇◇◇◇◇◇◇◇◇◇◇◇◇◇◇◇◇◇◇◇◇◇◇◇◇

Lucas gradually cooled down during the two-hour ride back to base, from the adrenalin high of battle to full-blown depression as he helped Kristian and Simon lift Max's stinking body out of the panzer. He had died instantly, the second-best outcome a soldier can hope for, but it brought home to Lucas the reality of death. As he laid the canvas bag on the ground, the humiliation of peeing his pants dissipated. Max would have laughed at him.

Depression descended like a blanket over Lucas. He wanted to see heroism in Max's death, but his mind told him there was none—heroism was for the childhood he had left and those who had never fought.

Max had died ignominiously, like a barking dog purposely run over by a car. His death had immediately generated a terrible rage in Lucas—a good man had died for nothing—someone had to pay for that!

He became the avenger, and it had nothing to do with honour, the Führer, or Germany. He had killed the men who had killed his friend, and he had done it joyfully.

He hadn't expected to feel regret at killing to save himself and his friends, but the euphoria he had felt when mowing down men who were his country's enemy now surprised and embarrassed him more than his wet pants. He had killed men and boys, people like him, Hartwig, and his father. He hadn't thought of the night of the bombing since joining the crew of 227, but standing beside the empty hole came rushing back. His shoulders shook as he tried to control the ache, and he thought of Corrine. Could he ever face her again? Could she love him when he told her how he had murdered dozens of men? A sob escaped, then another.

Klaus put his arm around Lucas's neck and spoke loudly to his men. "Let's go to the barracks before we eat. I need to clean up." He said softly in Lucas's ear, "Take as long as you need—we will wait for you."

It took Lucas 20 minutes to clean up, and he braced himself for a what he had to do. But when he joined his comrades, the feeling evaporated. They had survived, and he was a big part of the reason. Famished, he gave up trying to decide how he felt and headed for the mess hall with his new comrades-in-arms.

When they were seated, Klaus stood and lifted his glass. Every man in the hall rose noisily to his feet, and when Klaus lifted his drink, "Prost!" rang from every throat. They drank their glasses dry; Klaus clicked his heels and shouted, "Gentlemen, for Max...the Panzerlied."

Lucas stood at attention while the roomful of men began the song they all knew by heart. Klaus looked at Lucas and yelled, "Sing, Lucas!" Lucas knew and loved the anthem, and his unmistakable baritone voice rose to join his comrades. Klaus slapped him on the back and put his arm over Lucas's shoulder. He shouted in Lucas's ear, "My God, Lucas... you sing too?" Laughing, he rejoined the song.

Chapter Twenty

Christmas 1944

King Tiger

Only time and a brave mind are invincible; machines are not.

The Author

Max's replacement was half Italian, half German, and he came from the failing Italian front. Marcus Grünwald was tall and dark-skinned, affirming his Italian heritage, and as handsome as a Hollywood movie star. A Bavarian forester with an Italian mother, he had joined the Panzer Army as a volunteer in 1941. He was kind-natured and friendly, which drew Lucas to him from the first handshake.

Two-two-seven got a new front armour plate, new final drive gears, and new rings and bearings for the engine, and when 227's mini-overhaul and the training exercises were over, Klaus faced a difficult choice for his gunner. Marcus outranked Lucas, but Lucas was the better shot. He solved the dilemma by making the assignment of their duties mission-dependent.

Lucas kept his mouth shut, but he felt the only factor Klaus had considered was his age, and he thought it unfair but knew better than to complain. At times, Lucas was painfully aware of his immaturity and inexperience, but most of the time felt as capable as any man in the crew. He admitted to himself that Marcus's experience and age were enough to tip the decision, but his rank in the Waffen SS was the absolute deal-breaker for Klaus.

In late November, Panzer 227's crew loaded their tank on a train and moved with XXIV Panzer Corps to a confiscated Polish base near Kielce, beyond the range of the Russian guns at Sandomierz. Showers, bathing facilities, a dining hall and warm, dry rooms for the tank crews made the wait for the inevitable onslaught comfortable. Rumours of the Russian strength spread like oil on a hot griddle—millions of men, thousands of T-34 tanks and hundreds of thousands of guns. Lucas laughed when Marcus repeated the unbelievable numbers.

"Two million men? Hitler said that the Russians don't have that many men in all of the Eastern Front!"

They ate their Abendessen of black bread and marinated herring in the deserted dining hall, and Lucas was not in a good mood. He hated raw fish, and they had been late getting to dinner, eliminating a choice.

Marcus pulled a piece of Gouda cheese out of his pocket, unwrapped the cloth protecting it, and held it in his open palm. "If you don't like the herring, I will trade you a piece of cheese for it.".

"Done!" Lucas grabbed the cheese from Marcus and the pumpernickel bread from his plate before he slid it across the table to Marcus. He cut the edge off a piece of bread that had touched the herring and put it to one side.

◇◇

Klaus broke into the conversation. "If you believe the chief liar, Hitler, we should be home for Christmas! But the Russians are doing what they've done since we left Stalingrad. They attack us when they're ready, and we retreat. They fight us until they're exhausted, then rest while the people at home build more tanks and airplanes. When they're ready, they will do it again. And each time they repeat the process, their advantage becomes greater."

No one in the dining hall breathed. If the Gestapo was in the room, and they likely were, Klaus had just put a noose around his neck. He ignored the silence and charged on.

"Hitler is in a big office looking out on the Linden trees in Berlin, listening to his sycophantic pals—he doesn't know shit about Russians! Our pilots who fly over the enemy lines and the scouts who count the guns and men tell us they have four times our equipment and men—Katya rocket launchers, artillery, tanks, and soldiers, twice the numbers they've had since a month after Stalingrad and their equipment is better. What they lacked in quality until now is no longer the case." He waved his fork for emphasis.

"Whatever difference remains is more than made up for by their numbers and bravery. They have the quality and quantity of men and equipment to push us back until we are fighting in Germany to save our families."

He picked up a forkful of herring and slid it into his mouth, and Lucas had to look away to keep his supper down. Klaus swallowed with minimal chewing. He continued, "Their casualty rate has been four or five times ours, but even that hasn't been enough, and it's not true anymore. They win even if they lose because our intolerance for casualties is our downfall.

"Their T-34 tank is as good as our Panther, and their artillery can shoot as well as ours. But their most significant advantage is that they don't have the same attitude toward their soldiers as we have. They go to war expecting to die, knowing three or four are ready to take their place. If they lose a six-hundred-man battalion, gain a hundred metres and kill two hundred of us, they win. We don't do suicide missions because we know no one will replace us, and we said Auf Wiedersehen, not Leb' Wohl when we left home." Simon looked at Klaus as though he had committed treason but wasn't brave enough to accuse him.

"On the bright side, we are getting twelve new King Tiger tanks next week…they're on a train as I speak, and they are monsters! Speer says that a T-34 can't dent the front or side armour at point-blank range, and the eighty-eight-millimetre gun on the King Tiger will kill any Russian tank or destroyer three kilometres away." He slid another herring fillet between his teeth, chewed twice and swallowed. "If it's as good as they are telling me, most of us would sell our firstborn to ride out the rest of the war in one of those." Klaus repeatedly coughed, each time harder and louder, until a piece of herring flew from his mouth. He picked it up, picked a bone out of the glob, then swallowed the half-chewed mess.

Marcus smiled at his boss, looked at his herring, winced, and put his fork down. He said, "I was sitting in a Tiger I, with the same armour as the King Tiger, when an American Thunderbolt dropped a bomb on us. I can tell you that bombs will kill a Tiger as quickly as they will a Panther. I'm here because I survived, but only the commander and I did, and the commander won't fight again."

Klaus said, "The King Tiger is a different animal, but no tank can take a direct hit from a bomb." He looked longingly at Marcus's herring.

"If you don't want that, I'll eat it." Marcus gladly slid the plate in front of his commander.

◇◇◇◇◇◇◇◇◇◇◇◇◇◇◇◇◇◇◇◇◇◇◇◇◇◇◇

Klaus and his crew helped unload the new King Tigers from the railcars, then drove one to the base. When they reached their destination, they were over their "Tiger envy." The behemoth was slow; its sheer weight made it hard to maneuver. The "don't" list plastered on the bulkhead in front of the driver didn't inspire confidence.

Despite its shortcomings, a tank officer could feel safe in such a monster, and the devastation they could inflict on the enemy was chilling to imagine. Kristian sat in the driver's seat for five minutes after the rest of the crew had left, caressing the steering wheel that replaced the clumsy levers in the Panther.

When he climbed out, the crew crowded around for his assessment. He broke the tension with a smile. "It drives like a Mercedes, and I like the steering wheel, but it has no power and needs a hundred hectares to turn around. When I consider everything, I'm happy to stay in the Panther. If things get hot, a Panther will get you out of there in a hurry, turn on a Groschen and give you change…if you don't break a final drive."

Kristian waved his arm as he spoke. "The King Tiger's high ground pressure will make it useless in the fields unless they're frozen." He shrugged his shoulders. "But despite that, I believe that if we had a couple of thousand of them, we could push the Russians back to Moscow!" He looked at Klaus. "If you ordered them today, what are the chances of getting them before the Russians attack us again?"

Klaus laughed, and no one expected him to answer the question.

Marcus naturally evaluated the King Tiger in terms of its gun, the same as in the Tiger I, but with a longer barrel, making it more accurate. He examined it closely—it had the same sight as the Panther, but the barrel was six metres long and had a hole that looked twice the size of the Panther's gun. He said, "A thousand King Tigers would push the Russians somewhere!" He looked at the Panther sitting beside it and laughed. "The Panther looks like something a man would play with. A

T-34 might even be a better tank than a Panther in some ways—if it had a German crew and a Panther's gun. But the T-34's gun can't hurt the King Tiger unless it hits a track. The Tiger's eighty-eight-millimetre gun will take the T-34 out a kilometre before it can reach us!"

Klaus closely examined the monster tank while his men talked and then took the crew to the Kaserne for a beer. After his third, he silenced the chatter around the table with a gesture.

Klaus had encouraged Lucas to nurse a beer at the Kaserne so he would feel more like one of two-two-seven's crew, but Lucas still hated the taste and welcomed any excuse to put it down. He kept his fingers through the Stein's handle but left it on the table while Klaus talked.

"For those who think this is the Wunderwaffe promised by Hitler, we have twelve King Tigers and a bird told me they can build thirty a month." He looked at Marcus. "How long do you think it will be before we get another nine hundred and eighty-eight Tigers?"

He lifted his beer and noisily sucked the foam from the edges, an irritating habit, but no one wanted to be the one who mentioned it.

Marcus put down his beer after drinking half of it in one go.

"I heard there are more than a hundred Tiger tanks on the Eastern Front—maybe that's why the Russians have stopped."

A tank officer at a nearby table spoke up. "That sounds about right! A hundred Tigers could do a lot of damage!"

Klaus set his beer down but still gripped the handle. "Most of those are the Tiger One and not the King Tiger II. The Tiger I hasn't got a better gun than the Panther, and, as a matter of fact, my 75 mm long-barreled gun can kill a T-34 at a longer range than the old Tiger can."

Lucas was up to date on his tanks and their guns and followed the discussion as it went from tank comparisons to tactics.

Klaus drank another swallow before he went on. "The King Tiger weighs seventy tonnes, and the Panther weighs forty-five with the same tracks, transmission, and engine. Therefore, the Tiger's weight will seriously limit where and how it can operate. Berlin bureaucracy tells us we must conserve fuel for our Panthers and only start the engine to fight! If we have nowhere to sleep except in the tank, we can't run the engine to stay warm! And that begs this question: Where will the fuel for the thirsty Tigers come from if we don't even have enough for our Panthers?"

No one spoke while Klaus drank; they waited in silence.

"The ground is beginning to freeze, and that's a point for the Tiger, but a thaw would make the tank useless. The Russians will attack when they want to and not wait until we can drive a King Tiger on the fields. When they discover how useless the heavy tank is in the mud, they will deliberately attack us when the ground thaws! Their T-34s are much better on soft ground than even the Panther."

The Gestapo would undoubtedly have a set of ears in the room, but Klaus seemed not to care. The packed room appeared to go into shock as Klaus went on.

"What about the engine? It's barely adequate for the Panther, let alone another twenty-five tonnes. If I were driving a T-34, I would get close to the Tiger and keep moving until I could shoot him in the ass—give me a T-34, and I will kill your Tiger!" His audience waited without breathing while Klaus took a long draught of his beer. He wiped his mouth and chin with a napkin, then barged confidently onward.

"I admit that the Tiger II is an excellent gun platform, but we must protect them from the Russian T-34s, their artillery, and their heavy one-oh-five tank destroyers. Our tactics will have to change to take advantage of its gun. Our Panthers must drive on the fields to protect the Tigers' flanks and rear. The Tigers must stay on the roads, frost or no frost, firing beyond what we can reach with a Panther. As they do now, the scouts and Jäger companies will find and range the targets, but they will do it a thousand metres farther out. They will be useful if we adjust to their weaknesses and strengths, but they are no miracle weapon."

Murmurs rumbled from everywhere, and nodding heads all over the dining hall reminded Lucas of the great respect other tank crews held for his commander. He felt a pang of regret that his father could never meet him.

But Klaus's reservations about the new monster tank had planted a seed of doubt. There were days, sometimes several in a row when commanders were forbidden to start their Panthers due to the fuel shortage.

Klaus had openly questioned where the fuel would come from to feed the heavy Tiger, and Lucas wondered if, in a few months, his commander would look back on his clairvoyant remarks with regret.

◇◇◇◇◇◇◇◇◇◇◇◇◇◇◇◇◇◇◇◇◇◇◇◇◇◇

The new King Tigers dominated the conversation on the base for the next few days, and despite Klaus's public doubts, the new Tiger II crews became the subjects of their comrades' envy.

A demonstration of the tank's firepower using a worn-out gutted Panther for target practice stunned the Panther crews. A single shot, directly on the front armour, demolished the tank—pieces of steel flew everywhere. The condemned Panther was less than a hundred metres in front of the audience, and the King Tiger was barely visible behind trees more than a kilometre away, and only if you knew where it was.

Like the rest of 227's crew, Lucas sat on the frozen, snow-covered ground with his hands locked in front of his knees, and the sight of the Panther's destruction made his stomach churn. He wanted to ask questions but feared the answers. If an eighty-eight mm gun would do that much damage, what would the more powerful Russian tank destroyers' one hundred and five mm guns do?

Klaus spoke to his nervous men. "Remember, the Russians don't have the King Tiger: we do, and that's what matters here. We've always had to face artillery shells and tank destroyers with that much power and more—and we've learned that it doesn't matter how much power is in the shell if it doesn't hit you. The Russian guns and tank destroyers can't hit a moving target outside 500 metres; from outside a thousand metres, they seldom hit a stationary target as small as a tank. The reason they miss more often than they hit their target can be summed up in two words... lens quality. Their sights aren't as good as ours."

The men within hearing distance nodded and grunted; a couple of them snapped dry sticks they had in their hands, and others changed positions or stood up.

"The King Tiger crews came from Italy, where they crewed Tiger One panzers, and they are the best in the world. The King Tiger's gun has a six-metre barrel, a metre longer than the Tiger One. With our new high-velocity armour-piercing ammunition, flat trajectory and extreme range, the cannon has given the King Tiger an entirely new set of advantages."

He drained his beer.

"A T-34 at twenty-five hundred metres is about the size of a small bug in our Zeiss sight set at 5X, but the King has more than a fifty percent chance of destroying it with the first shot. On the other hand, the T-34 sight is only 4X, the optics are not as good as ours, the gunner must reset the range before every shot, and the gun and ammunition are not as reliable as ours. It is a fine thing to have the capability of destroying an enemy tank from a distance, but you must hit him before he hits you.

The gun on the King Tiger can destroy a T-34 outside the range of the T-34's gun, but first, he must find the target. That, comrades, is why we will drive ahead of the Tigers. We will contact the enemy, and the Tigers will take them out."

Klaus stood and brushed the dry, frozen snow off his rear end. "These tanks are a fantastic gun platform, but they are not impregnable, and we must protect them. They are heavy and slow—they can't run away as we can—and we can't leave them to defend themselves. From behind, from the side at short range, and in confined spaces, the Russians can kill the King Tiger, and the Russians have artillery and bombs that will destroy any tank!"

The silent men waited; Klaus summed it up:

"Do your best with what you've got; if you do that, we can succeed. Remember this every time you start your Panther—your panzer has the best-trained crew in the world, a Waffen SS crew."

Lucas proudly joined his comrades as they followed Klaus to 227, dreaming of wearing a black uniform with the cool Totenkopf on the sleeves.

◇◇◇◇◇◇◇◇◇◇◇◇◇◇◇◇◇◇◇◇◇◇◇◇◇◇◇◇◇◇◇◇◇◇◇◇◇◇

Klaus insisted on a complete check of the tank every day, and every man had his routine. Kristian checked the oil, started the engine, and checked every joint in the control system. Marcus swung the gun, greased the turning circle, cleaned the sight and examined the barrel. Lucas counted the ammunition, opened and closed the breach, and everyone checked for oil leaks and wiped down every surface in the area where they worked.

Simon ate an apple while he listened to the radio.

The routine took an hour, and Lucas forgot about his unanswered questions.

It took over a month of exercises to bring the new panzers and the men who would command them to battle readiness. Unexpected mechanical problems with the Tigers frustrated the tanks' crews and maintenance personnel. The final drives were no better than those on the Panther, and the undersized engine worked so hard that it was predisposed to overheating, even in sub-freezing weather. The King Tiger couldn't work at full load for more than a few minutes, and the advertised maximum speed was unattainable; the top two gears in the eight-speed transmission were useless unless the Tiger was running downhill.

The only part of the tank that worked perfectly was the gun. It had forty percent more destructive power and a thousand-metre longer range than any other tank gun, and Marcus noted that its turret swung noticeably faster than the Panthers'.

◇◇◇◇◇◇◇◇◇◇◇◇◇◇◇◇◇◇◇◇◇◇◇◇◇◇◇◇◇◇◇◇◇◇

The King Tigers were ready for battle by the middle of December, and with no fuel for further maneuvers, General Nehring parked them beyond the Russian artillery's reach.

Two days after Christmas, the Fourth Panzer Army received orders to prepare for a Russian attack across the Vistula River.

Hitler had ordered General Guderian to set up two defence lines. Unfortunately, he insisted on locating them close enough together that they were both within range of Russian rockets and artillery. The first line, the Grosslinie, was less than five kilometres from the Russian guns and Katya rockets, and the Hauptlinie was ten kilometres from them, still within range of heavy artillery.

Shortly after daylight, a few days later, Klaus had Kristian warm the engine on 227. The rest of the crew, except Simon, checked fluids, cleaned snow and ice out of the tracks, and Simon warmed the radio's tubes by listening to Radio Belgrade until Klaus ordered him to switch to Battle Command.

A few minutes later, Simon called Klaus down to the radio, and the tank commander clamped the headphones on his head. He asked

193

a few questions, his voice rising, and then threw the headphones at Simon without signing off. Simon said goodbye in the prescribed military manner and switched the receiver back to Soldatensender Belgrad.

Lucas had never seen Klaus lose his temper, but now his idol was so angry that Lucas feared him. Klaus climbed past Lucas, pulled himself through the rear hatch and threw his hat off the tank into the snow. He screamed at the trees:

"Verdammt Scheisse! We are the last line of defence between Stalin and Hitler's precious Berlin and that Arschloch has taken the Sixth Panzers to Hungary, including the Tigers! Half of our armour is gone! Is he insane? Guderian and Speer know better—hell, my wife knows better, and she's never had a serious argument—can't they reason with him? What the fuck does Hitler know about tank tactics?—we didn't even have tanks in the war he said he fought in! He was a damned corporal in the Great War, and the fucker thinks like a private! I've lost everyone—my parents, my wife, and my brother in his Scheisskrieg… that Sheisskopf doesn't give a shit about anyone but himself!"

Klaus sat down on the edge of his cupola and hung his head. The Panther's engine idled at 2,000 rpm to charge the batteries and warm the oil, creating a lot of noise in the steel cocoon and when Lucas climbed out of the rear hatch and sat on the rump close to Klaus, he was shocked to hear what could only be sobs.

The men, their chores finished, sat on the turret and rump, on steel warmed by the sun and the engine's heat. They looked away, at anything to keep from looking at their commander. Lucas dared breathe only hard enough to keep himself alive.

Klaus slid to the ground—Kristian climbed into the tank and shut off the warm engine. The rest of Klaus's crew retreated to the canvas lean-to camouflaged with spruce branches that had been their home for the past week.

A fire far enough in front of the shelter that the smoke could rise unimpeded radiated enough heat to keep the occupants warm. Sometimes, when the wind eddied in the wrong direction, the smoke forced them to retreat outside to cough the smoke out of their lungs and have a cigarette.

No one spoke as Klaus swore and threw whatever was loose back and forth across their living space. Lucas sat on his groundsheet, pulled his knees up to his chin and didn't move.

◇◇◇◇◇◇◇◇◇◇◇◇◇◇◇◇◇◇◇◇◇◇◇◇◇◇◇◇◇◇◇

Panzer 227, as part of the 4th Panzer Army, Panzer Corps XXIV, faced the bridgehead at Baranòw-Sandomierski as part of the Hauptkampflinie, the last line of defence. General Nehring had stretched the defence line that he was to defend back from ten to twenty kilometres from the Russian guns, and his main force safely waited there for the Russians. But he had positioned Klaus's 227 and a squadron of eight Panthers at a point slightly over ten kilometres from the bridgehead, not where Hitler's minions or Russian intelligence thought they would be.

Klaus's camouflaged Panthers waited in the forest—daily sorties by Russian tank-killer aircraft flew unchallenged, and a tank in the open had a short shelf life.

The crews settled into a routine of waiting, and with idle time and an artist's imagination, Lucas tried to imagine what the attack would look like. He pictured masses of Russian tanks and men charging across a field, the tanks firing, the men shouting their war cry as they ran through the snow. But then, Lucas decided that even the Russians described by Goebbels wouldn't be so foolish—Lucas knew what the guns on a Panther could do.

He tried to imagine the enemy scouts and hunters, similar to German Jäger companies that tormented the enemy, but he had never seen or heard of Russians behind their lines. He had seen a German Jäger company patrolling the woods near them because they sometimes met with Klaus, but he had never heard a shot fired.

The Jäger company commander met Klaus every two or three days, but none of the other crews had seen him. He and his men, dressed in white camouflage, were like ghosts; they disappeared and appeared unexpectedly out of the snowy nothingness, and Lucas decided he would not want Jäger soldiers hunting for him.

Chapter Twenty-one

Winter 1945

Beware the Sleeping Bear

When the bear wakes up, you had better have a plan.

The Author

W HEN THE SQUADRON FINISHED CHECKING the Panthers' camouflage of spruce boughs and white-painted canvas, Klaus gathered them together under the large tarpaulin covering 227's shelter. Closed on three sides and surrounded by tall spruce trees, it offered protection from the wind. The imminent battle meant fires were only allowed inside the lean-to, where they generated as much smoke as heat. Tarpaulins draped from the lean-to over the panzer's rump directed some heat to the engine, keeping it ready to start.

On the first day of January, the men got out of their sleeping bags an hour before dawn as usual, wished one another frohes neues Jahr and made the fires. As soon as the heat warmed the Panthers' engine, the driver started it, and the rest of the crew went through their checklist.

With checklists complete and engines warm, Klaus ordered all the engines shut off. The cold morning cooled the steel tank's interior in minutes, and the crew left for the shelter of the smokey lean-tos.

Klaus called his tank commanders to 227's lean-to and spoke to them as they crowded together under the tarpaulin shelter. Thirty-two of their cold and impatient men stood outside, stamping their cold feet, trying to hear what Klaus said.

"The scouts say the Russians will attack in the next few days, and if they follow the usual routine, probably before sunrise. They will begin the artillery barrage sometime between four and six, hitting the

Grosskampflinie forces closest to them first. They will hit the Haupt-kampflinie with the heavy guns just before daylight, and then they will advance." He looked around the group of faces and stopped on Lucas, who stood in a corner. "We will get up at four every day until they attack, warm up the engines and stay close to our tanks for the rest of the day."

Klaus spoke while watching the men's faces.

"As soon as it's light on the day they attack, the Russians will send out a probe of tanks and infantry, and we will ambush them. The Jäger company will set up the trap—I will coordinate with their Leutnant. Our objective is to wipe out the Russians as quickly and completely as possible so that the entire force disappears. The main Russian attack will then hesitate while they try to figure out what happened. They won't dare advance in great numbers until they know what we have. They will probably send out another probing force, giving us time to consolidate our defences based on what the Russians have done up to that point."

Klaus paused, leaving an opportunity for questions, and a tank commander grabbed it. "How many tanks will they have? What is a 'probe' in Russian terms? I came here from Italy a month ago, and the Americans always bombed from the air and then hit us with artillery before they attacked. There were no probes, just brute force!"

The worried men had all heard the "more than a million men, thousands of tanks, thousands of artillery" rumours. Klaus decided to explain the Russian strategy to the newbies and refresh it for those who had been fighting Russians for a few years.

"Ever since Stalingrad, the Russians have sent expeditionary forces to find out where and how strong we are. To accomplish that, they typically send between twenty and thirty T-34s and a hundred to three hundred infantry to test us, then run away if they can. If we can prevent that—if the force doesn't return or have time to send a message—if it disappears, the probe's purpose is moot. The main force will advance slower with little or no information, and they will be more tentative." He paused for effect. "Caution never wins the day, but when you don't know how hot or cold the water is and can't test it with your finger, you get into it slowly."

Lucas tried to sort out the inference, and Marcus voiced it.

"So, there will be no survivors?"

Klaus wagged his head. "Probably not. We are a mobile strike force, and we need to move fast. We can't handle prisoners, so the answer to the question is ultimately up to the infantry."

Lucas tried to imagine the alternatives; he could only imagine one, and it made him sick.

◇◇◇◇◇◇◇◇◇◇◇◇◇◇◇◇◇◇◇◇◇◇◇◇◇◇◇◇◇◇◇◇◇◇◇◇

It was always cold in the Polish winter at four in the morning. On the twelfth of January, the stars seemed so close Lucas had the strange feeling he could touch them, but the air outside his goose-down-filled sleeping bag was so cold he wasn't going to put an arm outside to try. He felt guilty, pretending he was asleep while Marcus started a fire with a cupful of gasoline and an armful of dry branches broken off nearby trees. When the flames began to crackle, Lucas crawled out of the bag and crouched beside him.

Despite burning eyes and choking smoke, the tank's crew spent every morning under the lean-to tarp tied to two-two-seven's rump. Despite the fire, the cold seeped through Lucas's heavy woollen clothing and thick double layers of mittens and socks. He decided he needed to move, picked up a burning lantern and started into the forest to gather wood to feed the fire.

Klaus waved his hand at him. "Hold up. I'll go with you."

Lucas slowed, held up the lantern and asked him, "When do you think the Russians will attack?" He shook the snow from a branch and held onto it while Klaus passed him. Klaus stopped beside Lucas and answered, "They will have to attack soon or wait until after the thaw—it always thaws sometime in January."

"What will it be like?" Lucas set the lantern in the snow, broke off a few dry lower branches from a spruce tree and jammed them under his arm.

"I can't explain an artillery bombardment with words; no one has invented any that would describe it."

"Do you mean the noise?" Lucas continued to break off the branches he could reach.

"Noise?" Klaus laughed. "Yes, but I can describe that. It's so loud you can't hear a man yelling in your ear. The sound is like a hard wall pushing against you; it hurts your eardrums, and I'm talking about real pain! Use the strips of cloth you are supposed to always have with you. Stuff them tight in your ears!

"Yes, I use them whenever I'm loading the gun."

Lucas noted that Klaus had only collected two small sticks. He watched his boss and mentor wind a branch in a circle—it was too green to break. Lucas wanted to tell him it wouldn't give any heat, only smoke, but held his tongue.

"Trees will fall…huge sharp splinters will split from them and fly around, killing men who aren't protected. Men will die all around you, some blasted into pieces too small to find, others without a mark on them. If a 105 mm shell hits our tank, we will all instantly die. Soldiers outside our tank will be wounded or killed if a shell lands within ten metres of them. Even if they are in a deep hole, they can die from the concussion if a shell lands within three metres of them."

Klaus finally broke off the branch, leaving a stringy strip of wood fastened to the tree. He added it to his meagre harvest and looked at Lucas while he spoke. "The rumours are true; the Russians have more than a thousand guns aimed at our men and tanks, perhaps several thousand. They know where our lines are, and on a clear day, like today, they will have hundreds, maybe a thousand aircraft flying over the battlefield." He looked at Lucas exactly as Lucas remembered his father looking at him when he wanted to calm him. "But they don't know where my tanks are." He pointed a stick in the general direction of the panzers. "The Russians won't find us until we want them to, and then we will kill them."

Klaus broke off a dry branch and spoke toward the tree. "Lucas, you don't belong here—you should be home with your girlfriend. But now I need you to do things that aren't natural to you and which you may consider wrong. You must leave the boy behind and become a man."

"How do you know I have a girlfriend?" Lucas smiled self-consciously.

Klaus turned around, an expression on his face Lucas had seen a thousand times before the bomb had killed his family.

"Because you never laugh at Simon's stupid jokes about women. You must like her a lot."

"Yes, I like her, but I don't know if I could live with her."

"An independent woman, or a mean one?"

Lucas laughed and turned toward the fire with his arms full of wood, the lantern dangling from a spare finger.

"If Corinne were here, she would be worth five men. She's smart, strong, and takes control, whether you want her to or not."

Klaus followed Lucas back in the tracks they had made into the woods.

"So why do you love this aggressive woman?"

"I didn't say I love her; I said I like her…."

"It's the same thing to a woman." Klaus interrupted, but Lucas kept the thought going.

"I like her because she has a warm heart and tenderness when she should be tender, but you cross her at your peril. Most of all, I like that she's honest."

"The perfect woman, as long as you intend to behave; the worst possible if you don't." Klaus smiled at Lucas's back.

"I will behave if I get home again." Lucas thought about it and decided he did love Corinne.

Lucas let Klaus pass him; Klaus slowed when he was alongside and looked into Lucas's eyes. "If you get a chance to grow up before the Russians kill you, she will love you too, and I'm betting that you will be a happy man." Klaus Paused, and Lucas waited. He guessed he was about to hear why Klaus went to get wood with him.

"This battle will be noisy and violent, but I guarantee that if you do your job, you will have a better chance to make it, and so will I. General Nehring is a 'hit-and-run' fighter; he will let us hit them and run away; we will never stand and fight until we die!

"I don't expect you not to be afraid—all of us are scared—but we must concentrate and do our job flawlessly!" He put his hand on Lucas's shoulder. "Two-two-seven is just a heavy piece of junk without the gunner and loader. You must do this as Max taught you, Lucas—you are still a child, but many lives depend on you!"

Thinking his mentor was done, Lucas got a slight sound out before Klaus cut him off.

"You will want to quit—you will want to hesitate to kill, but remember Max and how you fought! You shot everything that moved, and I need that again, Lucas, not the Kindersoldat you were a few months ago."

Lucas put his mittened hand on Klaus's. "Yes, sir, I will fight like the devil…I won't let you down."

Klaus hesitated, thinking before he said, "Remember that you are a man now—you are a good man—and it's not normal for a good man to kill other men. But you must not hesitate to do your duty for a second, or we will all die!"

Lucas added his wood to the pile gathered by the others, then sat on a log they had made into a bench. The fire was warm; radiant heat caught and held by the tarpaulin was enough to make them comfortable. Unfortunately, the smoke trapped in the tarp made it impossible to stay there for long periods. Lucas squeezed his eyes almost shut to keep them from watering and closed them when he didn't need to see anything. He slid down to sit on the ground, hoping the smoke was less there, put his sleeve against his face and breathed through it.

Simon opened his pack and pulled out canned army Wurst, bread, and boiled eggs. Kristian pushed a tin pot half full of water into the side of the fire, and in minutes, the water began to boil. When Kristian added a handful of black tea to the tumbling water, Klaus cringed.

Lucas looked at his watch, noted it was only twenty-five minutes before five, and wound it. He tapped the face, and the minute hand moved forward slightly. The dark morning before dawn passed slower than any part of the day. Lucas's brain told him that if it was dark, he should sleep. He had heard the war stories, the women stories, and the gripes his comrades kept in their memory banks. Even though the best storytellers added colour with each repetition, he found it increasingly difficult to pretend he was interested.

A twisted, nervous knot in his stomach occupied his attention, and he avoided talking. He didn't speak, convinced he was a coward and afraid his voice would break if he tried to join the crew's banter. He sensed that his comrades were looking for a reason to laugh, a distraction, and Lucas didn't want to be the one to fulfill that need. Kristian poured acidified tea into Lucas's cup and smiled at him. He said, "Don't worry, Junge, you will be fine!"

The high-pitched sound of air squeezing through a hole pierced the darkness, bringing Klaus to his feet—Lucas thought of a cross between a flute and an Oboe and guessed the note was an 'A' played by the Katya rockets he had heard about—someone long ago had nicknamed them Stalin's Organ. Within seconds, a wall of explosions between the Panthers and the river shook the ground, not quite drowning out the frightening screams of the next round of rockets.

"Katyas!" Klaus yelled above the racket and stood up. "They're hitting the Forty-eighth Panzers and our infantry. The guns will fire next, and then the Russian armour and infantry will move." He looked at Kristian, then Simon. "I want to get the engine started before I call headquarters."

Lucas gladly dumped the acidic tea out of his tin cup and was first on the tank, spurred on by the screaming rockets and explosions. He opened the rear hatch and barely heard Klaus yell his name over the racket. He looked back; Klaus was the only man standing up, and he was looking at him. The others were gathering the food and pouring tea into their canteens. With a smile, Klaus held up the flask Lucas had left behind and yelled, "Lucas, check the oil before you go inside. I'll fill your flask with tea."

Lucas closed the hatch cover and opened the engine's access door, controlling the urge to run. He pulled out the dipstick—the oil level was above the full mark by a millimetre. He looked at Klaus and yelled, "It's okay," then fumbled around in the dark, looking for the dipstick hole, finally using his fingers to feel for it.

Marcus laughed and shouted, "Do you want me to come up there and show you how to find a hole in the dark?" and Simon called out, "I can see why you're still a virgin, Lucas! But don't give up hope; Marcus has an ugly sister you can practice on." The men roared—Lucas thankfully found the hole and thrust the metal stick into its place.

"Make sure you've got it in as far as it will go!" Marcus laughed again.

"If your stick is too short, I can help!" Kristian laughed hard at his joke, but the exchange was losing its charm when Klaus said, "Check the coolant." breaking up the torment with his tone. He had his hands full and his foot on the wooden block they used as the first step.

Lucas loosened the cover and used his finger to verify that the coolant was near the top. He reinstalled the cap, checked to be sure he had it tight, double-checked that the dipstick was solidly into its seat, and closed the access door.

Just as Lucas opened the hatch, a sharper, continuous roar joined the organ, a sound that could only be artillery—with so many cannons firing that their explosions overlapped. Screams sliced through the wall of sound; hundreds of shells cut the cold air at a thousand metres a second, a soprano descant to the Stalin's organ contralto of the rockets and the low-pitched bass notes of the artillery. Lucas fought to prevent weakness from overwhelming him; he had to force himself to move. His chest tightened—he wondered if fear could kill him—if the horrible symphony would end his life.

Klaus yelled, "Don't worry, Lucas, they're firing at Nehring's fake headquarters." He turned to Kristian. "Start the engine and check everything. As soon as it's light, they'll have their tanks moving, and we have an appointment to meet them in a field northeast of here."

The Russian maps showed XXIV Panzer Corps's battle headquarters two kilometres from where 227 was preparing for a fight. Russian artillery shells rained down in torrents on a hundred empty tents that the Russians believed were home to five thousand German soldiers. Klaus smiled as he lifted the hatch on his cupola and said to himself, loud enough that Lucas's young ears heard, "So far, so good."

Just before closing the hatch, Lucas paused to look at the bright orange explosions creeping across the north and eastern horizons. German artillery well beyond the Panthers had begun returning fire, and as their shells passed overhead on their way to the Russian guns, the screams added a higher descant to the awful symphony.

The engine sputtered and kicked, and the batteries began to die, but just before their death, the engine caught on what sounded like a single cylinder, then two, and then the rest of them fired, one after the other, until all twelve had cleared their throats. The seven hundred horsepower V12 engine ran smoothly; the transmission whined, protesting—heavy cold oil offered little protection for the hardened steel gears and bearings.

The radio tubes warmed, and Simon called battle headquarters. A few minutes later, he handed division HQ's coded instructions to two-two-seven's commander, and he read them while Kristian coaxed the cold tank out of the woods. Klaus read what he had expected—he would take his two panzer platoons and join a company of Jäger infantry south of their position.

The tanks moved slowly, avoiding sharp turns and using only enough power to turn the tracks. Two-two-seven crawled out into the open—First and Second platoon's tanks forming a jagged line behind it.

They hugged the treeline as they drove east toward the Russian guns and the strategically vacant Hauptkampflinie.

An hour later, the panthers stopped, and a Jäger company of white camouflaged soldiers joined them. Half of the infantry climbed on the panzers, almost invisible on the white canvas and tree branches they used for camouflage. When the Leutnant in charge of the Jäger force climbed up to Klaus's cupola, Lucas took the rags out of his ears. Without them, he could hear the Leutnant through the open hatches.

Lucas heard the leutnant say that the Jäger scouts had located a force of twenty Russian tanks, two tank destroyers, and infantry already past the Forty-eighth Panzer and Sixty-Eighth Infantry lines and headed for what the Russians thought was the last German line of defence. He said the first line of German defence was no more, and the probe would test the second line.

The Leutnant assured Klaus that his men had dealt with all the Russian scouts in the area, and Lucas assumed that meant the Russian scouts were dead. As the Jäger spoke, his bearded face looked past Klaus at Lucas sitting in the loader seat. He obviously thought Lucas couldn't hear him over the engine, the whining transmission gears and the clattering tracks, but there were no clattering tracks inside the tank, and most of the engine noise went out through the exhaust. With his face turned toward Lucas, the Jäger's voice carried better than the Leutnant knew. Lucas was careful not to look at him or react as he spoke; he focused on the shells in the ring and listened.

The Leutnant asked, "Is the Waffen SS stealing children now? He looks as though he would have trouble lifting a dinner fork!" Lucas fought the urge to respond, forcing his eyes to look at the turret's floor.

Klaus's response neutralized Lucas's anger.

"Don't worry about him; he can load and shoot as well as any man I've ever seen."

Lucas smiled at the floor; his anger and half of his fear disappeared. He wondered, ...As well as any man he's ever seen? As well as Max? Marcus?...

"How old is he?" The Leutnant scoffed as he asked the question.

"Seventeen…well…he might still be sixteen…and you're right, he is too young to play soldier."

Lucas wanted to yell: You just said I was as good as any man you've seen! But he didn't want to give himself away. He pretended to be interested in a shell lying in the turret ring, scrutinized it, and checked that it was secured. He could see the bearded face in his peripheral.

"So are we all, but he is a child—one of Hitler's Kindersoldaten." The Leutnant's words reeked of frustration. "Our replacements are either children or old men…the bottom of the barrel! When the children are gone, who will Hitler send—their mothers?"

Lucas bristled, but his demeanour didn't change. A child soldier? Me, a child soldier? It was all he could do to keep his mouth shut. He touched one shell after another as though counting them.

The face disappeared, and Lucas relaxed and sat in silence, fighting the disappointment that had displaced his fear. He resolved to prove himself, preferably by killing half the Russian Army. Five minutes ago, Lucas had been terrified that he would freeze when it was time to load the gun. But the Leutnant had wakened a determination in him to show everyone that Lucas Schwartz was one of the best soldiers in the Waffen SS. Lucas committed himself to earning the black uniform, the tattoo, and the Totenköpfe. He would prove that he was worthy!

Lucas turned to the rear hatch and watched the Leutnant slog through the snow. He turned around and shouted something at Klaus—Klaus's tone was a little miffed when he replied. As Lucas watched the white figure's shadow doggedly trudge through snow halfway to his knees, he realized that his fear was now nothing more than nervous anxiety that his performance might not equal his expectations. Lucas told himself his skills were equal or superior to any man in the Panther except Klaus. He repeated to himself: Klaus said I can shoot better than Marcus or Max! When he examined the idea, he decided that he believed it.

✧✧✧✧✧✧✧✧✧✧✧✧✧✧✧✧✧✧✧✧✧✧✧✧✧✧✧✧✧✧

The exact location of the XXIV Panzer Corps' tanks and infantry was unknown to everyone except the tank commanders and General Nehring. Klaus silently congratulated his wise general whenever a Russian plane flew over. The only explanation that Klaus could find for previous bad experiences was that the Russians knew his orders and position. Because it happened too frequently to be a coincidence, Klaus's operational assumption was that the Russians intercepted every message he heard or read. As he decoded his orders, he sometimes felt that the Russians had already read them, and Nehring was the first commander who agreed with him. But today, based on false information, Russian Intelligence would believe they knew where Nehring's forces waited for them, but they would be wrong!

With mounting evidence since Stalingrad, Klaus had operated with the assumption that the Russians not only knew his orders but were also listening to everything he said on the radio. He had no idea how radio worked but figured they didn't call it 'broadcasting' without good reason. Consequently, Klaus kept radio chatter, even coded messages, to a minimum. Using what he thought the Russians knew, he had set successful traps and escaped from situations he had accurately predicted.

Klaus hated surprises; his world was well organized and predictable, and God had cut his Jäger friend from the same bolt of cloth. A veteran of the Sixth Army in Stalingrad, Leutnant Johann Finke liked to hunt Russians and was better at it than any other Jäger commander in the Wehrmacht. Finke hated radios and codes as much as Klaus did, and when he could, he climbed up on the tank to speak directly to the commander.

Finke's Company set off at a trot, split into two groups, and headed for the trees along the sides of the killing field. Klaus called on the intercom, "Simon, tell the other tank commanders to come to see me as soon as we stop; Kristian, stop the tank on the rise about a hundred metres ahead of us.

Chapter Twenty-two

12 January 1945

Cement Bombers

"I will only show mercy to the man who has shown mercy to me..." is the formula for a massacre.

The Author

The big Russian guns fired until the darkness retreated, and half an hour later, the Russian tanks arrived. The gray pre-dawn light starkly outlined their unmistakable shapes against the intense white covering the ground. Half the infantry waded through deep snow beside the slow-moving tanks and tank destroyers while the lucky ones rode on them. The T-34s formed a protective circle around two 105 mm tank destroyers, like an elephant herd protecting its vulnerable members. Klaus watched them through his "Donkey Ears" binoculars and noted the diminishing distance to the Russian tank he had chosen as 227's target. Klaus waited for the promised German artillery to fire—the signal for his Panthers to pounce.

Positioned in front of a barn, with his most trusted tank commander fifteen metres to his right, the unobstructed path to the slow-moving target meant that the T-34 would certainly die when Marcus fired. Two-two-seven was above the Russians and 500 metres from the centre of the killing field. Another barn 300 metres to the left shadowed two more Panthers, and the Russians passed four panzers—two that waited in the woods on each side of the ambush, along with a company of the deadliest soldiers and machine guns the Wehrmacht had. German artillery, sighted on a spot ahead of the Russians, completed the mantle of overwhelming power that would fall on the killing field.

When the first Russian tanks had passed the ambush point by a hundred metres, a German 88 mm gun two kilometres away fired. The sound didn't arrive until six seconds later, a second after an explosion of dirt a hundred metres in front of the lead Russian. Two seconds later, the scream of air parted by supersonic shells joined in the mêlée as ten 88 mm cannon shells landed in the huddle of Russian tanks. Most of the T-34s stopped, but a few turned toward the trees.

The next volley landed among the stationary T-34s, destroying three of them, throwing men in the air, and leaving Klaus's Panthers with seventeen confused tanks' soft sides as targets. Eight Panthers' guns hit eight T-34s, mortally wounding all of them. Artillery shells scored hits on two more as the infantry broke for the trees, but a steady rain of artillery, tank, and machine-gun fire cut them down before they had gone more than a few metres in the deep snow.

◇◇◇◇◇◇◇◇◇◇◇◇◇◇◇◇◇◇◇◇◇◇◇◇◇◇◇◇◇

Lucas had a shell in his hands when Marcus fired the cannon at the first target; he was breathing fast, mouth open wide when Marcus fired, and he rammed it into the barrel and slammed the breech shut. A shot from a tank destroyer struck the ground in front of 227, shaking it like a dirty rag. Marcus swore, then fired; Lucas reloaded, panting, hyperventilating, too busy to be frightened.

It would only take a small mistake, a shell dropped on its point, the breech not completely closed, a hand in the wrong place when the gun fired, and they would die in a flash of heat and light. Lucas moved his body precisely as Max had trained it—with smooth, skilful motions—a ballet inside a steel box where a clumsy mistake would kill five men.

He slid a shell into the chamber, slammed the breech, picked another out of the rack as the gun fired. He repeated the maneuver... Be careful, but move fast...don't bang the tip and kill everyone. The breech had to close and lock on the first try, or the recoil would drive it and the casing back, cutting off his legs. The gun fired; Russians died. Better them than me!

Lucas loaded his twentieth shell, but Klaus called a halt before the gun fired. Simon passed cannon ammunition to Lucas, who filled the empty, easy-to-reach bins. Sporadic bursts of rifle and machine-gun-fire continued as Lucas loaded the ring, and then, nothing. He had laid the last round in the ring when Klaus spoke quietly into the intercom.

"It's over. Everyone out."

Lucas swung the rear hatch open—he faced a wall of barn boards. He climbed onto the rump and stood up to see over the turret. Sudden tears streamed down his cheeks as though a dam had broken, and his jaw dropped to his neck.

Simon and Kristian followed Marcus out of the rear hatch to stand on the rump beside Lucas. Klaus still sat on his elevated commander's seat with his head above the cupola's open rim. Lucas wiped his face with his sleeve and lowered himself to one knee.

Bodies covered the field; frozen blood soaked the snow. Lucas had to fight the urge to throw up as his mind tried to imagine what had happened in less than five minutes. This was not how war was supposed to be; this was a massacre! He had loaded the shells; how many men lying in the snow were victims of those shells? He tried to imagine being on the other side, desperately trying to escape, but his mind wouldn't permit it.

Lucas remembered that Klaus had not allowed him to see the men he had killed in his first action, and Max's death had justified the fight. But as Lucas watched soldiers in white camouflage walk past hundreds of Russian soldiers lying in the snow, their dark red blood blotches on the white blanket, he felt a pang of intense guilt. None of the Russians had escaped, and none had lived long enough to fight.

Those men had been alive three or four minutes ago, joking about their girlfriends and quietly talking about their home, their sisters and their mothers. Now, they lay in a bloody swath from the tanks to the trees; none of them moved. Blood draining from their wounds soaked the snow around them.

The Jäger Company walked among the Russian soldiers, occasionally kicking one, sometimes firing a shot, then moving on, examining every soldier.

Not one Russian tank moved—most were smoking hulks. A dozen Jäger soldiers went from one to another, dropping grenades in the hatches of the T-34s that weren't burning.

Klaus ordered everyone back in the tank, and Lucas followed

Simon through the hatch, returning to his windowless burrow. Marcus closed the heavy plate and eased past him to the gunner's seat.

Marcus said, "Those Jäger bastards are an efficient bunch," as he pushed Klaus's right foot to the only place it could fit. "I've seen some messes, but that's the worst. Those men didn't have a chance!"

Lucas said, "I killed Russian soldiers when they killed Max, but it wasn't like this. They fought back, and I didn't kill wounded men...." He suddenly remembered gunning down the fleeing commander of a T-34 tank crew but pushed it aside.

Marcus didn't speak for a moment, turned to look at Lucas and said, "I heard about that, and I'm willing to bet everything I have that you didn't give any of those men a chance! You killed them as fast as you could, and if they tried to run away, you shot them in the back... am I right?"

The picture of the Russian tank commander running from his burning T-34 flashed back into Lucas's memory.

Marcus nodded and said, "I see that you did shoot at least one man in the back." He looked through his sight as the Panther began to move.

"It seems there has to be a little of the murderer in all of us, or we wouldn't survive. If we start thinking of our enemy as someone like us, we will all die, but don't we all know that the Russian soldier is at least our equal?"

<hr>

Klaus ordered his tanks to the trees on the north side of the field, where he met with the Jäger Leutnant. They spoke for five minutes but were far enough from the tank that Lucas couldn't hear. When Klaus climbed into his cupola and used the intercom to tell Kristian to go ahead, his voice was nervous, and Lucas couldn't help but wonder why.

At ten o'clock, the big Russian guns targetted the Fourth Army's artillery and the imaginary second line of defence, and the German artillery retaliated. Cannon shells screeched overhead on their way to one side or the other as Klaus's Panzer 227 led the squadron along the edge of a forest. The Jäger infantry stayed off the tanks, choosing to walk in the woods where the trees sheltered them from prying eyes and where the snow wasn't as deep. The tanks stayed as close to the forest's edge as possible, brushing the tree branches, stopping or driving into openings when spotters heard or saw aircraft. In the trees' shadows, a stationary camouflaged tank was difficult, usually impossible to find from the air. A moving panzer in the open, camouflaged or not, triggered something in the observer's brain, and the story usually ended badly for the panzer.

It was almost noon when Klaus parked his squadron in the shelter of thick spruce woods. Opposite the tanks, 300 metres from the edge of the forest, a creek had sluiced a deep gully out of the flat land, cutting a 50-hectare field in half. It was a perfect place for another massacre.

When the Russian artillery stopped firing, none of the Russian rounds had landed within a kilometre of Klaus's Panthers, a sure sign that the Russians hadn't yet found the panzer squadron. Their air reconnaissance would have located the missing probing force, and it was only a matter of time before a second probe came looking for them with murder on their minds and in their hearts.

Klaus said into the intercom, "This is where we wait for the Russians. Kristian—shut off the engine, and Simon, tell the rest of the squadron to do the same. Find someplace comfortable and relax...it could be a while." He paused with the intercom switch on, then said, "It won't be so easy this time!"

Marcus stayed in his slightly comfortable seat, but Klaus slid down the front and went behind a tree. Lucas couldn't sleep in the turret with its cold steel lumps and projections everywhere, so he opened the rear hatch, slid out and sat on the edge of the turret with his feet on the still-warm plates over the engine.

"Are you thinking about your girlfriend?" Klaus, buttoning his fly, walked to the side of the tank, crunching the snow with every step. He stopped beside the sprocket and checked the shaft seal, his head opposite Lucas.

Lucas said, "No, I was thinking about the Jäger soldiers killing those men. Why couldn't we have taken them as prisoners? They shot wounded men and..."

Klaus interrupted... "I watched you shoot men like rabbits, and I didn't hear any remorse afterward. Where was your pity for those men? And what about Max?"

Klaus drew on his fresh-rolled cigarette, took it out of his mouth, picked an errant piece of tobacco off his tongue, and returned the cigarette. He puffed on it for a few seconds, then put it between his fingers and pointed his hand toward Lucas.

"If you are going to feel sorry for the Russians, what are you doing in my tank?"

"But it's wrong to kill wounded men!" Lucas raised his voice unintentionally.

"It's okay if they're not wounded? I don't see the difference. If I were wounded, in pain, maybe with my balls shot off, I would pay you to shoot me!" Klaus looked around at his tanks, and Lucas suspected he was making plans.

Klaus put his hand on Lucas's leg and looked into his eyes.

"We are waiting here for Russian men with guns and tanks. They will outnumber us, and if we lose, they won't take any prisoners. If we win, what can we do with prisoners? Think about it, then tell me whether you want to warn them."

Lucas was losing the battle against Klaus's logic. But he instinctively knew there was something wrong with it.

"I just want to go home where there are no Russians."

"If we go home now, the Russians will follow us, and they will have a good time with your mother and girlfriend…I assure you that it's better to fight them here." He patted his hand on Lucas's leg. "Do you have a sister?"

Lucas shook his head. "No, sir, a British bomb killed my parents and my sister in Dortmund. My grandmother and my aunt died with them. I was playing the violin at a friend's house when the bombers came." He swallowed a lump in his throat, but a sound escaped.

Klaus pulled the last millimetre on his cigarette, then threw it in the snow when it burned his finger. He was silent for what seemed like a long time and then said, "So, that's why I won't have to write to your parents…" He looked up at Lucas. "Who should I write to?"

"I have a letter in my pocket. You can write to the people in the letter." He stamped his feet on the steel plate to warm them, and Klaus said nothing.

Lucas looked at his Wehrmacht boots and wiggled his toes. "There is no one else."

Klaus squeezed Lucas's shin and walked away.

A continuous stream of aircraft flew back and forth, mostly Ilyushin IL-2 Sturmovik, flying tank destroyers. Occasionally, one dropped down to fire at something nowhere near where Klaus's unit waited in the shelter of trees, but Lucas noted that Klaus was nervous every time one deviated from a straight line.

An hour later, the Jäger Leutnant's Demag returned from dropping off wounded soldiers, and Klaus had a heated discussion with the Jäger Leutnant. After much arm-waving, the Leutnant and four soldiers drove away to the northwest in the Demag.

Klaus called his tank commanders together and, following a short discussion, sent them to their Panthers. A few minutes later, eight Panthers' engines ran on fast idle, warming up for the coming battle.

Lucas's loader position got heat before anyone else in the tank, and he closed the rear hatch to hold it in. Fifteen minutes later, dozing in the warm turret, he woke when Klaus ordered Kristian to shut down the engine. When the temperature inside became colder than outside in the January sun, Marcus and Lucas joined Simon and Kristian outside, where they lounged on the warm steel like a bunch of cats.

Klaus had disappeared, and Lucas looked for him through eyes closed to slits to protect themselves from the light bouncing off the dry snow. The Demag had returned, and he found Klaus on its running board talking to the Leutnant. Four of the eight Panthers had vanished; tracks along the forest's edge disappeared to the northwest.

The Jäger soldiers spread out over a two hundred metre stretch of forest, stationed between the four Panthers on a line behind them. Even though he knew dozens of soldiers were there, Lucas could only find a few of them dressed in their white camouflage. Klaus climbed on the tank and reported that the Russians would arrive in less than half an hour.

Marcus asked, "Do we only have four Panthers? How many Russian tanks are coming?" Klaus smiled and said, "Look carefully across the field at the gully, and you will find the four missing Panthers—and we have another surprise for the Russians—a dozen eighty-eights are sighted on the field."

Lucas shaded his eyes and squinted. One after another, he picked out the tanks, with only their camouflaged turrets and guns exposed above the gully's rim.

"We will let the Russians get slightly ahead of us before we fire, giving them nowhere to retreat."

Simon said, "I'm glad I work for you and not the Russians..."

The Russians were on time; Lucas could hear their loud diesels and clattering tracks over 227's smoothly idling engine. He pulled a shell out of the awkward side bin and knelt beside the breech with it on his knee. Marcus grinned his approval.

Klaus spoke quietly through the intercom: "I can see about five hundred soldiers. Simon—hose them when the first artillery shell explodes, and Marcus, pick the last tank on this side of the field and hit him just below the turret. Your next target is the tank in front of him. The tanks hiding in the gully will take the lead Russians, and the artillery will pound the center. After that, we will shoot anything that moves!"

A few minutes passed before a single shot from a German cannon landed in the field. The explosion rocked 227, and Marcus fired as Simon's machine gun chattered. Lucas slid the round from his knee into the barrel and slammed the breech. Marcus fired again, accompanied by the muffled ripping-cloth sound of the MG-41 "Hitler's Saws," machine guns of the Jäger Company. The Panther shook from the explosions of German 88 and 105 mm artillery shells landing among the Russians over a hundred metres away!

A Russian shell exploded against 227's front armour—Lucas lost his balance and almost dropped the round in his hand. Even over the continuous explosions of battle and despite the cloth stuffed tightly in Lucas's ears, the sound was painfully loud.

He rammed the shell home, closed the breech and reached for another in the bins at his feet. He repeated the act five more times before Marcus stopped pulling the trigger.

"Stop firing!" Klaus ordered his squadron through the radio. Lucas slid the round in his hand into the barrel and slammed the breech home. A moment later, the artillery ceased firing, and a sudden silence fell on the battlefield like a heavy curtain. Marcus kept his eye in the gunsight and his foot on the swing pedal.

Lucas looked through his periscope to see what was going on, and despite the limited field of view, he could see men standing in the snow, scattered among broken tanks and a smashed tank destroyer. They optimistically had their hands up as Jäger soldiers walked toward them. Lucas's heart jumped when other Jägers went to the T-34s and let the crews crawl out before they dropped grenades in their hatches. The panzers in the gully drove across the field to surround the Russians in a semi-circle.

◇◇◇◇◇◇◇◇◇◇◇◇◇◇◇◇◇◇◇◇◇◇◇◇◇◇◇◇◇◇◇◇

Four Ilyushin "Sturmovik" aircraft emerged from the western winter sun, now low on the horizon. The sound of aircraft engines cut the silence, and 20 mm cannon shells exploded in a line in the snow, splattering through the men in the field and cutting down Germans and Russians like rabbits. Two Russian tanks exploded, one of the Panthers stopped, its track torn apart, and the aircraft dropped a bomb in the centre of the mélée. As it passed and pulled up, machine-gun fire from the rear gunner raked the soldiers on the ground, Russian and German soldiers indiscriminately. As the plane turned right in a steep climb, a second aircraft's cannon began its steady staccato rhythm; another followed it, then another.

When the slaughter stopped, three of the four Panthers were stationary, and no men were left standing.

And then, a black dot grew in Lucas's periscope until it became an airplane—flashes covered its wings as cannon shells struck the front armour plate, making a lot of racket but doing nothing more. The plane disappeared over the top of the periscope, and a bomb exploded behind it, fifteen metres short of 227, shaking it. Aircraft cannons and machine guns raked the line of tanks and men in the forest. Trees fell, and bombs exploded until, finally, the last Russian aircraft had exhausted its ammunition.

Lucas was amazed when men rose from the snow like ghosts, and the only Panther in the field that was still mobile swung its turret to clear imaginary unwanted passengers, then moved toward a still healthy-looking T-34 with its 75 mm cannon aimed at the Russian's rump. The T-34 remained stationary while the crew climbed out, and two white-camouflaged German soldiers climbed into the open turret.

About twenty Russians stood up with their hands over their heads, and the Jäger survivors herded them to the trees.

"We've got a mess to clean up," Klaus said into the intercom as though it were just another day, "Everybody out and help get our wounded on the tanks before those Russian planes return!"

It took an hour to sort wounded from dead and load those German soldiers with a chance at life on the tanks and into the Demag. The thirty-five Jäger soldiers who could still walk trudged behind the panzers, and thirty-two who couldn't, either sat or lay on the panzers and the Demag. A German crew drove the only T-34 that was still roadworthy as it moved out with five Panthers that could still fight. The Jäger Leutnant left a group of forty confused Russians in the woods with first aid supplies for their wounded.

It took all the remaining daylight and part of the night to reach a Lastwagen coming from the base at Kielce. When the Jäger soldiers had loaded the last man into the vehicles, Leutnant Finke and his remaining healthy men disappeared. Three hours later, as the sky lightened, Klaus parked his panzers in a patch of woods south of Kielce.

XXIV Panzer Corps' headquarters were in a Polish army barracks at the city's southern limits. Before sunrise, a Kubelwagen took Klaus to a staff meeting there, and it was mid-morning before he reported to his anxious men waiting beside their tanks. The crews from the five surviving Panthers and the commandeered T-34 stomped their feet and waved their arms in the traditional dance men use to keep themselves from freezing. Russian fighters flew reconnaissance day and night, selecting artillery and bomber targets, so fires were out of the question. During the day, rising smoke acted as beacons, attracting ground-attack fighters and reconnaissance aircraft.

Lucas stood beside Marcus, both doing the two-step to keep the blood flowing to their feet as Klaus looked around at the men who expected to die for him. Their breath left their mouths in clouds of frozen vapour as Klaus broke the anxious silence.

"I'll give you the bad news first. Since yesterday, the Russians have destroyed two-thirds of the Fourth Panzer Army's artillery, and a quarter of our infantry has been killed or captured. I can confirm that the Forty-Eighth Panzer Corps and the Sixty-Eighth Infantry have been totally destroyed—most of the infantry is on the casualty or missing list. Sadly, the Fourth Panzer Army has lost nearly two hundred thousand men." Klaus waited to let the numbers sink in.

Klaus kept his eyes moving from one man's face to another, and when he found Lucas's eyes, Lucas lowered his head and scraped his left foot on the ground so he would have something else to look at. He tried to imagine two hundred thousand dead, wounded or captured men, but the number wouldn't convert into human beings. Even the hardened Waffen SS soldiers around him looked at their feet and cleared their throats without speaking.

When the men finally lifted their heads and began to murmur, Klaus continued. "That was the bad news. The worse news for us is that the Russians are ten kilometres from where we stand, and now that daylight is on us, they are moving fast. With over five hundred tanks and a thousand guns, they will almost certainly trap what's left of the Fourth and Ninth armies in a salient pocket west of Kielce." He swiped his arm across the quadrant that represented the vulnerable area around Kielce. "The Fourth Panzers are not equipped to fight in the city, and we will certainly lose that battle if we try. So, we will buy time for our armies by fighting General Nehring's 'hit and run' defence... He knows, and I agree that we can't win a fixed-position battle.

"We will have three Panthers to replace our losses, and if we are to make a difference, our squadron must destroy or otherwise slow down a hundred Russian tanks. If we set up a fixed position, the Russians will use artillery to eradicate us from a distance our tank guns can't even reach."

Lucas, shocked at his sudden sense of vulnerability, immediately decided that if death were to be his lot, he would die heroically or, at worst, without complaining. Suddenly smitten with an exciting dose of patriotism, he stepped forward to salute Klaus and repeat a phrase he had learned in basic training; "I am prepared to die for the Fatherland!"

As the men around him snickered, Klaus caught Lucas's hand and pulled it down before his "Heil Hitler!" Marcus pulled him back, a few men laughed, and Lucas blushed.

Klaus laughed. "Oh, that would be a big help! Believe me, Lucas, our plan does not involve selling our lives, cheaply or otherwise, despite certain less-than-subtle suggestions from Berlin. In fact, I don't intend to die until I have a dozen grandchildren and lose my teeth and hair." He stepped forward and put his hand on Lucas's shoulder.

"No, son, we will not sacrifice ourselves. We will kill a few more Russians and then run away to fight them again and again until someone far above my rank stops this madness."

◇◇◇◇◇◇◇◇◇◇◇◇◇◇◇◇◇◇◇◇◇◇◇◇◇◇◇◇

Both of Hitler's defence lines along the Vistula River disintegrated as the Russians advanced, and Hitler panicked. He mobilized the German militia and conscripted boys as young as fourteen and men as old as sixty. They went into battle with only farcical training—none went to the Waffen SS.

XXIV Panzer Corps lost half their tanks and a third of their men in the following six weeks, but 227 was not among the casualties.

Chapter Twenty-three

February 1945

Poking the bear—Sonnenwende

Lucas and his comrades learned of the ongoing bombing attack on Dresden the night before "Operation Sonnenwende" began. Two-two-seven's crew, members of a privileged few, lived in a tent with cots. Cold but dry, Lucas lay in his sleeping bag on what the military called a bed, looking up into the dark.

He whispered, "Klaus, are you awake?" He was confused and wanted to talk to someone. Kristian and Simon were competing for the world snoring championship, and Marcus breathed deeply, but Lucas could hear Klaus trying to find a comfortable position.

"Yes, I'm awake." His fatherly voice again.

Lucas looked into a black void. He felt uncomfortable when he couldn't see his hands, so he closed his eyes.

"Do you believe that the British are bombing Dresden?"

"What makes you think they might be doing that?" Klaus's tone was sharp.

"Simon picked it up on the radio while we ran the engine. He said the British are firebombing Dresden—the whole city is burning. Goebbels himself spoke on the radio and said there are thousands of deaths; Simon said there are hundreds of thousands…"

Klaus interrupted, "Only a fool believes anything Goebbels says, and if you believe Simon…" He sounded peeved that Lucas had bothered him with something so trivial. "I don't believe anything I hear on the radio, half what I see on the battlefield, and nothing that I hear from Simon!" Lucas could hear him trying to find a comfortable position.

"Lucas, you must forget everything but shooting your gun and getting home alive. Just concentrate on your job." He paused, then said quietly, his words barely audible over the snoring chorus. "Adolph Hitler is the only one who can save the people of Dresden, or Berlin, or anywhere else in Germany, but he won't do it unless he benefits. Now, go to sleep."

◇◇◇◇◇◇◇◇◇◇◇◇◇◇◇◇◇◇◇◇◇◇◇◇◇◇◇◇◇◇◇◇◇◇

The following morning, Klaus announced, "We have a new objective." He had the men in his four-tank platoon assembled in their dining tent, sitting on benches eating breakfast prepared by the Goulash Kannone, the mobile kitchen. It was excellent, at least compared to the usual field rations of canned Wurst und Feldbrot, and, best of all, it was accompanied by a cup of real coffee.

"We are going to relieve the Army garrison at Arnswalde—the Russians have them surrounded, and they will soon be dead or working in Russian salt mines if we don't get them out of there."

Lucas felt the mood lift—An offensive and a rescue mission—finally, something worthwhile. For the first time in a month, they would attack the Russians, and for a noble cause. Klaus's tone was contagious.

"General Guderian has committed us to stopping the Russians at the Oder River, but not by the usual 'stand and fight to the last man' nonsense. We will cut the Russian army into two pieces and send them back to the Vistula River!"

Klaus got to his feet, raised his beer, clicked his heels, and every man who was sitting stood up. They raised their bottles and toasted loudly, "Prost!" Klaus shouted, "Heil Deutschland!" and every man repeated it with him, some noting the substitute for Hitler's name.

Klaus's voice took on a conspiratorial tone. "We have a new commanding General for Operation Sonnenwende, General Wenck, the best fighting general in the entire German army. I don't know how Wenck got past the boss, and I'm not interested." He lifted his empty bottle. "Lang leb' der General!"

Most of the men had never heard of Wenck but shouted, "Lang leb' der General!" anyway, to please Klaus.

Lucas, motivated by the men's sudden patriotic fervour, joined them in singing the first verse of the Panzerlied. He talked and laughed with his comrades as they finished their stew and listened with new vigour as they retold the best of their stories of home and battle to men who reacted as though hearing them for the first time. The story of Corinne trying to kill Hartwig with her Viola was a favourite, and with every telling, they teased Lucas about the dangers of choosing Brunhilda for a bride. Some even knew how that legend ended.

"Unternehmen Sonnenwende," the operation Guderian devised to relieve the German garrison at Arnswalde, split the Russian forces and deny them access to Germany, began before dawn, February 15th. The 11th Panzergrenadier Nord, Hitler's invention, to which the XXIV Panzers and Lucas now belonged, was the point of the spear, and the plan was to advance as rapidly as possible, reaching the objectives before the Russian bear awoke.

The day dawned gray and miserable, but on the bright side, the light rain mixed with big wet snowflakes would ground the Russian planes. The temperature rose during the night from a cold, damp minus-ten to a bone-chilling zero Celsius. The slightly above-freezing temperature generated a thin layer of wispy ground fog that hung over everything. As Lucas sat with Klaus on the turret's edge, their heads were above the mist, a thin shroud that blurred the ground. Lucas was happy to be in a warm, dry tank as he watched hundreds of infantry part the strands of fog when they climbed into the trucks that would take them to the jumping-off point.

The forward unit consisted of two King Tigers and four Panthers, protected by five hundred infantry. Five identical units with engines running made up an entire division waiting to advance. Two-two-seven had new final drives and a new front armour plate, and the detailed inspection Klaus had insisted upon that morning reminded Lucas of his father's unwillingness to accept anything less than the best anyone could do.

When the line moved out, the lead King Tigers drove toward the east side of nearby Stargard, where scouts reported the Belarussian northern flank would be. Wenck had allowed all his men, down to the lowest foot soldier, to know the battle plans. Every man bought into it as though they had personally planned the attack, and although Lucas was trapped in a steel box with only a tiny fixed periscope to connect him with the outside world, he felt part of something grand.

◇◇◇◇◇◇◇◇◇◇◇◇◇◇◇◇◇◇◇◇◇◇◇◇◇◇◇◇◇◇◇◇◇◇◇

The plan was for the first two Tigers to stay on the paved road to Arnswalde while the Panthers and infantry moved ahead on their flanks, across frozen fields and along service roads. General Wenck assigned the remaining ten Tigers to widen the slot behind the lead Panzer-grenadier Nord tanks. A Jäger scouting unit specializing in artillery and panzer warfare had located targets for the King Tigers before the action began. The Panthers were free to roam within their assignment to protect the King Tigers and to use their long guns to clear threats and open pathways.

The operation allocated three days' fuel supply and two hundred rounds of cannon ammunition for each panzer carried in supply vehicles following at a safe distance. The operation must take Arnswalde before those critical supplies ran out—a tall order, and every man knew it.

It shocked the 61st Russian Army to see German tanks bearing down on them from the direction of Stargard. The traditional artillery foreplay before every significant battle hadn't happened; the Russian scouts had not seen nor heard any activity that would have warned them. When excited Russian observers called the anti-tank field gunners with the attacking column's coordinates, the panzers were too close, and the German guns were too accurate, already sited on the Russians, thanks to the scouts. Thinking the Germans had lost interest in attacking, Russian artillery had not attempted to conceal themselves with camouflage. Adding confusion, Leutnant Finke's Jäger company had eliminated most of the Russian scouts and some of the scattered artillery during the night, leaving the remaining guns blind. The King Tigers and German artillery took care of any remaining guns from a range the Russians couldn't reach.

Russian tanks and destroyers were sitting ducks without eyes on their enemy and with German scouts behind every tree and building. The Jäger units knew precisely where the Russians lay in wait behind buildings or sparse lines of trees along the sides of the narrow roads. Leutnant Finke's radio reported their location to the advancing Tigers and Panthers three or four kilometres before the Russians could see them. From a range of two kilometres, the mighty 88 mm guns of the King Tigers and massive Elefant tank destroyers picked them off, one by one, taking time to guarantee a kill.

The Jäger units sent a constant stream of target coordinates, and

German panzers and artillery left the road and fields littered with wrecked Russian tanks.

The thick overcast touched the ground on every rise of land, keeping Russian IL2 tank-destroyer aircraft and reconnaissance planes away from the battlefield, and the column covered the thirty-five kilometres quickly, arriving in Arnswalde before the early winter darkness. To celebrate, the Goulash Kannone passed around beer with the hot evening meal.

In a state of euphoria, Lucas curled up in a corner of the turret he had found was a tolerable place to sleep. The night was relatively warm, approaching ten degrees, and Lucas was comfortable in his heavy coat and sleeping bag for the first time in months. He slept the sleep of the innocent, dreaming of his mother arguing with her sister over Brennestle soup. He woke up laughing when his mother burst into a Mozart opera aria extolling virtuous soup.

Panzergrenadier Nord tanks mopped up Arnswalde the following morning while Third SS Panzers widened the corridor to Stargard. Before noon, the Fourth Army panzers and infantry had taken the city and all Russian forces in Arnswalde had surrendered.

With 227 parked in the square opposite St. Mary Catholic Church, damaged by Russian and German shells as was almost every building in the city, the crew waited for Klaus's return from a staff meeting. Lucas sat on the turret facing the rear of the tank, and Marcus sat beside him, leaning against the cupola, discussing the successful operation.

Marcus said, "It's been too easy, Lucas. The Russians are not the best soldiers in the world, but they are better than this." Marcus looked toward the church. "If God hadn't blessed us with the fog and clouds...."

Lucas felt a pang of disappointment as he interrupted. "Klaus said that we would cut the Russian forces in two and drive them back, and we did. Maybe the Russians will ask for peace—they're a long way from Mother Russia—what would they gain by chasing us back to Germany?"

"Yes, the Russian soldiers want to go home in peace...ask any of the prisoners we've sent to work in Germany. But we're not shooting at Stalin, and he is the only Russian who matters, as Hitler is the only German who matters." Marcus put a cigarette in his mouth and lit it.

Lucas pulled out a package of cigarettes he had found and said, "The Russian soldiers aren't shooting at Hitler either, so where does that leave the people?" He put one in his mouth and pointed at the lit cigarette in Marcus's hand. "Can I have a light?"

Marcus snatched the cigarette from Lucas's mouth so fast there was no time to defend himself.

"Give me those cigarettes." Marcus snapped his fingers and stared at the package.

Lucas said, "I found them on the ground over there," and pointed at a bench where tired parishioners could sit in the shadow of their church.

"A young kid like you shouldn't smoke, and there aren't enough cigarettes for every German soldier who already smokes—you picked a bad time to start." Marcus snapped his fingers again, and Lucas reluctantly put the package in his hand.

"People who smoke die young." Marcus laughed. "You don't want cigarettes to kill you before the Russians get a chance, do you?"

Lucas smiled and kicked the side of Marcus's leg. "I suppose you want me to thank you for saving my life."

Marcus put the cigarettes in his shirt pocket. "Nope, I don't give a shit whether you smoke. I'm almost out of cigarettes, and this gives me another day or two to find some." He laughed again.

Lucas asked, "How much is a pack of cigarettes worth?"

"If you hadn't given them to me, and remember that you gave them of your own free will, the value of that package would increase every day until, if you auctioned them off, I would bid a month's wages, but I probably wouldn't get them."

Lucas tried to grab the cigarette pack from Marcus's shirt pocket, but he protected it with his hand. "You gave them to me! They're mine now, and you would just burn them up anyway!" He deflected Lucas with his arm and pointed at a figure marching across the stone courtyard. "Look, Klaus isn't happy."

Four Panther crews waited for their boss as he approached 227, waving his arms. When he arrived, he shouted, "That fucking lunatic has called General Wenck to Berlin so he can parade him in front of the fucking idiots who clean the Führer's boots with their tongues!" Every man in the square knew who Klaus was referring to. "The ground is thawing, the Russians know where we are going next, and we have momentum. The only thing we don't have is time! This is madness!"

No one dared open his mouth. They looked at one another, shocked to see their commander out of control. Lucas looked around to see if anyone else had heard the treasonous tirade.

Klaus toned down his voice, obviously embarrassed by his outbreak. "I can't tell you anything more until Wenck returns—hopefully tomorrow. You might as well go and rest; we aren't going anywhere before the day after tomorrow, and by then, we may all be going to hell!"

A day-and-a-half later, on the morning Wenck had scheduled for the offensive drive to Küstrin an der Oder, Klaus gathered his men.

The men knew Wenck and Guderian had designed the action to complete the job of splitting the Russian forces and stopping them on the Polish side of the Oder River. The key was to attack before the Russians could move men and equipment to a position where they could hinder them.

Timing and speed were the most critical elements of the plan, and they had been on track to accomplish the objective. Every panzer in Klaus's squadron of four Panthers and two King Tigers was full of ammunition and fuel, ready to fight, and the crews were high and confident of success.

They had gathered at the jump-off point, a farmyard on the north side of Arnswalde, anxious to get underway before the ground became a quagmire. The temperature was still well above freezing, a solid gray overcast hung a scant hundred metres above the ground, and the men were happy. They expected their commander's usual confidence-building pre-battle speech, but what they got was something else entirely—

Klaus spoke through clenched teeth. "Okay, I will give you the bad news first and then the worse news." Klaus was angry in a way that frightened the men.

"General Wenck and his driver drove for two days without sleep so he could lead this operation before the low clouds disappear and the thaw makes it impossible for the heavy panzers to operate." He paused and spread out his hands in a gesture of hopelessness.

"Last night, on his way here, General Wenck's car left the road and crashed. Wenck was driving and probably went to sleep. He is in a Berlin hospital, and won't be coming back to the front. Operation Sonnenwende is on hold until the man who fucked this up gets around to sending the general he wants to finish the job!"

The men looked at one another, and during the pause, Marcus asked, "Why can't the operation go on with Nehring?"

"That's the worse news. The idiot has appointed General Hans Krebs to replace Wenck, and we must wait until he catches up."

Marcus was becoming as agitated as his boss. He spoke too loudly and waved his arms too energetically. "Two more days of this weather will eliminate most of the side roads for the King Tigers, and we won't be able to turn a Panther in the fields." He pressed on. "Maybe we should wait until it freezes again."

Klaus shook his head. "It won't freeze without clearing the clouds out first, and then the Russians will replace them with aircraft. Our objectives are obvious, and while we stand here talking bullshit, the Russians are setting up their offensive. It's the middle of February, the sun is strong, and it probably won't freeze hard enough to carry the King Tigers or the Panthers again this winter. If we started our offensive today, I believe we could achieve our objectives, but every day we delay will cost us lives and equipment. The scales will tip for the Russians at some point, probably sooner than we think."

He waved his hands in a frustrated horizontal slicing motion. "I have no more to say."

The men returned to their panzers to talk and smoke, and when Marcus chose to walk with him, Lucas was pleased. The morning light was complete when they climbed on the tank and sat on the flat rump with their legs stretched out and their backs against the turret.

Lucas asked, as though he were the first to consider such a thing, "Why don't they make tanks that can drive in the mud? Wouldn't wider tracks work?"

Marcus looked at Lucas with something like pity. "I sometimes forget that you haven't been here long enough to experience the delight of the spring mud. No one can build a tank that drives on mud because the mud on this flat ground is like soup. Water can't drain away, and it has enough water that, most of the time, a boat would work better than a tank. The field mud is full of organic stuff like the roots of plants, and when that shit rots, you get slime. Today, you can't walk on the fields without slipping and sliding, but in a couple more days, the panzers will sink until their bellies drag. We will spend all our time pulling machinery out of the mud, and we will become sitting ducks for enemy artillery and bombers."

"So, I don't see why we don't just stay on the roads. I think we should stay off the farmers' fields and roads whether they're frozen or not!" Lucas realized that the comment was stupid before Marcus spoke—he hated himself when he reverted to the attitudes of a ten-year-old.

Marcus gestured to the sky with his fingers spread and arms extended. Lucas recognized the thick sarcasm in Marcus's first word.

"Lucas, just picture yourself in an aircraft attacking tanks... If you had your choice, how would you want them set up?"

Lucas looked at the bright spot in the clouds hiding the rising sun. The bottom edge was a band of bright light. "I would want them lined up nose-to-tail so I could fly down the line while I fired my cannons."

Marcus pointed his finger down the road, arm outstretched. "Precisely like they would be on a road like that one? And wouldn't you fly down the line from the rear so your thirty-millimetre cannon shells would penetrate their fuel tanks before they exploded? The infantry would have their backs to you, filling the gaps between panzers. Christ, even I could make a mess with that setup!"

Lucas wanted to stop the conversation. "Okay, I knew it was stupid when I said it."

Marcus leaned back and locked his fingers together behind his head. "Grown men who should know better say stupider things. Unfortunately, some of them are in Berlin!"

Lucas closed his eyes and leaned his head back, hoping Marcus would let it go, but he didn't.

Marcus said, "You are an exceptional boy, Lucas." He turned his head and cracked open one eye... "but don't let it go to your head."

Two days later, the Sonnenwende forces began moving in warm spring-like weather. Even the nights were above freezing, and soldiers sweated in their winter gear. Lucas left the rear hatch open partly to get fresh air and partly so he could watch the panzers travelling behind them.

The scouts had disappeared the night before to search for targets and make sure there were no surprises, and Klaus's Panthers travelled on side roads, moving parallel to the gravel road that the Tigers were using. The two King Tigers two-two-seven accompanied were visible through the hatch, travelling on a parallel road five hundred metres across open fields west of 227. The slow, steady speed, the warm turret, and the gray pre-dawn light soothed Lucas, and he was nodding off when Klaus's urgent voice on the intercom brought him back with a start.

"Kristian, stop behind the barn on our right. Everyone else, Achtung!" Klaus's voice woke Lucas from a dream with Corinne in the lead role. The sun peeked over the horizon, shining under the clouds into the hatch. Lucas looked at his watch and discovered he had lost half an hour somewhere.

Two-two-seven switched in an 's' turn to the right, then stopped. Lucas closed the hatch, noting before he shut it that the Panther travelling behind them had swerved into a line of trees on the other side of the road. Lucas removed the loader's seat and hung it on its bracket. He lifted a shell out of the bin, laid it on his knee and braced himself so he wouldn't accidentally drop it if Kristian had to maneuver.

Klaus climbed out of the cupola, his boots clanking down the front of the tank. Lucas wanted to look outside and was contemplating opening the rear hatch when Klaus returned a couple of minutes later, out of breath. He was barely in his seat when he said, "Kristian, middle of the road...now!"

Kristian released the clutch, pulled the left steering lever, then the right, and then stomped on the brake. Lucas straightened up enough to see through the periscope. The Panther's 75 mm cannon pointed straight down the centre of the road.

Marcus took two seconds to sight, then fired. Lucas slid the shell he held in his arms into the barrel and closed the breech. He reached for a round in the turret ring as Marcus swung the gun, and when the gun stopped, the shell was on his knee.

The second Panther fired; a round of enemy 75 mm from the opposition down the road exploded behind 227, and Marcus fired. Lucas rammed the round he had in his hands into the hot barrel and slammed the breech into position. He dove for another shell in the bin at his feet—if the turret swung, it had to be in his hands.

Klaus said into the intercom, "Okay, we got two T-34s, but one of the Tigers is in the ditch. We'll stay here until they get things sorted out."

Lucas laid the shell in his hands in the turret ring and slid the rear hatch open just in time to watch a Panther hook its tow cable onto the incapacitated King Tiger. The monster listed heavily, buried in the mud at the bottom of the ditch to the top of its left tread. A black-uniformed commander signalled, and the Panther spun its treads, moved sideways and slid down the bank into the ditch ahead of the Tiger. Lucas laughed at the ridiculous pantomime but stopped when he realized what it meant.

The second Tiger reversed down the road, turned around at a wide spot and backed up to the command Tiger in the ditch. Two men scrambled to hook a tow cable on the Tiger's rear hook, and the 70-tonne monster on the road eased ahead until it tightened.

The crippled Tiger, with the help of the Panzer on the gravel road, crawled slowly along the ditch, and when it swung to a forty-five-degree angle and began climbing the ditchbank, Klaus said, "He's going to make it!" while holding his Zeiss binoculars to his eyes. Lucas silently cheered them on. The behemoth slowly climbed the ditch bank, creeping toward the tipping point where it could crawl on its own.

Marcus asked, "What's going on?" He could not look outside except through the sight or the little periscope, but the turret pointed down the road ahead of 227, and the Tigers were behind and to the side.

Klaus said, "I'll climb out and sit on the edge of the cupola so you can see, but stay alert."

The gun crew watched the King Tiger begin to tip onto the road, and a small cheer filled their hearts. But just as reaching the hard gravel seemed a sure thing, its treads lost their tenuous sideways grip, and the Tiger slid back into the ditch. The commander waved both arms over his head, stopping the Tiger that was doing the towing.

Lucas slammed his hand on the steel edge of the hatch harder than he should have and said, "Verdammt Scheisse! What more can go wrong?" He rubbed his bruised hand, trying to put everything back where it should be.

"Give it time, Lucas," Klaus said from his seat next to the rear hatch, "I can think of a few worse possibilities than getting stuck in a ditch."

Following a quick conference, the towing panzer unhooked from the stuck Tiger and reset his tank so that his towing angle would be closer to straight across the road. The commander again gave the 'go' signal and, with the front of its tracks slightly over the shoulder, leveraging the tank's massive weight and black smoke belching out of both Tigers, the panzer on the road pulled the commander's Tiger around until it swung up the ditch bank as it moved backward.

Lucas tempted fate when he said, "They've got it now!" as the King Tiger crawled up the ditchbank with its seventy-ton partner straining on the cable.

Something resembling a shock of electricity went through Lucas's body when the cable snapped with a sound like a rifle shot. The instantly loose thousand-kilogram steel snake whipped through the air parallel to the ground, carrying all the energy the King Tiger had put into it. The 5 cm steel cable cut a soldier in two at his waist—his legs flew one way, his torso another, a string of blood, sinew and guts spraying everything within ten metres. Lucas opened his mouth, but there was no sound.

The crippled Tiger slid back into the ditch, and the towing Tiger, suddenly free of the fifty-tonne load on the cable that held it on the road, tipped into the opposite ditch nose-first, its cannon buried in the muddy field.

"Scheisse!" 227's crew swore in near unison, and a second later, the radio sprang to life.

"Jäger one to Panzer two-two-seven...thirteen T-34s and two destroyers approaching from the east. Range, three thousand metres and closing." The message was on the open battle channel; every tank and infantry commander heard it.

"Scheisse, Scheisse! Scheisse!" Klaus yelled into the intercom, "Thirteen tanks and two destroyers—Verdammt Scheisse, we need those Tigers!"

A few minutes later, on a ridge east of the stuck Tiger drama, Russian tanks charged across the open fields like a pack of wolves coming in for the kill, leaving the slow 105 destroyers behind. The T-34s' treads spread showers of mud in all directions.

<hr>

"Battle stations!" Klaus jumped into his raised seat, Marcus slid into his gunner's position, and Lucas climbed into the turret, slid the rear hatch into its place and locked it. He picked a 75 mm round out of the bin at his feet, leaving the turret ring full of shells he could use even if the gun were swinging.

Klaus ordered the second Panther to turn and confront the Russians, facing the thickest armour toward the anticipated return fire. A thin line of trees protected the Panthers from easy detection. The T-34s were still out of range for a moving target shot, but they would soon become vulnerable at the speed they were going. But the outnumbered Panthers would have to hit fast-moving targets!

Suddenly, Klaus's disbelieving voice said into the intercom, "The stupid bastards stopped. There are thirteen T-34s, but I don't see the destroyers! Wait, they're behind the T-34s—that's why they stopped."

Lucas crouched, a shell on his knee, ready to reload when Marcus fired.

"The range is over two thousand metres, a low-percentage shot. We'll wait until the destroyers are with the T-34s and moving forward."

Lucas shifted the shell on his leg, trying to find a comfortable position. He knew that at two thousand metres, even with the 5x setting on the sight, a T-34 was the size of a fruit fly.

The T-34s opened fire, followed by the solid sound of the heavier 105 mm tank destroyers' cannons. Both of their intended victims were stuck with their noses down too far to sight their superior guns, and the Russians, still unaware of the hiding Panthers, took their time, reckoning on a turkey shoot with the turkey tied up. The Russian tanks fired a half-dozen shots on a trial basis, but Russian sights weren't German Zeiss quality, and the range was outside their sure-kill zone.

Klaus said, "Those rounds landed short, but the next rounds won't. Marcus, shoot the T-34 nearest us. The other Panthers have their targets and will fire when you do."

Four Panthers fired. The Russians were at a forty-five-degree angle to Klaus's 227 and the Panther working the area with it, exposing their weakest point, and three of the four T-34s they targeted paid the ultimate price.

"We got three of them." Klaus said it as though reading a grocery list, "Marcus, shoot the one that stopped behind them." Marcus immediately fired, Lucas loaded, then pulled another round out of the bin.

"Du Lieber Himmel! You got him! Na Gut, work your way across the front."

Lucas rammed another round into the breech and felt the Panther heave as they took a direct hit. Marcus fired; Lucas slid a shell into the barrel and slammed the breech shut—Marcus fired again.

"They've stopped. A T-34 lost its turret...the Panthers on the other side of the field got two more."

Lucas loaded, then took a round out of the turret ring.

"They've had enough! There are only five T-34s left, and the destroyers are turning around. Concentrate on them!"

Marcus swung the turret and fired. Lucas loaded, panting, but still working smoothly.

Klaus said, "We've got them in a crossfire; they won't last long."

Marcus pulled the trigger. Two more panthers fired, and Marcus said, "That's it; they're running away! Load the gun, then come out and take a look."

Lucas slid the hatch open and crawled outside, followed by Simon and Kristian. There were a few dead soldiers around the Tigers, but the tanks appeared undamaged. The lead Tiger's commander called on the battle channel for the two Panthers on his right flank to come and tow his tank out of the ditch, and they immediately drove straight across the muddy field. Designed for these conditions, the Panthers were making good time when an artillery barrage began. Heavy artillery shells rained close to the helpless Tigers, but none near enough to damage them.

◇◇◇◇◇◇◇◇◇◇◇◇◇◇◇◇◇◇◇◇◇◇◇◇◇◇◇◇◇◇◇◇

Two-two-seven's radio came to life again. "Two-two-seven...Finke here.

There are twenty big howitzers straight ahead, and at least a hundred tanks and a battalion of infantry headed in your direction, and they're using the road you are sitting on!"

Klaus acknowledged, then ordered his partner to follow 227, driving as fast as he dared down a field road to where he hoped to flank the artillery. The Russian guns were only three thousand metres from the Tigers and would destroy them if Klaus didn't mount a distraction.

Lucas looked through the loader's periscope. The tree-lined road broke into the open in less than a kilometre, and as far as he could see, there were no trees or buildings on the flat land ahead of 227.

"Stop!" Klaus shouted, and Kristian dragged the tracks, stopping the Panther in the length of itself, banging Lucas's head on a steel rib. Lucas went back to his periscope, blood pouring from a cut somewhere in his thick hair. He ignored it as he watched infantry and tanks moving on the fields ahead of them. Russian artillery fired a steady rain of shells at the Tigers, and they disappeared behind a curtain of black mud.

◇◇◇◇◇◇◇◇◇◇◇◇◇◇◇◇◇◇◇◇◇◇◇◇◇◇◇◇◇◇◇

Russian observers spotted 227 and its wingman, and two heavy artillery shells exploded on the road in front of them, and flying dirt rose in front of the periscope. The Russians could raise the gun and fire in two seconds, and Lucas was sure his life was over.

Klaus yelled in the intercom, "Kristian—turn around, now! Get back on the main road!"

Lucas braced himself against the side of the turret, with one hand on the plate and the other holding a seven-kilogram shell against his hip.

Klaus shouted, "Simon, warn the Tigers that a hundred Russian tanks are coming...use the open battle channel!" Simon immediately transmitted and seconds later reported, "I sent it but got no confirmation from the Tigers."

"That's not good! Try again!" Russian shells landed on the road behind the fleeing panthers.

Explosions on both sides of the Panthers, now driving at full throttle on the main road in fourth gear, chased them as they ran toward the Tigers.

"Keep trying, Simon—ask for confirmation!"

Lucas turned his attention to their Panther wingman driving ahead of them—they were gaining on him.

Klaus shouted on the radio, loud enough that Lucas could hear him over the clattering tracks and protesting engine, "Number two, there are T-34s behind us...if you want to baby your final drives, get out of my way!"

The Panther sped up until 227 was losing ground.

"Still nothing." Simon sounded frustrated, as though the Tigers purposely refused to answer.

"Call Battle Command—tell them that we assume the Tigers are gone, and we are withdrawing..." He stopped to breathe,

"Kristian, is that all you've got?"

Kristian shifted two-two-seven up to sixth gear, running the straining engine at full speed and heading for a point opposite the trapped heavy panzers. The artillery shells fell well short as they searched for 227, and Lucas dared hope they would be relatively safe for at least a few minutes. Out in the open and stationary, the Tigers were not so lucky. Lucas risked putting his eye against his periscope in the thrashing tank, and when they came into his field of vision, he saw only smoking hulks. German infantry were in full retreat. One of the Panthers guarding the Tigers lay on its side; the other ran away, chased by cannon shells. Like 227, it was a difficult target for Russian artillery.

The Russian artillery lost interest in 227 and its partner and turned their attention to the fleeing infantry, now without support and caught in the open. Klaus said on his radio, "Number two, get in the trees on your right; we must slow the Russians down. Kristian, turn around and hide us behind the corner of the barn on the left."

Lucas tried to find a position where the round he held in his arms didn't dig into his hip and almost dropped it when Kristian spun the Panther neatly behind the corner of a barn. Lucas put his eye on the periscope, and a line of T-34 tanks appeared, running down the road toward them at full speed.

"Marcus, when I tell you, take the lead tank on our right...number two, take the left."

The Russians slowed, then stopped at the top of a low rise in the ground, looking for their quarry. Klaus said, "Eight hundred and twenty metres! Fire!" Marcus fired, and the T34 on the right stopped dead. Number two fired while the reverberations of Marcus's shot still lingered; the left T-34 lost its right track and swung sideways.

Lucas rammed the shell home, slammed the breech, picked another out of the bin, and had the next round in position when Marcus fired. He loaded and closed the breech, pulled a shell from the turret ring and was ready when the breech blew back—he counted aloud, "One-thousand-one, one-thousand-two...it was two-and-a-half seconds from shot to shot.

Klaus yelled in the intercom. "Five dead T-34s are blocking the road; it's time to get the hell out of here!" Gears ground steel against steel; Kristian cursed, but nothing happened, so Klaus yelled again.

"Kristian, we've bought the infantry enough time to get to the trucks and half-tracks. It's time to skedaddle. Get us out of here while the Russian tanks are blocking the road behind us! Now!" Kristian shouted, "Got it!" and spun the tank, a no-no for the final drives, and 227 led its partner at 55 kph, every bit of speed a Panther could make in sixth gear on a hard road, another no-no.

◇◇◇◇◇◇◇◇◇◇◇◇◇◇◇◇◇◇◇◇◇◇◇◇◇◇◇◇◇◇◇◇◇◇◇◇◇◇

The following day, the Russians attacked from two sides, driving the German forces back to Stargard, where the enemy attack finally stalled.

On February 23, two-two-seven drove through the battered city. During the retreat, fighting a rear-guard action ahead of the Russians, Lucas lost count of the number of abandoned German Panzers he had seen; a few mortally wounded, but most undamaged—stuck in the mud or out of gas and ammunition. He had two shots left in the ring, none in the bins, and Kristian said the engine was running on fumes.

Chapter Twenty-four

March 1945

Germany

Sometimes, a simple act of human kindness will put hope in a heart, stopping brutality in its tracks.

The Author

THE HUMILIATED, ONCE MIGHTY NINTH ARMY and what remained of the Fourth Panzer Army retreated toward Germany. A limited supply of ammunition, fuel and parts forced commanders to keep only the panzers in fighting condition and destroy those with severe battle damage. Only two of the twelve King Tigers in the Fourth Panzer Army remained after Sonnenwende; the others had been demolished or abandoned in the mud. As they passed abandoned tanks, half-tracks and Lastwagen, the crew of Panzer 227 became depressed, knowing they were members of a defeated army. They wanted to go home.

Klaus's panzer hadn't fired a shot in two weeks. Berlin had issued orders to avoid contact and preserve ammunition and fuel, and every soldier suspected that when the generals told them to evade the enemy, the end was near. Their fears became a certainty as they joined the tidal wave of people rolling ahead of the Russian advance. Two-two-seven's crew slept wrapped in blankets, five men's bodies squeezed into a cramped, cold steel box. There was no fuel to waste running the engine to keep the panzer warm.

◇◇◇◇◇◇◇◇◇◇◇◇◇◇◇◇◇◇◇◇◇◇◇◇◇◇◇◇◇◇◇◇◇◇◇

German Poles walking toward Germany had abandoned their homes. Their neighbours had no interest in protecting the people who had ravaged their country, and if the Polish Germans didn't leave voluntarily, their neighbours gave them to the vengeful Russian hordes.

Forced to give up everything they had, the desperate people headed southwest on the roads, hoping the magical line on the map that was the German border would stop the mass of soldiers bearing down on them.

The Russian air force indiscriminately strafed the refugees and soldiers clogging the roads; their low-level attacks hindered only by what defence the mobile anti-aircraft guns and battle-weary fuel-starved Luftwaffe could offer. The German Army took the right-of-way, forcing refugees to move to the shoulders or into ditches, woods, and fields. The refugees begged for food or a ride but soon learned to save their energy—there would be no help from the German Heer.

Lucas could not understand why Klaus would not permit anyone to ride on his tank—not even Wehrmacht soldiers, dragging their rifles, tired, beaten and begging for help. He drove the panzer past women, children and old men without offering assistance, water, or food.

Lucas asked, "What could it hurt to help those people?" as they prepared the Panther for another day of travel. He looked at the dipstick and noted that the engine would need oil as soon as they could find some.

Klaus shook his head. "No, Lucas, it's only a matter of time before aircraft or artillery attack us, and we must be free to move without dealing with riders. As for food, we don't have enough for ourselves, and I have no idea when or if we will get more. These panzers are all that's between the Russian Army and the miserable people on this road!"

Klaus was silent for a few minutes, and Lucas assumed the conversation was over, but as they climbed through the hatch—It was Lucas's turn to sit in the gunner's seat—Klaus began talking again.

"I spend all the daylight hours in my cupola where I can see what's happening around us; I see the misery; I'm not a stone. My orders are to keep going, and we must not stop or divert for anything except to defend the tank. I must keep two-two-seven rolling at the most efficient pace I can—there is no assurance of more fuel when this tank is dry. We cannot stop for any reason that doesn't involve danger to the tank."

Lucas made himself comfortable in the gunner's position and

steered Klaus's foot to its place. Klaus jacked his seat up as he continued the conversation. Marcus sat on the bottom of the turret, listening to every word.

"You can only fire the gun if you have a sure kill, and whatever you kill must be attacking us. I am responsible for four panzers that stand between the Russians and these people running away to Germany for protection. And don't forget our families in Germany—I must choose whether to help these people or the citizens of my own country." He paused again, and Lucas could feel him thinking. He finally said, "Lucas, you are not a soldier and could never be one. If I allowed it, your soft heart would get us all killed!"

Later in the morning, as Lucas watched through the periscope, an old man appeared in the middle of the road, trying to help his fallen wife get to her feet. He pulled on her arm, trying to drag her with one hand while he raised the other to ward off certain death as Panther 227 bore down on him at thirty-five kilometres per hour. His wife struggled to help but wasn't strong enough to make any difference. Finally, he put his arms around her and turned away from the oncoming tank.

Lucas took his eyes away from the sight, but his heart jumped when Klaus shouted, "Kristian, stop!" in the intercom. Kristian released the clutches and pulled on the brakes so fast that Lucas would have bet the month's pay the Wehrmacht owed him that he had begun before Klaus had shouted the order.

A cart, pulled by two women, loaded with their possessions and four children blocked the shoulder—there was no room for a three-and-a-half-metre-wide tank to maneuver. Lucas saw the terror in the old man's eyes before Kristian locked the tracks, halting forty-five tonnes of Panther in the length of itself, throwing him forward against Klaus's legs and the front of the turret. As soon as his body flopped back, he put his eye against the periscope. The man and his wife were nowhere in the field of vision, and tears burst into Lucas's eyes and down his cheeks as panic grabbed and held him.

Klaus put his head under the edge of the cupola, and his voice broke when he said, "Lucas, Marcus, help that man get that woman to the side of the road!"

Suddenly full of hope, Lucas banged his shin on the hatch as he climbed out behind Klaus and slid down to the pavement. He sobbed with relief as he reached the old man. He felt giddy as he helped Marcus carry the woman to the side of the road.

"Lucas, catch these." Klaus threw two cans of rations and a canteen of water to Lucas; he caught them and gave them to the old man. The old woman beckoned, and Lucas leaned over her. She smiled and said, "Gott segne euch alle," She wiped his tears with her finger and said, "Keine Sorgen, Junge. Alles wird wieder gut." "God bless all of you," and, "Don't worry, son, everything will be alright."

The line of tanks behind 227 stopped, but the radio remained silent. When Lucas and Marcus were back in their positions, Klaus said in the intercom, "Kristian, use third gear to save gas and the final drives. Simon, I want you to inform the squadron that they should do the same."

Lucas laughed, his face turned up to Klaus. "Leutnant, sir, you gave away Wehrmacht property and deliberately disobeyed orders not to stop—aren't you afraid they will shoot all of us—Sir?"

Klaus laughed, but there was no joy in it. He said, "Don't joke about such things, Lucas."

The Russian air force harassed the fleeing refugees and soldiers until they reached the Oder River, strafing and bombing them more or less continuously. Lucas and Marcus continued to alternate as gunner and loader, and Lucas was in the gunner's seat when a Russian Il-2 cement bomber started its run on the line of four tanks. It flew in a shallow dive, straight at 227, firing everything it had. A bomb hung under the fuselage. But the pilot had chosen the wrong direction...

Klaus ducked into his cupola as machine gun and cannon shells hit the Panther, exploding harmlessly against eighty millimetres of hardened steel, the thickest armour on anything but a Tiger. Lucas set the sight at 5X and 300 metres, and waited for the plane to fill the lens. Soldiers and refugees on both sides of the road ran for cover while Lucas pressed the machine gun trigger, hosing bullets into the fighter's face as the plane quickly filled the sight. He pulled the trigger on the 75 mm cannon when the wingtips touched the edges.

The armour-piercing shell that left the Panther's barrel met the

Il-2 in a head-on collision that would have destroyed the armoured fighter-bomber without the explosives. The high explosive powder in the shell was powerful enough to kill an armoured tank, and when it detonated against the bomber's twelve-cylinder engine, hundreds of pieces of Ilyushin 2 aircraft and two Russian airmen hurtled to the ground!

Surprised by the shot, Klaus yelled, "Scheisse!" and Marcus laughed. Klaus said, "...a bit like shooting a butterfly with a Mauser, isn't it?"

Lucas yelled back from Klaus's feet, "Not in the least; butterflies don't have cannons on their wings!"

Klaus said, "I guess that was worth a round, but don't tell the Führer I said that!" Lucas pulled his head back to see Klaus; he had a broad grin on his dark, dirty face.

◇◇◇◇◇◇◇◇◇◇◇◇◇◇◇◇◇◇◇◇◇◇◇◇◇◇◇◇◇◇◇◇

Two-two-seven crossed the Oder on the Schwedt bridge. Anti-aircraft guns stationed on both ends protected the soldiers and refugees covering the roadway, but they were unnecessary because the Russians had no interest in bombing the only bridge over the river and into Germany for fifty kilometres. Consequently, 227's crossing was slow and uneventful.

Once on the other side, the refugees scattered, some taking roads to Berlin, but most turned south to bypass Berlin and reach the Elbe River. The Ninth Army's orders took them southwest toward Berlin, now only ninety kilometres distant.

The following day, resupply trucks met them at a supply depot in the Frienwald forest, fifty kilometres from Berlin. Two-two-seven squealed to a halt under a canopy of trees, and Klaus got into a Kubelwagen that stopped beside it. Kristian guided a munition truck alongside and then helped Lucas and Marcus stow ammunition in the bins as fast as soldiers passed it to them.

In a pause, while the soldiers broke open another box, Lucas asked Marcus, "What do you think will happen now? Will the Russians stop at the border?"

Marcus answered while he worked—the soldiers were back in business. He passed a shell to Lucas, and he gave it to Simon, who filled the side bins at the radio operator's elbow with five rounds.

"Nothing will happen now, and I doubt the Russians would know a border if they tripped on one. In any case, we must change the final drive gears before we go anywhere. The brakes need adjusting, the oil is like tar, and we have half a dozen bent or worn-out track sections, probably more. We won't be ready to fight for at least a few days."

Marcus handed shells to Lucas like a robot. "And then, the crew needs a bath and a shave; that will take another two days."

Lucas chuckled. "I will vouch for that!"

When Klaus returned, Lucas and Simon were trying to drive a stubborn bent track pin out of a left track section. Kristian poured oil into the engine, and Marcus worked at tightening the 12 mm bolts on a final drive housing. Klaus jumped down from the same Kubelwagen that had taken him away, a box under his arm. He beckoned to the men as Simon took the whack that counted—the one that pushed the last millimetre of the bent pin out of the track.

Klaus said, "I've got good news and only good news. Let's finish loading the bins, and I will tell you about it while we eat our Mittagessen." No one protested the wait—any good news was rare enough to be worth waiting for.

While the rest of the crew finished loading the ammunition and pumping fuel, Kristian built a small fire under the shelter of thick spruce trees. He collected five ammunition boxes to use as seats, set them up in a semi-circle on the upwind side of the now-blazing fire, and distributed ration tins when the crew joined him.

Lucas opened a tin of Wurst and another of Feldbrot. He was famished.

Klaus opened the box he'd had under his arm and passed around bottles of beer.

"Is this the good news?" Marcus reverently examined his almost empty bottle of Herforder Pils. "If it is, I could use some more!"

"No," Klaus offered Lucas a beer, and Lucas gave it to Marcus. "The beer is just to get the party started." He took the opened cans of Wurst and Feldbrot that Kristian offered him.

"We are now the Eleventh Panzers Nordland, and we're in the Ninth Army. I'm sorry, all you men and Lucas, but we're now a reserve force and must stay here for at least a month!"

Kristian laughed. "Has Berlin consulted the Russians about that?"

Klaus shrugged. "We will take what we can get, but at the moment, they want us to go to Berlin for some rest." He put his hands up as though to fend off an attack. "I know, I know, we don't need or want a rest! We would rather fight the Russians, but those are the orders, and so, for the Vaterland..."

Everyone laughed. Behind so much irony, there had to be something terrific.

"In Berlin, we will stay in a beautiful house with bathtubs and a free bar!" Everyone cheered. "We will each have a private room, and female companionship will be available for those who want it. As your commanding officer, I must apologize—I'm afraid I accepted this assignment without asking how you felt."

Simon whooped and slapped Kristian on the back. "Now that's what I've been fighting for!"

Klaus said, "We will gather our things as soon as we eat. We go tonight at dusk, and Wehrmacht mechanics will finish the overhaul."

Kristian said, "I will finish putting oil in the engine." He wasn't as excited as Simon. "I drained it and want to be sure no one starts it without oil."

◇◇◇◇◇◇◇◇◇◇◇◇◇◇◇◇◇◇◇◇◇◇◇◇◇◇◇◇◇◇◇◇◇

Lucas decided that Hitler was giving them a holiday because the war wasn't going as badly as everyone thought. Perhaps the Russians waiting on the other side of the Oder were talking to Hitler, and maybe there would soon be peace. His theory seemed confirmed when, at dusk, three other panzer crews joined Klaus's men in a covered Lastwagen bound for Berlin.

Chapter Twenty-five

March 1945

Berlin

"In individuals, insanity is rare; but in groups, parties, nations and epochs, it is the rule."

Friedrich Nietzsche

It was midnight when 227's crew reached the house in Weissensee that would be their refuge for three days of rest. Located on the edge of a beautiful lake, the Nazis had confiscated it from a prominent Jewish family following Kristallnacht. The massive white-stuccoed three-story house, set aside for SS officers, was an oasis where they could wind down and recuperate from war.

Armed guards patrolled the grounds, and servants looked after the occupants' every need. Except for the now nightly bombers, the time Klaus and his men spent there would be quiet and luxurious. Waffen SS members and their guests enjoyed unlimited food, a free bar, a library, and private nightly entertainment.

Lucas immediately felt uncomfortable in such elegance. All he wanted was a bath, a real bed and a hot meal that had never been in a can. He bathed before dinner, ate a three-course meal, and slept in a soft bed. In the morning, Klaus woke him from a deep sleep.

Klaus asked the waiter at breakfast, "Some of those bombs last night came close. Is there a possibility the British bombers will attack the house? I'm sure they would love to kill a bunch of partying Waffen SS!"

Lucas looked up from his jam-spreading.

The waiter addressed Klaus. "You are safe here, sir. British Mosquito bombers visit Berlin almost every night, at unpredictable times, to keep us on edge. They've never hit the houses around the lake, and I doubt they will."

No one but Lucas stopped eating. He looked around the table and asked, "Bombs? What bombs?"

The waiter adopted the tone of a mother reassuring her child as he put his hand on Lucas's shoulder. "Don't worry, son; someone will come and wake you if you need to go to the shelter."

Everyone laughed but Lucas. He wanted to tell them he knew what British bombs could do but decided to keep his mouth shut.

<hr>

Lucas played chess with Klaus for an hour, and then they walked to the Berliner Allee, only a few blocks from the house. Kristian, Marcus, and Simon declined Klaus's invitation to join them—they were more interested in liquor, coffee, risqué magazines, and the luxurious lounge.

As they walked, Klaus talked about growing up in Berlin. He told Lucas that his family home was in the city's center and his father had worked in the justice department, but he had no idea what his father did. Klaus had been a member of the Hitler Jugend and had excelled in school, both academically and in military training.

Lucas turned up his courage and asked, "How do you feel about National Socialism?" hoping he knew the answer. "What are you fighting for?" Klaus didn't hide his feelings about the inefficiencies of the Nazi war machine and what he called the stupidity of Hitler's tactics. Still, as Waffen SS, he was a member of the Party, and Hitler was the National Socialist Party.

Klaus stopped, watched a sparrow chase a potential mate through the branches of a large oak tree, then turned to Lucas. "National Socialism is not what Hitler and our Nazi government represent. Socialism in its pure form is a good thing, but the Nazis have used it as fodder for fascism. As practiced by the Nazi party, socialism is tyranny, and nationalism is another word for unwavering trust in Hitler. The 'Party' selects who in society is worthwhile and who is not and discards those who oppose their doctrine. And that is the antithesis of socialism." He leaned against the trunk of a large oak tree and lit a cigarette.

Lucas thought for a minute. "If you aren't fighting for our Nazi government, then what are you fighting for?"

Klaus began walking again. "I joined the army as a way of living; I love the discipline, not necessarily the fighting. The military is as close to a perfect structure as man can create, and it is satisfying to me to be a part of it. I enjoy leading men, and I love commanding that part of the military machine.

"But since Stalingrad, I see our military being propelled and steered by insane politics, and now I'm fighting to save my family and country. But sometimes, when I think about it, even that is becoming a moot point. The question now is, who is worse, Hitler or Stalin? And I have no answer for that question."

That settled, Lucas asked, "What about the Jewish problem? Before I left Detmold, I heard terrible things about how we treat Jews. I heard that we are murdering them. Do you know anything about that?" Lucas waited anxiously for the answer. He had overheard Theo and Maria speak about Yvonne, a French Jewess who had escaped from Auschwitz, but they hadn't told him all of her story. What they had told him had given him nightmares!

"That's easy—there is no Jew or communist problem." Klaus raised his voice. "That is a lie started by Trotsky and other mad Russians so they could get away with persecuting Jews in Russia. Hitler used it in his book, Mein Kampf, refining it to be a conspiracy led by Jews and using communists to carry out their plan to take over the world."

He sucked the last millimetre out of his cigarette, dropped the butt beside his foot, and mashed it with his boot. He looked into Lucas's eyes and said, "I have not witnessed anyone murdering Jews, but I would have to be deaf and blind not to know that our soldiers are doing precisely that." Klaus paused, and Lucas tried to hold his commander's gaze. When he looked down, Klaus continued.

"There is no doubt that selected Germans murder women, old men, Russian soldiers, and even children. They are murdered by our SS, the Sonderabteilung, the Sicherheitsdienst, the Einsatzgruppe, or whatever the modern word for a gang of murderers is. The Gestapo also does their share, and when this war is over, the world will punish all those who took part, and we will be guilty as accomplices because we remained silent and let it happen." He looked away.

"As a member of the Waffen SS, the only question for me is, where will they stop? The Russians and the Jews could easily justify putting every member of the SS against a wall."

Klaus scuffed the sole of his boot on a raised stone, stopped and looked at it. "The Einsatzgruppe followed us through Russia, killing thousands of the villagers we had "liberated." He raised his eyes to meet Lucas's. "In the beginning, we didn't know what they were doing, but the time arrived when we knew but didn't admit it, even to ourselves." He looked down the middle of the street, visualizing something.

"We saw their starving victims working on the roads, mostly captured Russian soldiers, and we knew that when they became too weak, the guards would shoot them. At first, they were careful not to do it when and where we could see, but some did, and, eventually, those who saw and heard told someone else until finally, we all knew."

He waved his arms hopelessly, then pointed at Lucas. "We deserve no mercy, and the Russians, when they get to Germany, will show us what they think of men who kill Russian women and children and bury them in pits!" He was shouting—Lucas listened with his head down. Klaus kicked a stone off the sidewalk with much more force than required.

Lucas waved his arms, frustrated. "Why didn't you do something? When you knew, why didn't you run away or use your tank to stop them?" He cried, raised his head, unashamed of his tears as he looked at Klaus. "How is it going to end now…are the Russians going to kill every German? Will they kill Theo and Maria—will they kill Corinne?"

Klaus waved his hand toward something in the distance. "What does it matter how it ends? The only important thing is that it will end soon. I am Waffen SS…look at my black uniform…my little skull." He pointed to his sleeve. "I am one of the bad guys, and when the war is over, the Allies will call me a criminal because I didn't use my tank to stop the madness…and the truth is, I am still using it to protect those bastards hiding here in Berlin!

"The world expected us to revolt against Hitler years ago, but we told ourselves that we must fight for Germany, the greatest country in the world, and then Hitler became Germany!" Klaus stared at Lucas; Lucas kept his eyes level.

"You must grow up, Lucas, or you will get us all killed! We still have a lot of fighting in front of us, and survival is what we are fighting for."

The look on Klaus's face as he pushed past Lucas and walked the last block to the Berliner Allee told Lucas that Klaus regretted saying too much. Lucas hesitated, trying to decide whether to ask the question on his lips, then didn't catch Klaus until he stopped at the Allee.

Klaus was looking across the street when Lucas stopped beside him and adjusted the centre of his vision to look where Klaus had his eyes focused.

◇◇◇◇◇◇◇◇◇◇◇◇◇◇◇◇◇◇◇◇◇◇◇◇◇◇◇◇◇◇◇

A soldier stood in the bed of a Lastwagen that had stopped on the other side of the street. He had a rope in his hands. He expertly threw the rope over the arm of a lamppost while two soldiers pulled a struggling boy off one of two benches filled with wailing boys, all with their hands tied behind them. Klaus turned to Lucas and tried to push him back, but Lucas stepped around him, his eyes locked on the terrified boy's face. The soldier slipped a noose over the boy's head and knotted the free end of the rope into a loop just above the noose so the rope couldn't slide off the lamppost.

"Vorwärts!" The soldier shouted over the boy's screams; the truck stepped ahead, and the sound of the boy's cry stopped. His face turned blue as his kicking body swung back and forth. The Lastwagen stopped under the next lamppost, and the soldiers dragged another boy to his fate.

"We must get out of here!" Klaus grabbed Lucas's arm, but Lucas tore it away from him. Klaus hesitated, watching Lucas's face as a second Lastwagen drove behind the execution truck and stopped just past the boy whose kicks became weak as he slowly died. Lucas could see a soldier standing at the rear of the second truck, shouting at boys sitting on benches. "This is what happens to cowards, to every Verweigerer who refuses to fight for the Vaterland!"

"Nein! Nein!" Lucas screamed and tried to run to the boy, but Klaus caught him around the neck and pulled him to the ground. One of the soldiers in the second Lastwagen shouted, "Halt!" The truck stopped, and the soldiers watched Lucas struggle to get up.

"You can't help him!" Lucas heard Klaus's voice from far away. He flailed, but Klaus was stronger and more determined. The soldier in the Lastwagen worked the bolt in his Gewehr 98 rifle.

"Lucas, stay on the ground...you can't help them... You must help yourself!" Klaus pushed down on Lucas's shoulders until Lucas could no longer find the energy to fight. He closed his eyes and heard the first Lastwagen's brakes squeal, a boy's screams, the sound of the truck's engine, and the boy's choked-off cry as it stepped ahead. The open Lastwagen, full of crying boys forced to watch their friends die, stepped ahead, and Lucas heard the soldier repeat the promise Hitler had made to anyone who questioned his authority or dared to be disloyal.

Distance killed the sounds as the gruesome scene worked its way along the street. Lucas's body relaxed; his sobs became weak, like those of a broken-hearted child.

Klaus helped him stand; Lucas had difficulty connecting his legs to his brain. He held onto Klaus and forced himself to look at the now-still boy hanging from the lamppost across the street. There was a sign pinned to his narrow chest below his terrified purple face and bulging eyes. Legible even from across the street, it had a single word written across it—"Verweigerer," one who refuses to fight for the Vaterland.

Klaus whispered, "No, Lucas...don't look...don't look." He grabbed Lucas's chin and pulled his face around to look into his eyes. When he tried to look away, Klaus pulled his head again. Lucas closed his eyes, and Klaus spoke again from far away.

"He is like you, a Kindersoldat." With a bitterness that Lucas had never heard from him, Klaus said, "Those people are dangerous animals!" He squeezed Lucas's chin. "Open your eyes and look at me."

Lucas sobbed and opened them. Klaus's steel-grey eyes held determination, not sympathy.

"You must not fight them; it will do no good. You cannot win; you will just get yourself and probably others killed!" Klaus released Lucas's chin and pointed across the street. "Do you see the people on the sidewalk?" He pointed with his arm.

For the first time, Lucas noticed people on the sidewalks on both sides of the street. Some ran away; some stood with their heads up, staring at the boys; others lowered their heads. On the next block, where the trucks extended the line of kicking and screaming boys, a woman fainted in a man's arms. Two children buried their faces in their mother's skirt.

"Yes, sir, I see them."

Klaus released him and said, "Those people stood and watched their government kill those boys—I haven't seen a single person object. Why do you suppose they would stand there while their army murders their children in front of their eyes? Surely, they are not all animals."

Lucas knew the truth and said it out loud, bitterly.

"If they said or did anything, the soldiers in the Lastwagen would shoot them."

Lucas looked at the dead boy hanging from the post across the street and then at his mentor. He wiped his face with his sleeve. "I don't care if I die—I will fight these people! I must fight them!"

Klaus's expression frightened Lucas. When he spoke, the tone was as cold as the Russian winter, "Lucas, you will never win! You are just like those people on the sidewalk and the boys hanging from the posts. If you fight them, your foolish actions will kill everyone close to you, whether they join you or not." Klaus put his hand on Lucas's shoulder and squeezed so hard he winced.

"I don't want anyone in my tank who is fighting for anything but survival, and if you insist on changing sides, you might as well catch up to those bastards and let them kill you now. Who knows, you might kill one or two if you can find a gun somewhere!"

Klaus spoke to Lucas's bowed head and went on.

"You said that I should have used my tank to stop the SS or the SD from murdering Russian women and children..." He pointed down the street to where the Lastwagen had finally disappeared. The boys' screams had stopped. "Some of those murderers are not SS or SD, or SA—they wear the Wehrmacht uniform, as do you, and they murdered German children in front of you, me, and a hundred others... most of them good people. We were all witnesses to murder—German citizens walking to work, to the market, to visit their friends, and men fighting to save them from the Russians. Within weeks, the Russians will level their homes, rape the women, and take the children away. The soldiers did not attempt to hide their deeds; they wanted us to see and tell others. Hitler wants us to know that he can murder anyone who isn't prepared to die for him, and those who oppose him can do nothing about it! He believes that he is a God and has the power of life and death over others. He is afraid that if he loosens the reins of terror, we will revolt and stop this madness. And, of course, he is right!"

Klaus grabbed Lucas's shoulder and said in his Waffen SS commander tone, "I want to know who you are fighting for and against. If you don't care whether you live or die, I don't want you in my tank! I have to know that you will shoot whoever and whatever I tell you to shoot and do it without question or hesitation. You are a child like those boys, and I have no right to ask, but I need you to trust me."

Lucas thought about Corinne, Maria, Theo, and the men in the Panther. He knew what he had to say, and he said it. "I will fight to save my comrades, myself, and our panzer. I trust you and will follow your orders without question or hesitation."

Lucas knew his life had changed. Nothing would ever be the same.

Klaus turned toward the SS house and began walking. When Lucas pulled alongside, Klaus said, "Thank you, Lucas. You have earned the right to call yourself a man."

◇◇◇◇◇◇◇◇◇◇◇◇◇◇◇◇◇◇◇◇◇◇◇◇◇◇◇◇◇◇◇◇◇◇◇◇

When Klaus and Lucas walked into the room that served as a lounge and bar, Marcus looked up from his plush chair and asked with a grin, "How was the walk?" A glass of whiskey sat on a small table to his right.

Klaus got a beer and seated himself in a soft chair beside Lucas. He drank a quarter of the glass, then spoke carefully.

"We saw something all of you should see. Our brave SS and Wehrmacht are hanging boys from every lamppost on the Berliner Allee. They're pinning a sheet of paper to the boy's chests—apparently, they're killing them because the boys are Verweigerer; they dared to refuse to die for Hitler." Klaus looked from one man to another while he waited, and Lucas was surprised when he sensed Klaus wasn't sure how they would respond.

Simon spoke first, his deep, resonant voice loud in the quiet room.

"If we allow one soldier to refuse, others will follow! Without discipline, the army will collapse and then where will the country be? We can't win this war if we allow soldiers to choose whether or not they will fight!"

"They were children, not soldiers!" The edge in Klaus's voice should have told Simon to shut up, but the man's ignorance wouldn't let him hear it.

"You don't know that—did you see their Ausweis?"

Simon's ignorance blinded him to the signs of Klaus's impending explosion, and the stupid man waded into deep water.

"Hitler can't govern the country if he doesn't have the authority to get rid of anyone who refuses to fight for him. To disobey Hitler is unpatriotic—he represents our country, and if you ask me, it serves those Verweigerer right! He pointed toward the Allee. "The only reason I would go down there is to spit in their traitorous faces!"

Lucas hadn't expected the reaction; he had already decided that he hated the radio operator—now he knew why. He looked at Klaus as he started to open his mouth, and Klaus shook his head. Lucas decided to be quiet.

Marcus looked at Klaus, then shouted at Simon, "Jesus, Simon, are you crazy? They are children; they don't belong in an army any more than Lucas does!"

Lucas almost shouted, but his brain and Klaus's expression told him to hold his tongue.

Sitting in a comfortable plush chair, Kristian lowered his head and said nothing. Marcus picked up his jacket and asked, "Kristian, are you coming with me? I must get out of here before I do something I shouldn't!"

Marcus avoided looking at Simon, who was drinking his whiskey again.

Kristian nodded, grabbed his coat, and looked at Simon as he spoke to everyone in the room. "I don't think we should talk too loudly about this; eyes and ears are everywhere." Simon ignored the comment and concentrated on the magazine he had on his lap. Klaus left his glass on the bar, and Lucas followed him outside.

The following day, Simon returned from an early walk and announced that the boys were gone. No one commented or said "Guten Morgen" to him.

◇◇◇◇◇◇◇◇◇◇◇◇◇◇◇◇◇◇◇◇◇◇◇◇◇◇◇◇◇◇◇◇◇◇◇

Five days of rest passed quickly, and Simon's comrades gradually accepted the brutality that was part of his inherent stupidity and ignorant personality. But the gulf had widened between him and the rest of the crew. No one wanted to sit beside him at mealtime, and they ignored him when he spoke.

During the drive back to base, the men were quiet, and Lucas was happy to keep it that way. The night was dark and bone-chilling damp, and the cold, the darkness, and a light rain underscored the depressing mood.

Lucas thought about the death that likely awaited him—he couldn't imagine one worse than those boys had suffered. But his worst fear was that he might not see the men who had hanged the boys choking on the end of justice's ropes. The faces of the two soldiers putting nooses around the children's necks were forever burned into Lucas's memory, and he resolved to survive to tell someone what those men had done. He decided he wanted the Western Allies to win, not the Russians and certainly not Hitler. Lucas wanted Hitler dead!

The truck arrived at the barracks at midnight, and Lucas adjusted his life to the routines of war.

Chapter Twenty-six

April 1945

Seelow

"Compelled to become instruments of war, to kill and be killed, child soldiers are forced to give violent expression to the hatreds of adults."

Olara Otunnu

Klaus joined his men at their table in the dining tent. "I just came from a commanders' meeting, boys—vacation is over—we're going to Seelow."

Using his finger, Marcus steadied a big bite of hard-boiled egg on his spoon.

"What's in Seelow?" "Have the Russians crossed the river?" He pushed the egg into his mouth, grabbed his cup, and a gulp of coffee followed the egg.

"Yes, they started their attack on the first of three defence lines yesterday before daylight. General Busse had vacated it, so we didn't take many casualties, but the Russians took the position. They lost thousands of men and hundreds of tanks, but they didn't stop."

Simon spoke with his mouth full, wagging his spoon at Klaus. "It's about time we stood and fought the fucking Russians! That's what Hitler wants, but as soon as the Russians get close, those cowards we have for generals cut and run!"

Klaus grinned cynically and pointed at his radio operator. "You're right, Simon…when we get there, I'm going to give you a Papa and let you stand and fight the Russians while we cut and run." Everyone laughed, but their heart wasn't in it.

Klaus turned his attention to the men in the twelve-panzer squadron that would follow him to Seelow. "Intelligence says the Russians have over a million men, three thousand tanks, and seventeen thousand pieces of artillery on the Oder River near Seelow. And we must stop them with about a hundred thousand infantry and a hundred and fifty tanks. Realistically, all we can do is slow the Russians down; optimistically, we could hurt them bad enough that they will stop, at least for a while."

Simon broke in. "Yeah, and Hitler has a new weapon that will wipe out a whole tank battalion. If we slow the Russians, Hitler will destroy them before they get into Germany!"

Klaus looked at Simon as he would a child. "Simon, they're already in Germany, and there is no magic weapon. We will do what our generals tell us to do. Busse wants us to fight actions that will hit the Russians hard, then withdraw to fight again. A strategic withdrawal—if necessary, all the way to Berlin. That way, we give Hitler, Stalin, and the Western Allies time to stop this madness!"

Simon said something under his breath about Hitler never accepting the Russian surrender, but Klaus ignored him.

"We will defend the last line…Hitler calls it the Wotan line."

Lucas raised his hand like a student in school and said, "Wotan is the top God in Wagner's Ring Cycle operas."

"Sounds like a good choice." Kristian laughed. "We need a top God on our side right now."

Lucas didn't laugh. He said, "No, it's not a good choice. Valhalla, the home of all Gods, burned to the ground, killing Wotan in the last Ring Cycle opera."

Klaus gave Lucas a condescending look as the tank crews that heard the conversation stared at the foolish boy. Klaus spoke to his men, trying to relieve the tension.

"It doesn't matter what happened in an opera, and Wotan is not a God; he's a figment of someone's imagination. The Gods have deserted our battlefield and gone over to the Russians—if they were ever on our side, we did something to make them mad." Everyone knew what Klaus meant by 'something.'

◇◇◇◇◇◇◇◇◇◇◇◇◇◇◇◇◇◇◇◇◇◇◇◇◇◇◇◇◇◇◇◇

When the twelve Panthers under Klaus's command reached the battlefield, Leutnant Finke's Jäger Company led them through the woods to a forested ridge overlooking fields that lay between the low hill and the Oder River. Klaus's force lay in wait for the First Belarusians, the most significant armed force in the Russian Army and one of the largest in history. There would be targets galore, and Klaus's Panther squadron was in a perfect position to do maximum damage.

Klaus situated his panzers deep enough in the forest to hide them from prowling aircraft above and Russian eyes in the open fields below. The Jäger scouts predicted the arrival of a Russian probe at nine o'clock, and they didn't disappoint the German panzers. Thirty T-34s confidently worked their way toward the Wotan line, driving through the fields, spread out in loose formation. They escorted ten tank destroyers and five hundred infantry as they moved toward their first objective. They were the bait sent out to probe the resistance the main force would face when they attacked the second German defence line. The second line was five kilometres from the Belarussians' final objective—the northern flank of the Wotan Line.

The panzers' job was to discourage the Russians and buy time for the Wehrmacht and the politicians. A stalemate at Seelow could save Germany from invasion and Berlin from a Russian occupation.

The Belarussian tanks and self-propelled guns drove up the hill, unaware of Klaus's twelve Panthers and a hundred German artillery guns waiting for them to enter their killing ground. The German artillery had sighted their 88s on the field, five hundred metres in front of the centre of the Panthers' line, awaiting Leutnant Finke's command. Klaus's panzers waited a hundred metres apart in a thousand-metre stretch of woods. If a Russian turned to face one of the Panthers with his thickest armour, he left his side vulnerable to another Panther. In battle terms, the trap would expose the probing force to the Panthers' cannons and German artillery for a long time. Klaus's tanks could reload and fire many times before the Russians could get out of range.

Klaus said into the intercom, "Simon, tell the squadron to move to the firing position."

Simon repeated the order on the battle frequency.

Kristian squeezed 227 between two tall spruce trees, and Lucas put his sight on the rearmost T-34, designated as his first target.

Klaus spoke softly. "Range, nine hundred."

Lucas set the range and verified it using the T-34 dimension chart he had memorized and the small 'mil' triangles built into the sight. He adjusted the gun using the fine-sighting wheels, slowly moving the long barrel ahead, following the dark shape until Klaus shouted, "Fire!"

Lucas touched the trigger, the Panther jumped slightly, and twelve 75 mm high-velocity armour-piercing shells screamed as they parted the air at three times the speed of sound, travelling to their targets in less than a second. Ten T-34s stopped in their tracks; a few blew up, and two became flaming coffins. The remaining Russian tanks pivoted to face the Germans, exposing their sides to three of the Panthers' cannons.

The roar of 88 mm cannon shells landing among the Russians was deafening, even inside 227. German artillery fired from five kilometres away, and as Lucas's sight rested on a second T-34, it disappeared in a curtain of mud. When the curtain fell, Lucas saw that the direct hit had destroyed it, leaving no possibility of survivors. Klaus directed Lucas to a new target; Lucas picked it out in the melee and hit it full on the front armour, piercing the driver's compartment and igniting the ammunition. Lucas heard Marcus slide a shell into the barrel and slam the breech home.

Klaus said, "Lucas, use the machine gun on the infantry!" and Lucas sprayed a stream of bullets at men running for their lives, deserting their tanks. Many of the infantry, completely disoriented, ran toward the Germans. They couldn't see hidden Jäger soldiers firing MG 42 machine guns at them, and it was too late when they figured it out, turned and tried to run. The machine guns cut them down like sheep.

Using the 5x sight, Lucas searched the wreckage of tanks and guns that littered the field but could find nothing worthy of bullets, let alone a cannon round. Simon fired at fleeing Russian soldiers until Klaus told him to stop wasting ammunition.

◇◇◇◇◇◇◇◇◇◇◇◇◇◇◇◇◇◇◇◇◇◇◇◇◇◇◇◇

General Busse's Battle headquarters ordered Klaus's panzers to join the main force at the Wotan line as soon as possible. Klaus decided not to take his Panthers into the open and expose them to the dominant Russian Air Force—he would withdraw into the forest and travel northwest, taking a dog-leg route. Lucas stayed in the gunner's seat while the

Panthers crashed through the forest, holding onto whatever he could reach. The scouts led them on narrow forest roads where they existed, and the panzers raced across short stretches of open ground when there was no alternative.

They joined the rest of General Busse's 11th Panzergrenadier Nord Panzers at noon, a little later than planned, but without firing a shot. They were ten kilometres closer to Berlin, opposite the end of the Wotan line, where Busse had ordered them to stop the massive 1st Belarussian Army. If Busse's forces failed to halt the Russians there, Stalin would knock down Hitler's door in less than a month.

"Thank God that's over." Marcus opened the rear turret hatch and dragged himself onto the plate over the engine. Lucas joined him, and Marcus lit a match on his pant leg. He waited for the phosphorous flare to die and lit his cigarette. He drew smoke into his lungs, took the cigarette out of his mouth and said, "Next time, I take the gunner's seat, and you bounce around."

Klaus spoke from the cupola, sitting on the front edge with one foot on the rear and the other dangling inside. "Alright, Marcus, you can take the gunner's seat when we go inside." He was smoking a half-burned cigarette. "This one is not going to be like shooting rabbits. This morning's skirmish was an intentional sacrifice by the Russians to find out where we were and what we've got." He took a long pull on the cigarette, then crushed the short stub on five centimetres of steel plate. "Now, we will find out what they've got."

Marcus tried to put an optimistic tone in his voice, but the obvious effort ruined it. "We've got more than we showed them—they won't expect that." He puffed on his cigarette when Leutnant Finke and his sergeant approached the tank, then took it out of his mouth when Finke didn't waste time on a greeting.

"The Eleventh Panzergrenadier Nord has just over a hundred tanks in these woods, a thousand guns scattered two to ten kilometres behind us, and about a hundred thousand infantry, including the men on the Wotan line. We are waiting to meet the First Belarussian Army— about fifteen thousand guns, three thousand tanks and a million men. The Belarusians now know what to expect, and they will commit every tank, man, and gun to annihilate us. It's a perfect day to fly, and the

Russian Air Force will send every plane they have. We're all that's between them and Berlin, and it's a four-hour drive in a T-34. Are there any questions?"

Klaus asked, "Will you be fighting to the last man?"

Finke laughed sarcastically, "My Sergeant and I will mark out a retreat for when it gets too hot here. You can follow us or not—we will take you with us if you don't wait too long."

"We'll go when we're ready...I assure you that I have no intention of dying in this forest. Will you wait for us?"

"Depends... The Russians are going to hit you with artillery and bombs—let's see what your tanks look like in a few hours." Finke and his sergeant disappeared into the forest, away from the tanks and the Wotan line.

Lucas looked at the spot where they had gone into the woods. There was something about the Leutnant...

He asked Marcus, "How old do you think the Leutnant is?"

Marcus pinched the hot end of his cigarette and put the butt in his shirt pocket.

"He's not as old as he looks, but I would say at least forty-five."

"I thought I saw something familiar in his face, but I don't know anyone that old."

Marcus chuckled. "It must be nice to be so young you think forty-five is old!"

Lucas followed Marcus into the turret, closed the rear hatch while Klaus buttoned down the cover on the cupola and lowered his seat. He spoke into the intercom.

"Simon, tell the squadron to prepare for bombardment. No tank within five metres of another tank. Kristian, move us five metres sideways, away from the command tank." Simon confirmed and sent the message. Kristian reversed, turned left and drove ahead to increase the distance between 227 and the 11th Panzergrenadier Nord commander's King Tiger.

Twenty minutes later, the Russians confirmed Leutnant Finke's prediction when two thousand Russian artillery pieces fired their first salvo.

The deafening reverberation of explosions among the 11th Panzergrenadier Nord tanks swallowed the scream of shells travelling at over twice the speed of sound. Marcus's mouth said, "Hold on!" but the continuous thunder drowned out his voice. Individual explosions merged into a steady roar as the Panther shook.

Lucas grabbed the gun breach with both hands and held on. He swallowed, trying to find saliva for his dry mouth. Sweat ran into his eyes, he worked hard to breathe, and his stomach revolted.

An explosion rang the steel hull like a massive bell, lifted the side and let it fall back with a sharp jolt. Despite the strips of cloth Lucas had stuffed into his ears, the sharp sound of explosions cut painfully through to his eardrums. He focused on keeping his brain working—it was trying to switch off.

Lucas looked past the gun at Marcus, leaning against the side of the turret, lighting the short cigarette butt with one hand while holding on with the other. Lucas's fear diminished below panic levels, his stomach settled, and he began to win the battle with his brain.

The crews exchanged battle stories at night around the fires, and inevitably, they included descriptions of the bombardments they had faced during their retreat across Russia and Poland. Marcus had described in gruesome detail the American air bombardments he had experienced in the boot of Italy, particularly the one that had flipped the 70-tonne Tiger he was sitting in on its side. As Lucas watched Marcus suck on his cigarette until it burned his fingers, every story he had ever heard about artillery came back. When he listened to the stories, he had discounted half the drama as embellishment but now realized that exaggeration was impossible.

Terrified but determined, Lucas braced his feet and steadied himself with his left hand on the breech. He braced himself with his right hand pushed against the turret's roof and looked through the fixed periscope.

He saw men running through a curtain of exploding shells, flying dirt and branches. They dodged around trees and ducked flying debris. A man disappeared, then reappeared, flying through a curtain of dirt. The others still ran, but then two more fell. Three men ran a gauntlet of falling trees and bursting shells and disappeared.

A metallic explosion near 227 signalled the death of the neighbouring Panther; it split open like a can of Wurst. A shell landed in a shallow slit trench—there had not been enough time to dig deep ones—and men flew three metres into the air. Lucas was terrified, but the panic was gone. The tears that had threatened to overwhelm him dried up, and his thoughts returned to Detmold and Corinne.

Fifteen minutes of pounding ceased without preamble or diminuendo; the roar of the bombardment suddenly stopped. Lucas turned to Marcus, who was looking through his sight. He waited until Marcus pulled his head back, looked around the turret, and finally settled his eyes on him. Lucas wanted to believe he was misreading the fear in his mentor's face.

Klaus raised the hatch slightly, looked through the slits all around the compass, then cranked the cupola hatch tight in its groove and lowered his seat. Lucas met Klaus's stare, and Klaus spoke in the intercom.

"They stopped their guns because the bombers are coming. For the uninitiated, they will blast the tree canopy with the first wave, and then they will drop high explosives. It's probably a bad time to plan for the future. If you believe God will answer your prayers favourably, now would be a good time to ask him for help. It's for sure no one else can stop those bombers!"

Lucas recognized the distant sound of aircraft and raised himself to the periscope. Healthy men assisted the wounded, and he could see two undamaged panzers. Fallen trees covered the strip of ground in his field of vision, and two mangled soldiers' bodies lay partially covered with branches.

Lucas looked at Klaus and suddenly felt sick. His stomach surged; acid burned his throat and filled his mouth, and he forced himself to swallow. He left the periscope, wedged himself in his seat, and, despite his best efforts, he retched, spraying his boots and the shells beside his feet.

<hr>

The sound of engines and propellers had grown to a steady rumble when the aircraft released their bombs. Lucas tried to fight his growing fear, but he cried out when the first bombs struck.

The sound of explosions drowned out the crash of falling trees and the screams of men. When the first wave finished its work, the comforting sound of the Panther's idling engine filled the short pause. And then the second wave was overhead, dropping high explosives—the explosions were sharper and louder. Lucas closed his eyes, tears flowing down his cheeks, and said, "I love you, Corinne!"

Certain that this was his last opportunity, he tried to pray but found no comfort. Ten minutes of hell passed, and like a rabbit accepting its fate in the jaws of the fox, Lucas slipped into the trance-like peace that precedes inevitable death.

The forest suddenly became quiet—the sounds of aircraft diminished to silence, and Lucas tried to decide whether that was a good or a bad omen.

Marcus looked through the gunsight, flicked it to 2.5x, but left it stationary.

"I can see a mess out there, but if I'm going to see more, I need to swing the turret, and I'm not sure it won't break something."

Klaus wound his hatch upward and peeked through the slits under it. "Don't swing the turret or move the Panzer. We will give the Jäger scouts time to find us and remove a tree or two before we go outside."

A few minutes later, a rifle butt tapped the top of the cover, and a voice said, "Open the hatch; It's Finke." Klaus jacked it up, swung it aside, and the Jäger Leutnant's head appeared. The combination of face and name flipped a switch in Lucas's confused brain.

Lucas opened the rear hatch and stuck his head out. There wasn't an undamaged tree standing, and dead and dying soldiers littered the ground. It appeared that many soldiers had been killed by large splinters of wood and falling trees as well as from shrapnel or bomb blasts. The Panther couldn't move without running over a dead or wounded German.

Remarkably, soldiers stood up everywhere—more got to their feet than stayed on the ground! They immediately helped the wounded move out of the path the Panzers would have to take. The uninjured soldiers gathered in groups, checked their weapons, and readied themselves for the coming fight.

The attack had destroyed or damaged almost half the tanks Lucas could see, including the commander's King Tiger on their right flank. One of the Tiger's tracks lay beside it, the turret was askew, and the business end of its 88 mm gun was stuck in the ground. It was obvious no one had survived.

Lucas tried to listen to the Leutnant talking to Klaus. He clearly saw the Jäger's face when he raised himself to point to where the Russians would come. Finke was not an uncommon name, but Lucas was sure the face was the one in the photographs in Johann Finke's room! He looked older to Lucas, but war and a beard changed any face.

Lucas heard him say, "There are hundreds of tanks and hundreds of thousands of infantry over that hill, but I have worked out the escape route whenever you need it. The Russians will follow your tanks, and we found a perfect place to set up an ambush three kilometres from here." Leutnant Finke waved his arm in a northerly direction. "I lost my radio, so communication may be a problem."

Klaus nodded. "Simon has a radio you can borrow so we can stay in contact." Over the intercom, he asked Simon to pass up the radio, then turned to the Leutnant. "How many men do you have?"

Finke said, "As far as I know, four."

Lucas slid back into the turret, took the radio from Simon, and pulled himself out of the rear hatch. "Finke, you're Johann Finke?" He shouted louder than he needed to and pushed the heavy radio toward the Leutnant.

"Yes, I am. Who are you?" He leaned over to take the radio from Lucas, then passed it down to a Jäger soldier.

"Lucas Schwartz. Before I left Detmold, I slept in your bed at Gartenstrasse 18! I stared at your picture every night!" Lucas laughed. "Now that I see you, it may have been a picture of someone else."

"Lucas Schwartz... Yes, my parents told me about you in their letters." Johann paused, looked up and scanned the area before lowering his head again. His voice changed slightly. "Have you heard anything from them or Barbara?"

"We haven't gotten mail for a month...everyone was fine when I last heard..." Lucas intended to go on, but Klaus interrupted.

"Knock it off; we've got a war to fight!" Klaus stretched himself upward to see what was in front of the Panther's treads. He spoke to

Kristian through the intercom. "Kristian, open your hatch so you can see, then move ahead carefully to the edge of the woods. Try not to run over anyone." Leaving a short second of dead air, he continued, "Marcus, swing the turret slowly clockwise until the big tree falls off. You and Lucas will clean up the small pieces and straighten the camouflage as Kristian moves ahead."

Leutnant Finke turned to leave, but Klaus touched his arm and said, "We will have to slow the Russians down a little. My squadron will stay here to cover the withdrawal of the rest of the tanks and the infantry."

Johann jumped down, helped the men move the wounded and dead from the Panther's path, then disappeared. Marcus swung the turret until the tree fell on the ground, then climbed out the rear hatch and helped Lucas clear trees and branches from the hull. They heaved the end of another tree over the side as the Panther slowly eased ahead.

Lucas and Marcus cleaned broken branches off the canvas camouflage and strategically organized sticks and branches, tied where they would best hide the tank from the air. Klaus kept a steady stream of instructions flowing until 227 reached a point where it had a clear field of fire. As they carefully moved into position, Lucas counted sixty functioning tanks.

<hr>

The infantry soldiers worked fast and hard, building wooden walls of trees around their machine guns and mortars, digging shallow holes so they would be below ground level when they were behind them. Lucas estimated he could see a thousand men within a few hundred metres of 227, camouflaged behind branches and trees and invisible to anyone in the field in front of them. Some crouched behind MG-42 machine guns, others stood ready to feed ammunition to them, but most carried rifles.

Fifty thousand well-armed men and sixty Panthers spread out over a thousand metres was a destructive power beyond Lucas's imagination. He couldn't imagine a force that could move them. Without the panzers to stop the T-34s, the infantry line would crumble, and none of the panzers had enough fuel or ammunition to fight a protracted battle. The withdrawal's timing would be critical.

Empty open fields lay spread out for two thousand metres in front of the 11th Panzergrenadier Nord. But they only had to wait half an hour before an unbroken line of Russian armour, surrounded by clouds of infantry, flowed like a wave over the ridge at the other side of the field. When Lucas took his last look before sliding through the hatch behind Marcus, the juggernaut was a hundred metres deep, and specks still flowed over the ridge behind them.

Klaus said, "Lucas, you take the gun, and Marcus, you will load."

Marcus reluctantly grabbed the hatch handle. The inside of the tank smelled like stale puke. He took a deep breath and thought about leaving the hatch open but decided to pull it shut.

He grumbled to Klaus, "Don't you think Lucas should work in his own puke?"

Lucas, embarrassed, said nothing but slid neatly into the gunner's seat, and Klaus positioned his feet on both sides of his hips. Klaus left his hatch open so he could stand and range the shots using his 'donkey ears' binoculars. Fortuitously, it also kept his head above the stench.

German artillery began their barrage on the oncoming Russians before Lucas adjusted the range. He watched the Soviet line through the magnified sight as shells screamed overhead, and it disappeared into a wall of flying dirt. The field's fertile black soil created a moving curtain in front of the oncoming Russians, making sighting difficult.

Klaus said, "The range to the first line of tanks is fourteen hundred and fifty metres. Start firing, Lucas—pick your targets, and remember, we will need every shell we've got! Do not miss!"

Lucas swung the gun to find a target in the flying dirt, setting the sight according to Klaus's instructions. He picked a T-34 and was verifying the range using the horizontal triangles when an artillery shell blasted dirt in front of it. He chose another T-34 and, with everything already set, pulled the trigger when the tip of the triangle touched the center of its side armour. The tank stopped dead as a streak of flame squeezed under the T-34's turret—a bad sign for the Belarussian crew.

Over a thousand German cannons fired as fast as their crews could load them; the blasts from their exploding shells obscured the battlefield. Lucas had difficulty finding targets, but tanks and destroyers appeared out of the turmoil as the range decreased. Klaus continuously measured and shouted distances to the tanks, and Lucas picked them off as fast as Marcus could ram a shell in the barrel and close the breech. He found a rhythm: sight, fire, find a target, check the range, sight and fire again. Lucas destroyed tank after tank, one every four or five seconds.

Lucas lost count, but others still took their place, and infantry kept filling the space between them. The Russian tanks took no evasive action except to turn and face the German positions, targeting the general area where the Panthers hid in the smashed forest. Klaus twice backed 227 farther into the woods, and twice he moved his Panther sideways. Russian artillery kept up a continuous barrage on the general area where the German tanks wreaked such havoc, covering a wide area but doing little damage.

"Simon, tell everyone but our squadron to withdraw as planned… the infantry too." Klaus waited until Simon verified that the order had been sent and received, then said, "Report to headquarters that all but twenty Panthers and one King Tiger are withdrawing to the rendezvous point. We are low on ammunition but will defend this position as long as possible."

Seconds later, Simon said on the intercom, "General Busse confirmed receipt and wished us good luck." He didn't sound cheerful, and Lucas assumed he objected to the withdrawal.

◇◇◇◇◇◇◇◇◇◇◇◇◇◇◇◇◇◇◇◇◇◇◇◇◇◇◇◇◇◇◇◇

The retreating tanks took as many wounded soldiers as they could get on them; those who could run had to jog behind.

Klaus moved his twenty-one Panzers farther apart to deceive the Russian gunners. The Soviet Air Force renewed their bombing, but Luftwaffe fighters harassed them, causing the Soviets to miss their dispersed targets by a wide margin.

Lucas flipped his sight to 2.5x to widen his field of view as he watched another wave of Russian tanks and infantry appear on the ridge. Klaus said, "Range, a thousand meters; pick one."

Lucas flipped back to 5x, followed a T-34 and fired as soon as the sight synchronized on it. The tank stopped.

"How many shells do we have?" Klaus shouted above the din of battle. It was the loader's job to keep track.

"Twenty-two, I think..." Marcus answered breathlessly.

"Lucas, stop firing. Simon, call the squadron and tell them to follow me; then call headquarters and tell them we're withdrawing."

Marcus slammed the breech just as a shell hit the front armour, ricocheted off and whizzed past the cupola, exploding in the trees behind them. Klaus waited for the clang to die before he spoke. "Kristian, reverse straight back, slowly. Don't turn until I tell you."

While the Panther reversed, Simon passed Marcus the last of the shells stored in the lower hull, and Marcus laid them in the turret racks. A rain of explosions dug up the ground behind them; another 76 mm from the T-34s bounced off 227, and again the angled armour plating saved them.

"Okay, Kristian, turn around and get us the hell out of here before they get lucky!" Klaus wound the cupola hatch cover down to the slits as the blast from a near-miss blew off half the spare track segments hanging on the sides to augment the thin 50 mm side armour.

Two-two-seven turned, followed by twenty other panzers. Klaus's Panther and ten others looked like junkyard candidates, but everything worked so the fight would continue.

Lucas watched trees swing past his gunsight as the forty tonnes of steel turned; Kristian found a forward gear, drove ahead a hundred metres and stopped. Marcus opened the rear hatch, and a hand grabbed the edge. Marcus looked at Lucas and said, "It's Leutnant Finke and the Finn sergeant; they made it!" Lucas forgot the reality of his situation and let a jolt of joy take over when they climbed onto the tank's rump.

◇◇◇◇◇◇◇◇◇◇◇◇◇◇◇◇◇◇◇◇◇◇◇◇◇◇◇◇◇◇◇◇◇◇◇◇

Panther 227 led the squadron down a woods road, then left it to crash through a forest at breakneck speed, crushing trees and rotten stumps under its treads. The panzer rocked back and forth, from one side to the other on its soft torsion-bar suspension, throwing its occupants against whatever was next to them. The lone King Tiger fell behind, along with the sounds of German artillery pounding the Russians.

"The Russians are hesitating!" As they drove over a ridge, Klaus held the rubber cups on his binoculars tight against his face and announced, "They aren't going to catch us!"

Leutnant Finke and Viänü, the Finn, ducked behind the turret as trees and branches slapped the tank's sides. Lucas heard Johann yell through Klaus's open hatch, "Don't slow down... Follow the blazes... It's not much farther!" Klaus had his head below the edge of his hatch so the whipping branches wouldn't hit him. Kristian had opened his hatch to see without Klaus's help and frequently had to duck inside to avoid the trees he was knocking down. Lucas instinctively ducked when a falling tree whipped past the sight.

Leutnant Finke led the Panthers across a shallow stream flowing through the forest across their path; the bottom was firm, and the water, barely a metre deep, didn't reach the top of the treads.

Across the river, two-two-seven led eighteen Panthers on a narrow path straight ahead for five hundred metres and turned right through a field of stumps when their tracks were beyond the sight of anyone at the stream. Without slowing, Kristian drove into thick second-growth trees ten metres tall, following blazes up a hill.

When Panther 227 stopped, Lucas looked through his sight and saw that the Panther was between small trees at the edge of a cutover area. Across the clearing, less than three hundred metres from the tracks they had made when they crossed the creek, Lucas saw and understood the massacre Johann had planned.

When the Russians crossed the stream, they would have the German tanks on their right flank and above them, exposing their weakest armour to the Panther guns' first shot. Foresters had cut all the mature trees on both sides of the stream several years before, and the new growth was small and sparse, offering no cover for tanks as they crossed the strip of water and drove over the clear-cut area. The ambush would expose the Russians for a long time in the open. The soft spring ground and stumps at least forty centimetres in diameter and thirty centimetres high would make it almost impossible for the T-34s to maneuver.

As the slow Tiger reached the stream, Klaus said into the intercom, "Simon, tell the Tiger to follow our tracks past the stream before doubling back. I don't want it making any tracks that lead to us." A minute later, Simon confirmed the message had been received, and the Tiger followed the circuitous route the panthers had taken, joining them on the small hill, hidden behind a group of short spruce trees—a big cat lying in wait for its prey. Lucas shuddered when he thought of the damage that gun would do at this range.

In their lust to catch their enemy, the Russian tanks outran their infantry and scouts, leaving the tanks no information about what awaited them. Ten minutes after the Tiger was in position, they broke through the trees at the edge of the brook, crushing them under tonnes of steel. With testosterone-driven reckless enthusiasm, unimpeded and unprotected by infantry and blinded by hate, they were also oblivious to the disaster that could destroy them. Klaus's panzers had left a trail the reckless Russian tank commanders could follow at high speed, but it led to armageddon.

Klaus allowed thirty-two T-34s to cross the stream before giving the order to fire. Four panthers and the Tiger, all sighted on the two lead tanks, fired, and despite the targets' speed, the high explosive shells hit their marks, destroying them in a burst of bent steel and flames. Those behind them stopped, sealing their fate.

Eighteen Panthers and the Tiger fired at the stationary targets' exposed sides from short range, and the consequence was appalling. Fifteen more Russian tanks died. Most of the survivors turned to face their attackers, but two at the rear turned a hundred and eighty degrees and tried to flee, exposing their rumps and paying the ultimate price. Their crews died in a plume of flame as their fuel tanks exploded.

The thirteen T-34s still moving charged up the hill, driving over stumps and soft ground straight at the German guns. Lucas got his second kill with a head-on shot into the crack under a T-34 turret. The King Tiger demolished a Russian tank that had bounced a shell off the Tiger's armour. A charging T-34 hit a panther under the turret, lifting it off its mount, and from two hundred metres, Lucas fired a 75 mm armour-piercing shell through the front armour on the lead Russian tank.

The T-34s had run out of options—they had to continue up the hill or turn their soft sides to the Panthers and the King Tiger. But now, at less than two hundred metres, their front armour couldn't protect them from armour-piercing shells, and at that range, the 88 mm gun on the Tiger could shred a T-34 like a can of tuna! With an overwhelming advantage, the German panzers made quick work of their targets. Two minutes after the first shot, the forest was suddenly quiet—the German panzers had no targets.

Johann and Viänü climbed up to their perch behind Klaus's cupola while Simon fired his machine gun at fleeing Russian crews. Klaus shouted, "Stop that, Simon—they've had enough—save the ammunition!" Simon still held the trigger, killing Russian soldiers with their hands up. "Verdammt Scheisse! Marcus, shoot that bastard—Kristian, you will use the radio." The machine gun became suddenly silent.

Lucas added two tanks to his scratched list, bringing the total scratches on the inside of the turret to sixteen.

Klaus put his head down so it was under the hatch. "How many shells do we have left, Marcus?"

"Twenty, including the one in the breech."

"How many Russian tanks did we kill today?"

Marcus looked at Lucas and held up ten fingers.

"Sir...today...ten, but it could be more...we've been too busy to count."

Finke and Viänü climbed up on 227. Leutnant Finke spoke with Klaus, and Klaus said into the intercom, "It's time to go." Kristian put the transmission in gear while Klaus asked, "Kristian, how much fuel do we have?" He asked the question hopefully.

"Two hours in fourth gear, half throttle, maybe a few minutes more... How far are we going? It will be dark soon, and driving this thing in the woods at night is not a good idea!"

Kristian sounded worried, but Lucas had learned that Kristian worried about everything. When he wasn't busy, no matter how well things were going, Kristian invented awful things that could happen—until the action started, and then he did his job precisely, without complaint, and, as far as Lucas could see, without fear.

Klaus said on the intercom, "Leutnant Finke got a message on his radio...we will be fighting a little more before we go home. Fuel could be a problem—we'll do what we can."

Kristian opened his driver's hatch, put his head in the open, and made sure everyone heard him mutter, "So, this is what the air smells like without puke and farts."

He drove down the exact center of the woods road Leutnant Finke had led him to, but even then, the trees brushed the sides. Kristian put the transmission in fourth gear with only enough throttle to pull the tank. The drive took forty-five minutes, and Lucas used the time to wipe up his mess. The Panther's unpredictable motion knocked him around in the small working space, but eventually, he had the turret clean and threw the rags outside. He worked with every hatch wide open, and the smell of forest air flowing through the steel box soon had the crew commenting on improving air quality, then broadening the discussion to silly banter about farts and puke—anything to avoid facing the reality of another battle.

When they reached the new position, two-two-seven parked beside the King Tiger that had been following them around, one of fourteen King Tigers in all of Panzergrenadier Nord still capable of fighting. The number of Nord Panther tanks still moving numbered fifty-nine scattered through the forest, facing the labyrinth of tunnels and ditches that made up the Wotan line.

The sound of artillery cannons and explosions came from 227's left and right, at least a kilometre away and not aimed at them, so Klaus let his crew get some fresh air. Lucas and Marcus left the rear hatch open when they climbed onto the flat plate over the engine. Lucas sat next to Klaus with Marcus standing on his left. Lucas asked, "Who is firing at who?" Marcus shifted as though preparing to reply, but Klaus beat him to it.

"Who is firing at whom." Sitting on the edge of the cupola, he grinned at Lucas and went on. "The ones on the left are our artillery firing at the Russians coming up the hill toward the Wotan Line. The explosions on our right are Russian artillery trying to find our guns, but we keep moving them. The Luftwaffe is bombing and strafing the Russian guns and the tanks and infantry coming up the hill. Those are some of the explosions you hear on our left."

"Where was the Luftwaffe this morning?" Lucas's voice rose.

"This morning was not as important as this afternoon; like us, they've only got so much fuel and ammunition."

Leutnant Finke and his men worked their way along the edge of the woods, headed toward two-two-seven. The explosions to Lucas's left sounded like they were getting closer, and he guessed that Klaus would soon know what was happening. He asked his commander, "Will we die here? Isn't this the last chance to stop the Russians and save Germany?"

Klaus spoke quietly. "No, Lucas, this isn't the last opportunity to stop the Russians… We've often lost that opportunity since Stalingrad, and there are no more 'last chances.' And, for your information…" His voice, rising in volume and pitch, resounded off the trees. "The official objective is to sacrifice ourselves to save our Führer, not Germany. Hitler will sacrifice Berlin—hell, he will sacrifice the whole damn country and every one of his people to save himself!" Lucas was embarrassed, and Klaus's tirade added to the frightening feeling that this would be his last battle.

Marcus interrupted his boss. "That's what Hitler's been doing since Stalingrad fell; why would anyone expect him to change now? My parents burned in Cologne for that bastard, and that's enough! If he wants me to sacrifice myself for him, I will tell you right now that I won't do it!"

Klaus said, just loud enough for the crew to hear, "Leutnant Finke is determined to get us out of here alive. He has mapped out an escape route, but we must turn the Russians toward the front of the Wotan Line before we go. When they turn, we will have time to withdraw to the Spree Forest, where we will get fuel, ammunition, food, and hopefully beer."

"But with so many against us, how can we possibly win?" Lucas knew what was coming up the hill, and he was scared—and the adults seemed as frightened as he was.

Klaus said, "We win if the Western Allies get to Hitler and his helpers before the Russians get to us."

Marcus said, his frustration now under control, "Don't let his optimism give you false illusions, Lucas. We can't beat them, or we would have done it two years ago. Our only hope is to run like hell into the arms of the Americans. They are close to the Elbe River and could reach Berlin before the Russians. If we can get to them, and if they will take us in, we will live in an American prisoner-of-war camp for a while and then go home. But if we surrender to the Russians, they will execute us because we are Waffen SS soldiers!"

Lucas didn't think this was the time to remind Marcus that he was Wehrmacht, not Waffen SS.

Most of the Nord panzers were low on fuel and ammunition, but Klaus's panthers were more desperate than most. Simon and Kristian were smoking Russian cigarettes and leaning on the side of the Panther when Klaus said, "Kristian, don't start the engine until I tell you—we need to save fuel. Marcus, you will be the gunner; fire the big gun only at tanks—use the machine gun on the infantry. Simon, don't fire your machine gun until they are close enough to hit them." He looked at Lucas. "You will load. Put two rounds aside for our escape and warn me two rounds before you get to them. Don't use them unless I say so." Klaus looked toward the sound of the closest explosions. "Simon, tell the rest of the squadron to save the cannon for the tanks."

Lucas couldn't see them, but he was sure the Russians were getting close, and the look on his commander's face told him he was right. As he climbed through his hatch, Klaus said, "Okay, let's get ready," and slipped down to his seat.

When Lucas had closed the hatch, and everyone was in their seat, he selected the two shells furthest from him in the bin and laid them in the ring. Two-two-seven wiggled between the trees and into firing position. Klaus's squadron, scattered on both sides of the Panzergrenadier Nord command tank, waited for the enemy.

At seventeen hundred hours, with two hours of fighting daylight left, the Russians turned thousands of guns loose on the Wotan line. The Luftwaffe attacked the guns, using the last of their fuel and ammunition, but the rain of shells continued unabated. Wehrmacht Division Nord infantry waited for the Russians in the temporary safety of Wotan's deep bunkers. Through the loader's periscope, Lucas watched dirt thrown in the air by thousands of shells landing on the fortifications and felt guilty because he was glad it was them and not him. He did not envy them when the Russians eventually overwhelmed the line, as Klaus had said and as Lucas knew they would. There was nowhere for the trapped defenders to run, and the Russians could not be stopped.

◇◇◇◇◇◇◇◇◇◇◇◇◇◇◇◇◇◇◇◇◇◇◇◇◇◇◇◇

Lucas thought of Corinne and the life he longed to live with her and then, out of thin air, thought of Brahms' third violin sonata. Lucas positioned his chin to hold the violin, raised his left hand to the neck and curled his fingers around it to touch the imaginary strings. His right hand stroked the imaginary bow, and he hummed the romantically melancholy beginning of the Adagio movement. His fear subsided, and when tears blurred Lucas's vision, he closed his eyes and played the sonata as Johann's mother had taught him, successfully holding down the gall rising in his stomach.

Before the barrage was over, the fearless Russians steadily moved their tanks and infantry toward fifty-nine Panthers, fourteen King Tigers, and a thousand big guns hiding on their flank. General Busse's strategy gave the Russians two choices—attempt to bypass the end of the Wotan Line by charging straight into the guns and tanks of Busse's army or turn to face the minefield and trenches that were the last fortified line.

When the Russians were five hundred metres from the hidden Panzers, in position to run around the end of the battered Wotan defences, hundreds of German artillery guns in the small forest opened fire. As the barrage rained down, the line of dug-in MG-42 machine guns and infantry rifles at the edge of the woods opened fire. Each MG-42 fired twenty rounds per second, and there were thirty machine guns within two hundred metres of Panther 227.

Marcus and Simon fired 227's machine guns while Lucas moved a full ammunition box closer to Marcus's gun, anticipating the belt's end. It whipped through the turret machine gun's mechanism, and the gun became quiet. Lucas threw the empty in a corner, slid the new box in its place, opened the breech, fitted the end of the full belt in its position and slapped the breech cover down. He cocked the gun, yelled, "Fertig!" and the racket resumed.

Klaus announced, "I've got a tank destroyer turning toward us. Marcus, swing right ten degrees." The machine gun's chatter stopped, and Marcus swung the turret. Lucas picked a shell out of the bin at his feet.

Klaus barked, "Five hundred eighty metres," Marcus set the range, sighted, and fired.

"You got his track." Marcus waited three and a half seconds for Lucas; the breech slid shut; the Panther jumped.

"You got him, but another one beside him is slowing. I think he sees us."

The breech slammed, and Lucas yelled, "Fertig!"

"Same range." Klaus clipped his words. The Panther jumped.

"Marcus, fire at the tanks that turn toward us. Their armour won't help them at this range."

"I got the other destroyer!" Marcus yelled as he swung the turret.

"Five-sixty to the T-34." Klaus kept his tone steady and professional.

Lucas slammed the breech shut, the Panther jumped, and he reached for another round.

Breathing hard and concentrating on rhythm, Lucas had no time for fear. He slid another shell home, slammed the breech, and reached for another round in the ring.

"You got him!" Klaus paused, then, "The infantry, Marcus… turn them toward the line with the machine gun. Simon, keep firing."

"Changing the ammo box. Last one." Simon sounded angry.

Then Klaus said, "…Two T-34s are turning toward us. Shoot them, Marcus. Range four hundred and closing."

The Panther rocked. Lucas kicked a spent cartridge into the corner, slid a shell in the barrel, slammed the breech, and the Panther jumped again.

"Good shot, Marcus; a Tiger got the other one. Hold fire for now—they've had enough—they're turning toward the line. Lucas, how many shells?

He slammed the breech as hard as his numb arms could do it. "Ten."

"Range…six-fifty—pick a T-34's ass and shoot." The turret swung slightly, the gun fired, and Lucas fumbled, almost dropping the shell he had balanced on his knee. He found the hole, rammed it home and slammed the breech.

"Shoot one more before we leave the party." Klaus lowered himself and screwed the hatch down. A shell hit the front plate and exploded as the Panther jumped when the gun fired.

"I got the one that fired at us," Marcus said, pleased with himself.

"What about the one I told you to shoot?"

"One second," Lucas cried out, his strength gone. He struggled to slide the shell into the barrel, somehow found the hole, slammed the breech and instantly, the Panther jumped.

"Okay, he's done!" There was a triumph in Marcus's voice.

"Seven shells!" Lucas gasped as he staggered, lifted the seventh shell and found the barrel. He closed the breech and fell back against a steel bracket. He puckered his rectal muscles and desperately tried to hold his pee, but he could feel it leaking down his leg.

"Good job, Lucas and Marcus. Simon, tell headquarters 227's squadron is out of ammunition and fuel and is withdrawing." Lucas sat on the floor and leaned against the wall, sucking air into his burning chest. He relaxed for a second, and his stomach rebelled, firing a stream of vomit against the wall. He gave up holding it, and his bladder emptied itself.

Simon said, "Busse ordered Division Nord to withdraw two minutes ago." Simon sounded satisfied with himself. "I told them you were busy but that we would leave shortly."

"Tell them we've left, and tell everyone to get as many of our injured men on the tanks as they can. Healthy men will have to run. Kristian, reverse… I will guide you." The Panther backed for what Lucas thought was a long time, turned, and stopped. Over the idling engine, Lucas heard infantry scrambling all over the panzer like mice. Kristian and Klaus opened their hatches, and Lucas opened the rear hatch so fingers could hold onto the rim.

◇◇◇◇◇◇◇◇◇◇◇◇◇◇◇◇◇◇◇◇◇◇◇◇◇◇◇◇◇◇

Klaus said in the intercom, "Kristian, third gear; we will drive slow enough for the infantry to keep up; don't worry about the speed; I will tell you when to adjust."

Lucas sat on his little seat next to the hatch, lifted the earpieces of his headset and pulled out the sound-deadening rags. He could hear Johann shouting above the engine noise, instructing Klaus on the route. Exhausted, Lucas found his voice comforting. The engine's steady beat and the turret's warmth moved the battle to the back of his mind, replaced by Brahms's Second Piano Quartet. Corinne smiled at him over her viola, and Lucas imagined that the world was at peace.

Under the forest's dark canopy, darkness came quickly, like closing a door. Without lights, two-two-seven had to slow down to a fast walking pace. Sitting comfortably in the gunner's seat, Marcus leaned back so that his head was where he could see Lucas.

"You did a good job today, Lucas—I've never seen anyone load that fast!" Lucas woke, angry at first but then grateful that Marcus hadn't mentioned the stench.

Lucas thought of the men they had left behind. "What about the soldiers in the bunkers? Can they hold the Russians?" Lucas asked the question out of guilt. He wanted to believe they could beat the Russians if they stayed.

"No, the Russians will clear the mines in front of the line and cross the minefield tonight. In the morning, they will take the Wotan Line, and most of our men will become prisoners—the lucky ones will die."

"And what will we do? Where will we go?"

Marcus said, "Lucas, you worry too much. We will find the supply unit, fill up with fuel and ammunition and hide under the trees in the Spree forest."

"How long, Marcus? How long can we possibly hide sixty Panzers?"

"It's a big forest, with many lakes and lots of big trees, but if they want to find us, they will. We're not between the Russians and Hitler, so we can hope the Russians will leave us alone and concentrate on taking Berlin."

Chapter Twenty-seven

28 April 1945

Halbe

As Klaus hoped, the resupply unit met them before the Maybach engine died of fuel starvation, but the margin was only a matter of minutes. During the pitch-black night, Johann and Viänü found the unit in the middle of a forest. Unfortunately, the portable field kitchen was not with them—the horse that pulled it had sacrificed its life to feed hungry soldiers, there were no ingredients, and the Leutnant now in charge would not assign a precious tracked vehicle to tow it. Each man received one can of wurst and field bread, and all the rifle ammunition he could carry.

Lucas stowed cannon shells and boxes of machine gun ammunition with Marcus and Simon; Kristian took care of refuelling and inspected lubricant levels on everything. Klaus went begging for food and returned with enough for a week. Before daylight, the Panther was ready to fight—they had filled the ammunition bins and the fuel tank. They had changed the final drives, filled everything with oil and greased every joint. The camouflage was as perfect as they could make it, and they had replaced two bent track segments.

An hour after dawn, Johann led the 11th Panzergrenadier Nord tanks deep into the dark Spree forest. Under a thick canopy of spruce trees, the crews of the eight Panthers gathered around a small fire and listened to Klaus, who had just returned from a radio conversation with headquarters.

"The bad news first. The Russian army has completed the encirclement of Berlin, and Zhukow will now try to mop up what's left of the Ninth Army."

Several men dropped their heads and swore. Klaus waited for the finality to sink in.

"General Busse has eighty thousand men and seventy-nine operable tanks remaining, including fourteen King Tigers. The fuel, ammunition and food we have are all there is, and we are in a pocket surrounded by Russians." He waited. No one asked a question.

"On the positive side, the pocket is mostly thick forests, lakes, and not a lot of open terrain, making the price of fighting us high. They've seen what we can do, and they know that eliminating us would tie up a thousand tanks and hundreds of thousands of soldiers—men and equipment they will need when they enter Berlin.

If they take our capital, we will surrender, so why bother trying to wipe us out? And if they don't take it, we will starve or run out of ammunition and fuel."

Klaus looked from one man to another, knowing most would not fight to the last man for Hitler, but they had to stay out of the Russians' hands. Members of the Waffen SS had no future in Russia that was worth living.

Marcus said, with a bitter note, "So, we hide in the woods until Hitler surrenders, then off we go to a Russian Gulag! I guess it's a Russian vacation for us!" He laughed, but no one laughed with him.

Johann smiled at Marcus's sarcasm. "No, Marcus, I'm afraid there will be no vacation in Siberia. There are other plans."

Klaus was the man everyone trusted, and his men remained silent until he continued, hoping for a miracle.

"A couple of days ago, at a conference, probably the last, Hitler appointed General Walther Wenck as the commander of the Twelfth Army and told him to join the Twelfth and Ninth Armies to rescue Berlin..."

The men interrupted, talking over one another until Klaus put his hands in the air and got silence.

"A few of the generals present still believed that the German Army could rescue Berlin and Hitler, but the majority shouted them down. In any case, tomorrow, the Twelfth Army will begin the push to rescue the Ninth Army and open a corridor for refugees who are trying to reach the Elbe from Poland and Berlin. We will join Busse's main force and fight our way Southwest, with the Panthers on the flanks and the Tigers on the spear's point as we did in Sonnenwende."

"That's away from Berlin, not toward it." The voice silenced the crowd. "Aren't we going to rescue the Third Reich?" Every man knew where Berlin was, and they knew that Southwest wouldn't get them there.

Klaus broke the silence. "Now for the good news. While we move Southwest, General Wenck and his Twelfth Army will try to break through to us. He needs our help to protect the refugees trying to reach the Americans before the Russians cut them off. Together, we will keep a corridor open for them as long as possible."

Lucas could feel the men separating their allegiances to their families from their loyalty to Germany and Hitler. Klaus looked at Simon, the leader of the 'Save the Führer' pack.

"We can't help Berlin, and we can't save Hitler. The Russians are already in the streets, and, in a few days, they will march down Unter den Linden to the Reichstag."

Simon shouted at his commander. "What are you saying? Where are we going? We must help the Führer! That is our duty!"

"There is no German army to help the Führer—they are scattered everywhere with no structured command. The war is over! We will help the refugees, and then we will surrender to the Americans if they will let us. Our objective now is to survive, and the Americans aren't shooting their Waffen SS prisoners, but the Russians are!" Klaus smiled at Simon. "If you want to fight for Hitler, you are welcome to take a Papa—you can have mine. Join the infantry. I'm sure you can find a few Nazi fanatics around here who want to impale themselves on the Russian sickle. We won't need the radio much now; there is no battle command, and Kristian can take over for you. Go ahead; I'll even let you use the radio to find them."

Simon glared at Klaus, but Klaus smiled at him until he turned away.

◇◇◇◇◇◇◇◇◇◇◇◇◇◇◇◇◇◇◇◇◇◇◇◇◇◇◇◇◇◇◇◇

On April 28, following two weeks of fighting, Panzergrenadier Nord had only twenty-five thousand of its original eighty-thousand infantry who could still fight. Thirty-five tanks were mobile, including all fourteen Tigers, but they were low on fuel and wouldn't be fighting much longer without it.

Lucas hadn't eaten or slept in three days, except for short naps cramped in the loader's or the gunner's seat while Kristian drove through forests. His back hurt from bracing himself, and his arms were so tired he could barely lift a shell. Fortunately, there were no shells to lift. He cried privately for no reason and fought the urge to run screaming through the woods.

When Klaus spoke to the men through the intercom, he woke Lucas from a recurring nightmare about his parents. The Panther drove in the darkness of early morning, and only Klaus knew where they were going, or, more accurately, the crew hoped Klaus knew where they were going.

Klaus had received a radio message but hadn't told the crew what it meant for them. They waited patiently for news, and the wait became half an hour before Klaus told Kristian to stop the tank.

"Everyone out. We will eat whatever we have while I talk."

Everyone crawled out of Panzer 227, and the other crews in Klaus's squadron joined them on dry land under a pine tree. When his men had settled down, Klaus started to talk.

"I'm afraid this war is not over yet. Wenck has elements of his Twelfth Army waiting for us in Halbe, and they will have ammunition and fuel, and I promise that this will be the last we will get. The Russians are still between the Americans and us, but they don't know where we will break through, so their line is thin. Some of us will surely make it across the river."

"Right now," Marcus said, "all I want is food and sleep." He leaned against the tree.

Although Marcus could have pulled rank, he and Lucas rotated equally between the gunner and loader's seats, and both were exhausted. Marcus had given up; the last vestige of hope had evaporated, and Lucas had resigned himself to never seeing Corinne again.

Klaus cleared his throat, then said, "I'm sorry; I know everyone is hungry, but there won't be any food in Halbe. Wenck is using all he can find to feed starving refugees. When we talked over the radio, he told me he's feeding two-hundred-and-fifty-thousand people. We are hungry; they are starving, so when we meet the Twelfth in Halbe, there will be no food for us." Silence followed a loud groan.

Klaus cleared his throat again. "At the moment, all we can ask is an opportunity to survive. The refugees are in worse shape than we are!"

◇◇◇◇◇◇◇◇◇◇◇◇◇◇◇◇◇◇◇◇◇◇◇◇◇◇◇◇◇◇◇◇◇

The following day, Lucas and Marcus rode on the Panther's rump as it drove through the streets of Halbe to meet the 12th Army supply trucks. Lucas's mood dramatically changed when he saw citizens lining the streets with food and water for the hungry soldiers. Kristian parked the tank, and a small group of women crossed the street and offered food to the crew. They had somehow found cheese, bread, cooked potatoes, turnips and even wurst—Lucas suspected the townspeople would go hungry tonight, but he couldn't refuse the food. Like every man there, he lowered his eyes and said, "Danke schön." with a reverence reserved for a Saviour.

When the Panthers and Tigers parked in the street on the southwest corner of Halbe, SS infantry from scattered units gathered around them, but Klaus's men stayed with their small group.

Attrition had necessitated Klaus's promotion to the de facto commander of the Nord group panzers. Returning from a meeting with his commanders, he looked at the ragged men gathered around 227, climbed up on the tank and retrieved his and the gunner's machine guns. Lucas was standing with the crew, chatting and waiting for the supply trucks, when Klaus handed him the machine gun.

Klaus said, "I feel naked without one of these, and you should have one too." Lucas nodded, embarrassed that Klaus had given it to him instead of Marcus. Marcus kicked a stone from the road onto the grass. When he looked at Klaus, he was smiling.

Johann and Viänü joined 227's crew with their hands full of bread and sausage. The thirty-five men Johann now commanded had spread out around him, some on the grass, others standing in groups chatting about home and women.

Viänü pointed at Klaus's Papa. "Expecting a war to break out?" The Finn laughed at his own joke.

Klaus looked at the gun cradled in his arms. "I guess I've been

285

fighting them too long... My mind sees Russians everywhere." He let his eyes wander to the ragtag group of SS soldiers.

Johann nodded to the supply trucks moving from tank to tank along the street. "That's likely the last fuel and ammunition we'll see—one way or another, it will all be over soon."

A small SS infantry group crossed the narrow street to sit on the stone steps of an early nineteenth-century house opposite Panther 227. Lucas idly watched them, wondering what kind of people lived in the house that looked remarkably like Gartenstrasse 18. His thoughts wandered back to Detmold and then to his father, mother, and sister. He thought of Corinne, but the dreaded lump grew in his throat, and he dared not dwell on her for long.

Lucas's train of thought went off the rails when one of the SS soldiers shouted to his companions across the street near where 227's crew stood. "The fucking cellar is full of deserter rats! Bring the Panzerfaust!"

Klaus looked at Johann, then Lucas, and then tilted his head toward the soldiers across the street. Johann and Viänü racked their Papas as Klaus and Lucas headed off the soldier carrying the anti-tank weapon. Klaus cocked his gun as he spoke, and Lucas followed his lead. "What are you going to do with that?" Klaus's tone and the sound of machine guns racking a bullet into the barrel made his displeasure clear. The soldier looked at the SS rank insignia on Klaus's hat, then at his cocked machine gun.

The SS Private answered respectfully, "Sir, I am taking it to my commanding officer. He said there are deserters in the cellar of that house."

Klaus said, "We will accompany you," and headed toward the SS officer across the street with the soldier carrying the anti-tank weapon walking beside him. Johann and Viänü took the flanks, and Lucas walked behind the group, wishing he could be somewhere, anywhere else.

According to the badges on his hat, the SS officer standing at the top of the cellar entrance was a Hauptsturmführer, which meant he outranked Klaus. The horizontal cellar doors lay wide open on both sides, and the SS officer stared into the semi-darkness with smug satisfaction. Lucas followed the man's eyes to where terrified boys his age and younger looked up at their would-be executioner, and a boy's swollen purple face flashed into Lucas's mind, the child's eyes bulging, his purple tongue sticking out.

The officer took the Panzerfaust from the private, noted that Klaus had flipped the safety off his Papa and smiled. Lucas flipped the little lever and raised his Papa, forcing his sweaty hands to be still.

Klaus pointed at the Panzerfaust and said, "You won't be using that, not on them!" His tone left no room for negotiation.

Lucas looked at the frightened faces of the Kindersoldaten, barely visible in the black space under the house. For the first time, he noticed women with them. The women stepped in front of the boys in the vain hope they could protect them.

Four SS soldiers stood with their officer and trained their rifles on Klaus's group. Lucas stared at the soldiers and moved his machine gun from one to the other as though choosing the first to die.

The officer paused, then said, "You've got nothing to say about it. These are deserters, and I will lawfully kill them, along with anyone who helps them. Every German soldier must be prepared to fight and die for the Führer and the Reich!"

◇◇◇◇◇◇◇◇◇◇◇◇◇◇◇◇◇◇◇◇◇◇◇◇◇◇◇◇◇◇◇◇◇◇◇◇◇◇◇

Later, when Klaus told him what he had done, Lucas had no recollection of emptying his machine gun into the SS officer and two of the soldiers with him. Klaus told him the other two soldiers had dropped their rifles and put up their hands but had only survived because Lucas's Papa was empty.

The squeal of dry brakes took Lucas away from the bloody mess in front of him that, only a second earlier, had been an SS officer. He lifted his eyes; Johann smiled and put his hand on Lucas's shoulder.

Johann turned to Klaus and said, "We've got this, Klaus. You and Lucas can go back to your tank." Klaus looked at the frightened SS soldiers. He said pleasantly, looking down at the dead SS officer and the soldiers' dead comrades, "Doesn't it warm your heart to see German soldiers so eager to die for the Führer? If only more SS soldiers like those brave men would demonstrate their loyalty by giving their lives for Hitler..." Lucas stared blankly at Johann and Viänü. They smiled and pointed their guns at the soldiers, who closed their eyes and grimaced, waiting for the end while Johann and the Finn laughed.

The squealing brakes meant the fuel and ammunition trucks had arrived—Lucas stared at them, seeing nothing, and, in a haze, let Klaus lead him across the street to their panzer.

Without saying anything, Lucas worked like a machine, helping two-two-seven's crew fill the ammunition bins and fuel tank for what they feared would be the last time. The rest of the crew talked of women, mostly their mothers, leaving unsaid what every man knew—that when they fired the last shell or the engine stopped, either the Russians or the Americans would shoot them or take them to a prison camp.

Two hours later, with the fuel tanks, ammunition bins, and the crew's bellies full, Kristian started the engine, and they followed a King Tiger down the centre of the street. It was Lucas's turn to sit in the gunner's seat, and he watched through the cannon's sight as Johann and his men herded the SS soldiers away from the house. The street behind 227 was filled with infantry, and when he could no longer see Johann and his men, Lucas swung the gun forward, satisfied that the SS had lost interest in the Verweigerer hiding in the cellar.

◇◇◇◇◇◇◇◇◇◇◇◇◇◇◇◇◇◇◇◇◇◇◇◇◇◇◇◇◇◇◇◇◇◇◇◇

It was dark when, under heavy fire, the Nord panzers crossed the Berlin-Dresden autobahn, intending to guard Wenck's corridor and then fight their way to the Americans on the Elbe River. Artillery fire from the Russians was heavy but ineffective; Johann and his Jäger had removed the 1st Belarussian forward artillery scouts.

Klaus sent four Tigers across the moonlit highway to guard against interference from uninvited guests, and a squadron of Panthers was preparing to cross the road when the turrets of Russian T-34s began to rise from behind a low hill.

Klaus said in the intercom, "They don't see us yet, or they would stop." On the battle frequency, he told his squadron, "Panthers, hold your position and don't fire until the Tigers fire their first salvo." He spoke into the intercom, "Kristian, point us at the Russians; Simon, tell the Tigers to get ready—range about a thousand metres."

Klaus waited until he got a "ready" from the Tigers, and a dozen

T-34s had come over the rise in the ground, two abreast. The lead Russian tanks were at 800 metres when he said "fire" into the radio, and the front four T-34s stopped in their tracks, struck by King Tiger 88 mm shells. Two of them exploded, scattering pieces all over the road. The remaining Russians drove straight into the Panther's cannons at full speed, and the Panther's cannons fired with the Tigers' second salvo. Russian junk and shadowy figures suddenly littered the road. Klaus gave orders over the radio not to shoot the men running away from their tanks. When Simon asked him, "Why not?" Klaus said, "We need to save the ammunition."

The Panthers scurried across the road while the blind Russian artillery knocked down trees two hundred metres from the German Panzers. Lucas swung the gun as they crossed the last few metres of open area, looking for targets in the dim light, but none had gotten past the Tigers.

When the Panther reached the shelter of the trees, Lucas opened the rear hatch so infantry that climbed up on the rump could grip the edge, with the bonus that he and Marcus would have fresh air. Infantry capable of walking gathered around the tanks, and what remained of the mighty Ninth Army pushed on to Parey on the Elbe, where they hoped to surrender to the Americans.

◇◇◇◇◇◇◇◇◇◇◇◇◇◇◇◇◇◇◇◇◇◇◇◇◇◇◇◇◇◇◇◇◇◇◇◇◇◇

The clear weather allowed the full moon to cast its pale light through every opening, leaving coal-black shadows where trees wouldn't let it infiltrate. Fifty-four Panthers and fourteen King Tigers drove slowly through the forest, picking their way along narrow woods roads and hidden in the shadows. When the sky began to lighten, the Panzers parked where nosy airplanes wouldn't see them, and crews gathered around small fires built under the canopy of thick branches. Lucas and Klaus joined Johann and Viänü on groundsheets spread over moss and spruce needles.

Klaus spoke while digging a small hole in the moss with a stick. "Three days ago, the Americans shook hands with the Russians on the bridge over the Elbe at Torgau." He examined the hole and smoothed the edges with his hand.

"Yes, it's all over the camp," Johann confirmed, "The war is over, but the fighting isn't. Wenck won't quit until the last refugee is across the Elbe, and the Russians won't quit until they have Hitler's head on a pike!"

Lucas expected the conversation to continue, but when it didn't, he was confused. He turned to Johann, who was smoking his final cigarette, a gift from Klaus, who had vowed to quit and given Johann half a pack.

Lucas finally said, "I don't understand. If the Americans and Russians met on the Elbe River, how can we still fight? Who do we fight—the Americans or the Russians?"

Johann flicked ash on the groundsheet and pulverized it with his thumb. "Torgau is a hundred kilometres up the river. According to Wenck and Busse's intelligence, the Russians are tearing Berlin apart; they aren't leaving one brick still sitting on another. They want blood, and they're getting it!" Johann paused. The silence proved that the men listening were all making the same assumption.

"There is a reliable rumour that the Americans, the British and the Russians made a deal. Just like the Russians waited for the Germans to level Warsaw, the Americans and British agreed not to cross the Elbe until the Russians finish with Berlin. In effect, they are giving the Russians a license to kill Germans until their vendetta is satisfied. Unfortunately, just like Warsaw, it has stranded a million refugees who want to be on the American side of the Elbe. That meeting in Torgau was for the newspapers in America, Britain and Russia. The people in America think the war is over, and the Russians can satisfy their bloodlust without worrying about naive American interference."

Lucas did not attempt to hide his disappointment; the muttering around the fire confirmed that he wasn't alone. His mind snapped back to firing the cannon at empty houses in Warsaw and to women shot while trying to escape the brutality. He thought of Corrine and how desperately she would fight, and his imagination stopped there.

Klaus jammed the end of the stick hard into the hole he had dug, desperately trying to push it into the hard earth. He gave up, threw it into the trees and said, "We are fighting in the Kurmark Regiment under Wenck now. He is determined to keep a corridor open between the Americans at Parey and German refugees running for their lives.

The forests and roads are full of refugees from Poland and the parts of Germany the Russians have overrun, and the Russians are hunting them." He lifted the stick and jammed it down hard enough to break it. "Wenck gave me our official orders over the secret channel today, and our job is to help the Twelfth Army keep the corridor open and get as many refugees across the Elbe as possible."

Lucas opened his mouth but thought better of asking the question—Marcus asked it for him.

"So, we fight to the last man for refugees...most of them Poles? Why should we fight for them and not for Berlin?"

Johann's cigarette burnt the tips of his fingers as he put it between his lips, pulled on it until the burning tobacco touched them, and then spit it on Viänü's groundsheet. Viänü crushed it with the butt of his Papa.

Johann locked his fingers in front of his knees. "The Russians would like that—all of us in Berlin—they wouldn't have to spread their forces out looking for us—the lambs would come to the slaughter.

No, we cannot save Berlin, the Reich, or the Führer, but we can save women and children trying to get to safety. I would consider it an honour to fight for a just cause for a change..." He picked words out of the air... "otherwise, I have nothing about my part in this war that I would tell my grandchildren."

Lucas lay on the moss with the back of his head on his joined hands. Tiny bits of ivory light shone through the branches, and he wasn't afraid. He would live and marry Corinne. He had something to fight for.

Chapter Twenty-eight

Mayday 1945

Negotiating with death

"Diplomacy is the art of saying 'Nice doggie' until you can find a rock."

Will Rogers

Lucas and Marcus continued to rotate their duties in two-two-seven's turret. Leutnant Finke's Jäger company located Russian armour and infantry and planned traps and ambushes, taking a heavy toll on them. Unfortunately, Klaus's tanks had to sacrifice too much. When they helped Johann's men take out six Russian artillery pieces on Mayday, it left them desperately short of ammunition and fuel.

The King Tigers drank gas until they became stationary monuments to German mechanical ingenuity. Their crews abandoned them, leaving the most advanced fighting vehicles in the world for the Russians. Eight Panthers could still fight when Battle Command called and ordered what was left of Klaus's Division Nordland Panzers to Genthin to guard the refugee corridor. If it collapsed, the Russians would trap thousands of refugees and Ninth Army soldiers within ten kilometres of their goal. They would be at their mercy, although the Russians had temporarily suspended the use of the word.

Klaus's force reached the road north of Genthin and the Elbe-Havel canal, where Johann and his men waited for them two hours before dawn. The Panther's treads had barely stopped when Johann climbed up the front of the tank to sit beside Klaus's turret. Kristian shut off the engine to save fuel, and in the silence, from their positions below the commander's seat, the crew heard every word Klaus and Johann said.

Johann said, "The Russians are five kilometres east of us and driving down the road as fast as their infantry can walk."

"How long before they're here?"

A steady stream of people walked past the Panther, talking in hushed, hopeful tones, pushing their tired bodies as hard as they could. Many had walked for days, some for weeks. They had travelled hundreds of kilometres and were now a few hours from the Elbe River and the Americans. The Russians had never been far behind, but never this close, and the desperation in their demeanour was infectious.

Johann said, "Two hours—no more. The tanks will leave the road before the canal bridge and attack us from the south—there is no question they know you're here. There is no high ground, and you won't see them until they are less than a thousand metres from your position. I suggest you scatter your tanks along the edge of the woods fifty metres apart. Back them between the trees as far as you can,"

Klaus spoke into the turret. "Marcus, how much ammunition have we got?"

Marcus answered immediately—he didn't have to count it. "We have two rounds of seventy-five and a box of machine gun ammunition for Simon's gun."

"Kristian, fuel?" Klaus asked the question only to gain time to think.

"If they hit our fuel tank, it won't explode."

Klaus repeated the information to Johann.

Johann didn't speak for what seemed a long time. When he did, it was with a tone of finality that frightened Lucas.

"You know we should surrender—your men will die if we don't."

Lucas heard Klaus fiddling with the cupola's latch. Finally, he said, "We are Waffen SS—they will kill us anyway—what do you want to do?"

Johann said, "I'm not going to get home; nothing else matters now."

Klaus answered thoughtfully. "We will delay them for as long as we can. Every minute we buy will mean safety for another hundred people."

Johann cleared his throat, then said, "We've got a couple of ammunition belts and an MG-42 on the back of your tank. We'll set it up over there." He waved his hand vaguely to a spot on the edge of the woods.

"Johann, it's been a pleasure." Lucas heard sounds that could only mean that Klaus was shaking Johann's hand.

"Gleichfalls." As Johann slid to the ground, Lucas knew he would never see Corrine again.

In the morning twilight, a dozen T-34 Russian tanks, a 105 tank destroyer, and hundreds of infantry moved out of a narrow strip of trees into the open field, intentionally exposing themselves to Klaus's Panthers' guns. Eight camouflaged Panthers waited for them with only enough gas and ammunition for a brief skirmish; they were all that remained of Hitler's once-mighty Ninth Army. Both sides knew this would be the final battle.

The Russian armour tentatively followed their infantry across the field until they were less than a thousand metres from 227, intimidating the refugees on the road that ran beside the forest where the German panzers waited. The refugees took to the woods, passing behind Klaus's tanks. The Russians held their fire—the refugees disappeared.

Klaus spoke into the intercom with the same calm voice he had used in every action since Lucas had joined the crew.

"Simon, tell the squadron to start their engines. Lucas, range eight hundred twenty. Aim at the T-34 in the centre of the line, but hold your fire unless they fire at us."

Lucas set the range and the range triangle on the T-34, took a deep breath and watched the Russian tanks lined up to face him—if he saw a puff of smoke from a cannon barrel, he would pull the trigger. The engine started and ran smoothly, and Kristian set the idle at twelve hundred. Lucas tweaked the range and the gun to the exact centre of the T-34's turret.

"Range is now eight hundred, Lucas...but hold your fire."

"Eight hundred," repeated Lucas, "I won't fire."

Klaus clarified. "We won't fire unless they do."

"Understood." Lucas was puzzled—Klaus intentionally gave the enemy the first shot, something he had never done, but this was not the time to ask why.

A streaming mass of humanity approached from the east. There were too many to hide in the woods, and they poured into the field and onto the road in front of the Panthers, passing them without looking sideways. Those who could, ran, attempting to get past the battle before it began. The exhausted or injured put whatever energy they had left into getting past the Panthers.

Klaus spoke into the intercom. "A half-track is coming our way—it's showing a white flag—don't shoot." Lucas heard Simon relay the message to the squadron.

Klaus said, "Simon, tell the squadron Leutnant Finke and I will meet the Russians. If they do anything aggressive, fire at the tanks!"

Lucas looked through his sight—he could see his target clearly at 5x and knew his shot would blow the turret off the Russian. Klaus got out of 227 and joined Johann and Väinü. Half out of the rear hatch, Marcus told everyone what he could see.

"The Russians are talking, but I can't understand what they're saying. I'm catching a little of the translation, and it sounds like they are negotiating a surrender." Lucas's hopes jumped.

Klaus, Johann and Väinü talked with the Russians for a few minutes, and then the half-track started its engine.

"It's over; they're leaving and driving fast." Marcus crawled to his loader position. "We had better get ready."

Klaus, Johann and Väinü walked back to 227 and began a discussion. With all the hatches open, 227's crew could hear every word.

<hr>

"We all heard the translator, but what did the officer actually say?" Klaus's tone left no doubt what he thought the officer had said.

Väinü said, "The actual words aren't important. But, I can tell you that he will kill every man with a Totenkopf on his uniform, and if Johann and I are lucky, we will go to the gulags."

"What about the refugees?"

"He didn't mention them, but the Russians will attack them as soon as they finish with us—they were chasing them when we showed up."

Johann said, "We are not going to surrender. We will buy as much time for the refugees as we can."

Klaus stepped up onto two-two-seven's front armour. As he walked up the slope, he said, "I have no contact with headquarters, but I will send a message on a frequency the Russians listen to—they will think I am negotiating with Wenck, and maybe I can buy us some time."

Johann said, "You are a devious bastard, aren't you?"

Väinü warned, "Keep a finger on the trigger; that Russian bastard hasn't got a lot of patience! He's lost a lot of friends."

Klaus climbed into his cupola, leaving the hatch open.

"Simon, tell everyone to wait, then switch to the battle frequency we know the Russians have. I will talk from here."

Lucas heard Klaus's side of the conversation with battle headquarters. He asked for General Wenck and apparently would have to wait for him to return. An hour later, Klaus called Wenck again and discussed an "honourable" surrender of his panzers. At the end of the conversation, he joined Johann and Väinü, walking with them across the field toward the Russians. Marcus reported the half-track meeting them halfway, and then, after a short discussion, driving away in a hurry.

Klaus brought his negotiating team back to 227 and climbed through his hatch. Johann and Väinü sat on the flat rump.

Klaus said, "It's working out better than I thought." He sat in his cupola, looking toward the Russian tanks. "If we can keep them talking until just before dark, we may have the option of running into the woods before they know we're gone."

Johann said, "No, that's not going to happen...Russians aren't stupid. We will have to face the music one way or another before it's too dark to shoot. We must shoot before they do."

"And that would mean that every man would die." Klaus seemed resigned, crushing Lucas's hopes until Johann said,

"Not necessarily—if we hit them when they least expect it, we may have time to get far enough away that the infantry won't catch us. We could work out a plan that will get at least a few of us out alive!"

"If we give our men even a small chance, they will take it." Klaus spoke into the turret. "Simon, call the tank commanders and tell them to meet me in the woods behind 227. They must leave every five minutes, one at a time, as though they need to have a piss."

Klaus said to Johann. "I will go first. Follow me in five minutes." He stepped out of the cupola and climbed to the ground.

◇◇◇◇◇◇◇◇◇◇◇◇◇◇◇◇◇◇◇◇◇◇◇◇◇◇◇◇◇◇◇◇◇◇◇

An hour later, Klaus returned and immediately spoke through the intercom. "We have a plan. Our infantry will immediately begin leaving a few at a time while we wait for a guarantee from Zhukov that he will respect the Geneva Conventions if we surrender."

Lucas's spirits sank. He had heard horror stories about Russian prison camps and salt mines, and he would never see Corinne again!"

Klaus cleared his throat. "Of course, we're not going to surrender; we're going to delay the Russians as long as we can, and then we will hit them hard and run like hell! If this works, Johann and Väinü will lead us to the Elbe!"

Lucas listened to everyone express relief and hope, and the excitement in the Panther took him with it. His spirits soared as he checked the sight and adjusted it with the fine wheel, although it was precisely where it should be.

The bright light of day was fading when Klaus left his cupola to join Johann and Väinü on the road. Lucas flipped his sight to 2.5X, doubling the field of vision and putting the group at the bottom of the Zeiss lens. A half-track stopped beside them; a man in the back seat handed Leutnant Finke a piece of paper, and it drove off.

When Klaus and Johann arrived at 227, Lucas heard Johann say, "Did you see which tank he went to? The commanding officer is in that tank!" There was a pause, and then he said, "That's the frequency Wenck should use to contact Russian headquarters, but I think it's probably okay if you use it."

Lucas heard Klaus slap Johann on the back and say, "We are evil bastards, aren't we?" He chuckled as he said, "Two tanks to the right of centre."

Johann laughed, and Klaus climbed into his cupola and held out a piece of paper so Marcus could grab it. When he did, Klaus said, "Marcus, give that to Simon and tell him to dial it on the VHF—I will tell him when to connect."

Klaus leaned over until his head was just above Lucas's. "Move the gun two tanks to the right... I want you to sight on the turret. Your second shot will be for the one beside it. Take fifteen minutes to move the gun; the Russians will be watching."

Lucas used the manual swing a little at a time for ten minutes. It was a slow process without the engine, although the perfectly balanced turret swung smoothly. When he had the sight on the T-34, he said, "The second tank to the right of the centre?"

"That's the one."

"Then I am ready."

Forty-five minutes passed, and the light was rapidly fading when Klaus said into the intercom. "Everyone alert...I will send a message on the radio, and then I will give the signal to fire. Do your job, and when we fire the last shell, get the hell out of here. Kristian, start the engine now and go immediately to battle revs!"

Lucas heard the microphone click, the engine started, and then Klaus said, "General Zhukov?"...a pause, then... "Trakhni tebya voobshche!"

Klaus chuckled, then said through the intercom. "Simon, battle frequency on my microphone." Simon said immediately, "Ready, sir," the engine spun to battle revolutions, and Klaus shouted, "Schiess die Sheisser!" on the open battle frequency.

Lucas pulled the trigger and watched his target's turret upend onto a group of soldiers standing beside it. He touched the swing pedal, and the triangle stopped precisely on the adjacent T-34. He fine-tuned it with the wheel, heard the breech slam shut, and pulled the trigger before the reverberation stopped.

The armour-piercing shell fired by the second T-34 could not have penetrated the front armour of a healthy Panther from eight hundred metres, but the gunner got lucky just before he died. When Lucas's second shot penetrated the front armour plate of the T-34, the Russian gunner had already fired, and his shell struck 227 full on the front armour, precisely on a spot that had already taken two direct hits.

◇◇◇

The shell exploded on the transmission beside Simon, disintegrating his and Kristian's bodies. The shock wave blew upward into the turret, killing Marcus instantly and leaving Lucas singed but alive. The explosion bent the torsion bar tube at Lucas's feet, jamming his right foot, and the turret skewed off its track, pressing against his thigh so that he couldn't move. Stunned by the flash, he suddenly realized that Klaus had grabbed his shoulders. A terrible burst of pain shot through his legs as Klaus pulled. Lucas screamed, and the pulling stopped, but he felt his legs burning. Through the pain's fog, he heard Klaus say, "The torsion bar tube is bent upward, and the turret is off its track, jamming Lucas's foot. Try to grab his collar so you can pull with me."

Lucas tried to say, "No, you will hurt me!" but his collar tightened and choked off his air. Hands dragged him upward, slipped under his arms. He took a breath and screamed. Flames licked around the plate under his feet, reaching for his torso! He shit his pants and evacuated his bladder as strong hands pulled him out of the burning Panther.

The pain in his thigh and foot subsided, the hands beat out the fire on his pants, and Klaus and Johann put him on his feet. He whimpered and tried to stand, but his legs buckled. Bullets whizzed past; men ran; something exploded. He saw Väinü kneel, firing his sniper rifle as fast as he could work the bolt.

Johann pulled on one of Lucas's arms; Klaus took the other and yelled in his ear, "Run, or we all die!" Johann pointed with his free hand; Lucas worked his legs until he got them to move... He ran, terrified.

Johann talked while he ran, panting, "By now, they've figured out that we've run away...let's hope they've had enough of us!"

Explosions echoed through the dark woods as Viänü appeared with eight men. He said, "They are still firing at the Panthers. Without their commander, the infantry isn't interested in chasing us."

Klaus ran behind Lucas, pushing him when he slowed. They ran through gaps between the trees, avoiding paths or roads, until Johann breathlessly announced they could safely rest.

Lucas bent over, exhausted, trying to breathe enough oxygen to keep him from falling. Johann gathered the men around him in the fast-approaching darkness and laid out the route to the Americans. Lucas found some moss far enough from the men that they wouldn't smell him and sat down with his arms folded over his knees. He knew he stank; he could hardly stand his stench; it was the smell of cowardice.

Klaus left the group and walked over to Lucas. He smiled, his white teeth gleaming in the dark. He spoke quietly, like his father.

"Now you know real fear...that smell is fear; we have all smelled it."

Lucas hung his head. "I'm sorry."

Klaus put his hand on Lucas's shoulder. "Never mind; we're going home now...we'll find some water where you can clean up." He laughed in a way that told Lucas everything was alright and said, "We don't want the Americans to throw you back."

Klaus pointed to a spruce tree. "Sit down and let me see those burns, Lucas." Lucas got up and moved to sit with his back against the tree. Klaus reached for Lucas's left foot, lifted it, pulled up the pant leg, looked at it carefully, and lifted his right leg. "The burns are only superficial, like a bad sunburn, but they will hurt for a few days. The cut on your hip needs something to keep the dirt out." Klaus tore a corner off his shirttail to make a crude bandage over the cut, then helped Lucas to his feet.

"I want to apologize to Johann." Lucas started toward Johann before Klaus could stop him.

Lucas said, "I'm sorry, sir; I'm sorry I'm a coward." Lucas waited in tears for Johann's response; Johann responded immediately.

"It's alright, son." Then he added, chuckling, "Perhaps you should walk at the back of the line with Klaus."

<hr>

Russian artillery behind them began firing.

Lucas asked, confused. "What are they firing at? Aren't they firing toward the Americans?"

Johann put his hand on the young soldier's shoulder. "I'd say they're targetting the refugees along the river, and if that's the case, we can't help them." He pointed at a hole in the woods. "Through there... we had better get going."

Lucas tried to control the urge to cry, but tears sneaked down his cheeks. It was clear that Marcus and Kristian hadn't made it. Neither had Simon, but Lucas felt no regret about that.

Explosions roared from the direction that Johann had pointed. A cold rain began to fall, softly at first, then harder.

Johann said, "Those are ranging shots, Lucas; the real barrage will start in a few minutes." Everyone assembled behind him, and a few seconds later, the artillery fired at a steady pace. The shells exploded a long way ahead of them, and Lucas felt his fear subsiding as he fell in line behind Klaus.

Rain fell, becoming so heavy that Lucas could barely see Klaus, although he was only a few metres ahead. Soaking wet and with a sore foot, Lucas stumbled on a root, slipped and fell on the soaked ground. Fighting his way to his feet, Lucas said, "Klaus, I can't see you," and Klaus whistled. Lucas stumbled ahead as fast as he dared, and Klaus's shadowy form appeared before him, the length of his arm away.

In his fatherly voice, Klaus said, "It's okay, Lucas...you will make it. We won't leave you. Breathe, son; relax, and breathe."

Klaus's tone triggered a sense of calm, and Lucas realized he'd been holding his breath. Breathing in gasps, he fought to smooth it out, deliberately picking a rhythm. His heart slowed, and he found it easier to walk. He steered his mind to Detmold and the day he would put his arms around Maria and Corinne.

Klaus said quietly, "You're going to make it, Lucas—we won't leave you here."

◇◇◇◇◇◇◇◇◇◇◇◇◇◇◇◇◇◇◇◇◇◇◇◇◇◇◇◇◇◇◇◇◇

They walked in the rain for fifteen minutes, putting another five hundred metres between them and the Russian guns as a steady stream of shells screamed over their heads.

And then, the sound changed. Shells screamed from the opposite direction; explosions of shells landing near the Russians mingled with the sound of their guns firing.

"Do we have artillery near the Elbe River?" Lucas tried to fit the sounds into the situation.

"No, we don't have any artillery anywhere." Klaus slowed so quickly that Lucas ran into him. He grabbed Lucas's shoulder and guided him to where Johann collected the men.

When everyone had been accounted for, Johann said, "Those shells are coming from the west...the Elbe. There are no German guns between here and the river, so the only possibility is that the Americans are shooting at the Russians."

Klaus said, "Perhaps we should wait here until we know what's going on."

"Yes, I agree. While we're waiting, I've got dry socks and boots in my pack. All of my men carry dry socks, and we grease our boots, so let's get you and Lucas some dry feet, or we'll have to carry you. Tell us the size of your feet, and we'll see what we can do."

Lucas sat on a waterproof Zeltbahn that one of the infantrymen loaned him and removed his boots and socks. Johann's spare boots fit him perfectly, even the swollen foot. When he stood up, he felt a rush of happiness, and when he tried to return the infantryman's ground-sheet, a quarter-tent, the infantryman let him keep it, showing him how to wrap it around his neck like a poncho. He said he had a spare, but Lucas didn't see him put it on.

The Russians stopped firing, and seconds later, the scream of shells from the Elbe stopped.

Johann said, "The Americans wouldn't fire warning shots at the Russians unless they could fire accurately...so...they must have observers where they can see the Russian guns!" Klaus nodded, but no one said anything as they waited for Johann to go on.

The Russian artillery began firing, interrupting Johann, but immediately the Americans returned fire. The Russians ceased firing, and the American guns did the same.

Johann said, "If we find the American observers, we can surrender to them. They have to follow the woods to get back to the Elbe, or they would have to go across open fields—I don't believe they would do that. If I'm right, they have to pass us, so we could spread out and wait. I think we have a good chance of finding them... What do you think?" He looked at Väinü, then Klaus.

Lucas said, "Wouldn't they try to kill us?" and immediately regretted the remark.

Johann responded to what Lucas realized was a stupid question. "Yes, of course they would, if they could. But we will capture them before we surrender." He touched Lucas's arm. "Don't worry, this is what we do. You and Klaus will wait here, and we'll come back and get you when we've found the Americans." He and eight men disappeared soundlessly.

Minutes later, the rain stopped. Lucas removed his poncho, shook the water off and sat on it. After a few minutes of staring into the darkness, he suddenly realized he didn't know where he was. If he moved, he would likely go toward the Russians. He couldn't tell Russian artillery from American.

"How will they find us?" Lucas shivered. He wasn't cold, but he couldn't control it.

"How does a sparrow find the same nest, year after year?" Klaus moved closer to Lucas, put his hand on Lucas's knee, and the shaking stopped.

"Do you think Marcus and Kristian are dead?" Lucas couldn't hold the tears back.

"Yes, Marcus, Simon and Kristian are all safe now. It's over for them."

"It was quick for them, wasn't it?" Lucas shuddered, leaned against Klaus, and Klaus put his arm over his shoulder.

"They didn't feel anything." Klaus squeezed Lucas and was silent for a few minutes.

"We'll make it, Lucas; Johann will get us home."

The Russians began firing again, and a few seconds later, the Americans returned it. The Russian guns stopped, and the woods became quiet; even the wind had died.

"It looks like the Americans want the refugees to cross the river." Klaus shifted and locked his hands around his knees. "Some of the Russians will want revenge; they'll want to kill every German they can before an armistice. Most refugees are Polish Germans or Germans from the area around Berlin, and they don't have guns to defend themselves." Klaus leaned back on his elbows. "They're nothing but fodder for those Russian cannons."

Lucas shook, his teeth chattered, and he forced himself to be still. It started again, and he willed it to stop, but the sporadic shivering persisted.

They sat silently for another hour, and Lucas's mind drifted to Marcus. He wondered whether Marcus was married, if he had children, where he was at home before the war. He was embarrassed that he had never asked and was trying to remember whether he had told Marcus about his sister or his parents when a whistle from the woods startled him. Johann stepped through a wall of darkness and was suddenly in front of him.

"We surrendered to a couple of Americans. Viänü is staying with them until I bring you back."

Lucas stood; Klaus took his arm and guided him through the black wall behind Johann.

"It's better if you stay close to Johann. I will follow you."

Johann delivered Lucas and Klaus to two Americans sitting in the light of a small lantern. Viänü stood in the dark shadows with his men.

Johann held out his Russian machine gun to the American—the American said something, and Johann kept it.

The clouds broke apart; the night became brighter. Tiny patches of light became puddles, and then the waning moon peeked through enough that Lucas could see trees ten metres ahead of him.

Johann was leading the column with the Americans on his heels when Johann turned, took the American's arm, and pulled him to the ground. Lucas crouched and, encouraged by Klaus's hand on his back, flattened himself on the moss. Every man in the column was on his stomach, a part of the wet ground, except Viänü. He silently worked his way past Lucas to Johann's side. Johann put his mouth against his ear and said something.

Viänü nodded and melted into the woods with the eight Jäger soldiers. One of the Americans looked curiously at Johann, and Johann whispered something to him.

A few minutes passed, and Viänü returned alone. Again, he whispered in Johann's ear, and Johann whispered in the American's.

The American shouted something in English, and suddenly, the forest erupted with gunfire; Lucas tried to press himself tighter against the ground as bullets zipped over his head.

Viänü shouted something in Russian, the firing stopped, and the Americans tried to stand up, but Johann and Viänü pulled them down. The Russians again sprayed machine-gun bullets through the trees around Lucas.

Viänü shouted, "Shoot them!" and the woods near the source of the Russian bullets erupted in gunfire.

When the Jäger soldiers returned, Viänü nodded to Johann, and everyone stood up. Johann and Klaus spoke, and after a brief conversation with the American officer, the column moved on. Lucas had to step around a Russian soldier's body lying beside the path.

The Americans stayed behind Johann until three hours later when they walked out of the woods and into fields covered with refugees and

German soldiers. There were dead, wounded and dying everywhere, some with grotesque wounds. The Russian artillery had killed and wounded hundreds of helpless people, and Lucas felt a rage he hadn't experienced since the Berliner Allee.

◇◇◇◇◇◇◇◇◇◇◇◇◇◇◇◇◇◇◇◇◇◇◇◇◇◇◇◇◇◇◇

Klaus knelt beside a woman with a piece of shrapnel in her back, and she screamed when he yanked it out. He tore a piece of material from her dress and gave part of it to her daughter to press on the wound while he jury-rigged a bandage. Lucas worked with him as they moved toward the river, dressing wounds, stopping blood with tourniquets, and holding pressure bandages made from dirty clothes torn from dead bodies. The Americans used up their emergency medical kits in a few minutes but kept working with what they could find. Everywhere, people moaned and cried for help, and it took two hours to work their way downhill along the road in the direction of the Elbe. Finally, when there was nothing more they could do, they carried wounded children, joining the lines of people walking toward the river.

As he walked, Lucas had no idea what he would do but decided that surrender and prison camp could not be an option. Johann walked shoulder-to-shoulder with the American officer while the others trailed—Lucas caught up to him and pulled him to one side. The American took a little girl's hand and went to help her mother.

Lucas said, "I want to find my own way home... what should I do?"

Johann looked at the American; he was examining the mother's leg. The rest of the men were carrying wounded women and children to waiting boats.

"Pretend you need a leak, and I'll cover for you." Johann grabbed Lucas's arm. "Get rid of the uniform as soon as you can; you might get away with saying you're a refugee."

Johann checked that the American was still rigging a bandage for the woman's leg, let go of Lucas's arm and asked, "Are you sure about this? The Russians are also on the other side of the river, and right now, you are still wearing a Wehrmacht uniform. If you don't surrender here, the Americans or the Russians may shoot you if they find you running the roads. The safest place for a German soldier right now is in an American prison camp!"

Lucas said nothing—he kicked the ground with his Wehrmacht boot. Johann shrugged. "Okay, I see you've made up your mind. Let's hope you stink bad enough they won't want you within a hundred metres of them!" He laughed and squeezed Lucas's shoulder so hard it hurt. "Go upriver a couple of kilometres before you cross, then head due west and stay in the woods as much as you can. Travel only at night, and for about…" Johann looked at the river, then back at Lucas… "three hundred kilometres. You should be home in a week." He passed his compass to Lucas and saluted. Lucas was so surprised he could only wave a half-hearted attempt.

Lucas stepped to the side of the road, opened his fly, squeezed out a few drops and buttoned it up again. He waited for the group to disappear in the darkness, then walked up the river. He was alone for the first time since leaving Detmold, and he liked it.

A hundred metres along a narrow road running parallel to the river, a truck lay on its side in the ditch, the cab burned out but the load bed intact. Lucas opened the tailgate, crawled into the canvas-covered box, and checked for anyone observing him. In the sporadic moonlight, Lucas dragged crates of all descriptions through the back and opened them in the ditch. He had no idea what he was looking for, but he found boxes of ammunition, rifles, spare parts, and wooden crates full of cartons of cigarettes. Disappointed, Lucas crawled further into the truck and pawed through loose items but found nothing useful. He eventually found himself standing on the road, looking at the cigarettes. He thought of Klaus's and Johann's addiction, picked up the box, put it on his shoulder and started walking upriver.

Chapter Twenty-nine

1-2 May

The Way Home

"Every child comes with the message that God is not yet discouraged of man."

Rabindranath Tagore

THE AMERICANS BUILT FIRES AS BEACONS for those who sought refuge, and the Elbe River was a beehive of activity, covered with boats that looked suspiciously like American military equipment paddled by civilians. They moved back and forth across the river, delivering refugees and captured German soldiers to the Americans on the river's west bank. American soldiers didn't technically violate direct orders forbidding them to cross the river to help those fleeing the Russians when, in rectangular wooden assault boats, they rescued those attempting to swim the three hundred metres across the cold river. They came closer to the line when they picked up anyone who waded out to meet them.

Thousands of people in the fields and on the road had no idea what to do. Hitler had told the country that the Americans had joined the British and communists in a Jewish conspiracy to take over Germany and the world, and many Germans still worshipped at Hitler's altar. However, Stalin permitted and even encouraged his soldiers to take whatever revenge they wanted on the German people. They consequently left a trail of atrocities behind them that would invoke such terror that civilians left everything they held dear and fled. When they reached the Elbe, the enemy before the refugees didn't act like an enemy, and the brutal Russians behind them behaved like animals, so in the end, the refugees picked the lesser of two evils and ran to the Americans' open arms.

Lucas knew what was behind him but believed he could do better than an American prison camp. He asked himself: How long before they would let him go home? Would they have labour camps in America where German soldiers would have to work until they paid for the damage Germany had done? Undoubtedly, the world would exact revenge on his country, and what better place to start than with the soldiers who had killed their sons, husbands and fathers? Hitler's sins must be avenged!

Lucas turned left to walk upstream with a plan to swim across where there were no Americans or Russians. And then, even if he had to go naked, he would rid himself of every scrap of proof that he had ever been a soldier and walk to Detmold.

The number of desperate people thinned out as he walked along a narrow road parallel to the river, and when he reached a forest that began at the river's edge, he left the road for the riverbank. The water was high, leaving only a three-metre wide strip of sand that sometimes narrowed to less than a metre as he walked upstream, but there were no fires or lights on the opposite shore and, Lucas guessed, no Americans or Russians.

When he estimated he was two kilometres upriver from the Americans, Lucas stopped and sat with his back against a large beech tree, looking at the water, trying to gauge the water's speed by watching pieces of flotsam floating past. He was a strong swimmer, so he judged that neither the distance nor the current would be a problem. But the cigarettes were his only currency to get clothes and food—how could he take them with him? The air wasn't cold, but wet clothes would become a problem on the other side.

Lucas decided to look for something to float the box and his clothes and decided to walk farther upstream. He needed to find a farmhouse.

As he walked, his mind cleared and formed a more detailed plan. A kilometre upstream from the forest, only a faint glow in the sky marked the Americans' fires, and Lucas stopped to assess his options. The night was quiet on both sides of the narrow river, and the sandy bank made a perfect spot to launch whatever he found to float the weight of the cigarettes and his clothes. There must be a farm somewhere. He put the box in the long grass and walked inland.

Lucas eventually found a dark farmhouse with an attached barn a hundred metres from the river. The house had been damaged and the farm looked abandoned. He searched the barn and went outside, looking for a junk pile. Lucas's grandfather had been a farmer—he had a junk pile hidden behind a building, and he told Lucas that farmers never threw anything away.

But there was no junk; everything was neat, not even a piece of wood thrown on the ground. He found a shed built against the back wall of the barn that someone had broken into, leaving the door hanging precariously by one damaged hinge. He twisted it until the hinge's screws pulled out of the wood, then picked up one end. It wasn't as heavy as it looked—it would float the cigarettes, clothes, and more!

Lucas dragged the door to the water's edge, noting the solid feel and thick wood and wondering if it might carry his weight. He slid it into the water and the dry wood floated high, at least two-thirds out of the water. He put the box in the middle of the door and couldn't see any difference in the waterline. He grounded the door on the sand and sat down to remove his boots and socks.

A shadow coming from the woods moved into Lucas's peripheral vision. He waited, and the form, too small to be a man, cautiously approached him. As it took shape, it became a small boy and stopped three metres from Lucas. He stood still, looking at Lucas without saying a word.

Lucas asked, "Can you understand me?" and the boy nodded.

"Do you have people who are looking after you?" Lucas was afraid he knew the answer.

"Nein, Sie haben meine Mutter getötet." The boy answered simply in good German with a Polish accent. He wasn't over eight or nine years old and was unnaturally thin. He had yellow teeth with a wide gap in the front.

Lucas asked, "Who killed your mother?"

The boy sighed as though he were tired of telling his story, then said, "They hurt my mother and killed my grandmother. I tried to fight, but they laughed at me." He looked at his feet. "Mummy made me run, and we tried to get away, but they shot at her. I cried and tried to make her get up, but she couldn't."

The little boy looked up. "Mummy is an angel now." He pointed skyward.

Lucas fought his anger and tears. The boy looked into Lucas's eyes and went on in a monotone. "I got away because some men like you killed the bad men and took me to a road. Many people walked there, and I went with them, but they didn't have enough food for me. When I begged and cried, they chased me until I stayed away." The boy spoke without feeling as though he were reciting a poem at school. Lucas swallowed hard, then stopped to think while he watched the little urchin. The boy stood still, looked at his feet and waited for Lucas to decide his fate.

Lucas took time to think, and in a few minutes, the boy turned and started walking away.

Lucas asked his receding back, "Can you swim?" The boy stopped walking and wagged his head from side to side. Lucas said, "Then you must sit on the door." The boy turned to face Lucas, a pitiful glimmer of hope in his eyes. Lucas pointed at the door. "I want you to get on the door and sit down. I will slide it into the water, and you must stay still while I push you across the river. Can you do that?" The boy nodded vigorously.

Lucas took the box off the door, pushed it into the water, leaving the end on the sand, then motioned for the child to sit. Lucas saw that the door floated high enough to keep the boy dry, so he put the box between his feet and said, "I will take off my clothes and give them to you so you can keep everything dry. Can you do that?"

The boy nodded and silently watched Lucas wash the pants he had said he should keep dry. Lucas wrung them out, then gave the boy his coat, shirt, socks, and pants. The boy pulled them tight against his chest.

Lucas pushed the raft into the water and was happy to see it float high enough that the boy wouldn't get wet. He waded behind it until the water was up to his waist, then swam, using his legs in a frog kick. He supported his hands on the door, facing the boy.

The pale moonlight shone on the little boy's white, impassive face, and Lucas had to fight with his emotions as he thought of the horror that had buried itself in that little mind. He thought of Thomas and

Barbara as he tried to keep his focus on the gradually approaching shore, but a vision of the child's mother dying in front of him kept intruding.

◇◇◇◇◇◇◇◇◇◇◇◇◇◇◇◇◇◇◇◇◇◇◇◇◇◇◇◇

They drifted with the current flowing down the Elbe River, and Lucas gauged the deflection as he watched the glow from the American fires. He estimated they would reach the shore less than a thousand metres downstream from where they had begun, well north of any American soldiers.

As soon as he could get his feet on the bottom, Lucas stopped the downstream drift by standing up and pushing the door angled upstream to the shore. The bank's slope was gradual, and the bottom was smooth where the door grounded. Lucas gave it a last shove, pushing down so the end slid up the sandy bank. The boy waited until Lucas took the clothes from him one at a time and was fully dressed. Lucas pointed at the box, and the boy stood up, stepped off the door and tried to lift the box. Lucas laughed, lifted the cigarettes to his shoulder and began walking away from the river. He had walked twenty metres before he realized the boy wasn't with him. He looked back, and the child hadn't moved, so he stopped and said, "Don't you want to come with me?"

The little head nodded.

Lucas said, without thinking, "If you stay with me, I will look after you."

The tiny figure ran up the bank and wrapped his arms around Lucas's waist.

Lucas asked, "What's your name?"

"Thomas Finke."

Lucas put the box down and knelt to face the boy.

"Where did you get that name?"

"It's my name! It's my name!" The boy began to cry, and Lucas decided not to persist. He looked back at the river and then at the fields they had to cross. He pulled out the compass, levelled it, and the needle swung to point north. The silhouette of a farmhouse was ninety degrees to the left, west of where they stood.

Lucas said, "That's a nice name. I'll call you Tom. Is that OK?"

Thomas stopped crying; his little head nodded, and he wiped his eyes with his sleeve.

Lucas slowly walked toward the farmhouse, and the little boy put his tiny bony hand in his as he said, "Ich heisse Thomas Finke und Ich bin kein Jude."

Lucas put his fingers around the boy's and said, "I will call you Tom."

Lucas turned upstream to walk around the edge of a newly seeded field and found a narrow track heading away from the river toward the farmhouse. Two hundred metres along the rutted path, it widened and merged with another, more-travelled road and, a few minutes later, they stood in front of a large stucco farmhouse with an attached brick-and-beam-constructed barn. Lucas put the box on the dark doorstep and sat beside it. Tom shivered in his ragged clothing, and Lucas opened his coat and signalled for him to sit on his knees. The boy sat with his back to Lucas as he wrapped the coat around the tiny body and pulled the boy against him. Lucas couldn't decide whether to knock on the door, so he did nothing.

They had been sitting there for half an hour, and Tom was asleep when the door suddenly opened. Lucas turned to find a large man standing over him. He unwrapped the boy and stood up to face whatever was coming.

Chapter Thirty

2 May 1945

Manfred und Mechthild

"To change the world, we must be good to those who can't repay us."
Pope Francis

THE KIND EYES ABOVE THE BEARD AND SMILE eliminated any aggression as the voice said, "What are you doing here, soldier?" The musical baritone resonance of the man's voice was pleasant. Lucas decided to use the story he had worked out while sitting on the step.

"My name is Lucas Schwartz. My brother Tom and I are walking home. He's hungry and tired and needs to rest. I have cigarettes in this box, and if you would feed him and let us sleep in your barn, you could have some of them." Lucas looked at the kind face; its expression was sympathetic—and amused.

The man smiled, extended his hand, and stepped aside to reveal a fireplace on the other side of a large room. The embers of a dying fire glowed enticingly.

"You are welcome in this house. I will wake my wife, and she will find food for you, but you must leave before dawn. The Americans search our house every day looking for German soldiers, and although you are too young to be one, your uniform gives you away."

A match flared and lit a lantern on the other side of the room. The warm light illuminated a large woman with a cheerful face.

"Manfred, you know you can't get out of bed without me knowing it." She smiled and beckoned to Lucas and Tom.

"Come in, come inside. You are welcome here."

Manfred pushed them across the room.

"She won't bite. This lady is my wife, Mechthild, and my name is Manfred." He looked straight into Lucas's eyes, then at his wife. "This is Lucas Schwartz and his brother Tom." The man's amused stare told Lucas he didn't believe a word of his story and made him uncomfortable. Manfred remedied that with a warm smile as he asked, "Where is home when you aren't playing soldier?"

Lucas decided to tell the truth about everything except Tom.

"Detmold—it's between Bielefeld and Herford."

Manfred said, "I know where it is, and I know it's more than three hundred kilometres from here."

Lucas didn't flinch as he said, "Yes, I know that, and we will walk there."

The big man shrugged and looked at his wife; she nodded and said to her husband, "Okay, we'll have to find a way to get them there, but he won't get far dressed as a soldier."

Lucas was sure these kind people didn't believe him, but they didn't seem to care. He was surprised when the questions ended there.

A few minutes later, Mechthild had a kettle full of water on the stove and meat sizzling in a pan. The smell raised Lucas's hunger level to ravenous, and he wondered how long it had been since Tom had eaten.

Lucas remembered his manners and controlled his urge to ram the food into his mouth, but Tom began by downing two glasses of milk as fast as he could swallow, then devouring everything on his plate. Mechthild kept glancing at the boy as she buttered thick slices of bread and cheese, packing them in a wooden box as she shifted her gaze from Tom to Lucas. Manfred went to the adjoining room and returned with his arms full of clothes. He dumped them on a chair beside Lucas.

"The second of our two sons was killed in France last fall, and he was about your size. We have no more children to give to Hitler, and I want you to wear my son's clothes. There are also clothes for Tom, and I will burn that uniform!"

Keeping one hand on the pile of clothes, Manfred said, "Young man, I'm afraid you need a better story." Mechthild smiled at Lucas and nodded in agreement. Lucas looked at the floor, then returned the smile.

Manfred put his hand on his beard, looked thoughtfully at the floor, and said, "Let's try this: you are from Berlin, and Tom is a Polish refugee. Your father died fighting in France at the beginning of the war, and when you lost your mother to a Russian artillery bombardment, you left Berlin and joined the refugees." He stroked his beard. "You found Tom somewhere between Berlin and the river—close to the river works best." He grinned. "The Americans aren't interested in papers; they don't trust them, and their idea of order has something to do with bowel movements. Don't say too much, and stick to your story—the Americans appreciate a good story."

Lucas could feel his face burn.

"Yes, I see that works. We should get as close to the truth as possible. Am I close?"

"Yes, sir. I found Tom at the river."

"I won't ask why you brought him with you. We both know the answer, and that's the most believable and probably the best part of the story." He looked at Tom, then went back to Lucas. "Your grandparents live in Detmold, and you are taking Tom to live with them because he has nowhere else to go. That will pluck at the Americans' heartstrings."

He pointed at the door where he had gotten the clothes. "Change in that room, and join me in the barn—I've got something that might work well for you."

◇◇

Lucas dressed in the heavy clothing. The rough, woollen pants scratched his burned skin, but he didn't complain; he was warm and dry, the clothes fit, and they didn't resemble an army uniform. Tom's inherited clothes came from one of the sons at an earlier time. They were loose on his frail frame but worked nonetheless, and Tom's face beamed. Lucas had no idea how long it had been since the boy had felt warm and well-fed, but he was confident it had been more than weeks.

Mechthild sat beside Tom, cooing like a pigeon, brushing his long hair with her hand. His hair, curly and black, hung down to his shoulders. She looked at Lucas's straight, brown hair, and Lucas was happy to ditch the 'brother' idea.

When Lucas went out the kitchen door to the barn, he found Manfred with a black bicycle leaning against his ample belly. Manfred patted the seat and said, "This is an old chimney sweep's bicycle I bought for my sons—they could break anything, but not this bicycle. It's heavy, it's tough, and it will get you to Detmold."

The bicycle, built like a piece of farm machinery, had a sturdy tubular carrier frame fastened to the handlebars and a flat shelf behind the seat over the rear fender, already loaded with the box of food Mechteld had prepared. Manfred had fitted a 3-sided wooden box into the front carrier, and Lucas immediately saw Tom in his mind, sitting in the box facing forward with his legs through the carrier frame and his feet on the fender. Manfred picked up a hoe and held it up in front of Lucas.

"This is for you; Tom can hold it while you drive. The roads will have very little traffic, but the Americans will be everywhere. They're not stupid—they will know that a boy your age would likely be a soldier. If you hear them coming, you might fool them into thinking you are a farmer hoeing your field. If you hear a vehicle, jump off the bike before they see you and start hoeing and weeding." He smiled, "If they see you first, tell them you are going home after helping a neighbour. They only want an excuse to leave you alone—Americans are not interested in a Kindersoldat."

Lucas asked skeptically, "Are there enough cigarettes in the box to pay for this? I can't give you money. I haven't seen any pay for three months."

Manfred smiled. "I don't smoke, but don't worry, I have friends who do. They'll pay me for the cigarettes, and I'll make a handsome profit!" He put his muscled arm over Lucas's shoulder and steered him toward the kitchen. "Let's get you and Tom into bed for a few hours; I will wake you before the Americans come." He leaned the bicycle against a post and the hoe against a rail while a dozen curious cows watched from their stanchions. Manfred followed Lucas up the three steps to the kitchen, where Mechthild returned from the room where Manfred had gotten the clothes.

"Tom is tucked in and asleep. I bathed him and tried to cut his hair, but he wouldn't let me go that far." She smiled, and Lucas sensed Mechthild taking a victory lap.

◇◇◇◇◇◇◇◇◇◇◇◇◇◇◇◇◇◇◇◇◇◇◇◇◇◇◇◇◇◇◇◇◇◇◇

She looked solemnly at Lucas. "I found out what he's been through, and I know he isn't your brother unless you're a Jew. That little boy watched German soldiers in black uniforms rape and then murder his mother and grandmother. His mother tried to run away with Tom, but the soldiers shot her in front of him. Those Jews had probably been hiding in the barn for years, fed and cared for by the people who owned the farm, hoping the Russians would save them, but our soldiers found them first!"

"Black uniforms...those would be SS soldiers." Lucas looked at Manfred. "I'm a Wehrmacht soldier—but I was a gunner in a Waffen SS Panzer. I was the only one in a Feldgrau uniform."

Mechthild looked at her husband. "I find the rest very confusing. He said that German soldiers with grey uniforms killed the ones with black uniforms and rescued him. One of the grey soldiers gave Tom his name, Thomas Finke."

Suddenly, Lucas realized what had happened, but his mind rejected it as preposterous. But there was no other explanation—Johann Finke and his scouts had rescued the boy, and Johann had given him his son's name. The boy's real name must be blatantly Jewish.

Lucas looked from Manfred to Mechthild. "I think I know what happened. Wehrmacht Jäger scouts rescued the boy, and the Leutnant gave the boy his son's name. I know it sounds impossible, but I know that Leutnant and his son who has that name."

Mechthild nodded, accepting Lucas's statement as logical, and continued, "Tom said the soldiers took him to the road and paid a family of refugees to take care of him, but when the soldiers left, they would have nothing to do with him." She looked at her husband with tears in her eyes. "That poor child."

"Did he tell you his real name?" Lucas wondered what Johann had done. Had he and his men killed SS soldiers? Perhaps they just talked them out of killing the boy. One thing was unquestionable—if not for Johann and his men, the little boy would be dead, or worse.

And then, he remembered Halbe, the SS officer and the boys in the cellar—He had himself killed the SS officer and two soldiers, and Johann hadn't said a word.

"No." Mechthild wiped her tears with the skirt of her apron. "He became distraught when I asked him." She looked at Lucas, her eyes still wet. "Where did you find him?"

Manfred put his arms around her; Lucas stood to one side. "I found him on the other side of the river. He just appeared out of the darkness, and I couldn't leave him there, so I put him and the cigarettes on an old door and pushed it across the river."

It took Mechthild only a few seconds to right her ship. She said, "Gott sei Dank," then led him to the bathroom, where a wooden bathtub waited. It had been the scene of a battle between Thomas and Mechthild, and the result was a wet, slippery floor, a filthy, greasy ring of dirt in the tub, and a clean boy.

While the water heated, Manfred and Lucas cleaned the tub and wiped the floor. Lucas then had the luxury of soaking in fifteen centimetres of warm, soapy water. Mechthild stuck her head through the door to check on him, and he quickly yanked a towel over his private things.

She said, "I see you are not a Jew. Do you want me to wash your back?" He shook his head and laughed awkwardly. She giggled, then closed the door.

◇◇◇◇◇◇◇◇◇◇◇◇◇◇◇◇◇◇◇◇◇◇◇◇◇◇◇◇◇◇◇◇◇◇◇◇

Clean and wrapped in Manfred's substantial housecoat, Lucas crept quietly into the room where Tom was asleep. Mechthild sat on the bed beside him with her hand on his forehead. He whimpered and wiggled under the blankets, and she cooed to him until he became quiet. Mechthild gave Tom's hair a final stroke and looked at Lucas. "You take good care of this little angel. But if you don't think you can do that, we would love to keep him here with us. Manfred and I would raise him as the son we lost."

Lucas struggled with the idea of leaving Tom, and Mechthild waited for him to adjust to the possibility. Time passed until he could stretch it no further.

"I don't know what to say. You are very generous; I know you and Manfred would take good care of him, but I have to think about it. He really isn't mine to give."

Mechthild waited. Lucas made his decision. "The war isn't over yet; it's uncertain where Tom will be safer, and there is something about him that I can't explain. I know who Thomas Finke is; I played chess with him. I fought with his father—he was the Leutnant who rescued

Tom. He becomes upset whenever I try to find out who the boy is. I know it's not sensible, but I want him to meet Thomas Finke, and I want him to be there when Thomas's father comes home. I feel something special for the boy, and I think he is attached to me. That boy has had enough disappointment; I don't want to be another one."

"What about you, Lucas? You are a child and still need someone to care for you. Where are your parents?"

Lucas thought he should feel uncomfortable with these questions, but Mechthild and Manfred were the kind of people who made him feel comfortable.

"My parents, grandmother, and sister died in a Dortmund bombing raid, and my other grandparents died in the Wuppertal raid. I have no family now."

He decided to tell it all. "I have a girl in Detmold and want to marry her when I return."

He could see Mechthild's shiny teeth in the semi-darkness when she smiled. "That's wonderful, Lucas." She led him to his room, a loft above the kitchen. Strips of white cloth lay beside an open can of salve on the bed.

"I'm going to dress those burns on your legs. We use this salve on the animals. I guarantee no infection will grow with that on your wounds!"

She soaked a layer of cloth with salve, wrapped it around Lucas's legs, and then added a dry layer. She expertly plastered the ends with adhesive tape and looked it over.

"That should be alright. Don't take it off for at least four days."

Before she closed the door, she said, "We lost two sons in this war, and we have no one but one another. You are welcome to stay here for as long as you want. If Detmold doesn't work out, you and Tom have a home here if you want it."

Lucas felt sick when Manfred shook him awake from a sleep so deep he had to fight the curtain of unconsciousness, and it took several seconds before he remembered where he was. A wave of relief flooded over him when he recognized Manfred's kind face in the soft light of a lantern hanging from his raised hand. Manfred stepped back; Lucas rolled the feather comforter off, swung his legs over the board at the edge of the bed and waited for his head to sort itself out.

Manfred put his hand on Lucas's shoulder. "Mechthild is waking Tom, and breakfast will be on the table when you get dressed." His face softened in the lantern's light. He said, "When she asked you to stay with us, she was also asking for me. You and Tom are welcome here."

Lucas opened his mouth to say he must go to Detmold, and Manfred said, "Think about at least staying until Hitler is dead, and we have peace. The Americans won't bother you here."

Lucas was confused. Manfred was right, but the Americans might assume he was a soldier and take him to a prison camp. They came every day, and if he and Tom suddenly appeared... even if only Tom was suddenly there, the Americans would know he didn't belong there. What would happen to him?

The Americans seemed decent, but what happened to the soldiers who surrendered? Were they taken to labour camps? The Jews went to Hitler's labour camps like lambs, believing that they would soon be back home. Were the Americans so different from the Nazis?

He dressed and went to Tom's room, where Mechthild tried to coax him to the bathroom. Tom peed through the hole in boards over the barn manure, and then, over his protests, Lucas scrubbed the boy's hands and face in a basin of cold water.

Lucas left Tom with Mechthild and went to the kitchen, where a basket of boiled eggs sat in the middle of the table. Brötchen, jam and wurst piled on plates made Lucas's mouth water—food rationing obviously meant nothing to a farmer.

Lucas sat beside Manfred and broke the shell of a hardboiled egg with the back of a knife. Mechthild led Tom to a chair beside hers.

The boy's eyes opened wide when he saw the food, and he immediately went for the Brötchen. Mechthild buttered a half-bun before Tom could put it in his mouth, then slathered enough apple jelly over the butter to cover it. Tom reverently took it in both hands and said, "Danke schön," in a loud, grateful voice.

Mechthild cocked her head, smiled, and said, "Bitte schön, Mein Liebling!" It was painfully evident to Lucas that she had fallen in love with the little boy.

Breakfast was over in twenty minutes, and as they stood up, Mechthild said to Lucas, "I don't think we've finished with last night's discussion. Tom is welcome to live here if he wants to, and you will travel better without him. The Americans are here; they trust us and will stop for coffee in a few hours. He will be safer with us than on the road." She looked hopefully at him. "We would welcome both of you as our new sons. When Hitler is dead, you could even bring your girlfriend here!"

Lucas turned to Thomas and asked, "Tom, what do you want to do? I would be happy to have you come home with me, but I know you will be welcome and happy here. It's up to you, but you must decide right now."

Tom didn't hesitate. He took Lucas's hand and turned to Mechthild. "I want to go with Lucas." He looked up at Lucas. "He's my brother!"

Mechthild couldn't hide her disappointment when she said to Tom, "It's all right, Liebling, I understand." She wiped a tear from her cheek.

She sighed, turned to Lucas and gave him a small piece of paper. "This is our name and address. I want you to write and tell us how you and Thomas make out on your journey." She looked at Manfred, then back at Lucas. "I want you to know that if things don't work out for you in Detmold, we will welcome you back here whenever you want somewhere to stay." Manfred nodded in agreement, adding, "And bring your girlfriend."

Lucas offered his hand to Mechthild, but she put her arms around him. He hugged her, promised to write, took Tom's hand and followed Manfred to the barn.

The cows, their udders sore and ready for milking, complained loudly. One frustrated lady kicked the boards in her stall and banged her horns against the rail above her feed trough. The preparations for Lucas's departure had upset her sacred routine, and she was giving Manfred fair warning before she tore down the barn. Manfred assured her he would "be there in a minute" and wheeled the bicycle outside into the gray predawn light. He held it steady while Lucas lifted Tom into the front carrier—Manfred had added an old wool coat to soften the bottom. Two leather belts held the wooden box full of food on the steel shelf behind the seat.

"Lucas, are you sure you won't stay? The war will end in a few days, and then you can go home safely."

"The Russians are on the other side of the river, a few kilometres from here. I can hit a T-34 tank from that range, and I know that the Russians could crush the Americans if they wanted. As Lucas shook Manfred's hand, he said, "I want to get as far away from the Russian army as possible."

Lucas hated to see the disappointment on Manfred's face. The beard didn't hide the sadness in his eyes as he said, "I understand, and perhaps you are right."

Lucas smiled, "Please tell me the truth, Manfred. Do you have someone who will buy the cigarettes?"

Manfred laughed. "My friend will pay me that much for even one cigarette—but not until he runs out. His 'black' source has dried up because of the Americans; he has no more brown ration stamps, and I doubt he will find any for a while." He laughed, stepped back, and said, "Now, you must go, and I must milk the cows before the Yanks get here for their morning coffee."

The sun rose behind them, casting a long shadow ahead of the bicycle as Lucas pedalled westward toward home and Corinne. He was giddy with happiness and anticipation as Tom turned and waved at Manfred and Mechteld until they were out of sight.

Chapter Thirty-one

2 May 1945

Hunding

Gelernt ist gelernt
(what is learned in the cradle is taken to the grave)

LUCAS STOPPED AT THE FIRST FORK IN THE ROAD and studied a crude map that Manfred had drawn. It covered the first thirty kilometres, and Manfred had noted the narrow country lanes he thought would be safe for Lucas to use. The unpaved Waldstrassen and Feldstrassen skirted small villages, helping the boys avoid major routes.

Lucas decided to avoid the Magdeburg area, travelling south and west, exchanging greater distances for safety. He knew the general direction he wanted to go—they would stay north of Paderborn using woods roads in the hilly forests and agricultural service roads on flat land, circumventing the towns any way they could. Assuming the American Army would watch all the major routes and the flat open plains next to the Elbe River, Lucas planned to be in the hills under the protection of a forest canopy by nightfall.

He had thought about travelling at night, but now that he had Tom with him, they had the hoe, and they wore civilian clothes, he could see no problem with travelling during the day. There were significant disadvantages to being caught on the roads at night because the country was under curfew, and he couldn't think of an explanation for riding a bicycle in the dark with a little boy in the parcel carrier that someone with the intelligence of a mule would accept.

Twice during the morning, when they heard a vehicle approaching, Lucas and Tom jumped off the bicycle and hoed freshly planted fields. Both times, it had been a convoy of trucks, armoured cars, and American jeeps, and the Yankee soldiers had ignored them. Lucas chose paths through fields, well away from military traffic.

They were at the end of the map when the sun was high, and Lucas thought about asking for directions and decided it was safer to use the sun to keep going southwest until he reached the mountains. Lucas knew enough about the area that they couldn't be far from thick woods where they could hide. They needed a place to sleep, hidden from anyone on the road.

◇◇◇◇◇◇◇◇◇◇◇◇◇◇◇◇◇◇◇◇◇◇◇◇◇◇◇◇◇◇◇◇◇◇

Late in the afternoon, standing up on the pedals and rocking the bike back and forth, Lucas wheezed his way to the top of a long hill. When he heard a jeep approaching, it was already close, but the winding road through trees on both sides sheltered him and Tom from anyone's view. Lucas stopped beside a fence, lifted Tom from the carrier and threw the bike in the ditch. He set Tom and the hoe on the other side of the low wooden rail fence, jumped over and began hoeing. Tom knew the drill and knelt beside him, pulling what looked like short grass out of the ground.

The jeep with two soldiers in the front seats rounded the corner and stopped beside the bicycle with a squeal of brakes. A voice said something, gears clunked, and the jeep angled itself on the road so the hood pointed at the would-be farmers. The voice spoke again, and the American soldier driving the jeep shut off the engine. Both men leaned back and put their feet up on the dash. They laughed, pointed at the boys, and spoke so quickly in strangely accented English that Lucas's school English was useless to him. It was evident they were amused, and he was thankful when they remained in the jeep. As time passed, Lucas decided the Americans had no intention of arresting him, and the field was big enough to keep two refugees busy for the rest of their lives.

The sun disappeared behind the western hill in a final blaze of red, but the Americans were in no hurry—they sat in their jeep, smoking and talking as they patiently watched Lucas and Reuben. When they drank from their canteens and laughed, Lucas was so thirsty he wanted to surrender.

Lucas couldn't think of anything he could do that wouldn't raise the soldiers' suspicion. The bicycle was in the ditch beside the jeep, and leaving it behind would trigger a response and possibly result in the loss of the bike. Darkness was making hoeing and weeding a ridiculous endeavour, and the jig was up.

Lucas was about to throw up his hands when a voice from the other side of the field made him straighten up from his hoeing. A man stood at the door of a farmhouse at the foot of the hill and waved his arms, shouting, "Hans, Essen!" Lucas waved to him, then spoke to Tom.

"It's time to eat. Let's go."

Tom said nothing. He crawled under the fence while Lucas calmly climbed over it and then silently waited while Lucas picked up the bicycle. Lucas attempted to put him in the parcel carrier, but although the little boy wasn't heavy, the bike slipped sideways, and the boy fell hard on the ground. Tom rubbed his arm and screwed up his face but caught himself before he cried.

"Hey, let me help you." Lucas understood the simple sentence spoken by one of the Americans as he jumped out of the jeep. The American held the bicycle while Lucas put Tom in the carrier.

"That's quite a rig you got there, son." The soldier stepped back, patting the box of food. Lucas was afraid he would ask him to open it, but the man just smiled.

Lucas said, "Thank you, sir" in awkward English. He swung his leg over the low bar and put his foot on the pedal.

The soldier in the jeep pointed to Lucas's neat rows and said, "Y'all know that there's wheat, don't ya?" "In the yu-es-eh we-all don' hoe no wheat." He chuckled, close to an all-out laugh.

Lucas's English was adequate to know these soldiers knew something wasn't right, and he pretended he couldn't understand, which was not a long stretch of the truth.

He said, "I understand nothing you say." Lucas pushed the bicycle ahead, put all his weight on the pedal and rode down the hill toward the house.

The soldiers laughed, and a minute later, the jeep caught up and followed slowly behind until Lucas turned into the farmyard. The driver stepped on the gas, saluted, and tooted the horn. Lucas waved and could hear the GIs laughing as they waved their arms and drove off.

◇◇◇◇◇◇◇◇◇◇◇◇◇◇◇◇◇◇◇◇◇◇◇◇◇◇◇◇◇◇◇◇◇◇◇

The door to the house was open and Lucas leaned his bicycle against the old farmhouse's brick-and-beam wall, turning the bike so it pointed toward the road. The Fachwerk-style house seamlessly joined with the barn to make one building. The thick thatch roof spilled over the edges, and four small glass rectangles split four small windows. The thick, heavy fifty-millimetres-thick oak door, made hundreds of years ago, was low enough that he had to duck under the header.

A deep voice resonated from the semi-dark interior, lit only by a kerosene lantern. A fire in a stone fireplace and the evening twilight coming through two small windows added to the eerie scene.

"Come in and have supper with me." A deep, resonant laugh followed the invitation. "My name is Otto, and I would enjoy your company. And, of course, you must repay me for saving you from the Americans by helping me finish eating a pig. I have no ice; the weather is warm, and we must eat it tonight, or the flies will ruin it."

The first thing Lucas's eyes saw when they had adjusted to the dark interior was a massive, crudely built table with heavy square legs, probably as old as the house. Hand-hewn out of an enormous tree, two thick pieces of oak were joined in the middle to form the tabletop. The fifteen-centimetre-square legs braced on the corners that held the table up seemed barely adequate. The tabletop—finished as bare, hand-planed-wood had never seen shellac or varnish. Six chairs made in the same style, so heavy it would take two men to lift them, surrounded the table. Dark red material stretched over straw matting and nailed with large brass tacks covered the seats and backs.

Lucas thought it a perfect scene for the opening act of Die Walküre, the second opera in Wagner's Ring Cycle. He looked at two ancient tankards filled with beer sitting beside large unglazed clay pottery bowls filled with stewed pork and vegetables. A large cup of milk sat beside the third setting.

A huge man stood beside the table. He could only be Hunding, the evil host in the first Die Walküre scene. But this man had a twinkle in his eyes, and tiny wrinkles began there, then disappeared into his thick, graying beard and bushy head of hair. Lucas imagined himself as Siegmund, Hunding's mortal enemy whom tradition dictated Hunding must shelter in his home for the night.

Lucas opened his arms slightly and smiled, shaking off the association.

"Thank you for rescuing us from the Americans; I don't know how much longer we could have kept hoeing and weeding." He motioned Tom to sit down at the place with the milk. The huge chair wrapped around the little boy; his chin was just high enough to clear the table's edge. He put his hands on his lap and waited for Lucas and the giant man to sit down.

"Yes," the big man boomed happily, "that was interesting. I believe they knew very well that you weren't farmers, and I don't know why they didn't take you with them!"

"I thought my hoeing was going very well until one of them told me that in America, no one hoes whatever we were hoeing. I pretended I didn't understand."

The farmer's laugh came from his belly. "They were probably farm boys sent to fight the nasty Germans. Yes, they are correct; you were hoeing wheat, and no one in any country hoes wheat." He pointed at Lucas and laughed again. "And even worse, I could see, even from here, that you were hoeing the little wheat plants out and leaving the weeds and grass!" He roared the end of the phrase and laughed hard as he sat down. "Now, eat up and be thankful they were in a good mood and that you know some English. But first, we must thank God for your good fortune!" He bowed his head, and Lucas did the same, looking at Tom out of the corner of his eye—the boy understood and reverently bowed his head.

Otto thanked God for the food he had raised with his sweat and for helping him carry out the Lord's will by delivering these boys from the immoral American invaders. Lucas repeated the "amen," and the big man added, "Heil Hitler."

As they ate, the farmer introduced himself as Otto Kretchmar, the fifteenth generation of farmers to occupy this house and land, but he said he would be the last. His wife had died of heart failure the summer before, caused, he believed, by the death of their son at the hands of the American aggressors at Normandy.

Otto put both hands on the table. The twinkle in his eyes disappeared, and his beard jiggled as he spoke. "I will be sixty this week, and I've had enough of war! I have lost everything, and it's all for nothing. Hitler could have brought order and peace to the world, but his generals made stupid mistakes, and the people turned against him. Hitler must leave Berlin and rebuild the thousand-year Reich, and this time, the whole world will be against him!"

Lucas grunted a neutral response and ate his stew.

He helped Otto wash the dishes while Tom slept on a makeshift bed on the floor. Otto put the plates on a shelf above the sink and sent Lucas to the well for water. When Lucas returned, Otto was leaning over Tom, examining him. Straightening up, he took a last look at the sleeping boy and waved Lucas to the table, where he joined him and poured two tankards full of beer.

He said, "I brewed it myself," as he raised his beer stein.

Lucas raised his, said, "Prost," and swallowed as little as he could without insulting his host. It was "full-bodied," to say the least, and Lucas nursed a single mug for an hour.

Otto, sluggish and happy, left the room and returned with a Walthers P-38 pistol that looked like the one Klaus carried.

Otto waved it in front of Lucas's face and said, "My son gave me this pistol the last time I saw him. I keep it loaded, and I will shoot anyone, American, Russian, or Jew, who comes through that door without an invitation from me! The stupid Americans can't stop the Russians before they've taken all of Europe, and the English won't care as long as the Bolshevik bastards don't cross the English Channel."

Not convinced the safety was on, Lucas constantly maneuvered his head away from the waving muzzle.

Otto put his finger on the trigger and shouted, "God will help me take a few of the Scheisskerl with me before they take my farm!" He slurred his words as he waved the gun in Lucas's face, and Lucas noted with relief that it wasn't cocked.

Otto began to fade. He sat in his chair, hung his arms down so the gun's barrel almost touched the floor and let his head flop forward. His breathing became loud and regular, and Lucas hoped he had fallen asleep. Every instinct told Lucas to run from this man.

Otto's head drooped lower and lower, and Lucas slowly stood up. And then, just before the man slumped forward onto the table, he suddenly stood up and muttered something about milking the cows before daylight. He laid the gun on the table and crossed the room to show Lucas where he and Tom would sleep.

He had one hand on the wooden door handle when he looked at Tom's sleeping body and said, "I didn't get the boy's name—what did you say it was?"

Lucas said, "His name is Thomas, and he's my brother," as casually as he could.

"Thomas…that's my neighbour's name. What's the boy's last name?

"Moszkiewicz." the boy said the name softly as he sat up and looked at Otto with the innocence of an angel.

Otto shouted, "Das ist ein Jüdisher Name... Ihr Seid Saujuden!"

Lucas looked at Tom, panic-stricken. The boy suddenly realized what he had done and tried to fix it, speaking fast, almost shouting, "No, my name is Thomas Finke… Finke, that's my real name! Ich bin kein Jude!"

Otto stepped to Tom's side and carefully examined the boy, a cruel scorn replacing everything decent. His cruel bulldog face furiously contorted, the big man seized the little boy's arm and lifted him like a rag doll. Heading for the door, he said, "I will kill you outside; I don't want blood on the floor!"

Lucas tackled Otto's waist, but the man outweighed him by fifty kilograms. Otto opened the heavy door with one hand, threw Tom on the ground, and then turned to rid himself of the weight around his waist. Lucas let go, dodged past Otto, and the big man headed back into the house, cursing all Jews.

Certain that Otto was getting his gun, Lucas grabbed Tom, threw him into the parcel carrier, mounted the bicycle and accelerated out of the yard, standing on the pedals and pulling up on the handlebars to get as much leverage as possible. Lucas had reached the road and turned left when he heard Otto curse the gun. Lucas knew the drunken farmer had tried to fire without sliding the cocking mechanism and dared hope Otto wouldn't figure it out before they disappeared in the darkness. But the hope crashed and burned when he heard the metallic sound of the gun's slide levering a shell into the barrel. Otto cursed again as he pulled the trigger.

Even though he wanted to go right, left was downhill, and Lucas knew he could make Otto's shot more difficult when pedalling downhill. Otto fired five shots at the accelerating target, screaming obscenities each time he pulled the trigger, but the bullets whizzed past, too high to hit anything that didn't have wings. Lucas wasn't afraid of a drunken Otto shooting them in the dark even though a half-moon climbed slowly above the trees. Tom screamed with fright, and Otto aimed at the sound, but neither his luck nor aim improved.

Tom stopped crying a kilometre down the hill, and a few hundred metres farther, Lucas found a narrow woods road, barely wide enough for a team of horses. He drove the bicycle between the trees and past two bends in the gravel path, making sure they were out of sight of the main road.

Tom whimpered, "Why did he do that? What did I do wrong?"

Lucas made a note to talk to Thomas about his whimpering and whining.

"Tom, you did nothing wrong. Otto hates everyone who isn't like him because he's afraid."

"Why is he afraid?" Tom whined, half-crying, and Lucas cringed. "Is he afraid of the bad Americans? We aren't Americans, are we?"

"He's afraid of you, Tom. Many people are afraid of you."

Tom whimpered again, pushing his knuckles into his eyes. "I won't hurt anyone. Tell everyone I won't hurt them, and then they won't be afraid of me anymore!"

Lucas decided he couldn't stand it. "Tom, don't whimper—you're too big for that. I'll teach you how to deal with the people who want to hurt you, but you must be strong! Please, Tom, you must stop that whining and whimpering!"

Thomas was hurt, then resolute as he said, "I will never whimper or whine again, and I won't cry either." He clenched his teeth, "Never!"

"Crying isn't a bad thing when you need to…" Lucas paused, then decided to explain, "I cry when I have to, and sometimes it makes me feel better. You shouldn't be afraid to cry sometimes—but please don't whiiiine!" He whined the last word and smiled at Tom, jammed backwards in the parcel carrier in the dark. Tom tried to return the smile, but Lucas thought he heard a little sob. He felt as though he had just stolen Tom's favourite toy.

Lucas took the boy out of the carrier, stood him on his little feet on the ground, and laid the bicycle on its side. "The supper was good though, wasn't it?" He smiled, then laughed, remembering Die Walküre... Siegmund had run away with Hunding's wife.

Thomas wiped his eyes with his sleeve, and Lucas reached under the boy's skinny arm to tickle him. Tom laughed for the first time since Lucas had found him, and the mood infected Lucas, so they laughed together. Lucas lost control, sat down, and Tom pounced on him. They stopped laughing and lay on the soft ground, silently looking at the moon through the trees.

Lucas said, "It's beautiful, isn't it?" and waited for a reply, but none came. The boy was asleep, and Lucas laid his coat over him.

The night was warm for the second of May, and the stars shone brightly. The waning half-moon glowing through the trees would have created a romantic evening in another context, but tonight, Lucas preferred total darkness when he pedalled past Otto's farm.

Lucas lay beside Tom, trying to stay in a 'between' state, not quite asleep but not entirely awake. He dared not sleep until he took the bicycle up the hill past Otto's house.

Tom's legs twitched, his hands struck out at something, and he whimpered. Lucas sang a Brahms Volkslied and rubbed his back, and Tom lay still before he finished the first verse. Lucas lay back, looked up at the stars, and thought of Katrina, Hartwig, and Corinne.

The Brahms quartet seemed far away, but Lucas stayed awake by playing the music on an imaginary violin, finding a sense of peace he had forgotten. He tried not to become optimistic; he knew it was not time for that, but hope found its way into his mind as he imagined himself playing the violin. He missed music so much that the thought of playing again filled him with energy.

Theo, Maria, Barbara, Thomas and Gartenstrasse 18 were separate from his music; they existed in a different world, yet he needed them to take him back before he could make music again. He had killed men and done things that he knew they would not forgive—what would happen when he showed up on their doorstep? Lucas couldn't think of another possibility for the future.

◇◇◇◇◇◇◇◇◇◇◇◇◇◇◇◇◇◇◇◇◇◇◇◇◇◇◇◇◇◇◇

Lucas forced himself to wait until he was sure Otto would be asleep, and then he leaned the bicycle against a tree, picked up the sleeping Tom and slid him into the parcel carrier without waking him. Lucas wheeled the bike onto the road and pedalled hard uphill until he could see the end of Otto's barn.

He dismounted, listening for sounds from the house, searching the yard for movement. An owl hooted from the barn's vicinity, and a mouse rustled the leaves on the side of the road.

Lucas waited for his huffing and puffing to calm down, then pushed the bicycle forward.

Otto was no marksman, but he might get lucky, and Lucas didn't want to test him. He wasn't even sure he could pedal the bicycle up the steep hill faster than Otto could run. He slowed, looked for a twinkle of light, a movement, a shadow in the yard. Opposite the house, Lucas picked up speed, running as quietly as his Wehrmacht boots would allow. Tom woke, groaned, and Lucas shushed him. But no sounds came from Otto's lair, and the owl stopped hooting.

Two hundred metres past the barn, the hill wasn't as steep. Lucas mounted the bicycle and pedalled with all the strength he had until he was sure they were beyond the range of Otto's pistol.

When Lucas reached the top of the hill, his legs were numb, and he fought for breath. He was at the end of his rope when the bicycle crested the hill and coasted without his help. It quickly picked up speed, and Lucas had to use brakes on the turns for the next kilometre.

When Lucas was confident Otto was safely behind them, he slowed, searching for a path leading away from the road. When Lucas found one, he dismounted and pushed the bike into the woods. The roughness woke Tom, and Lucas stopped to lift him from the carrier.

They walked another fifty metres uphill until a small stream crossed their path. Lucas stood the bicycle against a beech tree and followed the stream uphill, hoping for a spring at the head of it.

334

They stopped at a dry knoll where the hardwood trees had left a thick blanket of leaves. Tom helped Lucas gather armfuls of them and then jumped on the pile, rolling back and forth and laughing. Tom lay still; Lucas spread his coat on him, then lay down and pulled leaves over Tom and himself.

The sun shining on his face woke Lucas from a dreamless sleep.

Chapter Thirty-two

3 May 1945

Yankees

"You can always count on Americans to do the right thing—but only after they've tried everything else."

Attributed to Winston Churchill

Tom was peacefully sleeping when Lucas awoke and started searching for the source of the water gurgling among the stones and leaves. Fifty metres up the hill, he found a spring bubbling from a small mound of rocks, pausing in a shiny pool before it ran downhill, joining other little streams to become a brook. Lucas knelt, cupped his hands, and drank. He splashed water on his face, and when he stood, he felt fully awake, sharp and optimistic.

Returning to the bicycle, Lucas opened the wooden box and took out the now empty milk bottle Mechthild had given them. There were still four pieces of buttered bread and a large piece of cheese in the box, and Lucas took the food to where Tom lay sleeping. He went to fill the milk bottle with water, and Tom was awake and staring at the food when he returned. They ate, drank, and were content, sitting on soft leaves in the warm morning sunshine. The more he thought about home, the more Lucas believed it was within reach.

He listened to birds flitting through the branches, chasing one another, and realized that, aside from Otto trying to kill them, he hadn't heard a shot in two days. There were no screams of the dying—only the bird's mating songs. For now, Lucas was in a place where there was no hate, no killing, and for the first time in what seemed an eternity, his world was a beautiful place where music was possible, and birds could safely sing. What Lucas felt now was more than hope; he dared to plan a life with Corinne.

<hr>

Finished with the food, except for a few small pieces of cheese that would be Mittagessen, Lucas closed the box, fastened it on the rear fender carrier and walked the bicycle to the main road. He listened for the distinct sound of American jeeps and, hearing nothing, lifted Tom into his seat and headed southwest, downhill.

As the bicycle coasted without input, Lucas began to think he might be travelling too far to the south. The sun on his left shoulder and a bit ahead told him the road was taking them more south than west. But Lucas had no choice but to follow it until he found one going more westerly.

The hills became mountains—the road became crooked and steep, uphill and down. It seemed much more up than down to Lucas's tired legs, and he and Tom started to walk up the steepest hills. The only traffic they encountered was a single American jeep that they avoided by ditching the bicycle behind bushes and running into the woods.

When the sun reached its zenith and started down, Lucas pushed the bike into a path in the trees, split the last pieces of cheese with Tom, and they drank and ate in silence.

A half-hour later, the road took them down a long twisting hill, and Lucas used the rear pedal brake and a touch of the front hand-brake to control the speed, hoping neither would fail. He let the bicycle roll as fast as he dared over two kilometres of steady downhill as Tom laughed, yelled, and held his arms out in the wind.

When they broke out of the forest, the road straightened to fit between rectangular fields on both sides. The bicycle flew on the straight, open road, and hiding was out of the question when a vehicle approached from behind. Lucas turned to see a jeep less than a hundred metres behind them. It was too close to avoid and too late to use the hoe. He pulled over to the shoulder, going too fast for the loose gravel, hoping the Americans would pass, but the jeep slowed to follow less than thirty metres behind.

Lucas didn't dare turn his head; it was all he could do to keep the bicycle upright on the loose gravel.

"Tell me what the jeep is doing and how many men are there." Tom twisted himself around until he faced Lucas and could peek around him.

"There are two men in it; they're the same ones as yesterday, and they're talking. I think they're laughing at us."

Lucas concentrated on what to do next. Perhaps the Americans would pass him, but why didn't they do it? The road was straight, and it was wide enough.

The gravel on the shoulder was too loose to keep driving on it; Lucas had to fight the front wheel to keep it from kicking sideways, and a crash was imminent if he didn't slow down. He braked harder, and smoke rose from the front brake, so he had to let the bicycle go.

Lucas kept his eyes on the track a few metres in front of the wheel, concentrating on keeping the tire on the narrow, hard-packed right wheel track. The farther Lucas drove, the more dangerous the narrow track became, and finally, in a fit of anger, he cursed, ignored the Americans and steered into the middle of the road. The road levelled out, the speed dropped, and Lucas decided it was safe to lift his head.

He looked down the road for the first time in five minutes.

◇◇◇◇◇◇◇◇◇◇◇◇◇◇◇◇◇◇◇◇◇◇◇◇◇◇◇◇◇◇

Two Russian soldiers carrying Papa machine guns stood in the middle of the road, watching him approach the intersection they were guarding, now only a hundred metres ahead of the bicycle. A half-track and a road car sat in the intersection, and the machine gun on the armoured vehicle pointed in Lucas's and the American jeep's general direction. His stomach churned, and his hands sweated as he coasted to the soldiers and stopped on their signal. One of the young Russians held out his hand and stated in heavily accented German, "Papier, bitte." Lucas noted that the young man wasn't more than a year older than he was.

Lucas shook his head. The truth wouldn't do—he would try Manfred's tale. "I don't have any papers because I escaped from Berlin with nothing." He nodded toward Tom. "And I found this Polish refugee when I crossed the Elbe River. We're going to live with my grandparents in Detmold." The baffled soldier looked at his companion, and Lucas added, "That's near Bielefeld."

He suspected that the soldier either didn't believe him or, more likely, had no idea what he had said. The young Russian waved at the road car. A third Russian soldier, older than Johann, stepped out of the car's rear door and walked over. He said in clear German, "Come with me. Leave the bicycle and bring the boy."

The Russian soldiers trained their machine guns on Lucas's chest. The safeties were off, and Lucas knew what those guns were capable of, so he laid the bicycle on the ground and took Tom's hand.

The little boy refused to move. Lucas pulled, and Tom leaned back and braced his feet. He whimpered, then cried at full throttle. One of the Russians pulled at Lucas's arm, trying to guide him toward the car, but Lucas planted his feet. The second Russian grabbed Tom's long hair and pulled. Out of the corner of his eye, Lucas saw a large dark spot spreading over the front of Tom's pants, and a stream of urine ran down the boy's leg onto his shoe.

The American jeep had stopped a few metres before the intersection, and while the Russians were busy with Lucas and Tom, they had gotten out of the jeep carrying their rifles. One of them walked into the intersection with his M31 cocked while the other covered him. The covering soldier leaned against the jeep with a microphone in one hand and his cocked rifle in the other.

The American soldier now in the intersection fired a single shot over the Russians' heads and gave instructions in what Lucas recognized as Russian. The second American said in English, "You're in our sector, boys, and we're here to tell y'all to get the fuck back across the river! You be good boys now and git back where y'all belong before somethin' blows you all to hell!" He held up the microphone he had in his hand while his buddy translated.

The American who spoke Russian waved his free hand down the road, and just as though they had rehearsed the scene, a Sherman tank appeared from nowhere, driving hell-bent toward the intersection. In full flight, it fired a shell over their heads, and it exploded in the field. The tank stopped a hundred metres from the drama, a range that meant certain death for anything the Sherman intended to kill, and the gunner levelled its cannon between the Russian vehicles. The gun moved to the car, then the half-track, then to the car, playing 'eenie meenie miney mo' with them.

The Russian soldier holding Lucas's arm tried half-heartedly to pull him toward the car, but Lucas freed himself. The tank and the seventy-five-millimetre cannon shell it fired had confirmed to Lucas that he correctly understood what the American had said. The Russian soldier aimed his gun at Lucas's head, and the American spoke into the radio. The Sherman fired again, head-high between the vehicles, and Lucas recognized the sound of armour-piercing munitions, as did the Russians. The shell exploded ten metres behind the Russian car, showering it with dirt and leaving a small crater. Small pieces of shrapnel rained down around the men in the intersection.

A Russian officer, older than Lucas's father, with bars on his sleeve, hurriedly bailed out of the car and started running across the field, and the Sherman fired its machine gun, digging up the ground at the Russian's feet. The man with the bars stopped, and the tank aimed its cannon and machine gun at the precise angle that would ruin the Russian's day. The tank commander shouted something, and the turret swung to the Russian armoured car, but the machine gun stayed on the now returning Russian who had decided it would be a good idea to raise his hands. Lucas noticed that the Sherman's turret spun twice as fast as a Panther's, and the gun's barrel was at least thirty centimetres shorter.

The Russian-speaking American spoke to the man behind the half-track's machine gun, pointed at the Sherman and made a throat-cutting motion. The soldier pointed his gun at the sky and got out of the vehicle.

The American appeared to threaten the Russian officer, and the officer snapped an order to his men. The soldiers immediately lost interest in Lucas and returned to their vehicles—the gunner on the half-track sat in the back seat. The American tank kept its guns trained on them until they left by the east fork of the intersection and drove out of sight. When they disappeared, the agile Sherman spun around and went smoothly down the road.

Lucas picked up the bicycle and lifted Tom into the carrier, but before he could get on it, the Russian-speaking American stood before Lucas.

"Not so fast, buddy! You understood English yesterday—how about today?" Lucas nodded and showed him his fingers with a couple of millimetres between his thumb and index finger. The soldier pointed at the jeep and spoke louder and slower. "Leave the bicycle, and you and the kid get in the back of the jeep. I'm pretty sure Colonel Feinstein will want to meet you."

Lucas shook his head. "No, I need the bicycle."

The American looked at his buddy, who had two stripes on his sleeve. The corporal nodded and said, "Okay, private; put it on the hood and tie it down."

When the private had stood the windshield up and tied the bicycle on the front of the jeep, Lucas and Tom sat on the steel seats in the rear. The jeep drove through forests and across fields for over an hour, reaching the town of Hersfeld without missing a bump. The cobblestone streets pounded Lucas's rear end until he thought it must be bleeding.

◇◇◇◇◇◇◇◇◇◇◇◇◇◇◇◇◇◇◇◇◇◇◇◇◇◇◇◇◇◇◇◇◇◇

When they pulled up to a building with the Wehrmacht shield over the main door, Lucas recognized it as a permanent German army barracks. The corporal beckoned Lucas to follow him, and Lucas began to untie the rope holding the bicycle. The soldier put his hand on Lucas's shoulder.

"No need to worry about your bicycle; private Hoskins will take care of it." The soldier spoke quietly, with no sign of aggression.

Lucas hesitated.

"Please, kid, let's do this the easy way. Just bring the boy and come with me—nothing bad will happen."

Lucas wasn't sure what the soldier had said but could see no alternative to following him. He went around the jeep to the tailgate, lifted Tom to the ground, and watched Private Hoskins drive around the building with his bicycle.

The inside of the barracks was bright; whitewashed walls defined a wide corridor lined with doors on one side and windows overlooking a pastoral landscape on the other. Manicured trees grew on a slope facing the building, and a small creek ran along the bottom of a hill parallel to the building. The late afternoon sun shone through the trees, and despite being in an army barracks, Lucas felt the war recede. The corporal stopped to talk to a fellow soldier going in the opposite direction, and Lucas stared at the beautiful scene, wondering if his next stop would be a prison camp. He felt safe, and no matter what happened now, he would get home somehow.

Lucas worried more about Tom than himself. He may have made a bad mistake when he didn't leave him with Manfred and Mechteld.

When the other soldier moved on, Lucas's escort waited and looked at the view with Lucas. "It is beautiful, isn't it?" He turned to Lucas. "Don't worry, Colonel Feinstein is a fair man. Tell him the truth, and he'll help you if he can."

Lucas smiled. He hadn't understood everything, but the name got his attention.

"Feinstein is Jewish name... is the Colonel Jewish?"

"Yeah, I think so, but I'm not sure." The corporal shrugged his shoulders and looked at Tom. "Who cares?" He looked at Lucas. "You don't, do you?" Lucas said, "No, I don't care," and the American began walking. Lucas took Tom's hand and followed.

As they walked, Lucas decided the truth would get him nothing good. He was a German soldier who had fought side by side with Waffen SS soldiers, and if the Jewish Colonel found out, he would throw him in prison. He must fine-tune his story.

The Colonel's outer office was a spacious, bright room staffed by a young corporal whose job was obviously to punish a typewriter. He looked up when the trio entered, happy to be interrupted.

The soldier put his hand on Tom's head and spoke to the typewriter torturer. "I've got a couple of boys here that I think the Colonel will want to see. Those damned Russkies are on our side of the river again, and he wanted me to report as soon as I got back."

The corporal lifted the phone, spoke into it, and had barely laid it on the cradle and returned to his typewriter abuse when the door to the office opened, and a friendly face appeared. The officer gestured to the corporal, then to Lucas, and Lucas steered Tom through the door behind the corporal.

Tom's eyes grew big and bright, fascinated with magnificence beyond his craziest dreams. The three-metre-high creatively plastered ceiling was as fascinating as the sky to a child who had not seen anything but barns and hovels for most of his life. Lucas almost tripped over him when Thomas stopped and stared at the ornate plaster on the snow-white ceiling, and all three men watched the expression of innocent wonder on the child's face. The colonel and his corporal waited until Lucas convinced Thomas to step out of the way using his finger as a prod, and the colonel touched the little boy's hair as he brushed past. He motioned for Lucas to sit in an oversized leather chair, and Tom stood beside him, his dark brown eyes focused on Colonel Feinstein. A tiny smile lit his face, and Feinstein grinned.

The corporal reported what had happened; the colonel grunted appropriately, asked for a few more details and said, "Thanks, and good work, Jack. See that George types that up for you before you leave." The corporal's salute was more like a touch of his hat, and he turned and left in a comfortable manner that looked like a relaxed walk in a park. Lucas was appalled at the casualness.

The door closed, and Colonel Feinstein sat behind his massive desk. "Now, let's talk about you and your companion." His smile was friendly enough, but Lucas's military education hadn't been wasted—he knew a clever, manipulative man when he saw one.

"I'll begin by telling you to be truthful. If you are truthful, I may help you. But if you lie to me, I promise you will go to a prison camp. Do you understand?" Lucas nodded. His school English was enough that he understood the point, and he decided to lie.

He said, "I will tell the truth."

While Lucas could understand simple English sentences spoken slowly, he had severe difficulty expressing himself. As soon as he began talking, he struggled to find simple words and realized his English wasn't good enough to tell his story. The colonel came to the same conclusion, picked up the phone and spoke to the corporal, George, the typewriter punisher, in the waiting room. He told the corporal to fetch Lieutenant Mundel, three coffees, and a glass of milk.

"It will be a few minutes, and I will read my mail while we wait." Lucas understood 'minutes,' 'mail,' and 'wait.'

Colonel Feinstein opened envelopes, shuffled and read papers while Lucas examined the room, noting the neatness of everything. Tom finished looking around and curled up, half on Lucas's knee and half on the broad arm of the chair. When he had read it, Feinstein piled the mail neatly in two piles, glancing once in a while at Lucas and Tom. Lucas guessed that Feinstein was assessing his prisoner based on what he saw. The questions would fill in the blanks later.

Fifteen minutes later, a striking blonde woman, not classically beautiful like Katrina but strong and capable like Corinne, came through the door and greeted the Colonel informally, then stepped up to Tom and Lucas with a glass of milk in one hand and a plate of cookies in the other. Tom instantly came to life, and she addressed him in perfect German.

"Möchtest du etwas Milch und Kekse?" Tom took a cookie in one hand and the milk in the other with a polite, "Ja, gern! Danke schön!"

She turned to the colonel and said, "He's Jewish, and he's a Polish-German."

Lucas understood enough to know that this woman knew what she was doing and assumed he was in trouble. Manfred's story was the one he would go with, but he would use Halbe instead of Berlin. He knew a little about Halbe but not much about Berlin.

"This is Lieutenant Mundel." The colonel smiled at her, then at Lucas. He added, "This young man is Lucas Schwartz, and the child is... "What is your last name, Tom?"

Lieutenant Mundel translated the question.

Tom said, "Ich heisse Thomas Finke," then shouted, "Ich bin kein Jude!"

The lieutenant smiled, touched Tom's hair and then turned to Lucas, all business.

"You must tell us who you are, where you were going, and why. I advise you to tell the truth." As she spoke, she passed him a cup of coffee, and the smile disappeared.

Lucas nodded his thanks. "My name is Lucas Schwartz, and my father was Andreas Schwartz, an engineer. We lived in Dortmund until a bomb demolished our house, killing my parents, my sister, and my grandmother. I have no other relatives in the area, so I travelled to Halbe to live with my grandfather. When the Russians attacked the city, he sent me to the forest and told me to follow the refugees and get to Detmold...I have a great aunt there. I walked through the forest for a few days, hiding from the Russians, and finally joined people walking on a road, trying to get to the Elbe River."

Lucas paused, and the Lieutenant asked in German, "What about the boy? Where did you find him?"

"I discovered a box of cigarettes in an abandoned Lastwagen, carried them to the river and found an old door to float them to the other side. I was busy getting everything ready when Thomas found me. He was alone, with no one to help him. I couldn't leave him there and added him to the cigarettes on the door. It floated high enough, and I swam and pushed it across the river near Jerikow, where there were no lights on either side.

When we got to the American side, I took a chance and went to a farmer's house. He and his wife were kind to us. They fed us, we slept, and I traded the cigarettes for a bicycle and food. Although he admitted before we left that he didn't smoke, he took the cigarettes anyway." Lucas looked down, adding a bit of drama for his audience. "Their names were Manfred and Mechteld, and they offered to keep Tom, but he wanted to stay with me."

Lucas looked up, straight into Lieutenant Mundel's eyes. It wouldn't hurt to repeat where he was going and why.

"We are on our way to Detmold, where I have an aunt and friends we might live with while I finish my music studies."

Lucas thought it all sounded reasonable, and the story contained enough truth that he imagined he might get away with it. He waited for the reaction while the interpreter relayed his story to the Colonel in English.

Colonel Feinstein rubbed his chin and looked out the window—Lucas knew he wasn't buying it—something about his story or perhaps his demeanour was telling the Colonel he was a soldier.

He began speaking as he turned back to Lucas, "Number one, all German boys your age were in the Hitler Jugend and were drafted into the military. Hell, we're holding fourteen-year-old children in our prison camps while we try to locate their parents!" His voice took on a sharp edge along with extra volume. "Tell me how you managed to get out of it!"

Lucas had expected and prepared for the response. "I'm a musician, and artists and musicians don't have to join the Jugend. When I travelled to Halbe, my grandfather didn't report me to the Bürgeramt. There is a big hole in the ground in Dortmund where our house used to be, and no trace of my family. The Dortmund bureaucrats assumed that the bomb that vaporized me along with my parents, my grandmother and my sister."

When Lieutenant Mundel finished translating, Colonel Feinstein asked the obvious question with his eyes, and Lucas answered it.

"I escaped because I was at a friend's house practicing a Brahms piano quartet. I am a musician, not a soldier—I know nothing about guns or fighting; I only know how to play the violin and the piano!"

That was the best he could do.

"All right." The colonel held up his hands, smiling. "But I'll bet a month's pay that's at least fifty percent lies. However, we happen to have a piano, and if you can play it, I will accept that bullshit for now, and we'll sort out the rest later."

He looked at Lieutenant Mundel. "Tell him I want him to follow me. We'll find out whether he's a musician or a soldier!"

"I understand, sir." Lucas felt his chances were better than they had been an hour ago, especially if all he had to do was prove he was a musician.

The lieutenant shook her head at the colonel, and Colonel Feinstein opened the office door, turned to Lucas and indicated with his hand that he should exit first. Lieutenant Mundel trailed, holding Tom's hand and carrying the empty plate while the boy took the empty glass. The cookies and milk were gone.

Lucas was confident as they walked down the wide hallway until it widened into a large room stretching across the building's width. Oak beams sloped from the ceiling's center to the room's edge, where black wooden posts supported them. Lines of chairs on both sides of long wooden tables filled the room, arranged in perfect rows. The solid wood floor, long ago painted grey, was scratched and worn by thousands of army boots.

Lucas was suddenly jolted out of his certainty. *Army boots... I forgot about my Wehrmacht boots! No wonder the colonel doesn't believe me!*

A couple of dozen soldiers sat at a few tables, talking, drinking beer or Coca-Cola with ice. They became quiet and interested when the colonel guided Lucas to a raised platform at the end of the room.

There was a grand piano on the platform but no bench. The colonel picked up a chair from the adjacent table and placed it in front of the piano. He motioned for Lucas to sit and pointed at the covered keyboard. He said, not hopefully, "You had better be able to play that thing, or you will be in prison before the day's end." Lucas didn't need an interpreter for that. He nodded and sat down.

A thick layer of dust covered the keyboard cover and the flat top of the piano. Lucas used his sleeve to wipe the dust off the cover before lifting it, exposing a perfect set of ivory keys and gold "Bösendorf" lettering. It was a beautiful piano, at least two metres twenty long and a much better instrument than Lucas had expected. He walked around the piano, wiped off the dust as well as he could with his sleeve, and then raised the top on the high stick.

In his element, Lucas sat down and ran through a few quick arpeggios to warm up his fingers and test the tuning, which turned out to be dreadful.

The colonel pointed to chairs at the table nearest the piano. Lieutenant Mundel sat down, setting Thomas atop her lap, but turned up her nose when she smelled his pants. When he wiggled free and sat on the chair next to her, she didn't resist.

Lucas had never played a better piano, and he hoped that its beautiful sound would compensate for the tuning. He lifted his hands and began Beethoven's 'Moonlight Sonata' amid the murmuring of bored men speculating on what would happen next. When he finished the first melodic line, the room was silent.

Lucas played the first movement and waited for a response—none came for at least three seconds, and then the room burst into applause, mixed with a few bravos, one of which came from the colonel's translator.

Colonel Feinstein walked over to the piano. "I know you are not who you say you are, but it's a sure thing you are a musician. If you'll stay here and play the piano for a few days until we figure things out and maybe get the truth out of you, I will try to get you home, wherever that is." He walked to where Lieutenant Mundel was sitting and sat down with a satisfied smile.

Lucas closed the lid over the keyboard and was lowering the top cover when Feinstein stood up and asked, "Can you sing?" Lucas nodded and said, "A little," as he stepped down to the floor.

"Okay, Lucas, Lieutenant Mundel will show you where you'll be living, and she will help with Tom. If you try to leave, we'll find you, and you'll go to a prison camp. Do you understand that, or do I need Lieutenant Mundel to interpret?"

"I understand enough, sir," Lucas replied in his best English, but Lieutenant Mundel translated anyway.

"Colonel Feinstein said that if you try to leave, he will find you and put you in prison. Is that what you understood?"

The lieutenant waited. Lucas said, "I understand. Can Tom sleep in my room?"

Mundel smiled and nodded. Feinstein interrupted the silence.

"Tell me the truth. Did you really pick that little boy up at the river and bring him with you?" Lucas could hear the skepticism in the Colonel's tone and tried to find words to explain himself but couldn't, so he told Lieutenant Mundel and let her translate.

Colonel Feinstein asked, "Why would you do that? I think you know he's Jewish, don't you?"

Lucas shrugged; he wasn't sure where Feinstein was going, but he knew precisely what the colonel had said and what he was insinuating. He said, "Yes, I know that Tom is Jewish—and I know that Feinstein is also Jewish. Is that bad for me?"

The Colonel precisely mimicked Lucas's shrug, smiled, and left.

CHAPTER THIRTY-THREE

4 MAY 1945

The Whole Truth

"Three things cannot long be hidden: the sun, the moon, and the truth."

Confucius

LIEUTENANT MUNDEL LED LUCAS AND TOM TO A LARGE ROOM with two wood-framed beds, a small oak table beside each, and a desk against the blank wall. There were two upholstered chairs at the foot of the beds. The green-painted wood floor was spotless. Watercolour paintings of German landscape scenes covered a significant percentage of the white-wallpapered walls, and Lucas guessed the room had previously been a German officers' quarters.

Lucas had a dozen questions as he admired the paintings, but Lieutenant Mundel sensed his curiosity and spoke before Lucas could ask.

"It's beautiful, isn't it? So is the whole town, and it is still standing because your German comrades surrendered to us, hoping we wouldn't destroy it. Two Bundeswehr soldiers carrying a white flag in one of your funny little jeeps met us ten kilometres before we reached the town. They gave Colonel Feinstein a letter from the German commander in Hersfeld, guaranteeing that no one would shoot at us. The Colonel put the soldiers, a driver and me in an American jeep and sent us back to the town.

I was there because I could speak German and assess the situation while I talked to the soldiers. They kept assuring me everything would be all right., but I was nervous even though the Colonel and a company of his men drove behind us."

She put her hand on Tom's head and played with his hair. Tom looked up at her and smiled.

"I wasn't entirely persuaded until we came to the barracks. Wehrmacht soldiers filled the yard, standing at attention in perfect lines, their weapons piled neatly beside the road. Their commanding officer gave his pistol to the colonel, an amazing show that saved the town."

Tom wrapped his fingers around the Lieutenant's hand.

"Colonel Feinstein told his soldiers that if they caused the locals to complain about anything, even spitting on the sidewalk or dropping a gum wrapper on the ground, he would have them cleaning bathrooms for the rest of their tour."

Lieutenant Mundel looked at Tom, who grinned at her.

She looked at Lucas, and he knew she was evaluating his reaction like his mother always had. The lieutenant's penetrating stare reminded him of her, and he was suddenly sad.

"Those soldiers who dared to come to us deserve a medal. They drove through our lines with nothing to protect them but a small white flag flying above the windshield."

Lucas said softly, "There aren't enough medals in the world for the heroes in this war," and immediately regretted having said it.

She touched his arm. "Where did you serve? Lucas, you can trust me!" She smiled, and Lucas said nothing—he didn't believe the trust part.

She took her hand back from Tom and opened the curtains on the only window. "My name is Elizabeth; I'm from Minnesota in the northwestern United States, and my parents came to America from Düsseldorf when I was a baby. I want you and Tom to call me Elizabeth, and know that I am your friend. You don't believe it yet, but so is Colonel Feinstein." She looked at Lucas, "And yes, he is a Jew."

Lucas felt her eyes watching him for a reaction.

Lucas looked into her eyes and saw softness. "I am one-sixteenth Jew. My father was an engineer in a steel fabrication factory; the Hoesch Stahlwerke, or the Nazis would have taken him away. You were correct when you said that Tom is a Jew, but he doesn't know what that means. Perhaps now we can hope it won't mean anything." From her expression, Lucas realized that his reaction was better than Elisabeth had hoped.

"Thomas is a strange name for a Jew or a Pole. You haven't told me everything yet." Elizabeth didn't wait for an answer; she clapped her hands, breaking the mood. "I have learned what is most important to the Colonel and me. We will talk about the rest later. Right now, let's find the showers. Both of you…follow me."

They walked two doors down the hall and entered a door still marked Duschen.

Elisabeth stopped at the door and spoke to Lucas while Tom waited. "I'll have someone bring clothes for you to wear for now. Leave the ones you are wearing inside on the floor, and I'll have them cleaned."

She pushed the door open, and Tom ran past Lucas. "I'll meet you in your room, and then it might be a good idea to put Thomas in his bed."

The 'good idea' sounded more like an order. It hadn't escaped Lucas that Elisabeth and Colonel Feinstein had surreptitiously noticed the stain on Reuben's pants.

Neither Lucas nor Tom had ever been in a shower. Tom laughed and played in the water, and Lucas enjoyed a luxury he had never felt. When the shower cooled, Lucas shaved the fuzz on his face at the sink, where someone had optimistically left a razor. The clothes were on the bench as promised. Thomas's were brand-new, and he smiled as he stroked his hand appreciatively on the oversized plaid shirt and summer shorts. Lucas put on an American Army summer uniform without insignia.

◇◇◇◇◇◇◇◇◇◇◇◇◇◇◇◇◇◇◇◇◇◇◇◇◇◇◇◇◇◇◇

The evening performance went better than Lucas expected; he was pleased that his fingers still remembered where the keys were. A young American soldier approached him in the first intermission and offered to help him learn the popular songs of the day. Lucas gladly accepted.

Early the following day—too early, considering Lucas had played until after midnight—someone knocked softly on the door. "Are you awake, Lucas?" Elizabeth asked the question softly, so Lucas ignored her. The morning twilight barely lit the window.

She waited ten seconds, then knocked a little louder. "Are you awake, Lucas?" was no longer a question. Lucas waited to see if she would retreat, but she persisted.

And then, with no pretense, she said, too loud to be anything but a command, "Lucas, you must get up! It's six o'clock, and breakfast is ready in the dining hall." She hammered on the door.

Lucas looked at Tom, who sat up and rubbed his eyes. Tom giggled when Lucas put his finger on his lips and took his time crossing the room.

"Lucas, I know you're awake…" Lucas yanked the door open just before her fist hit it. He grinned at her, and her face reddened.

"We were just getting up… Is there an emergency?"

Elizabeth tried twice to say something, then settled on, "Okay, We're going to have breakfast, and I will save a place for you and Tom. After that, we are going to talk." Elizabeth turned and marched down the hall. Lucas wasn't sure, but he guessed the 'going to talk' was added as a reparté to his insolence. But after last night's success, Lucas felt he was on solid footing.

◇◇

The best thing about breakfast was the scrambled eggs and orange juice, but it went over a cliff from there. Lucas ate a bite of toast made from pasty white bread and began work on tiny sausages that tasted worse than canned rations.

"You don't like American breakfasts, do you?" Elizabeth pointed at the sausage on the fork Lucas was trying to get the courage to put in his mouth. "It's because you haven't got enough jam on the toast or sugar in your coffee; that's the best way to kill the taste."

Elizabeth had eaten half of her eggs and none of the sausages. She worked on a piece of toast with ten millimetres of strawberry jam piled on it and a cup of coffee contaminated with so much sugar and cream that the spoon would almost stand up.

"We have a saying in Germany; it's a line from an opera…"

Elizabeth interrupted… "Yes, Hänsel und Gretel; 'Hunger ist der beste Koch!'"

"Yes," Lucas nodded and laughed. "Hunger is the best cook." He looked at Tom.

Tom stopped eating, looked at Lucas, then at Elizabeth, and then wolfed down a sausage and a bite of toast that Elizabeth had given the same treatment as hers.

Elizabeth laughed at Tom and drank a swallow of her coffee while Lucas polished off the last of his sausages.

She said, "We should talk now," with an expression that defined 'should' as 'must.'

A half-dozen men were in the dining hall, and Elizabeth had chosen a spot well away from them beside a row of windows. The rising May sun streamed through them, warming the room.

While Lucas fiddled with his coffee—the worst he had ever tasted, worse than Ersatz Kaffee—Elizabeth took Tom to the piano, raised the cover and showed him how to get a sound by pressing the keys. Fascinated, Tom pushed one, then another, then returned to the first one. Elizabeth played a short Mozart Motif and spent five minutes teaching the four notes to Tom. She left him to practice and returned to Lucas.

She stood opposite him with her arms crossed and said, "I need to know who you are and what has happened to you. I'm going to get two fresh cups of what this place calls coffee, and you are going to tell me the truth, or I will tell Colonel Feinstein that you are a soldier, and I will recommend that he send you to a prison camp in America."

She waited for Lucas to decide whether she meant it. He slid his cup across the table; she took it and headed for the counter. When Elizabeth returned, Lucas had decided to say as little as he could get away with.

"What do you want to know?" He dumped three teaspoons of sugar into his coffee and added a tablespoon of milk. He drank a swallow, but it still tasted like wet hay.

"Why don't you start with your parent's death in the bombing raid? Why weren't you killed too? I know you told us that, but humour me."

"I was practicing a Brahms piano quartet with my friends two houses up the street."

"Which quartet? He wrote three."

Lucas hesitated. "You listen to classical chamber music?"

"I know that Brahms wrote three quartets because I've played them. I play the cello when I'm not playing soldier."

"It was the second."

"A bit virtuosic for students. You are no prodigy on the piano, and that piece requires a piano virtuoso." She smiled, dulling the impact. "But, you are a good musician."

"My instrument is the violin. My friend Hartwig has a natural genius for the piano."

"There's no such thing as a natural pianist—the piano is a manufactured percussion instrument, and there is nothing natural about it. The human voice is the only natural instrument, and therefore, only singers can be 'natural' musicians with respect to their instrument."

"I've never thought of it that way. I think I like singing better than playing the violin, and perhaps that might explain it."

"You can sing for me later, and I will tell you whether you are a natural singer." Elizabeth walked to the window and stood for a long time, looking at the green world outside. When she turned back to face Lucas, she wore an expression that told him the lying was over.

"Lucas…your boots...I know the Wehrmacht must have conscripted you as a child soldier. How old were you? Fourteen, Fifteen?"

Lucas didn't look down. He decided to admit what was obvious and avoid anything more. "Fifteen. I was living with a conductor who is the music director in the Detmold Theatre, and he was teaching me." He looked at her with tears in his eyes, suddenly feeling helpless, his plan in shambles. "I lost my parents, my sister, my aunt, and my grandmother when a bomb landed on our house. As I said, I was just two houses away. A terrible fire burned most of the city but not our area."

Everything flooded back: the planes, the explosions, and the empty hole. Tears flooded his eyes.

"Hartwig, Katrina, Corinne and I were practicing in the living room when the bomb blew in the window, and we went to the shelter in the basement." Lucas tried to stop them, but the tears came in torrents. He sobbed, "When the bombers left, we tried to find my parents, but there was only a hole in the ground. My family was gone…not even a piece of clothing... Nothing. My parents, grandmother, and sister… now part of the air!"

Elizabeth moved her eyes down when Lucas looked at her; he wiped his face on his shirt sleeve.

"Corinne and I pedalled our bicycles to Detmold—she plays the viola, and I'm going to marry her." The tears stopped, and he sniffed to clear his nose. "Corinne lost her parents, too, so she has no one to look after her."

Elizabeth blew her nose with a white handkerchief and offered it to Lucas. He wiped his nose on his sleeve, and she laughed gently.

Tom banged furiously on the piano, playing variations on the little tune. He rocked back and forth on the chair, his head barely above the keyboard.

"Our little child prodigy." Elizabeth waved toward Tom. "I wonder who he is?"

"I don't know. Tom slipped and told a brute named Otto that his last name was Moszkiewicz, but he hasn't said it since. He will only say that his name is Thomas Finke, and I know that isn't true because I know who Thomas Finke is."

Elizabeth got up and began to pace; she stopped in front of him.

She said, "You know you must tell your story to Colonel Feinstein..." Lucas nodded—he had the story memorized.

"I'm going to find the colonel and bring him here." Elizabeth pointed at the little boy. "You'd better give Tom a piano lesson before he breaks the instrument."

Tom was on his knees on the chair, banging the piano so hard it was becoming difficult to have a conversation in the room.

<hr>

Tom turned his head to look at Lucas as he approached but didn't cut the volume even a little. He laughed and moved his hands up and down the piano as far as he could.

"You like the piano, don't you?" Lucas spoke loudly—Tom nodded, but gave the piano no quarter.

"Would you like me to play for you?" Tom stopped playing, nodded vigorously and began to climb down, but Lucas put his hand up in the universal stop signal. He grabbed a chair, slid Tom and his chair sideways, and sat down at the center of the keyboard.

Lucas decided to play "Golliwogs Cakewalk," the last movement of Debussy's "Children's Corner."

"Do you know what a golliwog is?" Lucas played the choppy, funny piece while he spoke, and Tom shook his head.

"A golliwog is a black-faced doll with a bright red coat and curly hair. My grandmother had a golliwog doll, and she kept it with her until she died." When he reached the end, he repeated the rhythmic dance.

"What's a cakewalk?" Tom put his hands on Lucas's and gently followed them as Lucas's fingers raced up and down the keyboard.

"A cakewalk is a dance my grandmother used to do in competitions."

"Show me." Tom jumped down.

"Okay, I think I remember how it goes." Lucas turned in his chair, and Elizabeth said from the far end of the room, "You play it, Lucas; I'll show him."

Lucas began playing the dance again, and Elizabeth wiggled and slithered her way through the alleyways between the tables. She arrived at the piano at the end of the piece and put her arms around Tom.

"Come on, Tom, I'll teach you the Golliwog's Cakewalk."

Tom took her hand, and, as Lucas played, Elisabeth leaned back so far it appeared her centre of gravity would make her fall backwards, then moved her head forward in a jerking motion, a little like a chicken. Tom imitated her perfectly.

"That's wonderful, Thomas Finke... you are a great dancer!"

"My name is Reuben Moszkiewicz. Mutti calls me Rube."

Elizabeth made a slithering motion, and the boy imitated it perfectly. She was facing Lucas, moving toward the piano, and Lucas could see the shine in her eyes.

"Reuben, that's a beautiful name." Elizabeth steered the boy back toward the tables, wiggling her torso like a mambo dancer while she slithered across the floor. Reuben returned to the chicken movement; Lucas kept playing, looping back to the beginning.

"Well, I didn't expect a party!" Colonel Feinstein's voice resonated in the live acoustics. "May I have the next dance?"

Elizabeth stepped sideways, whispered in his ear, and the colonel did a reasonable facsimile of the cakewalk alongside Reuben.

"I'm pleased to meet you, Reuben Moszkiewicz." The colonel stooped and shook Reuben's hand. "Can we be friends?" Elizabeth translated while Lucas resolved the middle of the piece to the final chords.

"Yes, sir!" Reuben said, making a good impression of a salute. Colonel Feinstein picked him up and hugged him. Reuben squirmed, trying to escape, but his heart wasn't in it.

Elizabeth slithered to the wide doorway, and Colonel Feinstein let Reuben go.

She said, "Reuben and I will cakewalk to his room, and then I will tell him a story."

"And Lucas and I will go to my room and have a little talk." Colonel Feinstein said it quiet enough that no one but Lucas could hear. Lucas closed the cover on the piano.

"Coffee?" Feinstein gestured for Lucas to follow him, "Real coffee?"

"I would love to have real coffee! I think they use cow dung to make it in America."

Feinstein headed for the doorway. "Follow me to coffee paradise."

Feinstein's room was magnificent, with a small kitchen nook, a private bathroom, and a sitting room with an upholstered sofa and two chairs. It took ten minutes to heat the water and pour it through a 'Malita' filter charged with coffee that smelled fantastic. While he waited for the coffee, Feinstein talked as he prepared a plate of pastries. He told Lucas about growing up in Brooklynn, where being Jewish was normal—in fact, he said, it was better than any alternative. But despite that, the U.S. government refused their visa application when his grandparents tried to get out of Germany.

He put the sweets on a small table and poured coffee into Lucas's cup.

Lucas put a teaspoon of pure white cane sugar in his coffee and poured in just enough fresh cream to lighten it slightly. Feinstein waited for Lucas to take his first sip.

Lucas put the cup to his lips, drank, and said, "I feel like I will live forever if I drink this."

"This is why I became a colonel... they ship me as much Jamaican coffee as I want. Only God knows how my Quartermaster does it. Truthfully, I don't want to know." He checked to see if anyone was listening, although they were alone in the room, and then whispered, "He told me that if I made him divulge his source, he would have to kill me." Lucas understood about half of the English, the most essential half.

Although obviously enjoying his coffee, Colonel Feinstein put his cup in its saucer and pushed it away. "I would like to ignore everything else, let you play the piano for a while, then send you home, but I can't.

You must tell me everything, and then I will tell you what I have. Perhaps we will then find a way to get you home."

Lucas tried to contain his excitement. "You will send me home?"

Colonel Feinstein reached for his coffee. "No, that is not what I said, and I need you to understand everything. We'll have to wait for Lieutenant Mundel."

Lucas's spirits fell like a stone.

"I made lots of coffee. Do you want another cup?" The cups were china, deliberately small, and both were almost empty. Without waiting for an answer, Feinstein stood up and took Lucas's cup from him.

When he returned, Lucas added less sugar and only enough cream to colour it. He took a sip. It was hot, and it had a more robust coffee flavour. He put the cup in the saucer, looked at the table, and then at Feinstein.

"I was gunner and loader in a panzer. My regiment is Waffen SS, but I am not."

"Yes, I've heard that's possible—you have to earn your way into the Waffen SS."

Lucas wasn't sure about his translation, but it sounded like a comment, not a question, so he decided to go on.

"I kill many Russians. We destroy twenty-six Russian tanks. My panzer was two-two-seven—a Panther. I join at Warsaw."

Feinstein wrote 227 on the table with his finger. "Two-two-seven, Panther? Yours?"

"No. Obersturmführer Klaus Riker is commander. Riker fight in Stalingrad, escape, fight back to Germany."

Lucas was thankful when a soft knock on the door interrupted him. Colonel Feinstein crossed the room to the door, and Elizabeth came in without Reuben. She flopped down in one of the soft chairs, and Colonel Feinstein brought his cup to the coffee table in front of the sofa. Lucas followed his example.

Elizabeth asked, with a bit of miff in her voice. "Aren't you going to offer a lady a cup of coffee?"

Feinstein was sitting when she noted his omission, and he jumped to his feet.

"Of course, Lieutenant." He busied himself with another filter and coffee while Elizabeth switched to German and spoke to Lucas.

"Have you two been talking?"

"Yes, we've been trying to, but my English is not good."

"What did you tell him?" She leaned forward with her hands together and her elbows on her knees.

"I told him I like this coffee, and I was a gunner on a Panzer."

"Did he mention Auschwitz or Dachau?"

"Dachau is near Munich, but I don't know where Auschwitz is. I'm sure he didn't mention them."

"Wait here." Elizabeth went to Colonel Feinstein, who waited for the last bit of water to flow through the filter. She spoke so softly into his ear that Lucas couldn't hear, and Feinstein shook his head. He said something to her low enough that Lucas couldn't understand, and then she returned to her chair. Colonel Feinstein put her coffee, cream, and sugar in front of her.

"I'm one of the favoured ones. Once a week, Colonel Feinstein lets me have a cup of coffee." She touched his hand affectionately as he returned to the sofa.

"She only comes for the coffee, and…" he smiled at her… "She is here more than once a week."

Feinstein's expression changed to something more serious. "I have something to show you, Lucas, and when you see it, you will know why I must have the truth from you." Elizabeth translated, then spoke to Colonel Feinstein.

"Do you think that's necessary? If we tell Lucas what we know, that should be enough without that."

"I'm afraid we must do this right now, and you must be the stenographer for the record."

Lucas understood that Elizabeth was trying to stop Feinstein from doing something, and he wanted to know what it was. He said, "If I am to tell Colonel Feinstein everything, I think he should show me everything."

Colonel Feinstein looked at him and stood up; Lucas sensed their pity. Feinstein said, "Yes, Lucas, I agree; you need to know what I know because you will know it eventually anyway. We will get to that, but first, I need you to answer a few questions that will lay the ground-work for what comes next."

Elizabeth translated, then crossed to a desk under the window. She found a drawer with a notebook on her first try, returned, and sat with pencil poised.

◇◇◇◇◇◇◇◇◇◇◇◇◇◇◇◇◇◇◇◇◇◇◇◇◇◇◇◇◇◇◇◇◇◇◇

Colonel Feinstein said, "I understand your Panzer, number 227, fought from Stalingrad to Germany. You joined the crew last summer about when the German Army destroyed Warsaw." Feinstein got up, crossed the room to the desk and returned with a brown folder. He spoke as he returned to the chair. "I want you to tell me what you did in Warsaw." He laid the folder on the coffee table and sat down. Lucas didn't need Elizabeth to translate.

Lucas fumbled with English, then switched to German. "Yes, sir. They sent our tank to Warsaw on the train, but we didn't fight the Russians; we didn't even see any Russians."

"Enough. Let me catch up." Elizabeth scrawled in shorthand, then translated for Feinstein.

When she nodded, Lucas went on.

"We drove our Panther to a street of what seemed to be empty hous-es. And then German soldiers shot a woman running out of one of them. A second woman tried to help her, and the soldiers took her away in a Kubelwagen. Klaus, our tank commander, was furious! I think he wanted to shoot those soldiers!" Lucas paused, remembering the shock and the look on Klaus's face.

"When the army finished taking away anything of value, we fired the big gun at one house after another, destroying them, setting some of them on fire."

Elizabeth translated while she scrawled.

Colonel Feinstein shook his head, bewildered. "With the Russians on the other side of the river, they ordered a Panther to waste ammuni-tion destroying empty houses?"

While Elizabeth translated, Lucas stared at the folder, wondering what was in it. He had gone too far not to answer truthfully, and he couldn't imagine what information could be in that file. If Feinstein caught him in a lie, everything would come apart!

Lucas nodded at the Colonel. "Yes, but I didn't understand why until Klaus told us. He said that Hitler destroyed Warsaw because of the uprising against us, and the Russians waited while Hitler did it because they wanted the Germans to destroy the Free Polish Army for them. He said that Russia wanted Poland after the war. Otherwise, they would have stopped chasing us at the Polish border."

Lucas stopped and looked at Elizabeth—she translated and nodded encouragement.

"Klaus told us to fire the gun as fast as we could; we should use the time to polish our speed, and Marcus and I took turns loading and firing. Trucks came with ammunition, and we ruined the barrel on our gun before the afternoon was over." Elizabeth translated as fast as she wrote. Lucas could not believe how easily she could simultaneously listen, translate, and write shorthand.

"Do you think Klaus did that on purpose? He would have known better than to fire so fast."

Elizabeth translated. Lucas nodded.

"Yes, he did it on purpose. After four or five shots, Marcus told him the barrel was hot, and Klaus said we should fire faster and let him do the worrying!" Lucas remembered Klaus's indifference when the barrel finally gave up. "We all hated to blow up people's houses with no purpose. We tried but couldn't find a logical reason for it."

"When you ruined the barrel, how long before they replaced it?"

"They loaded all the panzers on a train and shipped them back to the base, and it took almost a week to replace the barrel and sight the new one in."

Lucas shook his head slowly. "Klaus said that after we left, the Verbrennung und Vernichtung forces finished the job of destroying Warsaw." Elizabeth translated, and the Colonel went on, perplexed.

"What are "burn and destroy" forces?"

Lucas understood, and Elizabeth didn't translate. He said, "They specialize in using flamethrowers and explosives to destroy things— Klaus said Hitler sent them to burn the city to the ground."

<hr>

"Lucas, there were close to a million people in Warsaw, and I have information that now there are fewer than a hundred thousand, and most of them are refugees." The colonel leaned closer to Lucas while Elizabeth finished her translation. "Where do you think eight or nine-hundred-thousand people went?"

Lucas's mouth was dry—he became confused and asked himself, Why is Warsaw so important to Feinstein?

"That's not possible. We only saw those women; otherwise, only German soldiers and a few people looting the empty houses. The civilians must have been in another part of the city."

Elizabeth translated, giving her boss a warning with crisp diction and tone.

Feinstein moved to an upholstered chair that he turned around, so he was opposite Lucas and facing him. He put his elbows on his knees and leaned toward Lucas. "There is no other part of the city! Warsaw is level, destroyed, exactly as Hitler wanted. There are no civilians in Warsaw! They are gone! What we want to know is where?"

Lucas felt his resolve evaporate and spoke English, desperate to communicate directly with Feinstein.

"We did not kill Warsaw people. Klaus never ask us to kill people who are not soldiers!" Lucas looked at Elizabeth, and she nodded.

"The question is not whether you did; it's whether you knew. If you knew about mass murder and did nothing, you would be as guilty as those who pulled the trigger!" Elizabeth didn't translate; she spoke sharply to the colonel. She spoke slowly, and Lucas understood.

"You surely aren't accusing Lucas of murdering civilians! He brought Reuben here at great risk, and I don't believe he could kill an unarmed man, let alone a woman or a child! I find it hard to believe that he killed anyone!" Her voice had risen to the point of scolding the Colonel.

"Have you ever shot a prisoner?" Feinstein shouted the question at Lucas.

Tears came to Lucas's eyes. He understood the question and felt his anger rising, but more than anger was disappointment that this man, whom he liked and respected, would ask it.

"No, sir, I haven't, and our Panzer didn't kill any civilians or prisoners." He put his hands together, locked his fingers and bowed his head. "Johann Finke told me that SD Einsatzgruppe soldiers shoot prisoners and murder many people in villages after Wehrmacht soldiers leave. But he never does that, and neither did we!"

Elizabeth translated, then put her hand on Lucas's and asked, "Do you think your friend Johann killed prisoners? He was a special kind of soldier with a lot of freedom..."

"Johann killed many Russian soldiers. He was a Jäger; that's another name for a scout." Lucas shook his head. "Johann scouted for our squadron, and he would never shoot an unarmed man!"

Elizabeth took her hand away and scribbled, then translated.

Feinstein picked up the folder and pulled out several sheets of paper, "I have something here that I want to show you, but before I do, I have a question. Answer truthfully." Lucas nodded. "Do you know anything about..." the colonel looked at the paper... "Oswicem?"

"In German, it's Auschwitz," Elizabeth corrected. "Oswicem is the Polish pronunciation."

Lucas asked Elizabeth, "No, what is that—a town?"

"Yes, it's near Krakow—northwest of it, I think." She translated for Feinstein. He nodded.

"No, I've never heard of Auschwitz, but I have heard of Krakow. Johann saw SS soldiers near Krakow taking prisoners somewhere. He said the prisoners were mostly starving Jews, and he was sure the SS shot those too weak to walk. Johann and his men wanted to stop them, but he was on a scouting mission with only a few men and a Demag. They would have killed him, and he would have saved no one."

"So, he did nothing?"

"He did what he could. Johann and his men rescued a man and his wife when the SS soldiers were going to shoot the man. He gave them to the Free Polish Army, but Johann had only a few Wehrmacht scouts with him, and they couldn't fight the SS, so they had to leave."

While Elizabeth translated, Feinstein slid a sheet of paper before Lucas. It was the front page of the New York Times, dated February 3, 1945. He tried to figure out the story that Feinstein put his finger on but couldn't; there were too many words that he didn't understand.

Elizabeth didn't look at the article as she translated. "The article is from United Press International, translated from a Pravda report. Pravda is the Russian press."

She hesitated; Lucas thought it was because she hated to go on, and the Colonel said, "Go on…" when she looked to him for a way out.

"The headline is, Saved From Murder Factory." Elizabeth looked up at Lucas. "The Russians rescued thousands of Jews from Auschwitz, and the Jews Johann saw on the road likely came from there."

"A murder factory? What does that mean?" Lucas dreaded the answer.

Colonel Feinstein answered, "The Russians found records, and they document one million-five-hundred-thousand people murdered in that one camp, most of them killed in rooms filled with poison gas. The Germans running the camp kept very detailed records." He paused and then watched Lucas as he continued.

"Every day for the past four years, five trains arrived there full of Poles, Czechs and Russians, mostly Jews. Our intelligence believes this accounts for many of Warsaw's citizens, perhaps hundreds of thousands of them."

Lucas understood enough. He stood up and shouted at the walls. "No, that can't be! We would have known, and Klaus would have taken our Panzer to rescue them!"

Feinstein didn't wait for a translation. "Your commander, Klaus, is Waffen SS—most of the camp guards were SS soldiers." Elizabeth translated quickly.

Lucas cried, defeated. He knew the story was true—he had seen German children hanging from lamposts. He sobbed as he said, "The Waffen SS men I knew were soldiers, real soldiers, not murderers. They didn't kill civilians, but they were very good at their job, and their skill cost the Russians many men. I killed many Russians in tanks, and I killed infantry who tried to kill us." He paced to the window, and Feinstein waited. Lucas turned to face him, unwiped tears running down his cheeks and under his collar. "I don't believe the Russians! That article must be propaganda to make the Germans hate their army!" He knew he was grasping at a straw.

When Elizabeth finished her translation, Colonel Feinstein took another paper from the file and dropped it in front of Lucas. "I have more."

Lucas read: Chicago Herald-American, and the date, Mon., April 30, 1945. Then, Dachau, Germany, April 30, —(AP)—

Elizabeth put her finger on the print, following it as she translated.

"The United States Forty-second and Forty-fifth Divisions captured Dachau prison camp and freed thirty-two thousand prisoners. Two columns of infantry, riding tanks, bulldozers, Long Tom rifles, and anything with wheels rolled down from the northwest and surprised the SS guards in the extermination camp shortly before lunch. Scores of SS men were taken prisoner, and dozens were slain.

"The Americans were quickly joined by 'Trustees' working outside the barbed wire. French, Poles and Russians seized SS weapons and turned them against their captors.

"Jan Yindrich, a war correspondent and I saw the things that greeted our soldiers. Thirty-nine open-type railroad cars stood on a siding which went through the walls of the Dachau Camp. At first glance, the cars seemed loaded with dirty clothing. Then you saw feet, heads and bony fingers. More than half the cars were full of bodies, hundreds of bodies."

"Stop, bitte, stop!" Lucas shouted as he cried. "No, it can't be! No one is that cruel...."

"Read all of it." Colonel Feinstein left no room for argument. Elizabeth lowered the paper and looked at him; he said, "Read it to him, Lieutenant Mundel."

She looked at Lucas, her eyes wet, full of pity.

"Two SS guards fired into the mass of prisoners, betraying their presence. American infantrymen instantly riddled the Germans, and their bodies were hurled down into the moat amidst a roar unlike anything ever heard from human throats.

"In a barren room with cement floors, a mortuary, a hundred naked bodies were stacked in a pile. They had come from a room on the left marked 'shower bath.' It was really a gas chamber, a low-ceilinged room about thirty feet square. After fifteen or twenty persons were inside the doors were sealed and the faucets turned on, and poison gas came in. When they were dead the bodies were hauled into a room separating the gas chamber from the crematorium.

"There were four ovens with a huge flue leading to a smoke-blackened stack. Outside this building were tens of thousands of articles of clothing stacked in orderly piles.

"Typhus cases were scattered throughout the camp.

"The city water supply was reported contaminated from six thousand graves on high ground which drains into the Amper River.

"The GIs stormed through the camp with tornadic fury. A Swiss Red Cross representative and two SS officers came out of the building behind a white flag. General Linden said, 'The Red Cross man said the real heads of the camp had fled and placed these two fellows in charge of the camp last night. I accepted their surrender, loaded the three of them in a jeep and drove them down to the train and made them look. One SS fellow asked for safe custody.'"

Elizabeth said, "That's all of it," to Colonel Feinstein as she put the paper on the table. Lucas looked at the floor, his elbows on his knees.

Colonel Feinstein said, "Lucas, I need to know more about Johann and Klaus." He took the newspapers and put them in the file. "I've learned enough about you to know you are no Nazi, and you have had no part in anything that anyone could call a crime. However, I need to know what you have seen. It's all part of a puzzle we are trying to put together."

Feinstein paused, then said, "But that's enough for now. Play the piano for us tonight, and come to my office after breakfast tomorrow morning." He put the file in the drawer, then put his hand on Lucas's shoulder. "You are a victim, son, and I know enough that no harm will come to you. But now I need to know whether your Johann and Klaus are worth saving."

Lucas stood up, tears under control but too confused to function.

Elizabeth flopped her notebook closed and turned to Colonel Feinstein. Her voice had a hard edge. "I will write this up after I've taken Reuben for a walk, sir."

"That's fine, and take Lucas with you. He could use some fresh air and a friendly face."

Lucas stood up and bolted for the door; Elizabeth followed and caught him in the hallway.

He slowed and asked her, "That was all true, wasn't it?"

She nodded.

"How did Hitler become this…this animal? My parents weren't

Nazis—they said they would never join the party—but they believed in National Socialism. I guess I was too involved in my music to pay attention to politics, but I remember my father talking about what great things Hitler and National Socialism did for the country. They put men back to work and built roads, hospitals and schools. How could this happen?"

Elizabeth said, "Yes, Hitler talked about the working man a lot, but he and his government had a disease, an infectious disease called hate, combined with an addiction to power. He could have chosen to attack any group: immigrants, homosexuals, Muslims... But, because someone had already planted the seeds, he chose Bolsheviks first, then Jews. Romani gypsies and the mentally weak were add-ons."

Elizabeth took his hand in both of hers. "I am a psychologist by training and have read many books on the subject, and Hitler and his gang are not unusual. What is extraordinary is that he was successful—most sociopathic megalomaniacs are not. Not only Hitler but Himmler, Goering and Goebbels fit the description.

Hitler began with what appeared to be good intentions, but his fundamental objectives were beyond any evil the German people could have imagined or would ever have approved of had they understood them."

Lucas thought of his parents and their belief in a system that would benefit everyone. They could not understand why the world didn't welcome Hitler's ideas.

"Why didn't my parents see what he was doing? They voted for Hitler when there was a choice. They believed in the high principles of socialism."

Elisabeth stopped in the hallway outside Lucas's room. "Hitler talked constantly about the common people, the Volk, and all of Germany cheered when Hitler kicked the French army out of the Rhineland; and they cheered the reunification of Germany and Austria—the Anschluss. But for many, the Nürnberg Laws went too far. That is why, even though Hitler passed them, he refused to allow direct attacks on Jews until Kristallnacht.

The National Socialists had to identify who was and who was not a Jew according to the law before, step by step, the insidious persecution of them could begin. Some Jews saw it coming and left the country, but there were few places to go unless you had a lot of money. America would not accept any Jewish refugees who didn't have buckets of money, and many of those who died in the camps could have been saved had they been allowed to emigrate to America. After the war began, the Jews who remained accepted their fate and quietly left their homes, never to return." Elizabeth put her hand on Lucas's shoulder.

"I remember my father telling the family he was furious when Hitler abolished the communist party, and he couldn't believe that a criminal could become chancellor. A few years before, Hitler had tried to take over the country and failed, but his popularity let him get away with it. My parents cried when they read the papers the morning after the Kristallnacht."

Lucas put his hand on the lever that opened the door to his room and turned to Elizabeth.

"If I were the Allies, I would drive Germany into the ground and bury it!"

Elizabeth put her hand on Lucas's wet cheek. "Colonel Feinstein is right—you are a victim—evil is not in you, and it is not in the German people. The evil is in the men who manipulate the people and carry out those unspeakable atrocities. I don't know what will happen, but only time will heal this—a lot of time. I know Germans because I am one, and for your information, so is Colonel Feinstein—he was born in Frankfurt. Germany will survive."

She pushed his hand down on the lever, and the door swung open.

Chapter Thirty-four

7 May 1945

We fought the War to End Wars so we could have peace

"I am tired and sick of war. Its glory is all moonshine. It is only those who have neither fired a shot nor heard the shrieks and groans of the wounded who cry aloud for blood, for vengeance, for desolation. War is hell!"

William Tecumseh Sherman

LUCAS PLAYED THE PIANO AND SANG FOR A RAUCOUS HOUSE full of American soldiers, singing their simple songs as his friend had taught him using a phonograph. With a repertoire of only a dozen songs, and he needed help with half of them, he had somehow found himself teaching German marching songs to the willing crowd. Fourth was Erika, and Muss Ich Denn was a close third behind Lili Marlen, but the most popular, number one on their chart, was the Panzer regiments' song, the Panzerlied. Lucas sang it for them the second night, and immediately, they wanted to learn it. With the crowd's help, he translated the song into English interspersed with German, and a hundred men sang it every fifteen minutes until well after midnight. The songs became inescapable.

Lucas joined Reuben and Elizabeth for a late breakfast, which Lucas anticipated would be more of a therapy session than a meal. Reuben had utterly fallen in love with Elizabeth and ignored Lucas. Reuben's insistence on her attention forced Elizabeth to take him to the piano, where the boy's punishment of the beautiful instrument drove straggler coffee drinkers out of the large room.

With Reuben playing a background racket, Elizabeth turned her attention to Lucas.

"I know you've thought about what you saw yesterday. Why don't you tell me how you feel about that before we see the Colonel." She sipped her coffee and waited for him.

"I've thought about nothing else—I couldn't sleep last night. Why can't everyone live together as we do? I don't think of those American soldiers as my enemy, and I'm sure that the Russian soldiers are no different."

"Yes, but they are all soldiers…trained to kill on command. And on that note, I can't believe you got American soldiers to sing German military songs. Except for 'Lili Marlene.' I know it's a German song about a German soldier, but most Americans think Marlene Dietrich wrote it, and they know she's an American because she acts in Hollywood movies."

Lucas smiled; music was something he loved to talk about. Perhaps it was imagination, but he noted that Reuben's banging on the piano was getting closer to music than noise.

"Music is the language of souls, the only language spoken by every person in the world." He put quotation marks in the air. "That's from Theo Finke, Johann's father."

Elizabeth smiled. "A wise man."

"He has taught me so much…I can't believe that his son could be different. Johann's wife, Barbara, is an angel, and his son, Thomas, is a special little boy."

"He is lucky that his family has escaped the war. Detmold is a small town, and the war bypassed many of those towns."

Lucas lowered his head. "I wish that were so."

Elizabeth waited; he lifted his head and looked out the window at a male bird, carefully placing a twig in its nest while the female looked on. Elizabeth followed Lucas's eyes and watched her step impatiently from one foot to the other while the male rearranged the twig. She indicated her approval by bobbing her head, and he left to find another twig while she straightened up the mess he'd made.

"Johann had a beautiful daughter, Lisa. She played the violin… Maria, Theo's wife, was helping her work on the Mendelssohn concerto when Lisa died." Lucas swallowed hard. "She was at a birthday party with her best friends, twelve of them, when a British bomber dropped a bomb on the house." He looked at Elizabeth, his eyes wet. "The bomb killed Lisa and all her friends. Johann's sergeant told me that Johann can't talk about it."

Elizabeth put her hand on Lucas's. "Your Johann sounds like a good man."

"I hope I can someday be half the man he is." He smiled and wiped his eyes on his shirt sleeve.

Elizabeth stood up. "It's time for you to visit Colonel Feinstein; he's waiting for you, and I promise there are no more nasty surprises."

Colonel Feinstein sat behind his desk, fingers locked behind his head. He smiled, an encouraging sign.

"I've got a proposition for you, Lucas—but first, some coffee." He put the carafe on the table where two cups, cream and sugar awaited.

He spoke when they were both seated and had sampled the coffee.

"Strong enough?" Feinstein winked.

"Perfect!" Lucas forgot about rank, country, and enemies.

"In a few days, not more than two weeks, I'm going to a conference in Hannover, and I will have Elizabeth and my driver take you and Reuben from there to Dortmund, or Detmold if that's your choice. But I must warn you, there is a price." He waited for Lucas to react, and Lucas waited for the price.

"I have all I need from you from a military perspective, and I now believe I can trust you." He crossed his legs. "Elizabeth will be here in a few minutes, and I want you to tell me about your personal life. Tell me about your girlfriend, Johann's father and mother, and his wife." He leaned forward.

"How much did you understand?"

"We should wait for Elizabeth." Lucas's English had improved immensely, thanks to total immersion, but he still wasn't sure he understood what or why the colonel was asking. He didn't want to make a mistake at this point.

Elizabeth didn't knock; she just opened the door and arrived. Feinstein jumped up and began brewing fresh coffee while he told her what he had said to Lucas.

She translated, "He said I will take you home to Dortmund or Detmold, wherever you want, in a few weeks."

"He said something about a price. What price?" Lucas tried to restrain his excitement.

"Yes, he wants to know more about you and as much as you know about Johann and his family." She put her hand on his arm. "You should tell him about Lisa." She smiled her sweet smile, the one that Reuben had fallen in love with. "Trust him. He is working on something that you will like."

◇◇◇◇◇◇◇◇◇◇◇◇◇◇◇◇◇◇◇◇◇◇◇◇◇◇◇◇◇◇◇

It took an hour for Lucas to tell his story, beginning with the details of the bombing raid in Dortmund and up to crazy Otto shooting at him and Reuben. When he finished, he looked up—the colonel hadn't said a word during the entire tale.

When Feinstein finally asked Lucas a question, it was completely unexpected.

"Do you know the identity of the soldiers who took Johann and Klaus across the river?"

Lucas said in English, "Yes, sir, the officer was Lieutenant Johnson—I don't know the unit,"

Colonel Feinstein leaned toward Lucas and, out of the blue, said, "Tell me, this time for the record..." Elizabeth had her pad on her knee, her pencil poised... "Did you or a member of your family ever join the SS or the Nazi party?" The Colonel asked the question in an official monotone.

"I'm not sure, sir—my father may have had to join to keep his job. And the truth is, I would have joined if Klaus had let me."

The colonel turned to Elizabeth, frustrated.

"Lieutenant Mundel, we are off the record for now. Scratch that and begin a new page." He turned to Lucas. "Tell this naïve young man what to say. His father is dead, and he shouldn't besmirch his memory with speculation. And I'm not interested in what Lucas might have done!"

Elizabeth ripped the page out of the notebook and tossed it in the wastebasket.

"Lucas, this is not for Colonel Feinstein but for the official record. There is only one answer, and you must say only one word, two letters. NO explanations, NO guessing as to your father's affiliations. If you didn't see him swear allegiance to the Nazis, then you can't say that he did. Do you understand?" Lucas nodded hesitantly, and she said, "Okay, Colonel Feinstein will ask the question again." She looked at the Colonel, and he said, "We're back on the record."

Lucas waited until Elizabeth dutifully translated the same question. She looked at him when she'd finished, shook her head and mouthed, "No." He said, "No," as clearly as he could, then clamped his teeth together.

The colonel sat back with both hands on the arms of the chair. "We will have a document for you to sign tomorrow." He looked thoughtfully out the window.

"Klaus was a good man and a good friend to you. You'll only have one or two friends like that in your lifetime."

Lucas nodded and looked down again; memories from only a few days ago seemed a lifetime away. He wondered about Klaus and Johann—had they done something terrible before he'd met them? Then Lucas remembered the man running away from his burning tank, cut down by his bullets. Was that a crime the Allies would want to avenge? He decided not to talk about it. Not ever.

Colonel Feinstein got out of his official chair. "As soon as I can get everything arranged, you will go home, but in the next few days or weeks, someone will visit you regarding those poor boys hanging from the lampposts. I'll try to keep him out of it, but someone might visit Reuben to find out what happened to his mother."

Elizabeth translated, and Lucas raised his head. His voice broke when he said, "I don't know how to thank you, sir. I love Corinne, and if you let me go home, I will marry her someday if she'll have me."

Feinstein smiled at Elizabeth, then turned back to Lucas. "It's funny you should say that. You may have guessed that Elizabeth and I are more than friends. Until now, we have both put our energy into the army, and there is this damned war, so there is no wedding for us until we get this done. Because male and female officers are not allowed to marry unless one of them gives up their career, the army stands in our way until the war is officially over."

Lucas smiled at them. "I think even Reuben sensed that, and I'm guessing all of Hersfeld knows it."

Elizabeth punched the Colonel's arm. "I told you to stop looking at me like that!"

"Like what? He looked at her with a longing born of many months of self-control. He laughed and turned back to Lucas.

"There is something else you should know. Many years ago, my parents emigrated from Frankfurt to Chicago, then New York City, leaving their parents, sisters, brothers, and extended family behind. Elizabeth and I are working to find an endless list of missing persons supplied by the U.S. government, most of them Jews, and my extended family is among them." The colonel paused and took a deep breath. "Unfortunately, we now know where to start looking for them!"

Lucas tried to think of something to say but couldn't, and, for a moment, no one spoke. Elizabeth broke the awkward silence. "We'll see you in the dining hall tonight... I want to hear you sing."

The following morning, Elizabeth ran into Lucas's room with Reuben close behind. Lucas stood up from the desk where he was writing his daily letter to Corinne, and Elizabeth grabbed him in a bear hug, almost lifting him off the floor.

Rumours of ending the war had been circulating for days as unit after unit of the German forces surrendered. The evening before, unconfirmed news of a formal surrender in Reims, a small city in eastern France, had circulated among the men in the dining hall. Colonel Feinstein had stood up and announced that the rumours were accurate and the formal end to the war would be 'soon.'

Lucas played only songs of home from that point, and the excitement of impending peace added volume, if not quality, to the singalong.

Elizabeth shouted, "It's over, Lucas! The war is finally and officially over!"

Elizabeth retreated, red-faced, and Lucas could only think how lucky Colonel Feinstein was. He had used up his excitement the night before; the announcement of 'official' peace was an anti-climax. He had dreamed of Detmold and Corinne and had thought of nothing else since awakening.

"Does this mean that I can go home now?" He tried to think of why not, but nothing came to him.

"Yes, you will go home as soon as Colonel Feinstein officially hears from headquarters regarding your status. He is working on…something else." Though disappointed that he wouldn't go home immediately, Lucas sensed her excitement was more than the war's official end.

"David is taking us to dinner in Hersfeld this afternoon. I bought some clothes for you and Reuben, and you can try them out at our favourite Gaststätte." She smoothed her dress, turned and stopped at the door. "I left Reuben in David's office; I'm trying to get him used to children."

Lucas laughed. "Has he asked you yet?"

She nodded and smiled coyly. "Yes, a month after the U.S. Army assigned me to him."

"When is the day?"

"I wouldn't say yes until the war was over. I'm planning to give my answer at Mittagessen." Lucas caught her excitement, and his spirits soared.

"As soon as I get home, I'm going to ask Corinne to marry me!"

Lucas sensed her effort not to laugh. He opened his mouth to object, but she cut him off.

"The war has accelerated many things, but I think you should have a few more years on you before you take that step. Both of you need time to be young. You've lost too much, and you need time to adjust." Elizabeth smiled. "It's different for David and me—the war has delayed everything—but thirty is not too old for us to start."

Lucas bristled. "I'm old enough to kill men but not to get married? Is that the way it is?"

She shook her head. "No one is ever old enough to kill men, and putting you in that situation is criminal, no matter your age." She smiled. "You must adjust to life without guns and violence. Think about waiting before you do anything important."

She disappeared, and Lucas returned to his letter. He stared at the marriage proposal he'd already written, his declaration of undying love, his desire to have children with her, and his intention to adopt Reuben. Suddenly, he asked himself, what if Corinne says no? He crumpled the page, tore it into tiny pieces, and threw it into the wastebasket. He straightened, thought for a moment, retrieved the pieces and took them to the toilet. He flushed them, seeing every piece disappear with the swirling water.

◇◇◇◇◇◇◇◇◇◇◇◇◇◇◇◇◇◇◇◇◇◇◇◇

Colonel Feinstein and Elizabeth took Reuben and Lucas into the centre of Hersfeld, a few minutes by jeep from the barracks. Four armed soldiers discreetly escorted them to Zum Mückenstürmer, the most popular restaurant in town, where Colonel Feinstein spent a lot of time shaking hands.

When they stood for the fifth introduction, Lucas asked Elizabeth, "Does he know everyone in Hersfeld?" The parade to shake hands hadn't stopped when the food arrived.

"He's a popular guy around here. He goes to all the town council meetings but allows them to run the town as they wish. David answers their questions honestly, and when a problem concerns his men, he solves it."

The Germans in the room tried but couldn't hide their joy. Their sons, husbands, and fathers would be coming home, and they still had a town and families to return to. They treated the Americans in the restaurant more as liberators than conquerors—muffled joy was everywhere—and not a Nazi in sight!

Dinner ended without Elizabeth's answer to David's question. Lucas felt she wanted David to broach the subject, but Feinstein spent the night wrapped in the excitement of the war moment, bathed in the bright light of victory.

◇◇◇◇◇◇◇◇◇◇◇◇◇◇◇◇◇◇◇◇◇◇◇◇

Lucas played the piano every night until early morning, singing German folk Lieder, American popular songs, and war songs familiar to both sides. The Panzerlied stayed number one on the Hersfeld Barracks' chart, and Lucas had coffee with David every morning.

"Read this and weep." David showed Lucas a piece of paper, and Lucas read it while drinking Jamaican coffee. He spent a lot of time with Colonel Feinstein, and Reuben followed Elizabeth whenever she would let him.

Lucas read it twice. "It forbids anyone in Germany to sing the Panzerlied." Lucas looked up from the paper. "Your men sing that every night...I've taught them to sing it in German and English."

Lucas found his English improving daily and discovered that Colonel Feinstein had a limited but adequate supply of German vocabulary. Over time they made a pact: Lucas spoke English to David, and David spoke German to Lucas. They corrected one another when the mistakes were too drastic to ignore and completed one another's sentences to save time when the intent became apparent.

"Well, Lucas, this is complicated, and I must speak English. The new German authorities directed this at the German people. It is part of a larger plan by Germans to take their country in a new direction. The Allies rewarded anti-Nazis and the Jews who survived by reinstating them to positions they held before the war. The Nazis had taken their jobs, possessions, and dignity, but the new order is kicking those Nazis out of the houses and businesses they stole. Many anti-Nazis are being appointed as temporary government leaders, and, of course, they want to tear down everything connected to the Third Reich."

David retrieved a large poster on the table and held it up by the corners.

The poster shouted, REMEMBER THIS! across the top, and DON'T FRATERNIZE! across the bottom. Five pictures of emaciated bodies covered the space between the statements.

"This is straight from General Eisenhauer. I must hang this and a dozen others on the base. I am instructed to jail any member of my force who 'fraternizes' with the enemy—it seems that no one has told Eisenhauer the war is over!"

Lucas shook his head. "I have nightmares about those camps. The world will never forgive us…" He pointed to the poster in Colonel Feinstein's hand. "We will always be 'the enemy.'"

"No, Lucas," David shook his head, "That's not what is happening. This piece of propaganda is a military overreaction. The people of America are past that; they fill ships with food and clothes and send money to help Germans. And England, even though they were affected almost as badly as the Germans, sends whatever help they can." He shook the poster. "And our military sends me this!"

David shrugged and laid the poster face down on the table. "They should understand the obvious—that Nazi criminals do not represent the German people." He sat down in the upholstered chair next to Lucas.

"It's now certain that some of my relatives died in the concentration camps, and I'm afraid there may be more. And yet when Elizabeth and I walk on the Spa grounds because it is so peaceful, every one of the Germans who work there treats us like their King and queen. They know I'm Jewish, and they know what I've lost. The looks most of them give me are of compassion, not scorn or fear."

"So, did you just say we shouldn't sing the Panzerlied, or did you say we can if we want to?"

"I'm going to leave that up to you and the men. This order is for Germans, not Americans, but perhaps respect for the damage done by the Nazi's SS and their Einsatzgruppe is more important than that technicality."

"Don't forget the SD and the SA," Lucas corrected.

"Klaus told me that the Waffen SS he knows is a strictly military fighting unit, mostly foreign volunteers. Their units have infantry, armour, and artillery, and they are the toughest soldiers in the German army." Lucas's face oozed pride, but the feeling died when he saw David's expressiion.

Colonel Feinstein said, "Perhaps someday you could explain why a battalion of Waffen SS murdered and pillaged a dozen French villages while their comrades were fighting the Americans." The air left Lucas's balloon.

"The information I have doesn't distinguish SD from SS from Waffen SS... they are all criminal organizations, and the officers will be in prison until we figure it out. You were officially in the Wehrmacht, a legitimate army, and you are too young to prosecute. That's the only reason you are going home!"

"Does that mean Klaus is in prison? Klaus is not a criminal." Lucas tried to decide how sure he was.

"You don't know what Klaus did before you joined 227. I asked you many questions about him because your impression will carry some weight in the investigation."

"And Johann? He's in the Wehrmacht, and he hates Hitler and National Socialism..."

Colonel Feinstein smiled. Lucas tried to interpret the smile as the Colonel spoke.

"Johann is in an American prison camp in Bremen, and we will see how long he stays there. Klaus will go to a prison camp either in France or Texas."

The Panzerlied disappeared from Lucas's repertoire, but Lili Marlene, Muss ich denn, and Erika stayed. Days passed, which became weeks, and Lucas felt more and more at home with men who were so much like Klaus, Kristian, Max, and Marcus, but the turmoil within him continued. He learned their names, and during breaks, they told him their stories in exchange for his. They whispered stories of killing German soldiers when they had a choice to take prisoners, but Lucas didn't reciprocate by telling them of shooting fleeing Russian soldiers in the back.

As the weeks passed, his English improved to where he could carry on a normal conversation, and he understood most of the English words he heard. Colonel Feinstein came to the officers' lounge almost every evening and, without fail, bought Lucas a Coke with ice, a drink to which Lucas quickly became addicted.

A look from their commanding officer sent three GIs sitting with Lucas to a table on the other side of the room. Colonel Feinstein put Lucas's coke in front of him, then expertly slid Elizabeth's chair under her before sitting opposite Lucas.

"You're making me into an American." Lucas took his 'tall cold one' and slurped the first delicious mouthful.

Elizabeth said, "Sigmund Freud would say, 'You can only be changed if you want to change.'"

"Maybe I don't have to change that much. I like coke and ice; that's a start." Lucas felt very comfortable with Americans as long as he didn't have to drink their coffee.

David's suddenly serious expression killed the light mood, and Lucas waited while his new mentor played with his drink and arranged his thoughts.

"Lucas, I want you to know that putting those documents in front of you was the hardest thing I've ever done, and I regret it." He said it in English, and Elizabeth translated it out of habit.

Lucas responded in English. "Sir, you had to do it. My heart wants these things not to be true, but my parents told me they knew of many people who disappeared, many of them friends and neighbours, and they were all Jews. The whole world and I now know what happened to them! If the truth is out in the open, there is hope that it will never happen again."

Lucas thought for a moment while Elizabeth and David waited. He said, "Germans keep a paper record of everything…they must have Ordnung," He tried to find the right English word, gave up and went on, "They write everything down. Germans believe that anything on German paper is true if a Germans wrote it. Ink on paper is proof of almost anything!"

Neither David nor Elizabeth offered corrections or help, and Lucas continued. "I believe the newspapers you showed me told the truth. Many people have seen murders, thousands of murders, and when these people tell this truth, Germany must carry the guilt and find a way to atone."

They waited, and Lucas continued digging for words. "How did one man make my country a fool? Why didn't the country stand up… Why didn't the people rise against Hitler? The world will ask this question, and if we don't answer it, or if the world thinks only Germans could do this, it will happen again, perhaps someday in America!"

Lucas knew his words were not the best, but David's nod told him the meaning was clear. David shifted in his chair, but Elizabeth said in German before he could begin, "You are right, Lucas, and at least some of the criminals will be found and punished, but Germany will always carry the guilt. There is a lot of work to do before Deutschland becomes German again.

Elizabeth switched to English. "Let's forget about that right now. We have good news, and besides, you are too young to be bitter."

She looked at David, and he nodded. She said, "Lucas, tomorrow is the day you've been waiting for. Tomorrow, I will take you home."

Lucas, speechless, wiped the instant tears.

David said in English, "The men will miss you. Elizabeth and I will miss both you and Reuben, and truthfully, I was not looking forward to this."

Lucas played until the official closing at midnight before announcing his departure for home in the morning. Every man in the room stood up and applauded and only stopped applauding when Lucas began a boisterous introduction to "The Yellow Rose of Texas." Another half-hour of toasts, congratulations, and songs, ending with an 'acapella' rendition of "For he's a jolly good fellow," concluded the evening.

◇◇◇◇◇◇◇◇◇◇◇◇◇◇◇◇◇◇◇◇◇◇◇◇◇◇◇◇◇◇◇◇

Lucas lay on his bedclothes watching Reuben. The little Jewish boy peacefully slept in the pale starlight coming through the open curtains. The war was a month behind them, and everything had changed. The terror of fighting, the dread of making a mistake that would kill him and his crew, of muscles freezing for an instant, firing too late…too early…the fear… It was all gone. He thought of Klaus and Marcus— what a huge gamble it had been for them to trust him to do what must be done, and to do it right the first time.

He fell asleep without warning and became aware of a pounding noise moments later. He pushed it away, it returned, and he raised himself on his elbow. He looked at the American wristwatch his fans had given him... five hours had passed.

His father had said, "It's always darkest before the dawn." whenever Lucas thought the world was ending, and he had believed it until he had gotten up before dawn. The reality was the sky gradually lightened; the faint gray light became colourless, then brightened, and the rising sun slowly set the greyness on fire, reshaping it until the sun cleared the horizon and the light became colourless again.

The banging resumed, and Lucas could see the door move with every blow.

"I'm up," he lied, something he had learned to do well at a very young age. "We'll be ready in five minutes!" Another lie, but this early in the morning, everyone doubled their time estimates.

Reuben slid out of his bed and opened the door with the hand that wasn't rubbing the sleep out of his eyes. He had gotten to the door ahead of Lucas, and when Elizabeth wasn't standing before him, he jumped sideways, looked up and stared at the man looking down at him. He pointed at the man's face and said, "I know you! You saved me!"

Chapter Thirty-five

June 1945

Don't Worry, be Happy

Every parting gives a foretaste of death, every reunion a hint of the resurrection.

Arthur Schopenhauer

Lucas jumped out of bed and stared at the man whose picture he had seen every night on his bedside table in Detmold. The war beard was gone; he wore a pressed Feldgrau Wehrmacht uniform and a hat tilted to the side.

Lucas walked around the bed, stopped and contemplated a salute, but Johann took two steps and wrapped his arms around him in a man-hug. Lucas was so happy he couldn't speak.

Colonel Feinstein came into the room, put his hand on Johann's shoulder and said to Lucas, "I didn't tell you because I wasn't sure I could get this done." He put his other hand on Lucas. "Johann is going home with you." He backed up, and Johann grabbed Lucas's arms, pushing him to arm's length. "You look great, Lucas! And Colonel Feinstein told me you are the reason I won't spend a year in a French prison camp."

"Klaus..." Lucas turned to Colonel Feinstein... "What about Klaus?"

He shook his head. "Klaus is an officer in the Waffen SS, and any force with SS in its name will be investigated top to bottom. Members of the Einsatzgruppe and SS army units guilty of killing prisoners or guarding the camps are under indefinite arrest. Until we sort things out, there is no fixed date for their release. Klaus and many honest men like him are cooperating, and if that continues, he will be home in a year or two. He's at a prison camp in Attichy, near Paris, and will likely be sent to Texas for his own security until war crime trials begin in Germany."

Lucas, nodding slowly, dropped his gaze to the floor. "War crime trials? Klaus is not a criminal. He would never have killed prisoners."

When Lucas lifted his head, Feinstein was staring at him. "Do you believe that it's possible to fight a war with millions of casualties without producing war criminals from good men? However, Klaus has not been charged with anything yet, but he still could be a witness."

Johann shifted his feet, and Lucas thought he looked uncomfortable.

The occupying British Army set up their headquarters in Bad Oeynhausen, and because the winners of wars take what they want, they took possession of the town's centre. Feinstein's three-jeep American caravan passed through two roadblocks designed to keep unwanted persons out before they reached the administration building, formerly a hotel.

The British confiscated every shop within two blocks, including two restaurants. Fortunately, they hadn't brought English cooks with them—the personnel remained the same as before the occupation. The American soldiers travelling with them stood watch outside while Colonel Feinstein followed Elizabeth to a window table.

The menu was sparse, but the food was much better than the American slop that Lucas had almost gotten used to.

"A toast, my friends." Feinstein stood up and raised his wine glass. "To peace and the rebuilding of this great country!"

Lucas and Johann raised their glasses and said, "Prost!" but Elizabeth hesitated while waiting for more. The men drank, but Elizabeth remained standing, waiting for them to see their mistake, which they did with red faces. David tried to stand, but she pushed down on his shoulder.

"David, I swore I wouldn't do this, but I have waited as long as I am going to. Do you remember asking me a very important question six months ago?"

Colonel Feinstein's face revealed that he knew he was in deep trouble, but the 'eureka moment' wasn't there yet. He cleared his throat, painfully buying time while looking at the table, Johann, and then at

Lucas. No one could or would help him. The Colonel's expression told Lucas he didn't know what was coming.

"Uh…" he began, then stopped. "I give up. You're going to have to shoot me."

Elizabeth smiled, but not a smile David could take comfort from. Lucas knew Colonel Feinstein was about to go down in flames and decided to help him. He mouthed, "Marry me!" from behind Elizabeth. The Colonel looked puzzled, but a light went on when Lucas repeated the soundless words. He grinned, put on his longing expression and stood up.

"Uh…I was going to ask this later, but six months ago, when I asked you to marry me, you said you would answer me when the war was over, and I thought perhaps you were waiting for something else." He smiled like a Cheshire cat. "The suspense has been keeping me awake."

"I don't believe you—I think you forgot!" She pushed him back half a step, and he upset his chair. "For that, you will have to ask me again!"

The colonel looked at the hardwood floor. "The question still stands… why don't you just give me your answer, and we will toast the bride?"

"The toast to the bride is at the reception after the marriage ceremony. Don't you know anything about weddings?"

He asked, "Will you marry me, Elizabeth?" and everyone nodded—it sounded heartfelt.

"What about love? Shouldn't you say something about love?"

"You know how much I love you, Elizabeth. Will you marry me?"

The restaurant was the most popular on the base, the drama was heading for a climax, and just about everyone faced the action. Restrained snickers and more than a bit of out-and-out laughter spread throughout the room. Everyone sensed that Elizabeth wasn't done with him yet.

"Much better, but there is a magic word that you forgot. Your mother would be horrified!"

Lucas mouthed the first English word he had learned. "Please!"

Colonel Feinstein flicked his eyes from Lucas to Elizabeth.

"I love you, Elizabeth…Please, will you marry me and make my miserable life complete?"

Elizabeth faced her superior officer and said, "Yes, David. I love you too, and I will marry you." She leaned against him and put her mouth on his in a very sexy way. The good-humoured room stood up and clapped.

When dinner and excuses to delay the inevitable had passed, Lucas and Colonel Feinstein shook hands and promised to keep in touch. Lucas got into the jeep with everything around him a dreamlike jumble. Recognizing the significance of this day, he had vowed to organize and record everything in his memory, but his brain was a confused mess. Fortunately, Elizabeth had her camera and an idea for a feature story in the "Stars and Stripes," the American Forces newspaper.

Corinne, then Theo, Barbara, and Maria jumped into his mind. He imagined them waiting for him on the stone doorstep of Gartenstrasse 18, and his heart beat so fast he became dizzy. He took little notice of Elizabeth, buzzing around him with her camera.

Reuben sat in the jeep behind Elizabeth, and Lucas sat behind Reuben, facing Johann.

The jeep drove down streets untouched by war to Detmolder Strasse. Lucas pointed at the street sign. Johann reached across and put his hand on Lucas's shoulder, and they both smiled so wide that Lucas suspected he looked foolish.

A question jumped into his mind, something he had never considered: Where can I sleep now that Corinne is sleeping in my room? For a moment, he thought of sleeping beside her, then remembered Maria's sense of propriety. That wasn't going to work!

A light came on. I'll sleep in the cellar—beside the bathing room. Lucas rolled the idea over in his mind, satisfied he had found the solution. He would find some wood, build a bed and a table, buy a Schrank to hang his clothes in—a cheap used one. He had at least a month's pay coming, enough money to buy a new clothes Schrank and a bed if necessary. Sleeping in the cellar was better than sleeping in a Panzer or on the ground.

His mind wandered as the jeep's overworked little four-cylinder engine struggled to pull its load up a long hill, leaving a trail of oil smoke hanging like blue fog over the road behind it. Lucas watched the smoke spread, dilute into clean air, and disappear.

But what if Maria and Theo don't want me now that I've killed men? What if Corinne hates me? I've changed…I've killed men, young men like me, older men like Johann, with families like Johann's." Lucas didn't have any answers, only an overpowering sense of guilt.

He tried but couldn't rid himself of the vision of over a million people, so many women and children he couldn't imagine how many that would be, murdered, the murderers protected by the guns he fired. He had protected the men who built the camps and commanded them, the men who chose who would live or die, and the men his father and mother had elected because they wanted to restore Germany's prosperity and glory.

He braced his feet on the seat opposite him, and Reuben snuggled under his arm. The rear seats in the jeep had no backrests and faced one another across a narrow space. They had no cushions, and the steel was hard and slippery. Lucas reached over Reuben's shoulder and wrapped his right hand around the rod at the top of the frame on Elizabeth's seat. He braced his left hand on the edge of the steel bench.

Johann faced Lucas with a worried look on his face. Why wasn't he happy like Lucas expected he would be? Johann had a wife and son to go home to; what could he be concerned about?

The jeep steered around a hole, and Lucas accidentally kicked Johann as he repositioned his braced feet.

Johann forgave him with a smile. He said, "The Germans didn't build these roads for forty-ton tanks, and Americans didn't build jeeps for comfort."

Lucas returned the smile. "Panther two-two-seven rode better than this, even in the loader's seat." He decided to solve Johann's mystery, but Johann asked the question first.

"Are you worried about going home?"

Lucas figured out that his expression must be the equivalent of Johann's.

The jeep jumped like a rabbit, and Lucas and Johann bounced clear of the steel seat, remaining suspended while the vehicle moved under them. Gravity won the battle, and the jeep and its occupants landed with a crash.

"Scheisse…that hurt!" The tailgate had stopped Johann's rearward progress just before he left the jeep, and he pulled himself forward to grab the driver's seat frame.

The hand that Lucas wrapped around Reuben held onto Elizabeth's seat frame, saving them from going over the side, but his hip landed on the steel edge that ran along the outside of the bench before it slid painfully back onto the seat. The steel edge had cut into his thigh, and he grunted a soft curse. He looked down at a happy Reuben, ready for more fun.

"Sorry," the driver yelled above the little overworked four-cylinder engine, the whine of unsynchronized square-cut gears and the clatter of loose pieces of metal. Elizabeth turned her head to check on Reuben and smiled at him while holding onto a handle welded to the dash.

Lucas leaned ahead to look around Elizabeth so he could see the road. Mercifully, it was smooth as far as he could see ahead, so he turned to answer Johann's question.

"I don't know whether I have a home. Everyone in my family is dead, and I don't know whether Maria and Theo will want me now that I've killed people. I saw newspaper articles about Dachau and Auschwitz, and I am guilty of fighting to make that possible."

Johann nodded. "The Americans showed me what were probably the same articles. I told them that in 'forty-two, I knew that the SA Einsatzgruppe murdered Bolsheviks and Jews…in fact, I knew a man who belonged to that group of assassins, and I was instrumental in his timely death. Before the bastard died, he told me what he had done, and I told the Americans everything I knew."

"You didn't have any way to stop them. If you had tried, the Einsatz-gruppe would have killed you!"

"No, Lucas, it's not that simple. I ignored the truth—we all did. It couldn't have happened if we had not been silent. Those criminals count on good people being apathetic, and I lied to myself because I was afraid of the truth." He looked ahead through the windshield. "I don't know whether Barbara will forgive me when she knows every-thing. Perhaps you and I can live in a tree somewhere."

To Lucas, the thought of Barbara rejecting Johann seemed ridicu-lous. "Before you shaved and cut your hair, I might have believed that—you smelled like something that had been dead for a week—but the bath helped. You look and smell acceptable when you are clean and shaven, and the slightly used Wehrmacht uniform doesn't hurt."

Johann took the bait. "Corinne will like you in Yankee duds. American clothes, especially if they look used, are a magnet for women." Johann kicked Lucas gently on the shin. "Don't worry about where you will sleep—we have a spare room, and you can use it…we would welcome you as part of the family."

Lucas felt better, his spirits rose, and he laughed as he asked, "Have you ever heard me snore? Everyone stuffed their ears with rags every night when we slept in the panzer." Lucas looked at the jeep behind them, filled with soldiers who had nothing better to do than protect Elizabeth and her charges from a non-existent foe.

"Well…in that case, now that it's spring, the coal cellar will be empty…you can sleep down there."

"Careful, Johann, don't make promises without talking to Barbara. You have no rank now that the war is over." Lucas felt inexplicably buoyant, as high as he had been low a few minutes ago.

Johann killed his mood when he said, "Yes, we are unemployed now that there's no army and former soldiers have flooded the assassin market!"

Johann looked at the steel floor running down the middle of the jeep. Lucas's thought process stopped at 'no army.' He tried logic.

"But if we don't have an army, ships or airplanes to maintain, and the Allies run our country, can't we use that time and money to rebuild everything?"

"What are you thinking…that the Allies will give us money to fix our country?" Johann grunted as he landed hard on the seat, expelling air out of his lungs. "Scheisse! If they do, we can start by fixing this road!"

The driver, whom Elizabeth had introduced as Canadian, said, "Sorry," but didn't turn around. Lucas thought he heard a chuckle under his arm, looked down, and Reuben grinned up at him.

Lucas wondered if he should put a voice to his dream, then decided to share it with Johann. "I'm thinking about something your father talked about in his letters. He said the Palais would be a perfect place to set up a new music school." Lucas landed hard again; his hip landed on the bruise from the last one. He said, "Ach, Scheisse… Dass tut Weh!"

Johann was quick to respond. "What about money? Where would that come from? Germany lost the war, and we will have to pay like we did after the Great War, only this time, we can't just cancel the debt like Hitler did. This treaty…" he shook his head… "will make the Versailles Treaty look like a traffic violation."

Elizabeth turned, still holding onto the steel rod. "That's related to what David is doing in Hannover. The British and Americans are meeting to figure out the reconstruction, including the cultural institutions. David will have something to do with that. Of course, first will come survival… Germans need food, water, clothing—all the necessities of life. We must find thousands…no, millions of lost people. Germany needs so much it's hard to know where to begin! But punishing the people is not on the table. Unfortunately, the war with Japan isn't over yet, and it looks like it won't be for a while."

The jeep lurched sideways, skirted a crater, then struck the edge of another hole.

The driver said, "Sorry!" as he zigged again, and Lucas caught Reuben just before the boy went over the side.

◇◇◇◇◇◇◇◇◇◇◇◇◇◇◇◇◇◇◇◇◇◇◇◇◇◇◇◇◇◇◇◇

"It looks like the women aren't waiting for the men to figure it out." Johann pointed behind Lucas, and he turned around. Three women pulled a plough through the dirt, and another fought with the handles as she tried to steer it, obviously paying little attention to ploughing a straight furrow.

"Stop the jeep!" shouted Elizabeth, and the driver jammed on the screeching brakes. Two wheels dragged in loose gravel used to fill a shell hole, and the jeep behind barely managed to keep from rear-ending them. Elizabeth jumped to the ground with her camera, which was protected in a black box. She waved in Johann's direction. "The tripod is in the back." Johann untied it from the backs of the front seats, passed it to her, then jumped over the side and helped her set it up.

While Elizabeth took the pictures, Johann leaned against the jeep beside Lucas, still in his seat. Reuben jumped into Elizabeth's empty,

392

relatively comfortable seat beside the driver, turning his big, begging eyes toward him. The driver slid from the jeep, looked at Reuben, patted his seat, and headed for bushes fifty meters from the road. Reuben climbed behind the steering wheel, got his knees under him, grabbed the wheel, and made convincing jeep motor noises with his lips.

Lucas turned sideways to comfortably see Reuben out of the corner of his eye while simultaneously watching the women struggle with the plough. The steel point hit a stone; the plough stopped, and the women pulling it dug their feet in. They leaned ahead until their fingers touched the ground, pushing up piles of dirt behind their feet.

"Got it!" Elizabeth sounded ecstatic. The woman steering the plough pushed down on the handles. The ploughshare slid over the rock, releasing so suddenly the women fell on their faces. The camera clicked again as they got to their feet and wiped dirt from their cheeks, then again as they leaned ahead in their harnesses, each woman pulling with all she had. The plough moved, turned the sod, and Lucas and Johann watched the women drag it to the end of the field. Lucas heard Elizabeth snap three more pictures before the women lifted the plough out of the furrow and turned it around to go in the opposite direction.

She put the camera in its box and passed it and the tripod to Lucas. "I'm going to send these pictures to the press and hang a copy in David's office." She spoke to Johann and Lucas with one leg in the jeep. "Those pictures are worth more to you than you can imagine!"

◇◇◇◇◇◇◇◇◇◇◇◇◇◇◇◇◇◇◇◇◇◇◇◇◇◇◇◇◇◇◇◇◇◇◇

The jeep continued dodging holes and rocks for another hour until it reached Lemgo and stopped at a roadblock manned by British and American soldiers. An American pretended to check papers, appeared to read them mainly out of curiosity, saluted Elizabeth, and then a British soldier lifted the barrier. British soldiers, American soldiers, and German women and children searching for food mingled on the sidewalk. Children stood in front of soldiers, staring at them until they got a piece of Hershey's chocolate or an American quarter-dollar or both. As the jeeps waited, Lucas watched the children and didn't see a single soldier refuse. The child always got his quarter or shilling.

Ten kilometres and half an hour later, the jeep reached Detmold, rattled down the paving stones on Paulinenstrasse, past Bahnhofstrasse, and then Wiesenstrasse, two hundred metres from the hole in the ground that was Johann's daughter's unmarked grave. They drove parallel to Mühlenstrasse, one block east of Johann's home, and Lucas watched his eyes fix on the house roof, visible from Paulinenstrasse, until it disappeared behind the jeep.

Paulinenstrasse became Hornschestrasse; home was close. Then they passed the Lippischer Hof, where Aida's cast had marked Waltraud's death and celebrated her life.

When Johann directed the driver to turn right on Gartenstrasse, the first thing Lucas saw was the blooming golden rain tree across the street from Gartenstrasse 18.

The driver pulled up next to the curb at Gartenstrasse 18's iron sidewalk gate. The brakes squealed, and before the vehicle stopped, the house's stone steps filled with people running toward them. Lucas jumped over the street side of the jeep. Johann stepped to the sidewalk, then turned and lifted Reuben to the ground. Corinne passed Barbara, who flew into Johann's arms, then rounded the front of the jeep, skidding to a stop on the paving stones. She recovered in time to wrap her arms around Lucas. He buried his face in her shoulder and cried. Reuben looked up, a secret smile on his face.

Elizabeth didn't speak until Corinne let Lucas go and stepped back, and then she said, "Lucas, she is everything you said she is. Stop crying and Introduce me to her."

Lucas half-laughed, half-cried as he said, "Elizabeth Mundel, this is Corinne Krämer, the woman I am going to marry."

Corinne took his arm, and Lucas missed the look between the two women. Corinne said, "Elizabeth, I hope you have time for Kaffee und Kuchen, and tea, of course." She pulled herself against Lucas and led him toward the steps.

Elizabeth took Reuben's hand, and they had made it through the gate when Thomas passed them on his way to his father.

"Thomas Finke, is that you? I don't recognize you anymore!" Johann put his arms around his son, and Thomas reluctantly reciprocated.

"Father, I'm thirteen." Thomas was visibly uncomfortable and gently pushed his father away.

Johann, noticeably hurt, tried to hide it with a laugh. He put his hand on his son's shoulder. "I remember you as a child, but you are almost a man." He took Thomas's hand in both of his, then caught him in a quick hug. As they separated, Johann looked at Barbara and then at his son when she nodded.

"Son, I'm looking forward to getting to know you."

Barbara took Johann's hand, "It will take time, Johann. We will have much to discuss before we're used to being together again." She turned to Thomas. "Why don't you show this little boy your garden." She turned back to Johann and pulled on his arm. "Your parents are waiting." She pointed toward the house; Johann followed her hand to where Maria and Theo waited at the bottom of the steps. He took a dozen steps to meet them, slowing as he walked.

"Mother, I've missed you." He put his arms around her, and she didn't try to hold back her tears. "It's been so long!"

She sobbed. "My hair is grey, and I've got so many wrinkles I'm surprised you recognized me!" She smoothed her apron with her hands.

Everyone waited on the sidewalk while Johann embraced his father. "Dad, you were right: I learned to be a soldier and survived."

"Son, war changes everything and everyone it touches." He held Johann at arm's length. His eyes filled with tears, and his voice broke. "You will find life very boring for a while, and you will miss your comrades, but in time..."

Johann put one arm around his father's shoulders. "I just want my life back—I want to play my violin and get to know my wife and son again." He stepped ahead with his father. "Most of my comrades are dead. Fortunately, Lucas made it, and I've heard he is why I'm not in an American or French prison camp."

Thomas and Reuben had waited patiently to get past the adult reunion, but their patience was gone when Thomas touched his grandfather's hand and said, "Excuse me, Theo, I want to show Reuben the garden." Theo stepped aside, and Thomas guided Reuben past the steps, nattering as he passed.

Reuben turned his head and shouted to everyone over his shoulder, "Thomas has the same name I used to have!"

Chapter Thirty-six

13 October 1945

Ein Deutsches Requiem

"God is dead. God remains dead. And we have killed him. Yet his shadow still looms. How shall we comfort ourselves, the murderers of all murderers? What was holiest and mightiest of all that the world has yet owned has bled to death under our knives; who will wipe this blood off us? What water is there for us to clean ourselves?"

Friedrich Nietzsche

On her way to Maria and Theo's house, Barbara pulled her little cart into Strang's shop on Paulinenstrasse at seven-thirty. School on Saturday began early and ended at noon, with no afternoon classes, so the Finke family chose Saturday as their family day, and today, Barbara had her purse full of ration cards.

The allotted calorie limit was twelve hundred for adults and a thousand for a child. Children received extra rations for milk. Barbara had additional cards, traded with friends in exchange for bottled and canned preserves, and Maria had also made an under-the-table deal with Herr Strang that would get them enough meat for the party.

◇◇◇◇◇◇◇◇◇◇◇◇◇◇◇◇◇◇◇◇◇◇◇◇◇◇◇◇◇◇◇◇◇◇◇◇

The ration card allowance wasn't nearly enough for good health and left most people in hunger distress. However, Germans' industrious nature pushed them to supplement the cards with secret deals and hidden gardens, now that the punishment for such transgressions was no longer torture and possible death but a reprimand. Window boxes and flower pots grew vegetables; from the forest came mushrooms, ferns, berries, edible bark and roots of particular trees, boiled to a pulp, soaked with vinegar, and eaten for nourishment. Every day, people crisscrossed the forests and fields, searching for food.

Many people kept pigs, chickens and goats as family pets—biological lawn mowers, hidden in the house or an outbuilding and forced to sacrifice their cushy lives at an early age. Parents discouraged their children from naming or playing with these animals, but letting the children feed them was convenient. The animals inexorably grew, and when a cute little replacement appeared, the children knew that it would only be a few days before the resident animal made the ultimate sacrifice for their owners, and they swapped their allegiance. The killing happened when the children were in school or visiting cooperating relatives who benefitted from the booty. The nameless meat magically appeared on the table, and no one discussed the source.

The garden behind Gartenstrasse 18 was long and wide enough to grow a substantial crop of vegetables, and a chicken coop in the corner housed a sufficient number of laying hens to keep the family's need for eggs satisfied, with a few extras for the flourishing food barter trade. Two plum trees, an apple tree, raspberry and blackberry bushes, and two giant black current bushes added to the treasure, and sharing it with neighbours ensured their cooperation if the British asked questions.

Grünkohl, under normal circumstances and in any country but Germany considered a weed, became a vital vitamin source. Growing multiple crops in a season was easy, and the leaves looked deceptively appetizing. But Grünkohl, despite claims to the contrary and creative attempts to hide it, still tastes like an inedible weed. Grünkohl and wurst, sometimes with broad flowerpot beans, were cooked in a single pot so that the strong wurst and bean flavours overwhelmed the sharp weed taste, and the dish became a staple. A few onions, a splash of vinegar, lots of unrationed Maggi sauce, and the naïve, hungry children wanted seconds.

Cabbages grew everywhere—in window boxes, between trees, under bushes, and in flower gardens. Gartenstrasse 18's garden grew enough for themselves and their immediate neighbours. When it was ready to harvest, relatives and neighbours gathered around a giant wooden barrel, each with a job and a bottle of beer. Three weeks later, the sauerkraut was fermented enough to eat…two weeks after that, Theo and Maria, the chief conspirators in their little Sauerkraut Verein, bottled and distributed the vitamin-C-rich staple to their co-conspirators. As expected, someone evened the score with pork chops or its equivalent donated by someone's unnamed family pet.

Barbara pulled a handful of ration cards from her pocket and laid them on Herr Strang's counter. "I have sauerkraut, and my wish is a piece of Schweineshaxen to go with it, two if you can manage." Herr Strang pawed through the pile of ration cards, looking for meat rations. Barbara shook her head and touched her friend's hand.

"There aren't enough meat cards to cover it, but I will trade you, or I can bring more next week. Juliette and her family are coming to Gartenstrasse 18 this afternoon, along with Major McLaughlin and his wife, and I need to make them feel welcome. A woman and her son are also coming all the way from Heilbronn, and Maria and I want to feed them Schweineshaxen und Sauerkraut… perhaps you can help us with that?"

Herr Strang pulled a nearly-spent ration card out of Barbara's stash and put it beside the cashbox in the ration card box.

"That will do, Barbara. Maria stopped by yesterday and told me the story. I have four Haxen ready for you." He disappeared and returned in seconds, arms full of pork meat and bones tied in butcher paper. He slid the treasure into Barbara's cart, and before she could thank him, he disappeared again and returned in under ten seconds. "Flour and beet sugar—for such a distinguished party, you must have Kuchen." He plopped a sizeable white cloth bag and a brown paper bag on the counter.

Although he hadn't specified a price, Barbara put five precious marks on the counter. She knew he wouldn't tell her, so she guessed the amount that would cover it and said, "Thank you, Herr Strang; what would we do without you?"

Barbara's job at the railway station had disappeared with the Nazis, and Johann's teaching was not enough. Herr Strang reluctantly took the money.

Barbara trundled her little cart along Hornschestrasse and met Maria at the corner of Langestrasse. Maria was returning from the market with her cart filled with bread bought from Frau bitteschön, whose real name was Frau Nagel, and potatoes, green vegetables, butter and eggs at the farmers' stands in the square.

"I feel so spoiled when I go to the market—so many people have nothing." Maria's voice was soft and sympathetic. "Children are living in the ruins of our bombed-out cities with no parents, with no one to help them, begging for enough food to stay alive while we have so much!"

Barbara said, "I hear on the news that now the war with Japan is over, the Americans and British will send hundreds of ships with food, clothes and volunteers. Thank God for that because even with farmers giving what they can spare and people donating what they can from their gardens, we barely make a dent in the number of starving people. There is still so much misery, so many families without their men, with no way to earn money. We are fortunate to have ours home."

Maria led the way on the narrow Hornschestrasse sidewalk, and Barbara followed her around the corner onto Gartenstrasse.

Maria stopped to look at the perfect maple tree in her front yard and said, "Sometimes I think the music school idea is blasphemy when so many people are starving, living without a roof over their heads. Poland and Russia are even worse off than we are. There, people are dying by the thousands; they are worse off than they were during the war!" She clunked her cart up the stone steps, stood it up, pushed down on the door handle, and it swung open.

Annoyed, she said, "Katherine and Natasha never lock the door. After what Katherine has been through, you would think she would be more careful; there are many desperate people these days, and we only have the British Army to protect us. Not to mention the crazy vigilantes!" Maria opened her kitchen door with a push on the handle, and Barbara said, "Katherine teaches at the Musikschule this morning, and Natasha is at Leopoldinum Gymnasium until Mittag. Katherine knows about the party—she probably assumed there would be a lot of traffic in and out of the house."

Maria's tone took on a note of apology to the absent Katherine. "Yes, she's right; the door should be unlocked. I'm not myself today—I've only got peasant food to feed everyone, and I can't make kuchen without sugar and flour. How can we have a party without something sweet?"

Barbara closed the kitchen door, and they busied themselves unloading their carts while they chatted.

"Speaking of Kuchen, Herr Strang gave me a present for you." Barbara put the cloth bag of flour on the table, ceremoniously took the sugar bag from her cart, and put it beside the flour. She pointed at the cloth bag and then the paper bag. "Voila! Flour and sugar! All the Torte we want!"

Maria put her arms around Barbara, like a kid at Christmas. "Oh, thank you, Barbara! I have bottles and bottles of plums and apples. We will fill everyone with Torte!"

◇◇◇◇◇◇◇◇◇◇◇◇◇◇◇◇◇◇◇◇◇◇◇◇◇◇◇◇◇◇◇◇

Maria peeked into the bag of sugar, wet her finger and dipped it in. While Maria licked, Barbara asked, "When will Juliette and Marcel get here? It's been three years, and I can't wait!"

"Barbara, you know Juliette; she thinks the sun rises at ten. They're at the Detmolder Hof and will have breakfast there." Maria chuckled and pointed at Barbara, shaking her wet finger. "She's singing at the rehearsal at three, and the concert is at eight, so Theo said that you and Juliette will have to keep the talking to a minimum. You can talk tomorrow."

Barbara took the last bit out of her cart and straightened up. "I hear Major McLaughlin's wife Norma is a wonderful singer. Johann helps the British Army base with their little orchestra, and She will sing when he and Lucas play in the Christmas performance of The Messiah. I volunteered to sing in their choir this winter and met Willie and Norma at rehearsals. She made me cry when she sang Lili Marlene for us. What a beautiful singer!"

"What's he like? I can't imagine a British officer at our party."

"Major McLaughlin was a rear gunner in a bomber, and she was a singer in a pub near his base. I think she is better than Vera Lynn or Marlene Dietrich, and she sings classical music too!" Maria closed the flap on her cart and whisked both carts to the storage room in the entry vestibule before Barbara could protest.

401

Barbara dragged Maria's five-kilo cast-iron Schweineshaxen pot out of the cupboard and put it on the table. She dumped in a quarter-cup of contraband olive oil and laid the meat in it, exposing as much area to the bottom as possible. She spread a handful of pickle spices over the pork, covered two burners with the pot and slid the cover in place.

"What do you think…light the stove two hours before we eat?" Barbara asked Maria when she returned.

Maria put a large bowl on the table and made two piles of yellow potatoes, one on each side. "Yes, at about eleven. I have lots of sauerkraut in the storage room, and I will get two or three bottles when we need it." She sat down with a small knife and began to peel a potato. Barbara picked up a second knife, sat beside her and started peeling a potato from the other pile. Maria asked casually. "Do you mind if I ask whether Johann is still not sleeping well? Does he still thrash around all night?"

Barbara unbuttoned her high-neck blouse and pulled the edges down, exposing an ugly bruise.

"Oh my God, Barbara!" Maria touched Barbara's neck, "Did Johann do that?"

Barbara nodded. "Yes, he was fighting a Russian soldier. Johann has the same nightmare almost every week. When I woke up, he had his hands on my neck, and I couldn't breathe—I'm afraid I had to hit him as hard as I could before he would let go. He cried when he saw what he had done and insisted on moving to the sofa."

"I'm glad; I couldn't live with it if my son killed you!" Maria's knife slipped, and she cut her finger. She looked at it, put it in her mouth and sucked the blood. She said, "Ach Scheisse!" and took it out of her mouth to check the damage. It immediately dropped blood onto the potatoes.

Barbara looked at the finger and decided that Maria could take care of it.

"I'm almost as strong as Johann, and I fight him until he wakes up, but that one took everything I had!" Barbara stopped peeling and smiled while she looked out the window onto Gartenstrasse. "I'm afraid he has a black eye to explain, and I can't wait to hear it."

Maria began peeling again, but blood dripping from her finger stained the potatoes. She went to the sink and put her finger under running cold water. She spoke to Barbara with her back turned. "I'm glad he's on the sofa...you can't risk sleeping with him again until he gets over the nightmares."

"No," Barbara said emphatically, "I won't let him sleep on the sofa. I don't want him to get into that habit, and besides, if I'm not sleeping beside him, how will I know when he's safe? That bruise was the night before last, and it's the first time I've had to fight him in almost two weeks!" She smiled at Maria's back. "When he first came home, I had to fight him almost every night."

"Every night? Why didn't you tell me? He is my son, and maybe I could have helped!"

Maria gave up on the cold water, pointed her left arm straight up, and pulled gauze and tape out of a drawer with her right hand.

Barbara talked while she peeled. "Maria, please don't take this wrong, but Johann belongs to me now, and I will handle this my way. I will fight him, and I can't lose because that would kill him." Maria sat down, handed Barbara the gauze and tape and held out her bleeding finger. Barbara made a small pad, pulled enough tape from the roll to circle Maria's finger twice and cut it off with her peeling knife. "We will get through this if I hold his feet to the fire, but if I give him too much slack, I sense that he will give up. I want him back, but I don't want Johann to use the war as an excuse to ignore me."

"Has he been intimate with you? Between the fights, when he's awake, is he passionate?"

Barbara looked at Maria's finger. Blood soaked through the gauze but not onto the potatoes. "Your finger will be fine, Maria." Barbara stood up, put the gauze and tape back in the drawer, then turned to Maria. "Things are slowly improving in that department. We will make it, and I'm sorry I worried you."

Maria half-smiled. "I'm relieved. It wasn't easy for Theo—it took two years before the man I loved returned from those Verdammt trenches."

Barbara and Maria began to concentrate on peeling potatoes until, out of the blue, Barbara asked, "What about Lucas? How is he doing with Corinne? I hardly see him anymore."

Maria laughed. "Lucas has an angel looking after him. We don't say anything when he sneaks into Corinne's room. Theo and I hear them talking for hours, and we've decided that whatever else they do is none of our business."

Barbara dropped a peeled potato in the bowl and looked out the window at the leaves on the maple tree—a hint of yellow was beginning to colour them. She kept her attention on the tree as she said, "He doesn't want sex very often, and then it's because he thinks it's his duty, but he is more attentive. I think I'm winning, but I'm not sure."

Maria laughed affectionately. "Yes, of course, you are winning, and that's a good sign. Maybe you're right to stick it out, but you must be careful. Perhaps you should take a club to bed with you—put it under the covers where you can reach it quickly. A few smacks with that, and he'll stop whatever he's doing!" Maria winked.

"When you see Johann's eye, you'll forget about the club," Barbara laughed, "I will win this battle against his monsters, and in the end, I will have my husband back, not some weak left-over."

⬦⬦⬦⬦⬦⬦⬦⬦⬦⬦⬦⬦⬦⬦⬦⬦⬦⬦⬦⬦⬦⬦⬦⬦⬦⬦⬦⬦⬦

Colonel Feinstein and his new wife, Elizabeth, arrived early, in time to catch Maria, blood seeping from the gauze bandage, dumping sauerkraut in the cast iron pot. Immediately, Elizabeth turned on her heel and went out the door, and Barbara watched her climb into their jeep and pull out a brown package with a red cross on it.

When Elizabeth returned, she said, "Give me your finger, Maria." She examined the bandage. "That must be a very sharp knife; the cut is deep and clean. Take off that gauze, run cold water over it, and I'll dig out a fresh bandage."

Maria ran cold water over her finger; the blood slowed and then stopped. She held her injured hand over her head so the bleeding wouldn't start again and turned to Elizabeth. "I am so glad you and David could come. Willie McLaughlin and Norma will be here, and Lucas can practice his English on all of you."

David looked at the ceiling as though he hadn't heard, then out the window at the changing leaves.

Elizabeth translated. "David, Maria said that Willie and Norma are coming,"

David grinned. "I heard the names and got enough of the rest—but, my God, that language is hard!"

Elizabeth put her finger on David's lip. "We are going to raise a bilingual daughter, so I'm going to make you speak German to me like you did with Lucas."

"Son…I'm going to sire a son, and I can't say the wonderful things I want to say to you in that ugly language!"

"Daughter…I get to carry her for nine months, and, my dear, it's time I introduced you to Goethe and Schiller. Then we will discuss whether German is ugly."

"I order you to have a son. I can't teach a daughter how to be an officer in the army."

Elizabeth grunted and said, "Big mistake, Colonel. Her mother is the best officer you've got!"

Barbara laughed and put her arm between them. "Okay, okay, you two, enough arguing… Our young musicians are coming up the walk." The massive outside door opened and swung against the wall with a crash. "We're home!" Natasha shouted from the entry.

The kitchen door flew open, and three teenagers tramped through the kitchen and living room to Corinne's bedroom, chattering and ignoring the adults, leaving every door open.

Maria opened her mouth to comment, but Thomas and Reuben blew in through the open kitchen door before she could. They tried to join the crowd in Corinne's room but were summarily rejected. Reuben slid the pocket doors that doubled the size of the living room sideways and went straight to the piano. He dropped his bookbag beside the bench and began playing scales. Thomas closed the pocket doors and came to the kitchen, where he went to work on a bottle of raw sauerkraut.

◇◇◇◇◇◇◇◇◇◇◇◇◇◇◇◇◇◇◇◇◇◇◇◇◇◇◇◇◇◇◇

"Do we live in a barn?" Barbara sighed, headed for the hall to close the outside door, and met Juliette head-on. They squealed, wrapped their arms around one another, and Marcel, cradling a bundle in his arms, backed down the steps to give them room.

"It's been so long!" they exclaimed, stomping on one another's words. Marcel waited on the step until the passion level dropped slightly, then tried to slip past them into the house.

But Barbara wrapped her arms around him and kissed him hard on the cheek. "Marcel…but I guess it's Monsieur Durand now!" She let go and reached for the bundle. "And you're a daddy! Congratulations!" Marcel gave it to her without protest. The bundle squeaked, farted and smacked its lips.

Marcel edged through the door—Barbara followed him as he started talking.

"Yes, I'm a proud father. Peter is just over six months old and can already talk, but I'm the only one who can understand what he says." A voice shouted from outside the front door when he entered the kitchen.

"Unhand my wife, you beast!" Johann caught up to Marcel in the kitchen, and they engaged in a playful wrestling match greeting that ended in a handshake. Juliette and Barbara went into the living room to talk and play with the baby.

Marcel asked, "What happened to your eye? Did you lose a fight with a door?" He tried to touch Johann's swollen eye, but Johann brushed his hand aside as he said, "I don't want to talk about it." He headed for the living room. Marcel shrugged his shoulders and followed him.

Barbara interrupted them when they arrived.

"Johann, you and Marcel stop your nonsense and go to the Bahnhof. Marita Stephanie's train is due in twelve minutes; Theo isn't home yet, so you'll have to fetch her."

Johann stopped at the kitchen door. "How will I recognize her? We've never met."

Marcel pushed Johann ahead of him. "I know her, and I know her son."

Willie and Norma met them at the sidewalk gate. Johann hugged Willie, knowing full well how Willie hated it, and told him where he and Marcel were going. Willie waved Norma toward the house and said to Johann, in terrible German, "If you're going to fetch Marita and Walther, I want to go with you."

◇◇◇◇◇◇◇◇◇◇◇◇◇◇◇◇◇◇◇◇◇◇◇◇◇◇◇◇◇◇

The train, precisely on time, stopped with a door in front of Willie. When the door opened, he was looking at Walther Stephanie, and Marita stood behind him. While Willie searched for words, Walther stepped onto the platform and hugged him, and Marita walked over and put her arms around Marcel.

"Darling Marcel, it's been so long. I've been like a caged cat looking forward to this all day."

Marcel looked at her scarred face. "Juliette and I wept when we received your letter about Erik's death and your miraculous escape."

Marita took his hand in hers. "The war is over too late for Erik, but Walther and I are here, and our beautiful daughters are in Weinberg with Gunther and Annalisa. We are luckier than most."

Marcel stepped back, and Johann took Marita's hand, lifted it to his lips and kissed it. "Frau Stephanie, I am Johann Finke, and I'm proud to meet you. Juliette told us your story—what a heroic woman you are!"

"Heroic? Me? No, I didn't save anyone like Juliette; she's the heroine. I just ran away from a fire. A Gestapo Major who had no business saving me died so that I could live when he could have saved himself. I must tell you the story sometime if you would care to listen. My mother and I promised him we would tell everyone what he did in the last few months of his life."

Marita caught Johann staring at her scarred face. She touched her scars. "It is grotesque, isn't it?" She turned away from him. "This side of my face is how I looked before the bombs. I hardly notice the scars anymore, but most people are shocked."

"I've seen more than my share of grotesque things, and your face isn't one of them." Johann tenderly brushed her scars. Walther took his mother's hand and smiled at her, saying, "I think you're beautiful, Mutti."

Marcel picked up Marita's suitcase and waved everyone toward the car. "Enough talk... Mittagessen will be on the table, and it's my favourite." He turned to Walther. "Schweineshaxen und Sauerkraut. What do you think of that?"

"Wow! That's my favourite too!" Walther ran for the Bahnhof exit with his father's duffle bag bouncing on his back.

Marita laughed, and Willie ran after him.

⋄⋄⋄⋄⋄⋄⋄⋄⋄⋄⋄⋄⋄⋄⋄⋄⋄⋄⋄⋄⋄⋄⋄⋄⋄⋄⋄⋄

The consensus was that the buffet-style meal, eaten in every room but

Maria and Theo's bedroom, was delicious. Juliette moved through every room except Corinne's, which was inhabited only by teenagers and off-limits to adults, and finally connected with Lucas at the kitchen table, refilling his plate with pork and sauerkraut.

"Lucas, I haven't gotten a chance to speak with you." She smiled and picked out a plum-jam-filled croissant. "Barbara has kept me current since you went into the army. You should write a book someday."

"I hope you don't think it was all bad…there were many good days." Lucas put less sauerkraut on his plate than he had planned. "But there were days I can't talk about."

"Why don't we sit on the sofa?" Juliette picked up her cup and saucer and led the way to the most uncomfortable sofa in Germany. She put her tea on a low table and the plate with two croissants on her knees.

"Barbara tells me you have a beautiful voice."

Lucas reddened and leaned over his plate to hide it. "I like to sing, maybe more than I like the piano or the violin." He shovelled a forkful of sauerkraut in his mouth, tore a piece off his rye bread and stuffed it in behind.

Juliette said, "The Nordwestdeutsch Musikakademie has hired me to do monthly master classes in the new year, and Norma will teach regular voice classes next semester. I would like you to study voice as a student at the music school, and I want you to attend my master classes."

Are you that desperate for students? Lucas didn't say it, but the thought persisted. "But I have no training! I've never had a voice lesson in my life!"

"Lucas, you are already a musician with a trained ear for pitch and phrasing. Your voice is still breaking, and until now, voice lessons would have wasted everyone's time." She sipped her tea without raising her pinky.

Lucas felt a twinge of excitement. "I finish my Abitur in the spring and thought I would study violin at the Musikschule with Johann. Theo said he would hire me for his orchestra in the Sommertheatre and his church concerts." He put his fork down and turned all his attention to Juliette. "I need the money so I can pay Johann and Barbara something for my food and rent. And I'm saving so I can marry Corinne!"

"You can still study piano and violin and play for Theo. Norma and I need you to work on your technique for a half-hour a day, and in a second half-hour, you will learn all the repertoire you need right now. Can you give us that much? An hour a day?"

Lucas was trying to think of reasons to refuse when Norma sat beside him. He was already committed to playing in a small orchestra at Hobart Barracks. The British traditionally performed Händel's Messiah at Christmas, and Willie and Norma kidnapped young musicians from the surrounding area to play and sing. They had bonded with Lucas and helped him with his English; it would be difficult to fend her off.

Norma clamped her hand on Lucas's leg. "Lucas, I will give you your lesson schedule at the Messiah concert. If you think you can fight me and win, ask Willie how he did with that." Juliette chuckled.

Lucas wasn't hungry anymore. He glanced toward Corinne's room. Norma followed his eyes, reading his mind.

"Corinne already knows, and she approves. Don't worry, she will wait to marry you..." she chuckled... "until you're rich and famous. Singing will take your mind off… uh… things it shouldn't think about right now."

Carrying her empty plate, Corinne walked out of her room right on cue. She slowed and looked at Lucas as she passed. "Say yes, Lucas… You can't fight three women and win. In fact..."

"Okay, I'll do it." He stood, picked up his plate, turned toward the kitchen with excitement growing in his belly, then turned to look at Juliette and Norma. "I want to sing, but I'm afraid my voice won't be good enough."

"You let us worry about that!" Norma slapped his leg and extended her hand. "Let's call it a deal. You sing… we teach." Lucas shook her hand, then Juliette's.

◇◇◇◇◇◇◇◇◇◇◇◇◇◇◇◇◇◇◇◇◇◇◇◇◇◇◇◇◇◇◇◇◇◇◇◇

Theo walked to the middle of the floor, spread his hands, and the rooms became quiet.

"Before we go to the church for the rehearsal, I want to give everyone the good news.

"All of you," he looked around the room, "or at least most of you know what a financial struggle this has been. We began the Nord-westdeutsche Musikakademie with a small amount of money from the Prussian government, the land of Lippe and the city of Detmold. Most of the music schools in Germany are piles of rubble, and it will take a generation to reconstruct them—and only if the public will is there. That is why we opened our music school, and we've attracted the best teachers in the country. But with limited funds, we could not hire all those we should have." Theo shuffled his feet. "That's why the students in conducting and theory classes are stuck with me... I work cheap."

Everyone laughed, and when they realized that Theo's modesty was genuine, they applauded until he raised his hand.

"I will not compare myself with Herr Maler, our resident composer, or with Hans Münch-Holland, our cello teacher, and incidentally the best cellist in Europe, or with our piano virtuoso, Conrad Hansen, whose students are becoming legends."

He looked around the room. "With the rest of you, however...."

The laughter became relaxed and long, and Theo used his left-hand-cut-off to stop it instantly.

"Why don't you do that when I'm conducting?" Everyone laughed again but stopped before he cut them off.

"I cannot go further without recognizing the efforts and help of Franz Ley, who, hunted by the Nazis because of his Jewish ancestry, has remained in Oeynhausen and has chosen us to be the children he watches over. Of course, our Mayor, Richard Moes, has an affinity for the arts that has meant survival for the school."

Theo rubbed his hands. "Now, the future." He looked around the room, attempting to get the timing of the dramatic pause right.

"The Allied governments have listened to our new politicians and allowed Germany to begin the rebuilding process with the arts equal-ly alongside bricks-and-mortar. Colonel Feinstein..." Theo pointed at him, "...has called the arts, 'The bricks and mortar of the soul...'" The colonel smiled, and Elizabeth squeezed his arm... "That is going to be our watchword."

Theo acted like a schoolboy who needed to raise his hand. "The best news is that we will soon live in the state of Nordrhein-Westphalen, and the new state will finance our school as its own. We will need teachers, buildings, new pianos, renovation of the Palais, and, of course, a concert hall!" He paused. "And I might get a raise in pay!" He fixed a smile and wiggled his eyebrows.

Laughter and applause continued for a long time, and Theo finally cut it off with his patented move.

"Okay, we've got a Requiem to perform, and, of course, I will tell you why we are singing it." Laughter again, but only for a few seconds.

"Brahms wrote Ein Deutsches Requiem, not as a common liturgical mass in the language of the church, but as a requiem for humanity, in the language of the German people. When Brahms told Robert Schumann's widow, Clara, of his decision, she told Brahms that her dead husband had intended to use that title as the name for the Requiem Mass he wanted to write. Immediately, Brahms offered to name his work Ein Menschliches Requiem, a 'human' requiem, but Frau Schumann insisted that her husband would be honoured if Brahms would use the title he wanted and, of course, he did. This title and the work are painfully appropriate today.

"In this time of burying our dead and rebuilding our lost cities from the dust and broken bricks, our culture, the foundation of Western world culture, must also be reincarnated—It must rise from the ashes of our broken hearts and spirits. We need to think of this beautiful work, written eighty years ago, as intended for us, for this time and place. It is a lesson in hope, comfort, and peace. It is a prayer for the redemption of the German people."

Theo opened his arms toward Juliette. "Juliette is Belgian but has lost more than most Germans. She lost her husband to the Gestapo; her parents sacrificed their lives in the fight against Hitler, and Juliette lost her daughter, Nina."

Theo turned to Juliette with shiny eyes. "If you would sing Ihr habt nun Traurigkeit, Ich will euch trösten—I am sad, I will comfort you— words we all need right now, I will not ask you to sing it at rehearsal." He waited a short couple of seconds and added the kicker. "But of course, if you don't want to...."

Juliette smiled and nodded, trapped into singing without a warm-up, knowing he had lied about her singing exemption at the rehearsal. Theo went on.

"No one here hasn't lost a Peter, an Erik, a Lisa or a Nina." He looked at Reuben, and Reuben smiled, "…Or a mother." Elizabeth rubbed Reuben's black locks of natural curls and cooed in his ear.

Juliette waved her hand graciously at the piano. Theo went to the keyboard, already at the right angle and with the top jacked up on the short stick. Juliette joined him, standing in the crook with her hand resting on the edge of the cover.

It was the first time any choir member had heard Juliette sing the beautiful aria of grief and comfort, and her interpretation made them cry. They controlled themselves enough to sing the choral part with her, then allowed their emotions to overcome them again.

Johann sat on the sofa, remembering Lisa, crying tears he wasn't ashamed of. Barbara held him while they both cried. Johann tried to hate the men who had sent him to Russia, now dead or sitting in cells awaiting trial: Hitler, dead; Goebbels, his wife and six children, all dead; Himmler, dead; Heydrich, dead. But it wasn't enough. Hate couldn't bring back his men: Ian 'Cochise;' Wilhelm 'Geronimo;' and another hundred whose deaths he felt responsible for. He wondered about Viänü, now in a Texas internment camp with Klaus, and he could only speculate on whether they would ever get home.

The fight in the Stalingrad sewer flooded back for the first time. And Lisa, playing the Mendelssohn concerto, working so hard on the arpeggios. For the first time in over three years, her face was clear; the sound of her violin sang to his heart, accompanied by the explosions and screams of dying men. Johann had to work hard to keep from collapsing in a blubbering heap.

Standing beside Walther, Willie thought of the night over Heilbronn, the city burning below him, and he thought of Walther watching the tragedy from the Wartberg, believing his mother was in the flames. Walther had lost his father that night; Erik Stephanie died trying to stop the bombers before they reached his family.

Willie had met Erik Stephanie in the night skies over France. The vision of the night fighter and the burning cities still haunted him. He often awakened in the darkest part of the night, crying, not knowing whether he cried for his victims or for lost comrades.

He put his arm over Walther's shoulder—the boy looked up at him and smiled, accepting Willie's tears as natural.

Lucas thought of Max, Kristian, and Marcus. He hadn't cried for them, but now he couldn't control the flood that came when Juliette sang. Lucas hadn't told Corinne about their deaths, nor about Klaus standing beside him while strangled children swayed from the lampposts on the Berliner Allee. He needed to talk to her—and she squeezed his hand.

◇◇◇◇◇◇◇◇◇◇◇◇◇◇◇◇◇◇◇◇◇◇◇◇◇◇◇◇◇

Colonel Feinstein immediately stood and said, "Thank God the war is over!" and started clapping.

When everyone had shown Juliette their gratitude, they sat down… everyone except Marcel who said, "Is it over…or is this a pause?" He locked his eyes on the Colonel's. "There could be another Hitler somewhere, perhaps in America, waiting to grab the power of the atomic bomb! What if Hitler had built that bomb before America? What if a tyrant takes over the United States?"

The Colonel said, "No, that can't happen in a democracy guarded by the people. America would never allow a man like Hitler to run for dog catcher! There are too many safeguards. That's why the United States is the right country to have the bomb."

Marcel said bitterly, "Yes, America has the atomic bomb, making them the de facto rulers of the world. Are you insinuating Americans are smarter and more civilized than Germans?" He smiled, trying to cut the tension he could feel building in the room. "The power America has built during this war is absolute and can't be challenged…unless…" Marcel hesitated.

"Unless what? Go on, Marcel, what do you think America should do with the bomb?"

The room held its collective breath.

Marcel said, "Eleven days from now, on October 24, twenty-nine nations will ratify the United Nations Charter. President Wilson formed the League of Nations under similar circumstances, with the Treaty of Versailles as part of the negotiations. Ironiclally, that treaty

413

waas the reason Wilson's League of Nations dream failed. The League had no teeth—it had no army, so there was no means to enforce its mandates. President Woodrow Wilson predicted that would happen, and, as he feared, when the League confronted Hitler, he ignored them and they faded into history.

"Feinstein said, "And you think the United Nations should have an army…one that could defeat Russia or the United States."

"No, but perhaps America should give the atomic bomb to the United Nations. Japan is finished; Germany is done; and the last thing Stalin wants is to invade Western Europe. This is the time."

"So, you want the U.S. to prostrate itself before the United Nations. The people who paid to develop nuclear technology will never willingly give it up to a group of nations who, if they controlled the most powerful weapon in the world, would turn against the United States.

"President Trueman is proposing a world organization to control nuclear weapons, and that is more than any other country in the same situation would do!"

"That's comforting, but I've been around for Hitler's rise to power, and I have no doubt that such a man could wrest the same power from the American people. When he does, he will have the power to take over the world, and God help us if that happens!"

Feinstein put up his hand in the universal sign to stop.

"First, he must go through our election process, and I assure you a man like Hitler would never survive that—we are the oldest democracy in the world, with an educated electorate. The Weimar Republic was a fragile democracy at best, destined to fail at some point. Your country, Canada, has a robust democratic tradition based on the British constitution, as is ours. We have consulted with Great Britain, and particularly Canada, during the development of nuclear power, and we voluntarily agreed not to drop the bomb on Japan without Britain's permission. Churchill approved the dropping of both bombs. President Trueman nixed dropping a third bomb.

"Japan had several opportunities to stop the bomb and the war, including as late as ten days before we dropped the first one. They had another chance before the second bomb destroyed Nagasaki, and they still refused! In the six months before that, we had bombed forty

Japanese cities with incendiaries, killing many times as many people as we did in Hiroshima, and yet they wouldn't quit! The bombing of Tokyo alone killed twenty thousand more people than the nuclear bomb we dropped on Hiroshima!

"Look at Germany…the cities are piles of rubble, millions are dead, and yet Hitler refused to surrender! He allowed the British bombers to kill ten times as many people with bombs as we killed in Hiroshima, and when the Russians were knocking down the walls of his shelter, he complained that the German people hadn't done enough to save him. He enlisted children and old men, and yet, we are the bad guys!"

Marcel smiled. "I suppose it is ludicrous to expect the United States to give up control of the bomb, but it's either that or bury the technology. The genie is out of the bottle and no one thinks other countries won't figure it out!"

Feinstein softened his voice. "Tell me; now that the world knows it exists, who else would you trust with it? Great Britain has the plans for the bomb and nuclear power—we shared them. In a few years, the Russians will figure it out, and eventually, the rest of the world will have nuclear technology.

"Our hope is for a stalemate where no one dares to use it, and for the first time in history, there is a chance the world will never again witness a tragedy such as we have experienced. We have proven that we can eradicate life on this planet. No one can escape, not the politicians who, until now, could hide in their bunkers, and not the generals who order men to die for a misguided sense of nationalism. We must live together as brothers and sisters, or we shall all perish."

A heartfelt "Amen" came from everyone.

THE END

From the Author

I hope you enjoyed the book, and I invite you to read the first book in my next series, Pioneer Spirit. The series follows four generations of Canadians through a century of wars, depression, and prosperity.

But before you do, I have a favour to ask. Most people pick books by looking at the cover, reading the blurb, and checking the reviews. I write because I love to do it, but writing without feedback from readers like you is discouraging. You can help me by writing a review; your opinion will help others decide whether the book is for them.

My website is: thesongsofwar.com
My Facebook address is: Robert Faulk, Author
My email address is: robertfaulk@thesongsofwar.com.

You can join my newsletter on the website, or by sending me an email. I promise to keep you updated on what I am doing, along with giving you tidbits like chapters I left out of the book, historical context, and bits from new books I am writing.

Use the QR Icon to
go to the website

Muddy River

Book one in the series: *Pioneer Spirit*

BORN INTO THE SPACE BETWEEN TWO WORLDS, raised in the strict English methodist tradition, schooled by French priests and nuns, and thrown into battle to protect a land he didn't know, Joseph anchored his soul to his family.

His ancestors came to Canada from Germany, England, and Ireland. Their roots in the new world, planted by William Robinson, a methodist preacher who purchased fifteen hundred acres of land from the British government for eight hundred pounds sterling, grew in turbulent soil. The British acquired Acadia in the 1715 Treaty of Utrecht by defeating the French in Europe. But France's King Philip hadn't told the Acadian people and the French forts. Most of the Acadian French population refused to acknowledge their new landlords and British patience ran out after forty years of torment, and they evicted those who refused to swear allegiance to the British Crown.

The French had taken the land from the people everyone called 'Indians' at the time, and the British decided to begin their takeover there. They started their 'Indian' diplomacy in 1726 by signing treaties with the Mi'kmaw and Maliseet tribes and, by 1780, had treaties with all the tribes that would negotiate with them. They defeated the French everywhere and declared Canada theirs.

An adventurous William Robinson sold his English and Irish holdings and moved his family to the fifteen hundred acres he had purchased in Canada.

When William arrived, despite assurances that all the French had fled or been removed, he found himself in a land where everyone who would be helpful to him spoke a strange form of French.

William hired Acadians to help him farm and harvest timber on his land, and learned rudimentary Acadian French (Chiac, to those who speak it). The family clung to English but spoke the more practical Chiac in the outside community.

A hundred years later, when Joseph came screaming and kicking into the world, it was a confusing mix of cultures and beliefs. As he grew, he decided God was not Catholic or Protestant; he was neutral.

Joseph learned to speak Frenglish at home, and spoke the local version of Chiac everywhere else.

Joseph had no axes to grind, no preferences in religion, and hate hadn't entered his life when he rowed across the Petitcodiac River to sit in the Steeves's chaperoned parlour with Eileen. Work and love were all he knew when he married her.

In 1914, Europe staggered like drunken fools into a war that would be fought with exciting new technology that promised to increase the kill rate by several orders of magnitude. But, like a grass fire on a windy day, the fight got away from them and tore through country after country until foot-stomping and beating at the flames couldn't stop it. The fire became a conflagration, spreading to England and, by proxy, Canada.

A 'glorious and free' Canada eagerly joined the fight. Patriotic articles appeared in the newspapers, and posters appeared everywhere equating war and patriotism with Godliness and goodness. "This is your flag...Fight For It!—Women want men who will FIGHT!—Your chums are fighting...why aren't YOU!"

Joseph left his farm and family to join the newly-formed Twenty-Sixth Battalion, convinced that the 'Hun' would not last a year.

He fought the Germans until they quit, but it took three years of head-bashing, cutting and slashing, and shooting men he had no grudge against. When Joseph stepped off a ship in Halifax, the war in Europe was over, but he was not the man Eileen had cried over and never would be again. Joseph the idealist had died in the French and Belgian trenches, and a frightened stranger stood on her doorstep.

Joseph must now adapt to a peaceful, happy world when all he knew was chaos and murder.

AFTERWORD

German music schools located in all the major cities before the war were low-priority restoration projects after the bombings. The overwhelming priorities were food, housing and physical necessities. Germans hadn't lost the love of their culture, but there were life-necessary projects ahead of them. They had conductors, orchestra musicians and singers, but it would be decades before Germany could rebuild its music and art schools. Fortunately, the "Palais," a palace residence for royalty in Detmold, was untouched by war and became the Nordwestdeutsche Musikakadamie.

◇◇◇◇◇◇◇◇◇◇◇◇◇◇◇◇◇◇◇◇◇◇◇◇◇◇◇◇◇◇◇◇◇◇◇◇

Although the man who was my voice professor and friend at the Akadamie inspired Lucas, none of Lucas's actions or words are attributable to him. He told me bits and pieces of his story over time, and I have unfortunately forgotten so much that all I could do was try to inject the man I knew into Lucas.

The things that remain clear to me are these: his musical journey began as a pianist/violinist in Dortmund; he was drafted into the German Army at fifteen (possibly sixteen); he served in a Panzer during the Russian advance through Poland; he witnessed the hanging of Verweigerer from lampposts; and thirty years later, I pretended not to notice when he cried as he told me about it.

When a Russian cannon shell destroyed my professor's tank near Jerikow with only two survivors, he swam across the Elbe River with a box of cigarettes on a door and worked his way back to his home. Reuben's presence is fictional, but Manfred and Mechthild's are not. I also remember him telling me about the bicycle and hoe.

It is also true that American soldiers saved my professor from Russians at a roadblock, as they did in the book. They took him to an American base, and the colonel drafted him to play the piano in their officers' mess.

Lucas changed his music major to voice following the war, and when his career as a singer was over, he became a world-renowned teacher at the 'Akadamie.'

'Lucas' injured his back getting out of the burning tank, and the injury tormented him until his death. I visited him during his many trips to the hospital for days of treatment, and we enjoyed many chess games in his hospital room. I usually beat him—something to do with pain medication—and we sometimes talked about the war.

'Lucas' gave me voice lessons in his home on Tuesdays and Thursdays. After the lesson, we played chess between trips into his sweltering sauna, and sometimes we talked about the war.

A real-life Eddie, a Canadian, flew a bomber for the first time that night, but, unlike the Eddie in Kindersoldat, he landed successfully in England. As far as I can establish from the squadron records, a Canadian bomb-aimer named Eddie Sloan accomplished the feat despite having never flown a plane. The safe return occurred on the raid I depicted, but the aircraft landed in Burn, England, in the dark. Being a pilot, I appreciate the miracle Sergeant Sloan pulled off more than I can express in words. Following his miraculous performance, Eddie Sloan got his wish and became a bomber pilot, surviving the war.

I switched bombers in the book just before Eddie crossed the channel, but the Wellington that ditched in my account was also taken from an actual event. It had been on a raid to Bremen and had taken mortal flak hits. The pilot ditched on the beach below the high water line, and consequently, one of the forward crewmembers was trapped, and the tide was rising.

The incident was related to me by the man who mercifully and courageously shot the trapped Canadian crewmember. He was my doctor and friend in Detmold, and he told me the story during one of my visits to his office. With tears in his eyes, he described the local Dutch villagers working alongside the hated Germans to save the young man, but in vain. In the end, villagers and German soldiers cried together.

The Songs of War series has been a long cleansing journey for me; my life seems to have been a planned step-by-step journey to this place, but I suppose all lives appear to do that to some degree. I have cried with my characters but also smiled and sometimes laughed as they lived and fought through the worst tragedy in human history. I hope that their humanity, irrespective of their nationality, has come to life on these pages, and hope springs eternal in my heart that 'nationalism' will someday be replaced by a universal humanity.

As I write this, it is 2024, and I am 81. I still have stories to write—my imagination is young—and as I look forward, I see a world that becomes better for its human inhabitants every day. We become less likely to destroy the planet and more likely to unify under the banner of the human race. With the broadening of the internet and propagated by ignorance, conspiracy theories abound, but despite this formidable opposition, logic and thoughtfulness have gained a lot of ground since 1945, and a war like the one that inspired these books is difficult to imagine. As time reveals the foolishness of war, no major country would consider dropping a nuclear bomb or unleashing its full destructive power on another. The concept of "enemy" is fading as my grandchildren in Canada play chess against children in Russia, Saudi Arabia and China.

◇◇

And now, on to my next series. I've written the drafts for four books in Pioneer Spirit and am looking forward to rewriting them. The Spirit books, set in Canada, follow three generations through two wars and a depression. They are fictional, but as with The Songs of War, I drew from the life experiences of others.

About the Author

Robert Faulk, a Canadian, born on a farm and educated in a small rural school, grew up in a world of hard workers—men and women who farmed the land and harvested the forests and the sea. He studied engineering in university and worked in construction before taking his family to Germany to pursue a career as an opera singer. Over the next ten years, Robert met many Europeans willing to share still-fresh memories of the Second World War. Their traumatic and personal stories expose the most devastating cost of war—the human cost. Robert captures the spirit of these stories in a series of five books he calls The Songs of War.

We hope you enjoyed reading this title from:

www.blackrosewriting.com

Subscribe to our mailing list – *The Rosevine* – and receive **FREE** books, daily
deals, and stay current with news about upcoming
releases and our hottest authors.
Scan the QR code below to sign up.

Already a subscriber? Please accept a sincere thank you for being a fan of
Black Rose Writing authors.

View other Black Rose Writing titles at
www.blackrosewriting.com/books and use promo code
PRINT to receive a **20% discount** when purchasing.